"A WINNER!"
—*Rocky Mountain News*

"EXPERT PLOTTING!"
—*Chicago Tribune*

"A TOUR DE FORCE!"
—*Publishers Weekly*

"UTTERLY READABLE!"
—*Raleigh News & Observer*

"A TEX-MEX THRILLER!"
—*Kirkus Reviews*

"SUAVE, THOUGHTFUL, BELIEVABLE!"
—*The New York Times Book Review*

"EXCITING!"
—*Dallas Morning News*

MEXICO
WAY

A NOVEL BY

Robert Moss

A DELL BOOK

Published by
Dell Publishing
a division of
Bantam Doubleday Dell Publishing Group, Inc.
666 Fifth Avenue
New York, New York 10103

This book is a work of fiction. Names, characters, places, and incidents are either the product of the author's imagination or are used fictiously. Any resemblance to actual events or locales or persons, living or dead, is entirely coincidental.

ISBN: 0-440-21341-X

Reprinted by arrangement with Simon & Schuster

Printed in the United States of America

Published simultaneously in Canada

March 1993

10 9 8 7 6 5 4 3 2 1

OPM

for Pandora, Candida,
and Sophie

MEXICO
WAY

God punishes the scandal more than the crime.

—Mexican proverb

If the charge of forraine Espialls and Intelligences be committed unto you, take heede they deale not double with you and abuse you with toyes and matters of their own invencion.

—Instructions for a Principall Secretarie, observed by R.B. for Sir Edward Wotton, 1592

ONE

□ □ □

1

THE mover's truck lay on its side at the edge of a dirt road north of Amistad Dam. Bob Culbertson, the Border Patrol chief from Del Rio, sat in his clapped-out government mule, squinting at the truck, thinking that this was a helluva way to spend Friday night—the first night of the Memorial Day weekend. The driver—known as a "coyote" in Patrol lingo—had gotten out of the wreck intact, and hared off into the mesquite, running away from the river. One of Culbertson's men loped out of the scrub, sucking his thumb. Those mesquite thorns were wicked.

Culbertson got out of his car. "Throw up on that door handle!"

They wrenched open the back doors of the truck, and Culbertson's nostrils were assailed by the stench of puke and blood and feces. The *mojados* who could move struggled out into the glare of the flashlights, uncomplaining. Culbertson stared at the dark faces, the centerless black eyes. The women wore shawls, with the points trailing over their shoulders. One was lovingly woven with figures of birds and animals. These people had come a long way. From Oaxaca, maybe. Or Chiapas. Or farther south. Guatemala? What had they forfeited to get to this ditch by the road? A baby shrieked inside its mother's rebozo. The mother did not look up at the tall, hairy blond man—the *diablo tejano*—in cowboy boots, with a pistol on his hip.

Culbertson swung his flashlight into the interior of

the truck. There were a couple that hadn't made it, and a boy who was bleeding bad.

"You better call up Doc Lapham," Culbertson told Lew Rawlings.

"What about the others?"

"Shit. Push them back through the wire."

"They'll be back tomorrow."

"They always are." He stared across the chaparral, toward the black thunderheads that were leaning out of the north. "If those thumpers are working, we might catch that coyote tomorrow."

"We might," Rawlings allowed, without optimism.

"Let's clean up fast and get home," said Culbertson. "It's getting set to blow."

"See you tomorrow?"

"Not me. I'm dead to the world until Tuesday."

Culbertson climbed back into his car, slipped the clutch, and bumped south along the gullied road. Up in the hill country, the storm was already tearing up stumps along the river valleys, turning dry arroyos into boiling torrents. Against the paler sky to the south, he saw the black speck of a small plane, traveling low and slow without lights. Twin engine. Culbertson figured it had to be a doper, or one of those rich OTMs (Other Than Mexicans) who didn't care what they paid to get into the United States. He had caught an Albanian—an Albanian, for Chrissake!—only last week. Under ten thousand feet, those little birds were off the radar scope.

Culbertson toyed with his radio transceiver.

Why bother? If the plane belonged to a doper, he'd be in and out within ten minutes: a touch-and-go run or a parachute drop. Last time Culbertson had been over at Customs, they had a big map on the wall showing six hundred unlisted landing strips within a hundred-mile radius of the border.

Culbertson was dog tired, and he had better things to worry about than the monthly tally of confiscated drugs. He had received a tip that Internal Affairs were planning to pay him an unannounced visit after the holiday. Someone had been spreading word that he was on the take from coyotes.

He peered up at the plane. It was coming down over the dam, too fast and too soon. The wind wasn't *that* strong. Must be engine trouble.

They had the wheels down, apparently ready to try for a crash landing. The wind skirled down, and carried the roll of thunder. Culbertson could not see or hear what happened to the plane. He thought it had gotten over the dam, but it would have been a near miss.

He snapped on the transceiver.

"What can I do for you, hon?" came the voice of Pearl, the dispatcher.

"Get me Officer Rawlings."

Rawlings responded through the crackle of static. "Yo."

"What are you doing, Lew?"

"I'm trying to get me a date with one of these-here señoritas."

"Get your ass over to Amistad Dam. I'm on my way there now."

"I thought you were dead to the world."

"We got us a downed plane, and I don't aim to wait until they tote it back to Mexico."

That had happened before. A smuggler's plane had crashed on the American side of the river, on a moonless night, and Culbertson decided to go through the wreckage in the morning. Before his men got to it, scavengers from across the river had humped every usable piece of scrap back to Mexico.

He found the plane nose-down in a gravel pit off Route 349, the back road to Ciudad Acuña, behind the campground where those big German girls came on adventure tours and got the goat-rubbers all hot and bothered. The lightning flashed, and for an instant the scene was starkly defined. By some miracle, the gas tank had failed to explode, but the twisted metal around the cockpit suggested that the chance of finding survivors was slim. The plane looked like a four-seater Piper Navajo.

The rain was coming down in buckets. Leaving his headlights on as a guide for Rawlings, Culbertson hauled on his slicker and scrambled down the side of the pit. He wrenched at the door above the wing and it fell out into his hands. He jabbed his flashlight into the cabin, and saw the bodies of two men. The one in the business suit had died open-mouthed, in mid-scream. The aisle and the passenger seats were filled with brown paper packages, the size and shape of seat cushions. There must have been forty or fifty of them. The dopers had made no effort to camouflage their load, but Culbertson reached for his hunting knife and slit open one of the packages, to be sure. It was good stuff. Inside the yellow plastic wrap, smeared with some doper's code—"Baby-3," scrawled by a felt marker—the cocaine hydrochloride was as fine as confectioners' sugar.

Culbertson's attention returned to the two dead men; both their IDs were probably bogus, but they would have to be checked. The man in the suit had a Florida driver's license. The pilot had some kind of Mexican police badge. That, at least, might be genuine, though the *Judiciales* would deny they knew him.

The suit had a satchel between his knees. He was gripping it so tightly that Culbertson broke two of the dead man's fingers before he got it free. It had to contain money.

The satchel had a combination lock, but Culbertson didn't bother with that. Slitting the box open, he found to his chagrin no cash; only a copy of the *Wall Street Journal* and an odd-looking pouch, sheathed in something like oilskin, with a wax seal on the back. The pouch was barely bigger than a legal pad, but there were strange protuberances inside. It occurred to Culbertson that the thing could be booby-trapped.

Jeez. What could be worth so much that you hid it in a booby-trapped pouch—the kind of things spooks went in for—when you left thirty or forty million dollars' worth of cocaine lying about on the floor?

"What we got?" Rawlings drawled as he walked up behind Culbertson.

"Look for yourself," Culbertson said as he quickly slid the pouch under his slicker. So far as he knew, it didn't contain money or dope, so he didn't feel guilty about taking it. He couldn't have said at the time why exactly he was concealing material evidence, but he would say later that he acted on gut instinct, the same kind of hunch that tells you to get out of a bar before the quiet guy in the corner decides to do a job on your kidneys. Bob Culbertson relied a lot on gut instinct.

Besides, unless he was mistaken, he had seen something like this pouch once before—when he'd been called in to help a hotshot CIA type who'd got himself into trouble down at the Motel Alaska in Acuña, where the Soviets liked to hang out.

"Start making an inventory," Culbertson told Rawlings. "I've got a call to make."

"You fixing to bring in the Customs boys? DEA's gonna want a piece of this too."

"Yeah? I figure they can sleep in late tomorrow."

By tomorrow, of course, more agencies than you could count off with the fingers of one hand would be crawling all over the scene of the accident. Unless, of course, the thunderstorm and the fact it was a holiday weekend slowed them down. The FAA was supposed to be on the scene of a plane crash within eight hours. The guys from the National Transportation Safety Board would want to poke around too. Under Texas state law, the Department of Public Safety—in other words, the Highway Patrol—was supposed to make out a report. Four Customs men would ride out in a black car, or maybe a chopper if the weather permitted. The presence of drugs meant DEA, if not FBI too. And if they had nothing sexier to do, the Air Force Intelligence types from Laughlin might want to be in on the act as well, since they were in the neighborhood. On top of all that, any number of people with radio scanners might have picked up the signals from the doomed plane—or from Culbertson's call to Rawlings. Newshounds had scanners too. If they hadn't learned of the crash already, they'd hear soon enough. *Everyone* would want to talk to Culbertson, the first man on the scene.

He was starting to get a headache.

He decided to stop for a quick beer at the bar of the campers' hostel before calling anyone.

A sexy pink-skinned, yellow-haired girl stood by the jukebox; Culbertson gave her an automatic wink and ordered a Corona.

As he sat nursing his beer, his mind focused on the pouch still nestling inside his slicker. The tight seal, the odd shape—everything about it reeked of CIA. All of which made Culbertson doubly determined to find out what was inside. Still, he would prefer not to be dismembered by a charge of plastique.

With his second beer came a bright idea, and Sam Yardley's name was attached to it, in neon lights.

Sam ran the Fit-Rite Shoe Store downtown, about as high-tech as you got in Del Rio, and Sam had a fluoroscope.

Culbertson called him at home. "I need you to meet me at the store."

"If you think I'm going out in this weather for anything less than what Dolly Parton had before she went on a diet, you're crazier than a peach orchard boar."

Sam worked on his reputation as a local character. Having pissed away the family money and reduced himself to measuring fallen arches, he was entitled to cling to something.

"Sam," said Culbertson. "You do this for me, and I'll lend you my two-seventy. I'll even lend you my wife."

"This must be serious."

"About as serious as it gets."

"You're sure about the two-seventy?"

"What about my wife?"

"I've seen her. I'll take the gun."

As Culbertson rode downtown, he remembered to make his check-in call to Pearl at headquarters. He tried not to make the plane crash sound too exciting. The longer it took the other agencies to muscle in on the case, the better it suited him, but he also had to ensure that the logs left him looking clean as a whistle. With Internal Affairs on his tail, all he needed was for someone to report that he'd ripped off part of a drug deal.

Culbertson squatted among the shoe boxes, while Sam set up the fluoroscope.

"It's all yours," Sam announced.

"Shit, this ain't nothing," Culbertson mumbled to himself after he had taken a good look through the fluoroscope. The booster for the dynamite charge inside the pouch looked like a fountain pen. It was rigged so that if any outsider broke the seal, his face would be churned into hamburger meat. It took Culbertson less than five minutes to disconnect it.

Later, in a booth at Billybob's saloon, Culbertson inspected the contents of the pouch. They consisted of a tight wad of single-spaced, typewritten pages. No spelling mistakes, so far as Culbertson noticed. He did not grasp much else, except that this was heavy stuff. Government stuff. Although the initials appeared nowhere, the document had CIA written all over it. And he had lifted it from a doper's plane.

Culbertson experienced a sudden lift, a burst of euphoria. He ordered a chicken-fried steak, heavy on the gravy, to celebrate.

He had something on Washington. And he knew just where to take it.

2

THERE was dense cloud cover over Washington, a miserable start to the long weekend. Everything looked out of focus. The river was clothed in olive drab, like a soldier trying to keep his head down in a trench.

Bob Culbertson took a taxi from the airport out to the Virginia suburbs. The driver wasn't sure of the address, but Culbertson said, "It's off Dolly Madison," and that was good enough.

It had occurred to Culbertson that Cousin Phil—as in Philip Taylor, the Commissioner of Immigration and the boss of Culbertson's immediate boss, the chief of the Border Patrol—might have taken his family away for the weekend. He had opted not to call ahead, however, sensing that to do so might have guaranteed that Cousin Phil wouldn't be home. Culbertson knew full well that his cousin regarded him as one of the less desirable of his poor relations.

Taylor lived on a winding road of grandiose villas constructed for the capital's *nouveaux riches*. The houses parodied—and miscegenated—every style from Tudor to Greek Revival to neo-Moroccan, mostly in red brick. The trees on the lots would not throw shade for another ten years, assuming that the lots had not been subdivided by then.

"Pretty fancy neighborhood," said Culbertson to the cabbie. "Guess these places sell for a couple of hundred Ks."

"You got to be kidding! A million! That's to get heat and running water. What's the number again?"

"There." Culbertson pointed to a mock-Georgian creation with an oculus above the door. There was a three-car garage at the side. The gates were down. No sign of life anywhere. The hall light was on, but people always left that on when they went away. As if burglars were as dumb as their marks.

"Do you mind waiting?" Culbertson asked.

"It's your money. The meter's running."

Culbertson got out of the cab, trotted up the steps, and rang the bell. No response. Culbertson looked at his watch. Nearly 3 P.M. If only he could have caught the earlier flight! He had turned his back on the door before it opened.

"Yes."

Culbertson swiveled around. There was Cousin Phil, larger than he remembered, in a bathrobe and with huge bags under his eyes.

"Phil!"

"Who is it?"

"You gone blind, or you just stopped talking Texas friendly?"

"Oh God!"

"Well, that's more like it! You mind paying this ol' boy who brung me out here? I don't seem to have none of your Yankee money."

Whatever Commissioner Taylor's initial mood may have been, it had not visibly improved by the time he had gone back inside the house and returned with cash to pay the cabbie.

"What the fuck are *you* doing here?" Cousin Phil demanded, as soon as he was alone with Culbertson. "I'm supposed to be in Ocean City, with Trish and the kids."

"Don't let me hold you up."

Phil Taylor narrowed his eyes into the kind of stare you reserve for your partner's divorce lawyer.

"I don't care who she is, Phil," said Culbertson, with his natural diplomacy.

"I had to get through some paperwork."

"I understand, Phil. Really."

Culbertson strolled through the living room, advancing on the bar and making free with a bottle of Jack Daniels.

"Make yourself at home," his cousin said sourly.

Culbertson killed a jolt of the sour mash, set his teeth, exhaled slowly, and handed his glass to Commissioner Taylor for a refill.

"This had better be good." Phil Taylor's patience was being sorely tried. He was a fattish, placid, moderately concupiscent man who had risen on Harry Butler's coattails—a good deal higher than his native talents could have carried him. He had known the President since they were in the Roy Miller High School together. He had carried Harry's bags—off and on—since Butler was a fresh-faced young district attorney with a tenuous claim to a social conscience. Inside the Beltway, Taylor's appointment was viewed as one of President Butler's many payoffs. Certainly it was meant to be a low-profile, low-pressure position. Few people—most especially Commissioner Taylor—had anticipated that because of the ruckus over the new tide of drugs and illegal aliens from Mexico he would end up sitting on one of the hottest seats in Washington.

Culbertson swiveled his head around the vast room. "Nice place you got yourself, Phil. The cabbie said these houses go for a million and up."

"Eight-nine-five," Taylor said almost as a reflex. "Now what in hell's name are you doing screwing up my weekend?"

"I got something here in my pocket, Phil, that's going to knock your socks off. I guess it's going to blow off the boss man's jockey shorts."

He handed Taylor the document he had retrieved from the wrecked plane, and settled back to enjoy its effect.

Commissioner Taylor put on his reading glasses. His frown deepened as his eyes traveled over the first page. He went back to the beginning of the second paragraph and reread it:

Objective A: *To exacerbate conditions within ZU/ BANKRUPT.* It will be necessary not only to work within the social structure of the area of principal concern but to augment operations in this sector with those elsewhere. The conditions within ZU/ BANKRUPT at this time are such that with minimum outflow of funds and timely coordination conditions can be generated that will neutralize the resources of the security structure.

Objective B: *To have in place to assume leadership functions those persons you have indicated you wish to be dominant in the new structure.* They will require professional guidance. To this end we will establish a command center with the appropriate communications. It will be located in the immediate area of your concern. We have already centralized the necessary procurements. You will receive a list of recipients.

Objective C: In addition to commo gear a certain depth of proquip has been ordered and stored in strategic locations in proximity to our areas of interest.

Commissioner Taylor flattened the pages against his knee.

"I don't get it. I don't understand a word I'm reading. What the fuck is proquip?"

"I figured you'd been inside the Beltway long enough to talk gobbledygook like the rest of them bureaucrats. Stick with it, Phil. Long about the last page, you might get a better notion."

Taylor grumbled, but he read on:

Objective D: On your instructions we have established an office which will issue bulletins and reports as the situation is developed. Such reports will be distributed to priority lists of officials and opinion-makers. This office is now functional.

Objective E: While modernization of ZU/BANK-

RUPT communications has made interruption of these facilities more difficult than before, we have assigned technicians to be in place to sever communications between ZU/BANKRUPT center and our immediate areas of interest on an effective though temporary basis.

Objective F: After recent soundings at SAFARI-1 and SAFARI-2 we have reason to believe that they have assured themselves of adequate support within the armed forces and that in those cases where support is not forthcoming they will prevail since our proquip will be superior.

Objective G: While we feel assured of success, we are preparing E&E channels, without which we believe our professionalism would be called in question.

Phil Taylor had had enough. "E&E! Proquip! ZU/BANKRUPT! These guys don't talk American! Are you going to translate this garbage for me or are you just going to sit there killing my whiskey?"

Culbertson took his time about clipping a cigar from his cousin's humidor and firing it up. He was enjoying the feeling of control that came with his cousin's confusion.

"Hell, I thought they would have given you some kind of clearances, you being Commissioner and all."

"I have all the access I need."

"How about CIA? You ever talk to those guys? You ever read Bob Woodward or Jack Anderson?"

"I've been to CIA briefings. I see the Director socially. Are you saying this is a CIA document?"

"They're the only outfit I know of that produces poop like that." He walked over to the sofa where Taylor was sitting and jabbed his finger at the top page. "See that?" He indicated the prefix ZU. "That's what the spooks at CIA call a diagraph. ZU/BANKRUPT is the code name for the target country."

"What country?"

"Well, that paper came from Mexico, and Mexico is as bankrupt as a Houston real estate developer."

"So is most of Latin America," Taylor snapped, but the implication of what Culbertson had just said hit him hard. It was one thing for the CIA to go fooling around in a tinpot country like El Salvador. But Mexico—that was another matter.

"See that?" Culbertson pointed to some words in the opening paragraph. "That's the name of the operation. Project Safari. A lot of this other stuff is spook talk for what you need to put a paramilitary job together. Proquip is protective equipment—could mean Uzis, could mean laser-guided smart bombs. We're talking mercs and shoot-em-ups, Phil. Heavy stuff."

"In *Mexico?* I can't believe it!"

"Wouldn't be the first time. Ever hear of San Jacinto? Or Zach Taylor? Oh, yeah. E&E—" he riffled through the document to find the reference on the last page. "That's Escape and Evasion. Getting your ass out if you screw up."

"How do you know all this stuff?"

"I do my homework." Actually, Culbertson had placed a call to a gun dealer he knew who boasted that he'd done some paramilitary jobs for the CIA out of Miami and the Florida Keys. Whether he had or not was debatable, but he knew the lingo.

"You're telling me . . ." Commissioner Taylor bit his lip, and tried again. "You're telling me the CIA is planning a coup, or something like a coup, down in Mexico? That's insane."

"I'm not telling you one damn thing, Phil. It's all in that paper."

"What do you expect me to do with this?"

"I think you should call up your friend Harry Butler."

Taylor stared at him. "If I take this to anyone, I'm taking it to the Bureau."

"You wouldn't want to do that, Phil."

"I wouldn't?"

"Let me try to walk you through this. Whatever's going down in Mexico, the President either knows about it, or he needs to know about it before he reads about it in the newspaper. Am I right so far? Okay. Now, if you sit on this thing, come Tuesday—at the latest—the FAA and Customs and Willie Nelson's fairy godmother are all going to be crawling over that wrecked plane demanding some answers. So you don't have all that much time. You want to run this thing by the Bureau? You do that, Phil, and I'll tell you what's going to happen. The thing's gonna leak. Then you'll have a hundred senators wanting to piss all over the guys who put it together. I guess old Harry Butler wouldn't be too pleased about that. On the other hand, I reckon old Harry would be mighty grateful to a man who wiped his backside for him."

"You're a gross, crude—"

"You gonna call the man, Phil?"

The Commissioner was wavering. He mumbled something about the President's being out of town.

"I read about them White House telephonists in *Reader's Digest*. They can reach you anywhere."

Taylor assumed a sullen expression, which generally meant he was thinking. He'd been under fire recently because of the invasion of illegal aliens from Mexico, and he'd been worried that Harry Butler might make him a scapegoat for the Administration's indecision. If Culbertson was right about the importance of the document— and if he took it to Harry as a gift—he could expect a reward.

He walked across the room, thinking, still troubled. He turned back to Culbertson and asked, "What's in this for you?"

Culbertson said something vague about good ol' boys sticking together. Taylor narrowed his little eyes, waiting with growing impatience.

"Okay," said Culbertson, "I could use a little help."

He explained about the Internal Affairs investigation. He allowed that they might have something on him —something to do with his cozy relations with a certain *comandante* in the Mexican police who had an indoor swimming pool and a Mercedes 450SL.

"You know, I'm only ten months away from retirement, if I want to take it," Culbertson concluded. "I figure the government owes me a pension, right?"

Taylor's mouth turned down, but he made the call. The White House operator said all she could do was to pass on the message to the President's staff. Was there something specific the Commissioner wanted to communicate to President Butler?

"Comanche Moon."

"Excuse me, sir?"

"Tell him Comanche Moon. The President will know what it means."

"Very well, sir."

It had been a boyhood signal between Phil Taylor and Harry Butler and a handful of other Texans, born out of racial memories of bloody days on the old Indian frontier, when the Comanches would ride a hundred miles, in the full moon, to ravage the Texas settlements. It was a phrase you used when you had totaled your father's car or were trailing the other team by fourteen points in the last quarter. It meant trouble.

The President responded within forty minutes, his call patched through from Camp David. It was raining hard up there; Harry Butler groused that he'd had to cut short his afternoon ride.

When Commissioner Taylor mentioned the phrase "Safari Project," the President cut him off.

"This is not a secure line, Phil. I'm going to fly back to Washington. I want you to meet me at the White House before dinner."

Taylor hung up the phone and remarked to Culbertson, with a kind of slow wonder, "I guess you weren't bulling me."

CULBERTSON insisted on accompanying his cousin to the White House, and Taylor finally agreed, on condition that he shave and put on a tie. They entered the White House through the West Lobby. There was a yellow ribbon on the door, in tribute to the U.S. hostages who had been grabbed by Palestinian terrorists in revenge for the humiliation of Saddam Hussein; somewhere in the world, there always seemed to be American hostages. Culbertson, who had never visited the White House, gawked like a tourist at the Boehm porcelain birds in their cabinet, at the flattering portrait of Zachary Taylor, at the huge gilt eagle over the clock.

They were led down a hall lined with color photographs of the President and his family: Harry swinging a golf club, Harry brandishing a bonefish on the end of a line, Ann at an Oscar awards ceremony with a producer in sunglasses, Ann among schoolchildren demonstrating for a drug-free America.

Outside the Oval Office, the walls were covered with paintings by Catlin of Indians, including Comanches fording a river. The door to the Roosevelt Room—the Chief of Staff's domain—was shut.

Aaron Sturgiss, the White House Counselor, came out of the Oval Office smoothing his hair. "He's waiting."

The President was standing behind the partner's desk in front of multiple layers of Plexiglas, treated to ward off bullets and laser hits and directional microphones. He was wearing a light summer jacket over his polo shirt.

He dismissed his aide and listened intently while Taylor explained Culbertson's role.

"Where is it?" he demanded before Taylor had completed his introductions.

Culbertson handed over the Safari paper.

President Butler leafed through it quickly.

He nodded and said, "You did right to come to me. Don't worry about it anymore. I'll handle it. Are there any copies of this?"

Taylor deferred to the Border Patrol man, who said, "No, sir."

"Who else has seen it?"

"No one, sir."

The President rewarded Culbertson's discretion with his celebrated smile. He slipped the Safari document into his desk drawer. He said, "I'm taking this under consideration. Do you gentlemen have any conception of what it means?"

Commissioner Taylor cleared his throat. "I guess we're talking national security here, Harry."

"Right on the money. So we don't need to say anything more about it, do we?" He looked at Culbertson. "Any questions, Chief?"

There was one possible difficulty, Culbertson observed. Nobody had seen him remove the pouch from the plane, but if somehow an investigator from one of the other agencies did hear about it, he'd be on the spot. Culbertson did not mention his friend in the shoe store, but he was thinking that Sam Yardley had a loose mouth when he was drinking.

"No problem," the President said. "If anyone starts asking questions, you'll give them the document."

"Sir?"

"It may not read the same as the one you gave me. You take my meaning, Bob?"

"I guess I do, sir."

"Would you be willing to join in a little—uh—shaping of the truth to help out Uncle Sam?"

"You bet," said Culbertson, without hesitation.

"You're my kind of Texan, Bob." The President threw his arm around Culbertson's shoulder as he walked his visitors to the door. "I'll remember the consideration that has been extended. If there's anything I can do for you . . ."

"Well, sir . . ."

The President winked at Phil Taylor. "The Commissioner and I will talk about that. Since we both seem to be stuck in town for the weekend, Phil, I thought we might knock a few balls around tomorrow."

4

ANN Travis Butler had flown back from Camp David with the President in Marine One. She found the Maryland retreat dreary in any season, and she had a sneaking suspicion that her husband's sudden decision to fly back to Washington was connected with his extracurricular activities. She did not grudge Harry his one-night stands, as long as he kept them discreet. For her own part, she had always found sex with Harry marginally less exciting than having her legs waxed. But she was conscious that Harry was restless, and all the pressures and obligations of his public life were not enough to hold that restlessness in check. And restlessness could lead to indiscretion. Yes, she was glad she'd come back. He needed watching, especially on a long, drizzling Washington weekend.

She had ordered a fire to be lit in the upstairs parlor —even though the air conditioning was on—because a fire was always company, and Ann Butler always felt cold. She was in her dressing room, brushing her jet-black hair and sipping at a martini, when she heard Harry come into the parlor. Then she smelled burning, more acrid than wood smoke.

"Harry? Are you smoking up here?"

She had laid down a strict ordinance that the private quarters were a no-smoking zone.

When she received no reply, she swept out into the

parlor, martini glass in hand, and found Harry burning something in the fireplace.

"What's that? A love letter from one of your whores?"

He looked up at her wearily while feeding the last sheet of the Safari document into the flames.

"You're not my conscience, Ann."

"Then you ought to rent one." She saw that the pages were typed. "What *is* that?"

"Nothing you need to worry yourself with, my dear —just something I need to lose."

TWO

□ □ □

1

THE National Security Adviser came into the West Wing early on Sunday, and started skimming through the intelligence digests that were waiting on his desk. Admiral Enright was pleased with the look of the Pentagon's *Early Bird,* a clippings job pasted together between 1 and 5 A.M. Pride of place, on page one, was given to a story lifted from an obscure newsletter whose mailing address was a box number at Union Station. It was entitled "Mexico: Noriega Next Door." It named top Mexican government officials who were allegedly involved in drug dealing and the murder of political opponents. It dovetailed precisely with Admiral Enright's conviction that the mess in Mexico was becoming a major threat to American security—and an excellent opportunity to scare Congress into voting to restore cuts in the defense budget. He would have to call the article to the President's attention. Harry Butler was a Texas President, and to any Texan, what went on in Mexico was a family concern.

One of the Admiral's aides, a good-looking Alabaman in faultlessly starched Navy whites, stuck his head around the door.

"Sir, the President has just called up the chopper. I thought you'd want to know."

Admiral Enright consulted his wristwatch. Where was President Butler going at six-thirty on Sunday?

The National Security Adviser hurried out to the South Lawn. The rotors of the white-capped Sikorsky VH-3D were whirling. A doctor, a pair of Secret Service

bodywatchers, and an Army officer with the Football—
the black case containing the codes authorizing a nuclear
strike—were already on board.

President Butler came marching across the grass. He
was wearing sunglasses and a baseball cap. The heavy
dew streaked his suede loafers.

"Mr. President?" Enright shouted above the roar of
the rotors. "Anything you need, sir?"

"I need some goddamn time to myself," Harry Butler growled.

"Sir, I have that update on the Mexican elections
you requested. It's worse than we thought. Looks like the
government is fixing to steal the voters blind."

Harry Butler's response was swallowed by the noise
of the helicopter.

"Excuse me, Mr. President?"

"I said, Get off my back!" Harry Butler bellowed.

FROM Camp David, the President punched out a number
in northern Mexico on an NSC-issue portable scrambler
phone.

"This is Cottongin," he announced. "You fuckheads
just dropped some mighty hot paper around Amistad
Dam. I guess you know that, huh? The plane that went
down just happens to be full of dope. Now, I want you to
listen to me very carefully, Raúl. First of all, it looks like
you guys don't know how to keep a secret. Second of all,
I don't give a shit how you pay your bills. But I don't buy
anything that's tied in with drug traffickers."

Raúl Carvajal tried to interject. His English was im-
peccable, with a trace of Oxbridge in the accent and ca-
dences. He was cut off, however, after only a couple of
words.

Harry Butler's voice grew in volume, until he was
shouting down the line.

"I know I said I'd cover for you guys! I just did it. I

just buried Safari. As far as I'm concerned, it stays buried. Now I'm turning off the water.''

THE President's words echoed in Carvajal's mind as he walked the long patio of his colonial mansion outside Monterrey. He experienced a momentary ache in his lower back, but his head was clear. He reminded himself that he was always at his best—and his calmest—in moments of crisis. He found stillness when the world about him was blowing apart. Lack of sleep, lack of time, the intensity of his purpose combined to lend all of his problems a curious clarity, almost transparency. As if he could reach through them to seize a solution from a different dimension, a hidden order of events.

The plane crash was a serious blow. The cocaine his associates had provided would have supplied enough money to finance a revolution—and buy half the generals in the Mexican army. But the money could be found somewhere else, from his partners in Houston, if not from the original source. The loss of President Butler's support was more serious. Everything the Mexican had worked and planned for these past months depended on the active intervention of the United States, and Butler's friendship was the key.

Raúl Carvajal and Harry Butler had been friends since college days. The Mexican hoped, still, to bind the President to his cause through shared loyalties and shared interests, but if he shied from the starting gate, the Mexican had the means to spur him back.

He stood with his hands on his hips, drinking in the sweep of *his* mountains, purple and bronze in the morning light. He had too much at stake to even consider the possibility of failure.

He went to his study, unlocked a file cabinet, and took out an NSC-type scrambler phone identical to the one President Butler had used to call him. He punched out a number; in Kendall County, Texas, a phone rang.

"John?"

The oilman sounded surly. "Jeez, Raúl. I was up half the night in a poker game."

"We may have a cash-flow problem."

"Tell me about it. I'm leveraged up to my ass."

"We need half a million to keep things on schedule. We need it by midweek. I'll put up half if you put up the rest."

"Shit. I got bankers hammering on my door. Those sons of bitches aren't the same sons of bitches they used to be. You've hit me too many times, Raúl. And I don't see any results I can use. I'll tell you, if I want to blow another quarter million, I know a lot more fun ways of doing it."

"Everything depends on timing," the Mexican said patiently. "We've been over this repeatedly. After the elections, everything will come together. I guarantee it."

"What about your fat-ass friend? The one who looks like Pancho Villa? I thought he was going to fill up the war chest."

"There was an accident. A plane crash, near Amistad Dam."

The oilman swore profusely. "That was our plane? Hell, they were flying in dope. It's all over the goddamn newspapers. The Governor's making a big thing out of it. He's ordered a crackdown right along the border. Surveillance blimps, spotter planes, the works. I told you not to trust that fat clown Carranza. Now he's got us mixed in with the druglords! If that shit is linked to Safari, you can kiss good-bye to any help from Uncle Sam."

"I don't think you are in any position to get priggish about drugs, John," the Mexican said carefully.

There was silence at the other end of the line. Since his financial troubles began, the Texas oilman had been happy to generate cash by laundering hot money out of Mexico through corporate subsidiaries.

"There is only one link to Safari," the Mexican continued.

"Goddammit! When I see Carranza, I'm gonna cut him in half!"

"It wasn't Carranza's fault," the Mexican defended his partner. "It was your man. The gray man who likes writing memos. He wanted to send you a progress report. He's damn lucky he decided not to hand-deliver it."

"There was a Safari document *on the plane?*"

"An indiscretion." Raúl did not need to labor this point.

"Where is it?"

"It's in Washington. Cottongin just phoned me about it. You might say we've been lucky. I prefer to believe we are being rewarded for making the necessary preparations."

The Texan wheezed. Raúl pictured him gulping too much smoke from his cigar.

"What's Harry gonna do?"

"He says he's done it already. He's buried it."

"Praise the Lord."

"But there's a problem, John. He's not happy about the plane. I think he prefers not to know us, just now, and we can't let that happen."

"You're gonna use the woman, right?"

"Only if I have to. Only at the right time."

"Have you talked to her about it?"

"That's my affair."

"Listen up, Raúl. I'll raise my half of the money. You just keep Carranza and those goddamn cokeheads out of—"

The Texan's voice was replaced by a sound like water running through a trash compactor.

"John?"

"You hear me okay?"

"You sound like you're talking from inside a submarine."

"I'm in the pool. With a lady friend. She picked a helluva time to get cute."

"You said you were up half the night."

"Can't blame an old bull for trying. Raúl? Why don't you do all of us a favor? You've got Harry by the balls. *Use the Bitch.*"

ONCE off the phone, however, John Halliwell did not return immediately to the young woman lounging next to him in the pool. There was a call he had to make.

Admiral Enright had sensed from President Butler's tone that something was drastically wrong; Halliwell's call confirmed it.

"Dammit, Enright, I don't know how it got so fucked up, it just did," the oilman said as levelly as he could. "What I want to know is how Butler is going to deal with this and what we can do to keep this from blowing up on us."

"I suspect this whole thing will go away, John. They're probably blaming it on the CIA, and if that's the case, they'll just let it drop. Whatever, I'll watch out for it."

"But what about the CIA, won't they have to look into it?"

"John, let me deal with this," Enright said. "The guy who heads up the Agency operation in Mexico, Jim Kreeger, is a little bit of a maverick, or so I hear, so it may be easy to let him absorb the blame. Also, we've got one guy there who is giving us full cooperation, so you needn't worry."

"Enright, you'd better be right about this. We've got too fucking much at stake here to blow this thing now."

2

IN the foothills beyond Cañon Huasteca, twelve hours' drive from Mexico City, Raúl Carvajal reined in his stallion. He swung smoothly off the Arabian and with the next motion, he was at the side of his beautiful companion, helping her down. He eased the strap of her riding hat away from her chin and freed her tawny-gold hair, allowing it to blow freely in the dry wind from the north, gusting down from Texas.

His lips brushed her hands, the pearly slope of her neck, that shining mane.

What would you say, he spoke to her with his mind, if I told you John Halliwell calls you the Bitch? He says it as if the word had a capital, as if it were coined for you.

He murmured, "You are magnificent. I want you now."

He seized her by the waist. One of his hands thrust between the buttons of her blouse and under the cup of her bra, gripping her breast.

Shelley laughed and slapped her crop against the calfskin of her riding boot, hand-tooled by Lobb's in London. It was a throaty laugh. It rustled like fresh linen bed sheets.

He was pawing at her jodhpurs, which buttoned like a man's.

Shelley said, "I'm an old woman, Raúl. I'm going to be forty. Have you ever slept with a woman that old?"

He rubbed against the whole length of her firm, hilly body, and groaned softly.

"Wait. Not like this." The Mexican was too fast, darting like an eel, then gone. She had tried to teach him patience, without success. His idea of foreplay was still to grope for tits and ass, like a drunk in the front row at a strip joint. For all his poise, his skill with words, Raúl

Carvajal made love like a hasty adolescent. Harry Butler had made a better pupil. It had been painful with him at first, the big man pounding away, oblivious to her rhythms. She had mastered him gently, harnessing his force to her needs. The memory was vivid enough to make her soften under Raúl's renewed assault.

She told him to spread the blanket from her mare over the rocks, while she stripped and folded her clothes neatly. He looked more impressive on horseback. On the ground, his cowboy boots discarded, she stood nearly half a head taller. She enjoyed her advantage, as he pressed his lean, tanned face into the gully between her breasts.

She made him lie under her, where she could control his movements better, alternately coaxing and curbing with the pressure of her fingers at the root of his member. When she permitted him to come, waves of pleasure coursed through her body, cresting and breaking. She was thinking again of Harry.

Still she panted in time with Raúl, then whinnied and buried her teeth in his neck, holding on until she tasted salt blood.

He was grateful for the show.

As he pulled on his boxer shorts—she never trusted a man who wore any other kind—he said, "I have a birthday present for you. I've been keeping it."

"It's not my birthday yet. When it is, I think I'll go into seclusion."

"It's a Rauschenberg." He dressed very fast, as if he was late for an appointment.

"The one at the ranch?" Shelley was trying to remember the prices she had jotted down at her last swing through the New York galleries. An early Rauschenberg must be worth six figures. She followed the prices for modern American paintings the way a Wall Street speculator studies stock options. She calculated she had made a four hundred percent annual return on her collection—mostly of the minimalists the Japanese loved to buy—

over the past three years. Most of her paintings were in a vault in Manhattan. She did not intend to retire without a very soft cushion.

She rewarded Raúl with a kiss on the lips. Raúl Carvajal was a generous man. On that count, she could not fault him. She wondered, at the same time, what he was going to ask for next.

"My polo friend from Brazil—do you remember him?—he has a name for a woman in her prime. He calls her a *balzaciana*. Don't you like it?"

"Your Brazilian friend wears too much cologne. And a *balzaciana* sounds like a cross between a meringue and an over-the-hill hooker."

He was off into one of his postcoital bouts of sentiment. He descanted to her about ripeness, about how a woman who knew life and the world could bring its finest distillation to a man.

Shelley laughed. "Sometimes you talk like one of those Mexican soaps. You should be writing scripts for Fatal Passions, or Marriages of Hate."

"The male of the species is the romantic. I swear it. Why are you women always so down to earth? Why do you have to be so pragmatic?"

She considered his question, at the same time contemplating his lean, taut figure, appearing as a silhouette against the grainy pastels of the mountains, slowly turning to burnished copper with the rising sun. Raúl Carvajal was short, even in his Lucchese boots, but he was well-knit, and he moved with the pride that horses stir in men. The wings of gray in his dark hair lent distinction. The men of the Carvajal family—a dynasty of brewers and glass-makers and entrepreneurs—ran to flesh early. Raúl was an exception. He looked poised to vault into the saddle, or to dance with the bull.

A sunburst from across the sierra divided his face into light and shade, and reminded Shelley that Raúl's was a troubled lineage. There had always been dreamers in his family, and few of them had died in their beds.

Shelley had vague recollections of Raúl's father, a big, boozy bear of a man, the brass-lunged enemy of the political establishment in Mexico City. He had died in a spatter of machine-gun bullets on the steps of the Gran Hotel, courtesy of Fernando Ramírez, now the Minister of Government and the most powerful man in Mexico, next to the President.

Raúl stirred, and his shadow fell across Shelley's heart.

She said, "Women have to be practical. The survival of the species depends on us."

"Is that why you stay with me? Because it's practical?"

"We suit each other."

"Nothing of love?"

"You're kind to me, Raúl. Kindness is more dependable."

"And with Harry?"

She folded her arms beneath her breasts and turned away, to stare at the milky haze that drifted over the smokestacks of the Carvajal steel mills and the Carvajal phosphates plant on the plain below, to the east of the city of Monterrey.

She had first met Raúl here, in the lee of those snow-capped peaks. Harry—then Senator Butler—had urged her to come for a weekend at the ranch, away from paparazzi and prying eyes. He had introduced Raúl as an old friend from college, a classmate at Texas U. Shelley had been flattered when the elegant Mexican had looked her up, affecting surprise that she had broken up with Harry.

"How long is it since you saw Harry?" Raúl was asking.

"It was the morning after his acceptance speech. I haven't counted the months."

No, but she remembered. She remembered Harry's strong, square-jawed face—a Texas face, too tanned for

Massachusetts, in any season—turned away from her, the voice as remote and monotonous as a tape recording.

"I can't go on any longer, Shelley. It would destroy both of us. You must understand, I never lied to you. I couldn't see into the future, that's all. If you don't understand me now, I pray that you will. I am not the man that I was. I am a different person."

On and on, that voice that did not belong to the man she had loved, but to a hologram that lived on the airwaves, an emanation of Boss Tube, who ruled the party machine and the polls and all that went with them.

And inside her, a lead weight had fallen, its descent so slow she thought it would never touch bottom. When it did, after he had left her room in the hotel, her disheveled bed, it drove up cold waves of nausea from the pit of her stomach. She lay face down on the bed, seeking sleep without dreams and not finding it. The circus of the party convention trampled on without her.

Through forethought, or the lack of it, Harry Butler had left his sleeping pills behind, on the bedside table. Shelley did not use them. She had a daughter to provide for, a daughter now in the tenth grade at a private school in San Diego. Women are required to be survivors.

Raúl was trying to read her face.

"Look up there." Abruptly, he seized her arm and wheeled her so she was staring straight up the sharp ascent of the nearest peak in the sierra.

The morning light played tricks with the stone. High up, above whorls of pink and brown, it played on the hooked beak and huge, intent eyes of an eagle. Or was it only the mask of an eagle? The head of a bird-priest, incised in the rock?

"This place was sacred to the Indians," Raúl said, slipping his arm across her shoulders. "They came here to dream. To soar like the eagle. Here it is possible to go beyond the commonplace.

"In Mexico City, they drag everything down, into the swamp, into the sewer. Everything of the higher man is brought low, into their crawling evil. The north is different. You know it in these mountains. Here a man can rise, soaring with the eagles."

Words, words! The men in Shelley's life were so full of them! And nowhere on earth was the gulf between words and actions so immense as here, in Mexico. Now Raúl, dressed in his tailored safari suit, stood prattling about eagles, and Indian dreamers, his voice formed in a mid-Atlantic accent acquired at an expensive boarding school in Switzerland. In an hour's time, he might be on the phone to Dallas, arranging to import wheat that could not be sold in the United States because it had been contaminated with carcinogenic chemicals—for resale, at vast profit, to the *chilangos* of Mexico City he reviled. Or on the phone to the White House, to cadge a favor from his college friend and sometime business partner, President Harry Butler, whose jilted mistress he had courted assiduously until she allowed herself to be bought for a price few men, on either side of the border, could have afforded: her own house off the Calzada San Pedro, its garden a splash of color in a city without flowers; the condo in La Jolla; the reserved suite at the Presidente Chapultepec in Mexico City; the charge accounts at Bergdorf Goodman and Bulgari in New York; the doctor and dentist in Houston; the generous allowance she usually deposited in a Texas bank.

Shelley Hayes felt no guilt about the worldly goods she extracted from Raúl Carvajal. Other men had used her like a whore. For the first time in her life, she was exacting a price. She had a daughter to protect, and a life after Raúl to provide for.

Life after Raúl might begin any time. Raúl played with people, as with causes, and he broke his toys when he was bored with them. Shelley hoped she had learned enough about men to anticipate that moment, and make the break before he did. Raúl was still an ardent lover, and he enjoyed showing off the *güera*—the natural blonde—who could talk high politics with the air of an insider to his friends. All this would change, or else Raúl would succeed in hurling himself off a mountain on his horse, or would sail into the side of one in his Piper Cherokee—he was as much a madman in the cockpit as in the saddle. Or he would die like his father, cut down by an assassin's bullets. The Carvajals never could stay out of politics. As the head of the clan, Raúl carried the burden of his father's causes and his father's enemies. Part playboy, part businessman, part bomb-thrower, he loved to ride where the earth is narrow.

Shelley said, "You spoke to Harry, didn't you?"

Raúl fretted the side of his boot against a smooth boulder. He said, "Harry has disappointed me. He stands aside, and allows us to be treated worse than Mongolian peasants."

"What makes you think he will see me?"

Raúl shrugged. "Why do you suppose Harry will have any say in the matter? A chance encounter, at a reception. Perhaps at the home of a friendly senator. Such things can be arranged."

"To what end?"

Raúl took both her hands, lifting them so the morning light flashed on her rings, on her diamond-and-ruby bracelet. He was reminding her that he was not an ungenerous man. "I may need to send a message to Harry in a way that he will listen."

"A message? Do I look like a carrier pigeon? Why don't you send Felix—" Raúl winced, ever so slightly, because Felix was the trusted employee he used to carry large sums of cash to banks across the border.

"The nature of the message is such that it really ought to come from you."

He made her sit beside him. Together they watched the sunlight stream down into the dry bed of the Santa Catarina river. To begin with, as she listened, Shelley wondered if her lover was altogether sane. With the accumulation of names and details, she felt giddy and breathless, scared and exhilarated in the same instant:

the way she had felt when she first went skydiving, before the parachute opened. She began to understand the secretive huddles that had been taking place at the ranch and at Raúl's office; the furtive arrival and departure of couriers in twin-engine planes; the drilling of armed retainers, out in the sierra.

"President Carvajal," she tested the words out loud.

"It fits. At last we will have a country that is ready for the twenty-first century."

"But the risks. Raúl, they killed your father. They'll kill you as soon as look at you."

Raúl laughed and squeezed her hands. "Would you be so desolated? You'll have your Rauschenberg."

"That's not fair."

"Life isn't supposed to be fair. It's a game to be fought and won. Besides, my family is used to risks. All we need is Harry. His support; his cooperation. Harry is the trump."

He added, "You see the depth of my feeling. For you, and for my country. I have put my life in your hands. Are you available?"

An available woman. In the part of south Texas where Shelley was raised, that was maybe a step up from being called a whore.

She said, with the ghost of a smile, "I guess you could call me that."

3

BOB Culbertson was swilling from a longneck bottle in the 1900 Saloon, across the river in Ciudad Acuña, Mexico, fighting the temptation to tell his friend Sam about his session in the Oval Office. From time to time, he reached down to scratch the painful bumps behind his right ankle. This summer, nothing that gave off heat was safe from fire ants.

"Mean little boogers," said Sam sympathetically. "They got my dawg."

Bob Culbertson wasn't listening. He was looking at the newcomers who had just walked into the bar. Three of them, dark and chunky, sporting lots of gold jewelry. The one in the middle, in the white silk jacket, was as wide as he was tall. Culbertson knew the one on the right, in the black T-shirt and loose-hanging leather coat. He was Manolo, the cop from Coahuila who drove a Mercedes.

As the Mexicans settled themselves into a booth, Manolo shot Culbertson a quick look that traveled past his shoulder, indicating the men's room at the back.

Culbertson took the hint. He drained his beer, and ambled to the rear of the saloon. He was washing his hands in the men's room when the Mexican cop walked in, bolted the door behind him, and checked the stalls.

"Hey, Manolo. Long time no see."

"I phone you, *mano*. I ask you to come see me. Why you not come?"

"I got held up."

"I got something for you, *cuate*." He pulled an envelope out of a side pocket. It wasn't even sealed. Culbertson could see the wad of twenties and fifties inside.

Culbertson pushed the Mexican away, hard enough to send him crashing against the swing door of one of the stalls.

"What the fuck is the matter with you, *mano?*" Manolo protested.

"What the hell is wrong with *you?* You wearing a wire or what?" Culbertson groped under the Mexican's jacket, and found only a moneybelt and the butt of a .357 magnum, which he confiscated.

"You out of your head? Bob, this is *me*. We are friends, no?"

"Look, I don't know what you want out of me, but

I'm not interested. We got us a sticky situation back home right now. There are some major investigations going down, and Feds all over town, and the last thing I need is for some dickhead out of Coahuila to start handing me dirty money. Jeez, it looks bad enough already, you and me in the shithouse with the door locked. You want to talk to me, you make a goddamn appointment. Who are those guys you came in with, anyway?"

"You are talking about a very important man."

"The one in the fancy threads?"

"He needs to talk to you, Bob."

"Who is he?"

Manolo hesitated. The rattle of the door handle, followed by loud knocks, apparently persuaded him to spill it all.

"He is Carlos Quintero."

Culbertson stared at him. Carlos Quintero—known as "Chocorrol" because of his girth and his eating habits —was the godfather of one of Mexico's most notorious drug families.

"My friend, you have definitely lost it." Culbertson was starting to enjoy himself. "Your pal Quintero is under indictment in the States. There's no way I'm gonna get caught dead talking to him."

"Quintero is an impatient man," said Manolo.

"He owns you, right?"

"He pays for security. This is natural."

"So why come to me, for Chrissake?"

"He believes something was stolen from him. It was on a plane."

"The one that crashed by the dam."

"He does not believe the story about the crash. You were the first man on the scene. It was in the newspapers. He wants to hear it from you. I would like you to do this one thing for me, Bob."

The hammering at the door stopped abruptly.

"If you do not talk," the Mexican proceeded, "Quintero will think it is because you have something to hide. This would be most unfortunate. Trust me in this."

"So you're threatening me now."

"I give you friendly advice. Mexico is a friendly country." It was an unsubtle reminder that Culbertson was on Manolo's turf.

"Okay. We'll talk. But not here."

"Then where?"

"In the van." Culbertson had driven across in Sam Yardley's minivan, which was upholstered in blue plush and had wooden drink holders for every seat. "I'm an American. Americans think better on wheels."

Quintero complained about the arrangement, and Manolo bitched about the fact that Culbertson insisted on holding onto his gun till the end of the conversation, but they went along in the end. They were confident of their ground. Front and back, the van was escorted by black Fords loaded with armed Mexicans—soldiers for the Quintero family, or cops from Manolo's unit, if there was any real distinction. Sam Yardley was not at all happy when he heard what was up, but Culbertson took him aside before they left the saloon.

"If I remember right," said Culbertson, "there's a bounty posted for this Quintero. I figure it must be worth at least a hundred grand. I wouldn't mind splitting it if things turn out right."

"You had too many drinks, Bob. Them chili-eaters are all over the place. I bet they've got Uzis and all kinds of shit."

"You got the two-seventy, right?" The hunting rifle Culbertson had promised to loan Sam was in the back of the van. "I guess you might as well get some practice."

They took the blacktop road through mesquite country, past the radio tower and the big warehouse where Mexicans sorted the coupons handed in at American grocery store check-out counters. Chocorrol Quintero sat in the front passenger seat, munching candy bars. The other Mexicans sat in the row behind, sipping whiskey. The godfather wanted to hear, over and over, the exact details of the plane crash. He wanted to know how many sacks of cocaine had been found on board, and which law enforcement officials had had access to them.

"I guess you don't trust your partners worth a damn," Culbertson remarked, removing one hand from the wheel to take a pull from the vodka bottle he held between his knees.

Off to the west was the huddled form of Sleeping Lady Mountain. The road made a wide curve, leading toward the back door to Del Rio.

"The plane came down just over there." Culbertson jutted his chin toward the bridge where the river joined the dam. "I don't mind if we take a quick look. You might spot something I missed."

This led to hasty consultations in Spanish. Sam was in one of the back seats, affecting not to hear anything that was being said.

The lead car had come to a stop. They were only a couple of hundred yards from the Mexican Customs post.

"*Muy peligroso*," said Quintero's bodyguard, who had not been introduced. He reached over Culbertson's shoulder, and flicked the high beam on and off. The lead car swerved in a U-turn.

Culbertson seized his moment. He pulled Manolo's pistol out of his waistband and rammed it up against Quintero's teeth. In the next instant, he slammed his foot down on the gas pedal and yelled, "Let's go for it!"

He heard the click as a safety catch was released, felt the chill of cold metal at the base of his neck.

"You do that, boy," he said without turning, "and your boss gets it too."

He was less confident than he sounded, because the bodyguard's hand was shaking. The man was nervous enough to do anything.

Manolo, unarmed, was plainly deliberating whether to make a grab for Culbertson's gun hand.

"Don't think about it, pal," Culbertson said to him.

"Whatever your boss is paying you, it's not enough. You're not wanted for anything in Texas. Yet."

They were almost at the Aduana. Culbertson continued to accelerate. The Mexicans on duty yelled but did not shoot.

The bodyguard got an armlock around Culbertson's windpipe, and reached over him with his free hand, grabbing for control of the wheel.

In the same instant, one of the black Fords sped past them and veered wildly to the right, seeking to force the van into the guardrail. The van skidded from side to side. Culbertson was trying to ram the lighter vehicle, but he could neither see nor steer properly. He felt the pistol wrenched away from his failing grip.

Behind him, Sam Yardley swung the hunting rifle like a club. Culbertson heard the dull thud, and felt the bodyguard slump forward, a dead weight that he shrugged aside. He focused on the road, and saw that the van was hurtling straight toward the U.S. Customs booth in the middle of the bridge.

"Stop it *now!*" Chocorrol Quintero screamed in English.

"Do it, Bob," said Manolo. He had reclaimed his magnum, and was pointing it at Culbertson.

The Border Patrol chief glanced in his rear-vision mirror and saw Sam Yardley crouched in the aisle, with the .270 hunting rifle at the ready.

"Hey, Manolo. My friend Sam don't say much, but I figure he's got the drop on the both of you and he's scored the first down."

He swung the wheel to the right, and braked to a shuddering halt beside the U.S. Customs booth.

A gum-chewing Customs official leaned into the driver's window.

"Pretty fancy driving, Bob. Anything y'all might need before you start telling us what it's in aid of?"

"Yeah. I need to use your phone. Long distance."

"I don't know about that."

"I gotta call Judge Renwick up at San Antone. I just got him a birthday present and a Christmas present too."

The Customs man shook his head, but let Culbertson place the call. The judge was a household name in south Texas. They called him the Hanging Judge, though it had been a long time since anyone had been hanged by due process in Texas.

4

THE fat man flew in to the Carvajal ranch on his private Learjet. He was dangerously flushed. His breathing was fast and shallow. He had no time for small talk.

From the verandah, Shelley Hayes saw him being driven in from the airstrip in one of Raúl's Land Cruisers. She beat a hasty retreat to the shady cabana by the pool. She had no desire to spend one minute more in the presence of Paco Carranza than was strictly necessary.

Carranza sat with Raúl in his air-conditioned study, and gulped scotch and soda like water. Raúl viewed this red-faced, foul-mouthed *hacendado* from Chihuahua, with his pendulous gut and his overgrown mustache, with a patrician's disdain. But he regarded Carranza as necessary. The man was highly motivated, and generally effective. He could mobilize conservative landowners all across the north. In addition to their money and hired gunmen, Paco Carranza was Raúl's principal channel to the Quintero drug family, which was wealthy enough to buy and sell governments.

Paco Carranza was one of the first Mexicans that Raúl had recruited for the Safari Project. There was no other Mexican, outside Raúl's own family and household, who knew as much about the project's true agenda. Raúl was less inhibited with his Texas friends than with his own countrymen, perhaps because he was more at home with Texans than with Mexicans. Then, too, Texans had practical experience of founding a new republic. It was in their blood. To a certain kind of Texan, the Safari Project—which would be reviled as worse than mere treason by many in Mexico—summoned up images of the glory days of Sam Houston and San Jacinto.

Now, watching the fat man sweating as he slopped his whiskey, Raúl wondered if he had made a bad miscalculation in bringing Carranza into his inner circle. The fat man was badly rattled. He had the wind up, because of a stupid incident at the border involving a bounty hunter, an off-duty Border Patrolman named Culbertson.

"They took Chocorrol Quintero to San Antonio," the fat man repeated. "Do you understand what that means?"

Raúl Carvajal sipped his wine. "If Quintero has good lawyers," he suggested, "it means nothing. He was kidnapped. Our government—" his lip curled at the phrase, "—will have to make an official protest. Gringo courts are fanatical about technicalities. They will have to release him."

"Maybe not. The judge in the case has vowed war on *narcotraficantes*. He has promised in public to put Chocorrol behind bars for thirty years."

"What is the name of this judge?"

"Hugh Renwick." The fat man pulled the silk handkerchief out of the breast pocket of his rumpled linen suit and mopped his forehead. His sweat had seeped through his jacket, making dark patches under his shoulders.

Raúl wrinkled his nose. "It's quite a fascinating problem, don't you think? Judge Renwick is our friend. At least, he is the friend of our associates in Houston."

"*Hijo de puta!*" the fat man swore. "He knows us! He knows both of us! We met him at that fucking safari park!"

"Exotic game farm," Raúl corrected him.

"Can we control him?" Carranza demanded.

"I don't think we should show our hand. Not if the

judge is as exercised about drugs as you maintain. We must let American law run its course."

"That's easy for *you* to say. It's *my* ass that's hanging out."

"What do you mean?"

"Chocorrol Quintero can name me in court. Trades. Payoffs. Enough to hang me."

"You mean you dealt with him face to face?"

The fat man's eyes were hot with anger between the puffy folds. "It's the only way, fuck-your-mother! Principals deal with principals!"

"Who else did you deal with?"

"The younger brother. He called me. He expects our help. He's a wild man, Raúl. They call him El Loco. He's capable of anything."

"I see. What exactly do you propose?"

"Call Houston. Maybe there's a way around the judge."

Raúl agreed to consider it. Later, he made the call in private, from his study, while the fat man was taking a siesta after a five-course *comida*. Alone in the room, Raúl reflected on the venality of the men he had chosen for his purpose. The Houston oilman was propelled by ravening greed: by the lure of a vast new oil field, hidden from the world beneath the waters off the coast of Tamaulipas. The fat man, too, pursued the dream of fabulous wealth, to be milked from the drug trade and to be torn from the peasants who would one day be herded off their collective farms. The gray man who had written the Safari document was a mercenary, impure and simple.

In his own view, Raúl belonged to a different breed, and worked toward higher ends. He was a man of honor, engaged in a private war to avenge his murdered father and to free the northern states—the harsh lands colonized by Luís de Carvajal, his *marrano* ancestor—from the vicious tyranny of Mexico City. Raúl would accept any means that served this end. Despite his education, he had no sympathy with word games. He would not entertain the thought that the means always subvert the ends.

After talking to Houston, he found Carranza snoring in a hammock on the verandah. He put a finger across the fat man's nostrils. Carranza snuffled, and woke with a start.

"Is it done?" he demanded, when he saw Raúl.

"Let us say we have expanded our options. Our friend the judge has a daughter. A very pretty one, I am told."

THREE

□ □ □

1

THE whine of the telephone drilled into the left lobe of Kreeger's brain. He groped across the stirring body of his wife to claim the receiver. The fuzzy green digits on the radio alarm clock read 3:57.

Jesus. Nobody calls at four in the morning except to tell you someone has died. More people are born than die at 4 A.M., but the proud fathers usually let you have coffee and juice before they phone you about it.

"Yes."

Kreeger listened to a flow of rapid Spanish.

It was a Mexican operator, asking if he would pay for a collect call from a Señorita Kreeger.

Kreeger felt a cold puff of air at the base of his neck. "Dad?"

Jim Kreeger pulled the phone as far across the bed as the cord would allow. But Karla was already sitting up, alert and worried. She reached for the lamp on the night table.

"It's Lucy, isn't it?" she said, with a mother's instinct. "What's happened?"

Kreeger put his hand on her shoulder, trying to make sense out of the cascade of words on the other end of the line.

"Take it slow, honey. Where are you?"

Lucy was calling from one of the smaller border towns, a few hours' ride from San Antonio. Kreeger remembered it from his youth, a place where a hill country boy old enough to drive went to get a taste of life. It hadn't changed a hell of a lot. The honky-tonks were still painted aqua green and flamingo pink. You could still buy a Coke in a glass bottle built like Mae West.

"Dad, I'm sorry."

Nine hundred miles north of Kreeger's rented house, located in the Bosques de la Herradura, an affluent northwest suburb of Mexico City, his daughter was crying her heart out. He was torn between anger and the need to reach out and comfort her. He could picture the whole thing. That guy she was dating—Brad—must have driven her down from Austin with a bunch of college friends. There'd been some kind of accident. The local police were involved, and would have to be bought off. Damn it. He had ordered Lucy never to cross the border without giving him notice. Every crooked police *comandante* and druglord and leftist crazy in Mexico knew that he was Chief of Station, and the CIA is a lot less popular with Mexicans than the National Lottery.

"Put Brad on the line. That young man has some explaining to do."

Through a burst of static, he heard Lucy say, "They think he's going to die."

What she said next reminded him of the maxim he had lived by for twenty years: Never think what you want to think until you know what you need to know.

Lucy said, "They took Donna."

"Donna Renwick? You mean she was kidnapped?"

The blood drained from Karla's face. Kreeger massaged her shoulder. He spoke evenly into the phone. "Honey, I need you to tell me the whole thing, from the beginning."

When she had gotten her emotions under control, Lucy gave him a coherent, graphic account. Four of them had driven down from Austin for the weekend—Lucy and Brad, Donna Renwick and another boy. Lucy was careful to specify that the girls were rooming together. Her father didn't believe it, but there was no point in making an issue of that now. They had checked into a motel on the U.S. side, and walked across the bridge into Mexico. They ate chilies rellenos at Mario's and drank beer at Crosby's, and were walking back to the United States when a carload of thugs in a black Grand Marquis cut them off and made a grab for the girls. Brad used his fists, and one of the attackers made a hole in his belly with a pump-action shotgun. Kreeger had seen wounds like that; there's not much a doctor can do. The hoods threw Donna in the back of the car and took off. The one Lucy saw most clearly was sporting a diamond bracelet and a leather jacket with a rhinestone scorpion on the back.

"Nice," said Kreeger.

The hospital wanted money up front, and the *Judiciales*—the state police—didn't want to know. Except that they held her and the second boy incommunicado for three hours, making them look over musty books of mug shots before they allowed her to call her father. In three hours, Kreeger reflected, the kidnappers could have driven halfway to Sinaloa. There were also many other awful things they could have done.

"Give me an hour," Kreeger told his daughter. "I'll get someone to bring you out."

"And a doctor for Brad. An American doctor." Her voice was shaking again.

"Yes. Everything's going to be fine. Hold on. Your mother's going to talk to you."

Kreeger passed the phone to Karla as he jumped from the bed and began to dress. He had his pants on when he heard his wife announce that she was going to take the first flight up to San Antonio. They were discussing whether to meet on the border or at the Renwicks' house.

Kreeger slid his .38 short into the waistband of his trousers. The little Smith & Wesson was a Stone Age weapon compared with the high-tech armories of druglords and terrorists, but Jim Kreeger believed in instinct more than technology.

Karla was off the phone now, and the room seemed unnaturally quiet. Kreeger wrapped his arms around his wife. They had not been close for a long time—Karla blamed his job and he didn't contradict her—but a threat to a child serves to bind a couple together.

"I'm taking the Ford," he told her. "Ultimo will take you to the airport."

Ultimo was Kreeger's chauffeur-cum-bodyguard, one of the square-built Mexican security types the CIA station chief referred to as Bookends. He was generally reliable, if a little torpid after lunch, but beyond any shadow of doubt Ultimo's heart belonged to SIN: which is to say, the Servicio de Información Nacional, the Mexican secret police.

Karla was still a handsome woman, even with no makeup and her eyes red and swollen.

"I keep thinking," she whispered, "what if it were Lucy? That poor Donna. What will those men do with her? Such a pretty little thing. Who's going to tell Hugh and Marion?"

Kreeger did not say what he had said at the office when the last DEA agent went missing: When someone disappears in Mexico, you abandon hope.

He said, "I'm on it. I'll get Donna back."

Karla said, "You can't lie to me, Jim. When you lie, it lights up on your forehead."

2

THE Kreegers' house, located in one of Mexico City's few neighborhoods where the air remained somewhat clean, stood as a kind of urban fortress, its back to the street, ringed by a high security wall. Kreeger unlocked the gates and eased the Ford LTD out into the narrow road. Ignoring the relative cool of the early hour, he turned on the car's air conditioning, hoping to stave off for at least a while the sickening stench of the smog that deepened the further he got into the city. He knew his efforts were futile. Only a couple of miles from his home, Kreeger felt the first symptoms of nausea.

At seven thousand feet, the air in the Valley of Mexico was thin enough to begin with. The effluvium vomited by the world-city was driving out the oxygen that was left. Mexico. In Nahuatl, the language of the Aztecs, the word meant the Navel of the Moon. Maybe the rulers of Mexico would end by making the valley of their capital as uninhabitable as the moon. Mexican schoolchildren—so Karla told him—shaded the sky smog-gray in their coloring books, even in pictures of the Garden of Eden, because that was the color of the sky they knew.

The atmosphere was not conducive to good humor or calm reasoning, especially when, like Kreeger, you had a mild hangover from a round of stupefying but unavoidable diplomatic receptions the night before, and were trying to figure out why a bunch of hoods had attacked your daughter and abducted her best friend. And why the local cops weren't looking for them.

Donna Renwick.

He remembered a cute little blond girl, not much over five feet tall, vivacious as only Texas girls can be. A few years back, weary of fighting turf wars and chasing phantoms through the files of the counterintelligence division of the Mausoleum at Langley, Virginia, he had taken his family on vacation into the limestone hills above the Balcones Scarp, into the landscapes of his boyhood. Jim Kreeger always returned to the Texas hill country when he needed to breathe. In the hill country, you seemed to breathe a larger air. Donna had come up from San Antonio to join them. For three generations, the Kreegers and the Renwicks had been friends; Hugh Renwick and Jim had shared their childhood. Wild, rawboned Hugh Renwick, as stringy as Kreeger was broad and muscular, had somehow managed to pass his law

exams and had made his ascent from Small Claims Court
to the status of U.S. District Judge.

Judge Renwick. Kreeger smiled at the thought, remembering Hugh as a beer-swilling, skirt-chasing, hell-
raking cardsharp and all-round good ol' boy.

His mind was jolted to the present as he was forced
to swerve into the middle of the Avenida del Conscripto
to avoid running down the military policeman in dark
olive who was waving a tiny red Alto sign at his windshield.

Kreeger sat with his foot on the brake pedal while a
black car, an LTD like his own—SIN loved them—
wheeled out from behind the high wire fence of Campo
Militar Numero Uno, which sprawled for a mile or more
along the left side of the road. Through the powdery
dark, Kreeger caught a glimpse of the driver. The shades
made him look like a hungry mole. No doubt some poor
devil had spent a night as horrible as Lucy's friends had
endured. The SIN used a building at the back of the
Campo Militar to conduct special interrogations.

The MP advanced on Kreeger as if he meant to give
him a piece of his mind, or at least extract a *mordida*, but
stamped away in disgust when he noticed the blue-and-
gray diplomatic plates.

Allowed to resume his journey, Kreeger again undertook a mental assessment of the situation he faced.

Donna Renwick was not just another tourist. Her
father was about to open the trial of a notorious Mexican
doper, Carlos "Chocorrol" Quintero. According to the
press reports, Quintero had been grabbed on the Mexican
side by a bounty hunter, a cowboy from the Border Patrol. Hugh Renwick, as the ranking judge in the district,
had issued a preliminary ruling denying bail and announced he would hear the case in person. He would
also tell reporters that he thought the bounty hunter deserved a medal.

These reflections brought a flutter of hope.

If the cartel was holding Donna Renwick, they were

holding her for trade: her release in exchange for Chocorrol Quintero's.

How would Hugh Renwick respond to an offer like that?

How would *I* respond, Kreeger asked himself. Would I damn those scumbags to hell, and let my daughter be tortured to death?

He smiled grimly and resolved, If those dirtbags want to trade, I'll give them a trade.

3

KREEGER took Calle Homero down to the Paseo de la Reforma, lined with tiny bronze heroes, statues that stood like potted palms. The city was still dozing. Even the shoe-shine stands were deserted. The newspaper kiosks would be shuttered until eight or eight-thirty. Mexicans feel no urgency about reading the news the government deems fit to print. Kreeger looped around the Angel of Independence and slipped into the tight one-way street between the open-air car park and the anonymous bulk of the American Embassy. The five-floor building was utterly featureless apart from the security ramps and the shed with antennas up on the roof. Kreeger drove down into the basement garage, where he abandoned the Ford and boarded the elevator reserved for the top floor.

The first thing Kreeger did when he entered his office was to turn on the Muzak. The built-in sound system covered the walls of the Station Chief's office, one of many devices employed to thwart eavesdroppers. The musical score had been selected by someone who obviously spent a lot of time in hotel elevators.

Eddie O'Brien walked in, with a Styrofoam cup in his hand.

Trim and blue-eyed, with a thatch of light brown hair that wouldn't stay off his forehead, Eddie was very popular, especially among the single women on staff. Today he was wearing a bold check shirt, and a red tie that hung at half-mast. Usually he had a smile for everyone, but he wasn't smiling now.

"Lucy's fine," he announced. "I'm afraid the boy didn't make it."

"Shit." Kreeger's bum knee throbbed. Lucy had just turned twenty. The boy might have been a year older, but no more. "Any word on the judge's daughter? Donna Renwick?"

"Zip from our friends the *Judiciales*. But it looks drug-related. Judge Renwick told the Bureau he got a call around midnight—and he changed his unlisted number last week. Do you know where your daughter is? That kind of stuff."

Eddie studied his shoelaces.

"Something else?"

"The Bureau guy said they got the judge's dog yesterday. Slit its throat and pulled the tongue out the hole. Guess that's what they call a Colombian necktie."

"I know what it's called." Kreeger remembered the dog; he'd been part of that family for more than a dozen years. They shouldn't have done that.

Easy, Kreeger cautioned himself. He had to take this case one step at a time. He was Chief of Station, with more than forty case officers to protect. He also had to consider an intricate web of relationships with the Mexican government. He wouldn't get off with a verbal rebuke if he handled this one wrong. And if he miscalculated, he could make every member of the station, and their families, targets for killers.

"Tell me what I can do," Eddie said.

"Get me anything you can turn up on the Quintero family—who they are, where they are, who their friends are."

Eddie could smell action a hundred miles away.

Kreeger recognized in this thirty-year-old something of a younger self. Eddie had played baseball for Hofstra, and was good enough to be offered a contract for the Mets; he decided the CIA was more of a challenge. He was a natural operations man. If he were ordered to spend his days poring over files, he would just shrivel up and die. Eddie would go a long way—if he had guiding rails. Kreeger had made him head of the operations support section, which handled stake-outs, surveillance, and technical jobs. Officially, Eddie checked visas in the consular office.

Eddie said, as if he could read his chief's mind, "I'd like to be in on it, boss."

"I'll let you know."

4

For the first part of the working day, Kreeger stuck to routine. He chaired the normal meeting of his section chiefs in the Bubble: a twelve-by-eighteen secure room, elevated above the floor, sheathed in metal like a bank vault, with its own air-conditioning system and a battery of electronic devices to baffle any attempted probe from the outside world. In addition to Kreeger, seven men and one woman sat in on the meeting. Bow-tied, pipe-smoking Maury Atthowe III was deputy COS, a throwback, Kreeger thought, to the Agency's anglophiliac infancy. Maury was not one of Kreeger's favorites, and Kreeger had already determined that whatever he decided to do about the Renwick kidnapping, he would not share his decision with his number two.

The lone woman was an attractive divorcée of Czech origin named Lois Compton. She had joined the Agency as a lateral entry, out of a DA's office in Southern California. Several of the men in the Bubble gave Lois more of their attention than her role in discussions seemed to justify. Now in her early thirties, Lois held one of the toughest and least popular jobs in the Station, that of head of the counterintelligence—CI—section. Because of her flair for languages—and, undeniably, also because of her looks—Kreeger often called on Lois to cultivate Soviet and East European targets in the social round of the Mexican capital.

Kreeger kept this morning's in-house meeting briefer than usual, not even mentioning the Renwick affair. Maury Atthowe and the Mexico specialist discussed reports indicating that opposition groups, on both the left and the right, would launch an armed uprising if the government stole the presidential election on July 1, as they all expected.

After the meeting, Kreeger asked George Camacho, his liaison officer, to stay behind.

"I need to see Fausto, this morning if possible."

"Okay. You want me along?"

"You take Fausto his money last week?"

"Yes, third Friday of the month, one week before the Israelis pay him, one week after the Japanese."

"Are we sure about the Japanese?"

Camacho, a lively, olive-skinned Cuban-American, put a finger to one eye and drew down the lower lid. "*Ojo.* The Soviets aren't our only competition here, Jim."

"George, let me ask you a hypothetical. If you needed to mount an action operation—a unilateral operation—here in Mexico, who would you use?"

George liked the question. He was too young to have fought in the Bay of Pigs, but he was a Cuban—one of the ones Castro called *gusanos*—and he had signed on with the Agency to fight Communists. Tactical considerations were a specialty of his.

"Nobody from the Station," said George.

"Right. That goes without saying. The station cannot be compromised."

"What are we talking here, Jim? You want someone knocked off?"

"Now, George. You know that's illegal. We don't do that kind of thing anymore."

"Hell, we should have done it in Panama. And Baghdad. It would have saved our guys from being shipped home in body bags. It would have saved a helluva lot more Kuwaitis." He paused. "You want an action operation, you want Cubans," Camacho told him. "One call to Miami, and I got you twenty guys who'll do anything you want."

Yes, Kreeger thought, and once the job is over, we'll be left with a new pipeline for cocaine traffic in and out of Florida.

"Any other thoughts?"

"I don't know. I mean, you want to do this outside channels."

"That's the general idea."

"Unilaterals," George suggested.

The station rented a network of Mexican agents—unilaterals—inside the local police and security organizations. Most of them belonged to SIN. In theory, their association with the CIA was unknown to Fausto, but Kreeger suspected that several, if not most of them, kept their boss fully briefed on their dealings with the station.

As they had talked, a plan had started to form in Kreeger's mind. Maybe the idea that had been shaping itself was madness, pure and simple. Maybe it was because he was tired and hung over. Maybe he had been carried away by emotion, by the memory of his daughter's grief-stricken voice. Maybe hearing about the performance of that cowboy up at Del Rio had given him the idea. Whatever, he knew what he had to do.

"Shit," Kreeger said suddenly, "those sons of bitches shouldn't have killed that dog."

AFTER Kreeger's morning meeting with the Ambassador, Eddie O'Brien brought him a photograph of a punk identified as Arsenio "El Loco" Quintero, the godfather's kid brother. The younger Quintero's face was lean and pinched, mean as a coyote's, and framed by a tangle of frizzy hair. He wore a three-day stubble, and his eyes were wild, as though he were high on drugs, perhaps from smoking *morenita*—peachy-brown cocaine base, milder and smoother than crack. The crazed eyes were almost more menacing than the gold-plated butt of the Colt .45, embossed with a diamond motif, that protruded from his belt, over his belly button.

Overall, a weak face, Kreeger thought. That kid would drink human blood, but only if he had an audience to impress.

Clipped to the photo was an aerial shot of a fortified compound near Cuernavaca, south of Mexico City. The deed to the place was in the name of a lawyer who worked for the Quinteros. There were several armed guards in sight in the picture, and a blockhouse by the gate that looked as if it might contain a mortar emplacement, or at least a heavy machine gun. A Bell helicopter squatted on a pad behind the stables. The battery of antennas was designed for more than pirating the Disney Channel. It struck Kreeger that there was little hope of getting in and out of that compound quietly.

Not without Fausto.

5

KREEGER let George Camacho drive him to the SIN headquarters, though it might have been quicker to walk. Mexico City traffic lurched rather than flowed, spewing exhaust fumes.

Fausto's command center was an unmarked concrete blockhouse at the corner of Calle Ignacio Ramírez and the Plaza de la República. With its broken windows and filthy, neglected walls, it could pass for an abandoned warehouse.

The SIN command post was in better shape, however, than the Monument to the Revolution, positioned on a rise across the street. Under a vaguely Oriental cupola, the stout columns dedicated to the heroes of the revolution had been blackened by the smoke from charcoal fires, where homeless squatters toasted their tortillas.

George squeezed the Honda into a narrow slot between Porsches, Audis, and Trans Ams in the sticky courtyard at the basement level of the SIN headquarters. The two CIA men walked up to the lobby, where SIN Bookends made them show their IDs and sign for laminated visitor's passes.

They rode the elevator up to the third floor of the four-story building, where Fausto's office overlooked the courtyard—or would have, had the room's windows not been permanently shuttered. Kreeger turned to his liaison officer: "George, would you mind waiting for me? I need to talk to Fausto alone."

A stuffed black panther, frozen in mid-leap, greeted Kreeger from the left side of Fausto's doorway. The cavernous room was filled with other predatory felines, painted, sculpted, or stuffed. The pelt of a Siberian man-eater sprawled across Kreeger's path. To his right, he saw the glass-fronted cabinet against the wall that held two of Fausto's treasures: a jaguar-knight, filched from a Mayan tomb in the Yucatán, and an ancient Olmec figurine, strangely contemporary in the abstraction of its design, that seemed to portray a man changing into a tiger—or a tiger transforming into a man.

Fausto García liked to remind his visitors that the servants of SIN called themselves *los Tigres*.

Fausto's private office was empty of other furnishings, except for a big leather swivel chair lifted from a barbershop, or a dentist's office—neither origin held pleasant associations for an involuntary guest—and a small bar stocked with a single-malt scotch and Stolichnaya.

Fausto slid from his dentist's chair and greeted Kreeger with a ritual *abrazo*. He moved with feline grace, in the second skin of a midnight-blue shantung suit. The diamond-studded Rolex on his wrist was worth more than the Mexican President's salary. His tiny feet—a dancer's feet—were shod in gleaming cordovan leather. His complexion was ruddy; his wavy hair and his clipped mustache might have been dusted with ginger. The eyes were hazel, flecked with green. Fausto did not look like Hollywood's idea of a Mexican. That had been Kreeger's first impression—that, and the intensity of the stare. Kreeger wondered whether Fausto practiced it in front of a mirror.

"Qué onda, cuate?" Fausto greeted the Texan in the slang of his street agents. "What's up, pal?"

Fausto's secretary brought a chair for his guest.

"Andale, Jim. What do you want to know? Whether Comrade Fomin of the KGB is screwing a *puta* from the Plaza Garibaldi? Whether our next President from Harvard—our Mr. Rafael Paz Gallardo—will be able to govern this country? I will tell you a great secret, Jim. Politicians are all the same, in my country or in yours. After three days in office, they begin to stink."

Ignoring Fausto's somewhat garbled attempt at badinage, Kreeger got right to the point. "I have a problem with the Quinteros."

"It is a common name."

"I mean the Quintero family. The drug dealers."

"Those Quinteros are not my concern." Fausto's eyelids fell a fraction. "I am not a pharmacist."

"I am informed," Kreeger said, his voice void of expression, "that when Chocorrol Quintero was arrested, he was carrying credentials of your service. As well as the badge of a *comandante* of the Jalisco state police."

Fausto shrugged. "Such things can be forged. I would be shocked to discover that any officer of my service would consort with drug dealers. Besides, it is my understanding that this Quintero was not arrested. He was kidnapped. It is an outrage against the sovereignty of my country."

Ignoring Fausto's obvious posturing, Kreeger proceeded smoothly.

"I have a special interest in the youngest of the brothers. The one they call El Loco. It is my information that he uses a villa outside Cuernavaca, and is frequently in the capital."

"What is the nature of your interest?"

"Chocorrol Quintero is under indictment before a U.S. Federal Court."

"Don't play with me, Jim. Is this Company business?"

"It's *my* business. Is that good enough?"

"It's better. Go ahead, Jim. I'm listening."

Kreeger told him all he knew about the abduction of Donna Renwick, explaining that this was a matter involving his friends and family. Fausto García listened intently. Fausto was a man who believed in family obligations. He had invited Jim Kreeger to attend his eldest daughter's *quinceañero*—her fifteenth birthday celebration—in a churrigueresque church in Guanajuato. Kreeger had found he was the only man inside the church, since the government was ferociously anticlerical, at least in show; Mexican officials did not dare to show their faces anywhere that smelled of incense. That Fausto had six or seven illegitimate children by his various mistresses—supported, in part, by his CIA subsidy— did not make him any less of a paterfamilias, at least in his own estimation. All his children went to private schools.

"I understand your concern," said Fausto, when he had heard the account of the kidnapping. "The assault on your daughter, and the daughter of your friend, is unforgivable. As you know, I am a family man. How can I help?"

"I want Arsenio Quintero. El Loco."

"Is this man under indictment in the United States?"

"Not yet."

"It makes no difference. We do not extradite Mexicans." He paused. "Let me understand you clearly. You want me to take this man—El Loco—and hand him over to you."

"That is more than I can ask."

"And more than I can give. This Quintero is a Mexican. He has important friends. You know what our supernationalists would say if they found out that I did this for you, Jim. They would call me a *vende-patria*. A hired traitor."

"A favor demands a favor. You know we would show our gratitude."

"You, Jim Kreeger, maybe you! But your government? Your government is—inconstant."

"I'm not asking for my government. I'm asking you as a friend."

"*Pues.*" Fausto spoke with a perceptible lisp, which added a faintly sinister catch before some of his consonants. He ejected himself from his dentist's seat and inspected the teeth of his stuffed cats.

"What I like in you, Jim, is that you are not a luke-warm-water man—not like so many men in your government, and mine. I will tell you this plainly, Jim, man to man. I cannot touch Arsenio Quintero, or any of his clan. These are Mexicans."

"They are animals, Fausto, and you know it."

"Perhaps. But there are animals in the United States as well, animals who have a license to roam the jungle. Am I wrong?"

"Maybe you can at least point me in the right direction," Kreeger said.

Fausto considered this for a long moment before replying. "I would need to know all of it. If you take El Loco, what will you do with him?"

"I will trade."

"With whom? With the brother who is in jail?"

"With whoever is holding the daughter of my friend."

"Do you know who that is?"

"I think El Loco will know. Or be able to find out."

Fausto walked to the bar, and sloshed whiskey into two cut-glass tumblers. "I think we should have a drink."

There was a small disturbance outside. Fausto's secretary put her head through the door, to tell her boss it was the man from the Presidency.

"Con permiso." Fausto handed Kreeger his drink and walked out, to take delivery of a fat envelope from a sleek man in a dark suit with an attaché case chained to his wrist. There was no secrecy about the ritual, at least among friends. It went on at least once a month in the office of every cabinet minister, and every top-level official crucial to the survival of the government. The payoffs came direct from the Office of the Presidency. Kreeger wondered how much Fausto's cut was worth at the current black market rate. A hundred thousand dollars? Probably twice as much. It put his three thousand dollars a month from the CIA into perspective. Maybe Fausto had timed this visit from the presidential bagman to do precisely that.

Fausto stuffed the envelope into the safe in his outer office, and returned to his visitor.

He savored his malt whiskey for a moment. "Money is always made in dark places," he remarked. "Your *norteamericanos* make too much of a drama out of narcotics. Why do you make such a noise about countries that merely give your people what they want? You look for foreign demons, but you have made your own hell. You rattle guns at South America. You rattle words and travel advisories at us. We all know where the problem is. It is in your own houses, in your cities. El Loco Quintero—" he snorted, "—what is he? *Me importa una mierda.* Not worth a shit. You take one Quintero, there will always be another. As long as you invent them."

Kreeger agreed with more of Fausto's words than he cared to admit. He said, "Are you telling me you'll help?"

"Officially, no."

"Unofficially."

Fausto observed that government wages were low, and there were always men—professional, serious people—who might be engaged for protection work in their off-duty hours. Many of them were part of his own command. What his people did in their own time was not his concern. As for El Loco's movements, well, it was possible that someone might hear something. Mexico had many ears. If Kreeger should receive a phone call . . .

"I'll be ready," Kreeger completed the thought. "And thank you."

"A favor demands a favor, Jim."

"I understand. Anything I can do for you?"

"Nothing at all," Fausto laughed. "I just want you to remember."

This thought made Kreeger a little more uneasy than he might have been had Fausto asked for something expensive, but specific. Fausto was running a tab.

FOUR

□ □ □

1

Lois Compton was sitting with Kreeger in the Bubble when the call was patched through. Kreeger had not had much time for Lois that day, even though she was itching to tell him something about his favorite subject: Peter Fomin, the Resident Director of the KGB. It had been closer to six than five when she had gotten in to see him, and already she had lost his attention. She crossed and recrossed her perfect legs, in mild irritation.

"Yes," Kreeger spoke into the receiver.

"You know the Fantasma Club?"

"In Polanco?"

"The *pollo*—the chicken—will be there after midnight. *Póngase trucha.* Make like a trout."

Fausto's caution needed no translation: Be quick, and be slippery.

Kreeger turned to Lois. "Look, I'm sorry. I just don't have time for this now."

Her lips formed a straight line. She was disappointed. She had spent a whole week studying and collating the files on Fomin until she had built her case. The evidence suggested that the KGB *rezident*, in person, was the case handler for a Soviet Illegal living in the United States—an agent who had clearances in Washington way beyond Top Secret, Noform, and Nocon. What could be sexier than that?

She smoothed the hem of her skirt down over her knees. That Kreeger didn't seem to notice only added to her frustration. She indulged occasional fantasies about her boss. You couldn't call him handsome, but he had a natural authority that made the younger men in her life seem soft and unformed. And he was physically powerful; the linebacker's muscles had not been completely obliterated by years of cocktail parties and five-course dinners. If she could get the chief out on the tennis court, Lois thought, she could fix the damage in no time. But Jim Kreeger didn't play tennis. In fact, he had played tennis only once in his life, and that time only because of a woman. That woman was long dead. Lois knew nothing of her; hopefully, Karla didn't either. The fact, however, that Lois reminded him of her was one reason he kept their relationship confined to business, between office walls.

"Are you going to tell me what's up?" Lois demanded.

Kreeger looked at her speculatively. She wasn't sure what that look portended, but at least she had his attention.

He said, "Do you like to dance?"

"I guess."

"How about tonight?"

"You serious?"

"Sure. You got something sexier to wear than that suit?"

"You're putting me on."

Kreeger, however, didn't look like he was kidding. In fact, he looked grim, Lois thought, like he had misplaced his sense of humor.

She said, "It's not a social invitation."

He shook his head.

"Go on. I can take it."

Once again he detailed the abduction of Donna Renwick, concluding with the tip-off that the Quintero brother would be at the Club Fantasma after midnight, explaining the plan he had been pulling together. He had realized that there was a gaping hole in his scenario. He needed a woman—an attractive woman—as cover for the operation. If necessary, to divert the doper, or some of his friends.

"Bait." He didn't say it, Lois did. "I guess I should be flattered."

"Think you can handle it?"

"You want me to come in a body stocking?"

"It could be dangerous. It *will* be. This guy is high half the time. He's completely unpredictable. You can't figure which way he'll leap."

"Hell, the most dangerous thing I've done lately was to crack a nail trying to get a staple out of the damn Xerox machine. I'm in."

GEORGE Camacho had hired the muscle.

Kreeger inspected the Mexicans he had selected in an indoor parking lot off Avenida Juárez, down from the National Lottery.

He counted seven men, including Cuco Salazar, who held the rank of *comandante* in the SIN. Salazar was bigger than the average Bookend—almost gross—but he could move his weight around as deftly as a sumo wrestler.

Casual wear, for these Mexicans, meant loose-hanging brown or black leather jackets, tight black pants, and cowboy boots. They had brought along whatever sidearms had taken their fancy. The favorite was the micro-Uzi machine pistol. But one of the Bookends sported the new Korean-made USAS-12 assault shotgun. Another favored the Mossberg bullpup. It was hard to avoid blowing your adversary in half, from across a room, with either. Cuco Salazar had a pair of grenades clipped to his belt.

"Okay," Kreeger addressed them. "I don't need to teach you guys your business. George picked you because you're the best, right? I just want you to remember we're not out to blow the whole suburb away. Though if you should happen to drop one of those grenades over the wall at Five Fifty-four Masaryk, I wouldn't rat on you, Cuco."

Everyone chuckled, because 554 Avenida Masaryk was the address of the Cuban Embassy.

"I need you to make some noise when I give you the signal," Kreeger went on. "Then we're in and out of that club like a jackrabbit on his bunny. Okay?"

Okay was universal language.

2

THE Fantasma Club occupied a converted mansion in Polanco, overlooking the unkempt park with the deserted aviary where Hermann—a notorious Soviet Illegal based in the United States—had been caught chatting with his KGB paymaster. Come midnight, Mercedeses and Lamborghinis, Citroëns and a canary-yellow Rolls-Royce were blocking traffic on both the road and the sidewalk, under the complaisant eyes of several uniformed cops who were in attendance to collect their tips.

The pulse of the music vibrated for several blocks, beyond the shuttered flower shops and fish markets around Calle Oscar Wilde.

Lois thought the bouncers at the door must have been schooled at Studio 54 in New York, in the bad old days. The one who was dressed as a Babylonian demon, with blowfly wings, took in Kreeger's old check sportcoat and thinning hair and gave him the evil eye.

"It's okay, Pop." Lois winked at her boss. "We'll be home before dawn."

The bouncer's scowl softened as he took in the blonde with the half-buttoned blouse and the long, long legs. He even deigned to pocket the ten Kreeger slipped into his palm.

Under pink and red downlighters, the dance floor

looked to Kreeger like the chest of a patient undergoing quadruple bypass surgery. Papier-mâché spooks and winged skeletons whirled overhead, blurring the background murals that were the one wholly Mexican touch: ersatz Mayan princes drawing blood from their tongues and penises, or from the bodies of their captives.

On a tiny revolving stage, a girl in black high boots and a lizardskin shirt dress that reached just below her crotch lip-synched the words of the songs that were blared from the amplifiers and screamed *"Qué padre!"* in the gaps between numbers.

A bottle blonde with two-inch fake eyelashes stared at Kreeger's shapeless old check coat and started giggling.

Kreeger grumbled to Lois, "I was born too old for this. Let's get a drink."

He barreled through to the bar. The bartender might have been rented from Chippendale's. He was barechested except for hot pink suspenders and a clip-on bow tie and detached collar.

"I'm glad you have a dress code."

"Mande?"

"I'll take a Presidente with soda."

The bartender gave him a dirty look.

"This is a class joint," Lois said. "They only serve imported brands."

"Okay. Give me a manhattan."

"Make it two."

They started screening the dance floor.

Lois spotted their quarry first, and pinched the inside of Kreeger's thigh. "Isn't that our boy?"

Kreeger followed her gaze, and spotted El Loco Quintero swaying between two women, a redhead and a brunette. The man's pants were tight enough to give him a hernia, and his crimson silk shirt hung open to his waist, exposing enough gold to fill the Bulgari display window at the Hotel Pierre in Manhattan. Although he continued to dance, El Loco wasn't paying much attention to his lady friends. He was giving Lois the eye.

"Watch this," Lois said to Kreeger. Coolly, she ran her eyes over El Loco, as if she were mentally stripping him from top to bottom. She arched an eyebrow, puckered her lips, and turned away.

"Two minutes," she told Kreeger. "Time me."

It was nearly three before the band reached the end of the set, and El Loco sloped off to the bar.

He ignored the big gringo in the check coat.

He leaned over Lois. She smelled him. Beneath the cologne, she sensed something rank and feral. He took her hand, and raised it to his lips. Despite his gyrations on the dance floor, his skin was moist but cold.

"Dance with me," he spoke to her.

"Hey, you just hold it, boy—" Kreeger gave his impression of a short-tempered tourist. "The lady's with me."

"Demasiado jamón por dos huevos viejitos. Too much ham for two stale eggs," El Loco sneered at him.

Kreeger affected not to understand the insult.

El Loco said, in passable English, "The lady decides."

"You mind my seat for me, honey," Lois said to Kreeger. "I'll be right back."

Kreeger feigned impotent irritation, watching as Lois led El Loco to the dance floor. Whoa! Kreeger thought. Where had Lois learned to dance like that? She moved with a sensual abandon to the thump of the new fast-beat Brazilian dance.

Kreeger turned from the spectacle on the dance floor, looking for El Loco's protection. He counted three probables, and two likelies.

He looked back. El Loco was touching Lois too often, with hands and hips and chest.

In the middle of a set, Kreeger saw the doper take Lois by both hands and swing her off the dance floor. He was shunting her up a flight of steps on the far side. Two gold-draped goons peeled off after them.

It was happening too fast.

Kreeger bulled his way through the barflies.

"Hey!" he yelled through the hubbub. "Hey! Where d'you think you're going?"

"Later, old man," El Loco laughed at him. The bodyguards blocked Kreeger's path.

He shrugged, as if accepting defeat. When he turned his back on them, he allowed his right hand to fall, in a sudden, raking motion.

The Bookend posted by the door caught the signal, and eased his way out.

Kreeger counted to sixty, slowly. One—one thousand. Two—one thousand. . . . He tried not to worry about all the things that could happen in the couple of minutes Lois was with that creep in one of the private rooms upstairs. He pictured George Camacho and Salazar moving outside. They had already picked out El Loco's car, the fire-engine-red Lamborghini. In his mind's eye, Kreeger saw Salazar pulling the pin, saw the grenade rolling under the car.

The boom was louder than he had expected. It came like the thump of a mortar, firing at close range. It was followed by a second explosion, one that shook the nightclub. The bartender vaulted over the counter, barely avoiding the bottles that came crashing down behind him. Women screamed.

Kreeger ran for the stairs.

Behind him, the Babylonian bouncer was brushed aside by men who flashed the badges of the Federal Judicial Police—the *Judiciales*—the mortal enemies of SIN. Fausto's men made sure the bouncer got a good look at their fake ID. The men from SIN wanted the Quintero gang to remember who was to blame.

Kreeger took the stairs two at a time. Glimpsing a shadow dart across the hall, he slumped back into the stairwell, just in time, as bullets dug holes into the wall. Fired through a silencer, they made the soft plop of corn popping in a microwave oven.

Moving on his knees, Kreeger cranked himself around the corner, using his left hand to steady his right, which held the little Smith & Wesson. He squeezed off two rounds, and saw El Loco's man crumple like a punctured balloon. He wasn't dead, to judge by the groans and curses, but he was near enough not to be a problem for now.

Kreeger hurled himself on the door nearest the wounded man. It splintered under his weight, though he felt as though his shoulder had splintered too.

Lois had her back to the window. Her blouse hung off her in ragged strips. In front of her, as a shield, she was holding El Loco Quintero. She had his head pulled back by the hair. The snout of her pistol pushed in behind his windpipe, angling up under the bony outcrop of his chin.

One of El Loco's hoods had her covered. Two more had wheeled to confront Kreeger. The nearest of them was cradling a pump shotgun.

For an instant, the whole scene was frozen. Then Kreeger heard pounding feet in the corridor. He made the mistake of glancing back. He saw Salazar running with George Camacho at his heels—and everything exploded into violent life.

Kreeger found himself stretched full-length on the floor, a powder burn nipping his cheek. Salazar was shooting across his body. Kreeger heard splintering glass, saw Lois spinning back into the room like a rag doll.

"Lois! God, Lois!"

Nothing was moving in that room except smoke. Kreeger crawled to where Lois had fallen.

He smelled blood. He groped for the source, and found an open wound along her thigh.

"Easy, boss. We don't know each other *that* well."

"Lois, Jeez—"

"Just a scratch. El Loco must have pulled a knife. I didn't have time to check if he was carrying. Sorry."

George Camacho was at the window, yelling in Spanish to the Bookends stationed outside.

"Just get that motherfucker. Will you do that, Jim?"

El Loco had lost his fancy wheels, but his bodyguards came to get him in an armored van—a real war wagon, Kevlar-plated, with portholes for shooters in the back.

By the time Kreeger had satisfied himself that his CI section chief wasn't bleeding to death and had raced downstairs, El Loco's war wagon was already three blocks away.

Kreeger and George Camacho jumped into an unmarked Chevy, with a souped-up engine. Two of the Bookends were in the lead car, the inevitable LTD, giving close pursuit. The one in the passenger seat leaned out the window, aiming his Uzi at the tires of the doper's van. He knocked out the left rear tire, then the right. The war wagon skidded crazily across the road, swung into the left lane, then back onto the sidewalk on the right, but continued moving on the metal rims, throwing sparks.

The chase ended when El Loco's driver succeeded in wrapping the van around a lamppost.

Luckily, El Loco was riding in the back, because there wasn't much that could be done with the hoods in the front.

Kreeger was inspecting the state of the goods when two Mexico City squad cars homed in on the scene, sirens blaring. Salazar dealt with them smoothly. He showed his fake badge as a *comandante* of the Federal Judicial Police. The cops straggled away, with the disappointed expressions of coyotes driven from a carcass by wolves.

In the back of the van, El Loco crouched, knife in hand.

Kreeger picked up the tire iron lying on the floor.

He said, "You better send your soul to God, boy, because your ass belongs to me."

KREEGER left it to Salazar to extract the phone number from El Loco. The ways of SIN were not subtle, but sometimes they produced speedy results.

"I didn't leave a mark on the *hijo de chingada*," Cuco Salazar reported. "All I had to do was tickle him with this."

Salazar held up an ice pick, which they had retrieved from one of El Loco's hoods. Bone-picking was a favorite with the dopers. They stabbed through to the bone with an ice pick, and made music with the nerves.

With El Loco squeezed into the back seat, pinned between Bookends, they drove through El Satelite and took Federal Highway 57 north. There was a roadblock just south of San Luís Potosí—federal highway patrol. Cuco Salazar flashed his badge, and the cops let them by.

El Loco regained some of his cockiness and started eyeballing the men in the car. His meaning was plain: I am recording your faces for the undertaker.

Then he started shaking, and broke into a cold sweat.

"Give me something. I gotta have some stuff."

"You won't need it where you're going," Kreeger told him.

"You're all dead men," El Loco spat. "You and your whore."

Kreeger wasn't going to hit a man in handcuffs. He just reached back, took El Loco's right hand, and squeezed until the bones creaked together.

They made the first phone call outside San Luís, from an all-night truck stop along the highway. Kreeger and George Camacho tuned in while El Loco repeated the prepared message.

His life for the girl's. The girl would be turned over

on the U.S. side of the border. If she was not intact, El Loco's captors would exact compensation. They would call again, to arrange the time and place of the trade.

"*La puta está limpia,*" El Loco reported. Donna Renwick had not been touched. Or so they claimed. The way he said it made it very hard for Kreeger to resist the desire to smack him across the face.

They drove on, through the predawn light—the twilight of the wolf—into Mexico's cowboy country, through cactus forests and dusty flats, with flat-capped mountains rising in the direction of the sunrise.

El Loco's spirits seemed to lift.

"You. Gringo." He leaned forward toward the front seat, where Kreeger was stretching his legs. "You are *pinche rinche*, no? Fucking cop. DEA?"

"I'm a Texas Ranger."

"Listen, *pinche rinche*. You're a dead man."

"You said that already."

"You're a dead man, fighting a dead man's war. You can't do nothing to me. I'm not an outlaw. Outlaws hide. You want to stop the drugs? Stop the white death? You can't stop La Blanca. She is beautiful. She is our revenge."

"You're out of your skull, boy."

"No, listen to me, gringo. The White Lady—the *cocaina*—she is our nuclear weapon. She is our hydrogen bomb. She is the vengeance of Latin America on the *yanquis.*"

Kreeger stuffed a rag in the man's mouth.

4

DAWN had broken when Kreeger and his team drove into Matehuala, a scrabble of low buildings in the desert of cactus.

Kreeger listened in while El Loco made the second call. Donna Renwick was to be handed over at the Ice-breaker Motel in Del Rio, on the U.S. side of the river. Once she was in the hands of the American authorities, El Loco would be set free, at the Motel Alaska in Ciudad Acuña, on the Mexican side.

The people at the other end of the line were suspicious. How could they be sure the men holding El Loco would honor their side of the deal?

"Put Salazar on the line," Kreeger instructed.

Salazar introduced himself as a captain of the Judicial Police, sympathetic to the problems of his fellow Mexicans. A friend of the Quintero family. Then he told the unknown party on the other end that, regrettably, the friends of Chocorrol Quintero had gone too far with the abduction of the gringo judge's daughter. It was bad for business. They should be thankful that matters could be put right with a simple exchange. He gave his word— the word of a *comandante* of the Federal Judicial Police!— that no tricks would be played on this side. But if his friends, the Quinteros, failed to honor their obligation, to the letter, then—*Quién sabe?*—terrible things could happen. Life for them in the Republic of Mexico could become very difficult.

They drove on, down from the plateau through the steep mountain passes winding down toward Saltillo. Morning light glinted on the snowcapped peaks of the Sierra Oriental. At a truck stop that advertised *pan de pulque* and nutty empanadas, they placed the last call.

The deal was on.

Kreeger let the others escort El Loco back to the car while he tried to raise Karla. He had gotten her message the previous evening. She and Lucy were spending the night at a La Quinta inn near the San Antonio airport.

The phone rang in Karla's room four or five times before it was answered, and then it sounded as if Karla were gargling with mouthwash.

"Honey?"

"Aaargh."

"Sorry I woke you."

"Jim?"

"Listen. I have to make this short. I'm getting Donna out."

"Jim, that's wonderful. How—"

"Just listen. Please. Someone is supposed to call you to say that Donna's unharmed. I'll phone you later to make sure. Stay in your room, okay?"

"Lucy's here. You want to speak to her?"

"Sure."

"Daddy?"

"How are you, sweetheart?"

"Hangin' in there."

"That's my girl. You talked to Donna's family?"

"Yes. Oh, Dad—"

"Lucy, I want you and Mom to call Donna's pa, all right? You call now, you might get him before he leaves for the court. You tell him everything's going to be fine. I'm on it. When it goes down, I need him to keep quiet about it, that's all. Did you get that?"

"Yes. . . ."

"I can't talk any more now, sweetheart. I'll see you soon."

WHEN they reached Ciudad Acuña, the sun was almost at mid-sky. Coyotes and document-peddlers ranged the Plaza Mayor, in front of the church. Indian women from far to the south squatted in doorways, palms outstretched, babies nestling in their rebozos. Sharp-eyed juvenile pickpockets worked among the tourists in street markets filled with leather goods, shoddy ceramics, and machine-made antiquities.

The Motel Alaska was a cheerful place by the river. The seats in the restaurant were covered in bright orange plastic; the walls were hung with touristy souvenirs from five continents. The whitewashed walls across the street were daubed with red hammers and sickles and Marxist slogans. Hadn't anyone heard that communism had died?

Kreeger set up his operations center in a shady room behind the parking lot. The first time the phone rang, it was a wrong number—or so they said. The next time, it was Karla.

"Jim?"

"Is Donna out?"

"Someone called me—I guess he was Bureau?"

"Uh-huh."

"He put Donna on. She's scared, but she's okay."

"Fine."

Kreeger had El Loco make the last call. He didn't wait to see them come to collect him. He left El Loco gagged and trussed, balled up on the floor of the motel room.

He said, on parting, "This time, you live. You cross my path again, you're dead. Remember that, asshole, or I'll show you a worse place than the room in hell they've got reserved for you."

He left George Camacho and the Mexicans at the checkpoint. The old wooden bridge was rotting away into the shallow brown river, next to the new metal bridge that Kreeger strolled across. Hiring a car on the U.S. side, he picked up Donna Renwick at the Icebreaker Hotel, bought her a chocolate chip ice cream, and headed for San Antonio.

They sped past Fort Clark, the last U.S. Army post to keep horses, past Bracketville and the movie-set Texas of the Alamo Village, and on through Uvalde and Knippa. Mesquite flats spread to left and right. Here and there you could see a cotton patch, or a clump of ceviche bushes, whose pink blossoms flew open at the first sign of rain, more reliable than any TV weatherman. The road stretched straight and *clean*—not even a sandwich wrapper in sight—through the sunburned, homespun towns. Ahead, the gray blur of the hills beyond the Balcones Scarp. Comanche country. Country the Kriegers—borderers from Alsace who spelled their name the right way—had settled when Texas was a Republic, threatened by Mexicans on one side and Indian horse-warriors on the other.

Donna and Kreeger didn't have much to say to each other. They were drinking it in. They were going home.

That evening, after Kreeger had scrubbed off some of the dirt he had carried out of Mexico, Karla said, "Why don't you put in for early retirement? We could try setting up that winery in the hill country, like we've talked about for years. I talked to the Renwicks about it. They want to go in with us. You know Hugh would do anything for you. Especially now."

Kreeger toweled his back. "You ever heard of a vintage Texas wine?"

"Come on, Jim. They started a winery over in Fredericksburg."

"That's blush wine. I'm not making any pinko brew."

They both laughed at the absurdity of his statement.

He kissed her, and the towel dropped around his ankles. "I still have a job to do."

She glanced down and said, "I didn't know you still cared."

Later, when they thought again about what came next, about going back to Mexico, the fear returned. "Jim, they saw your face. If they find out who you are . . ."

"They won't. Not for a while, anyway."

He counted on Fausto for that. His role at the Club Fantasma would fall without an echo—like many things —into the netherworld where Fausto ruled.

FIVE

☐ ☐ ☐

1

JUDGE Renwick wanted to say thank you for the safe return of his daughter. He called Kreeger at the motel that Friday night and announced that he had booked the two of them into a cabin at the YO Ranch for the weekend.

"We'll get back in the saddle and sip some whiskey. Hell, Jim. You need it more than me. All that time in Washington, all that cloak and dagger stuff. You're getting detribalized, is what. You don't hardly talk Texas friendly anymore."

Kreeger was uneasy about extending his unauthorized visit across the border into a long weekend, and he said so, but Hugh Renwick would not be put off.

Kreeger recognized the urgency in his friend's voice when the judge added, "There's more to this damn Quintero business than you know. Frankly, there's more to it than *I* knew until a couple of smartass attorneys in thousand-dollar Eye-talian suits walked in on me this morning. I'd appreciate some advice. After all, you've made it your business too."

Kreeger could not quarrel with that.

THEY drove up into the hill country behind Kerrville in the judge's Lincoln Town Car. They turned off Route 41 onto a paved drive that ran for a mile and a half to an unmanned security gate where the judge had to phone through for the combination on the lock. Behind the high wire, gemsbok and antelope darted across the drive. Across the sprawling game park, giraffes and elands, scimitar-horned oryx and Armenian red sheep browsed among the dwarf cedars.

Hugh Renwick seemed in no hurry to talk about the doper whose trial was set to begin on Monday, and Kreeger did not push him. Both families had been traumatized by the events of the last two days. When the shock of her boyfriend's murder had sunk in, Lucy's doctor had placed her under heavy sedation.

The men dumped their bags in a log cabin decorated with longhorn skulls, and rented a couple of horses from the ranch manager. They spent most of the morning jouncing along the back trails; Kreeger discovered muscles he had not used in years. From a knoll, they watched a movie star in a ten-gallon Stetson and tailored safari kit miss two easy shots at a white curly-horned oryx. For fees ranging up to $7,500 a trophy, the rich and famous could shoot exotics at the YO Ranch year-round.

The judge swung his horse's head around in disgust. Kreeger clipped his mount's flanks with his heels and trotted after him.

"We got some serious drinking to do," the judge called over his shoulder.

Back in their cabin, they relaxed with a bottle of Jim Beam, and the judge proceeded to talk about boyhood escapades, family and friends, Texas politics, a barbecue dinner with President Butler—anything and everything except the issue he had raised on the telephone. Kreeger sensed the depth of his friend's unease. Why did the judge keep holding back? Was he still afraid for his wife and children? Had he received new death threats since the kidnapping?

"Hughie," Kreeger attempted to call him to order. "It's great to sit here shooting the breeze. But you said you needed to talk to me about Quintero."

"That son of a bitch." The judge popped an ice cube between his teeth and bit down hard. "How much do you know about him?"

"I know he's big time. One of the major players. And I guess he likes to eat, since they call him Chocolate Roll."

"Quintero has probably poisoned more American kids than anyone since the Medellín kingpins went down. If I had my druthers, I'd put him on death row. The best I can do is thirty years, hard time."

"And you've got a tight case."

"Tight as a virgin's ass."

"So where's the problem?"

"Quintero wants to deal. About an hour after we heard Donna was coming out—get this, Jim—the Eye-talian suits come strolling in, smooth as cat puke. Offering names. Talking plea bargains."

"That's not your style, to deal."

The judge crossed and recrossed his legs. He had developed a facial twitch, below the right eye, that Kreeger did not remember. Kreeger did not like the way his friend looked.

"What's Quintero offering?" Kreeger asked. "Crooked cops? Mexican officials? What's the bait?"

"Quintero has been doing business with some very important people, on both sides of the border. The way his attorneys tell it, he's ready to leave a few of them twisting in the wind."

"You want to run some of those names by me?"

The judge poured himself a stiff jolt of bourbon, and

drained most of it before he said, "Paco Carranza. He's a big rancher down in Chihuahua. A political type, in big with the Mexican opposition."

Kreeger had heard something about this Mexican called Carranza, but he couldn't place him exactly. He caught the blurred image of a florid, overweight blow-hard denouncing the Mexican government at some rally near the border. How could he be that important?

"Who gives a rat's ass about this Carranza?" Kreeger asked. "Seems to me Quintero's fancy lawyers aren't of-fering you much of a trade. Guys like Carranza are a dime a dozen. And he's on the wrong side of the border. I thought the least Quintero would do would be to offer you a U.S. bank president and a couple of DEA guys."

"Then you really don't know." Hugh Renwick was reaching for the bottle again. When he next spoke, he sounded abstracted, as if he was working something out in his own head. "I guess they must have bypassed Mex-ico Station for security reasons."

"Security reasons?" Kreeger echoed, incredulous. "Sounds to me like someone's been spinning you a line, Hughie. You better give me the whole of it."

"I guess I've said too much already."

"*Hughie!* This is *me*, remember?" Kreeger had never seen his friend look so uncomfortable.

The judge cleared his throat. "I met this son of a bitch, Carranza. I met him here, at the YO Ranch." The judge peered about nervously, as if the Mexican might be hiding in the bathroom.

"Don't tell me he used to be one of your campaign contributors when you were running for state judge."

"Nothing like that." The judge hesitated. He needed to let something out, but he was no longer sure of his footing. He was visibly upset that Kreeger did not know all about Carranza, and Kreeger could not figure out why.

There was a rap on the door, and the judge hurried to answer it, welcoming the interruption. A ranch hand in denims and a broad-brimmed straw hat stood framed against the white heat outside. There were no telephones in the cabins. The ranch hand had been sent down from the Chuck Wagon, where the guests ate at trestle tables, to tell the judge he had an urgent call.

While his friend went to answer the phone, Kreeger strolled across to the Lodge and made an inspection of the trophy room. Beneath wagon-wheel chandeliers was a mass of years of hunters' trophies—a golden eagle with wings outspread, a stuffed bear, assorted heads. Kreeger pushed through double doors leading into a courtyard which contained a stone wellhouse converted into a beer cooler. He was sucking at a longneck bottle, and worrying over unanswered questions, when Hugh Renwick found him. The judge's expression had changed. He looked relieved and guilty, at the same time.

"That Quintero thing?"

"I hear you."

"I guess we can forget it. Chocorrol Quintero was just found dead in his cell."

"*What?*"

"No signs of violence. The marshals say it looks like a heart attack. Of course, we won't know for sure till the coroner's had him opened up."

"Goddamn convenient timing," Kreeger observed. "You don't expect me to believe that Quintero died of natural causes the day after he offered to blow the whistle on his friends."

The judge bridled. "Listen, Jim. I had Quintero locked up tight. We were holding him in an isolation cell under my own damn courthouse. I had U.S. marshals watching him day and night—guys I've known for years. No visitors. No roughhouse."

"Yeah? Well, if this had happened in a Mexican jail, I'd sure know what to call it."

"I take exception to that, Jim."

Kreeger noted that his friend was avoiding his eyes. He was also sweating more than seemed normal, even in the warmth of the early afternoon. Damp patches had spread from his armpits across the front of his shirt.

"Who else knew that Quintero had offered to deal?" Kreeger demanded.

"I don't have to answer that. As a matter of fact, I think we're starting to get on each other's nerves. I'm sorry I dragged you up here."

Kreeger grabbed his friend's forearm. His patience had just run out.

"I want some straight answers from you, Hughie. I risked my goddamn neck getting Donna out, and now you tell me there was no need, because Quintero decided to give up the ghost the weekend before the trial. And you're standing there in a puddle of sweat, and you won't look me in the eye. I think I deserve better."

The judge's long, lanky frame seemed to contract. "I guess you do, Jim. I'm sorry." He eased his narrow buttocks onto the lip of the well. Whatever Hugh Renwick wanted to conceal, the direct appeal to friendship—and obligation—could not be denied. They had been reared in the same hard, inconstant border country, where friendship was the one thing you could count on.

"Okay. So let's start over."

"Your call," said the judge.

"How do *you* think Quintero died?"

"He had food sent in from outside. From restaurants and such. He was a big eater. One of the marshals says he got a box of candy this morning. I guess he ate the lot."

"What are you telling me? That Quintero was poisoned?"

"Could have been strychnine," the judge reflected. "Looks natural enough. Maybe the autopsy will show. Maybe not."

"Didn't any of your men check what was coming in?"

"U.S. marshals aren't food-tasters, Jim. Look, nobody in these parts is going to shed tears over a Mexican doper. Maybe whoever sent the candy did all of us a favor."

"You're going to leave it at that, aren't you? I don't envy you your conscience. Who are you trying to protect? Who else knew that Quintero wanted to trade? Did you call your friend Carranza?"

The judge shook his head. Kreeger could feel him closing up again, and risked everything in a brusque, brutal assault. "What's in it for you, Hughie? Are you on the take? Has this Carranza got something over you?"

The judge straightened his spine. "I have never taken a penny that wasn't owed me, and if you think different, you're no friend of mine."

Kreeger believed him. "Then what are you hiding?"

"It's a national security matter, Jim."

"National security is *my* business. Either you spit it out now or I hitch a ride back to San Antone. Who else did you talk to yesterday?" Kreeger made a performance out of consulting his watch.

The judge opened and closed his mouth. Then he said, "I talked to old John Halliwell."

"The oilman?" Kreeger frowned. He had a vague recollection of John Halliwell, an oversized good ol' boy in alligator boots, showing off at one of the guest ranches around Hunt. It had been many years back, when Halliwell had made his first millions in the oil patch and Kreeger was a high school kid trying to earn a few bucks by cleaning pools and mucking out stables for the rich crowd who came up in summer to escape Houston's fog and muggy heat. The men, he remembered, talked money in boxcar numbers. The women drank gin fizz or mimosas with breakfast and flirted with the help. Kreeger was quite sure John Halliwell had never noticed his existence. How did a Houston oilman fit into the Quintero puzzle?

The judge responded to the unvoiced question. "It was John Halliwell who set up the meeting at the YO where I met Carranza and some other fellers."

"What was this meeting about?"

"It had to do with how things were going to hell in a handbasket down in Mexico. Crooks in government, commies waiting in the wings. A few ol' boys had a notion of how we could sort things out, so to speak."

"So to speak? You mean these guys are cooking some kind of political operation?"

"I didn't get too involved."

"Then what were you doing at the meeting?"

"I guess John Halliwell wanted to show me off to his Mexican friends, seeing as how I was Harry Butler's finance chairman and all back when he was running for the Senate. Show the pro-American people in Mexico that there's sympathy for their cause up here. You know how it works. I guess old John might have wanted some legal advice, too. Problems with the Neutrality Act, that sort of thing. Though I can't see as how they have any real problems, not with Washington behind this."

"Behind what, exactly?"

"I guess they figure on changing the government down in Mexico, if the bunch in power steal the elections."

"And how do they plan on doing that?"

"I wasn't in on all of the sessions. I shot me a couple of whitetail bucks."

"But you mean they actually plan to get us involved in the Mexican elections, that they've got an operation all set up and ready to go?"

"They call it Safari."

Kreeger didn't speak for a moment. Some things were finally starting to make sense. Specific queries to his office from some people in the Butler administration—questions that had no relevance, made no sense at the time. But surely this thing couldn't have gotten that far out of hand.

"Okay, this Safari operation, what gives you reason to believe that it has Uncle Sam's blessing?"

"Why, one of your high panjandrums from Langley came down specially."

"From Langley?"

"That's what they told me. Talked like it, too. Didn't say one damn thing in honest American."

"Did he have a name?"

"Cantwell. Mr. Cantwell."

Kreeger had never heard of a CIA officer called Cantwell. Of course, the Agency was a large bureaucracy. It was possible also that Cantwell was a work-name. Or camouflage for a flimflam artist. As the judge told it, Cantwell's message to the gathering at the YO Ranch had been succinct. The U.S. Administration and the intelligence community had given their full endorsement to a covert operation designed to install a reliably pro-American government on the south side of the Rio Grande. In this effort, the U.S. government was counting on private enterprise for funding and support, because of the constraints imposed on Washington by "un-American" elements in Congress and the media.

"That's about the sum of it," said the judge. "It sounded like a pretty good idea to me, as long as they can keep it under wraps. But nobody contacted me after I drove away, and I didn't give the thing much thought until Quintero's lawyers came up with the name of this asshole Carranza. He didn't say much at the meeting. He seemed to be mostly there for the honey hunt."

To anyone familiar with old-time Texas hospitality the phrase needed no elucidation. A honey hunt was a game of hide-and-seek played with hookers.

When Kreeger had a chance, he jotted down the handful of names the judge could remember. Besides Carranza and Halliwell, Renwick had mentioned a couple of Texas bankers, a high-priced attorney who was reputed to be the Governor's fixer, and a string of Mexicans whose names he did not recall, except for a Monterrey fat cat who was introduced as Raúl.

If Kreeger had heard about the secret meeting at the

YO Ranch under different circumstances, he might have felt more relaxed about it. Every time there was trouble in Mexico, well-heeled rightists from across the border huddled with their Texas business partners to talk conspiracy and revolution. Nothing had come of it for more than a century. The mental pictures Kreeger formed of a small squadron of Learjets and Piper Cherokees parked at the YO's landing strip, of stretch limos circling the Lodge, of good ol' boys panting after hookers through the mesquite, were colorful, but hardly more than that.

What riled him was the mysterious Mr. Cantwell's claim to speak for the CIA. Cantwell, no doubt, would prove to be just another one of the swarm of con men and Beltway bandits who used the CIA for a cover. Kreeger would be a great deal less happy if Cantwell turned out to be a bona-fide CIA officer, because that would mean the Director had decided to cut Kreeger and Mexico Station out of a clandestine operation on their own turf.

What made Kreeger quite certain he needed to follow up the judge's leads as hard and fast as he was able was the fact that there was blood on the floor. A Mexican doper had apparently been killed in his cell, to stop him from disclosing the names of one or more men who were part of something called Safari. Maybe Safari was a blind for a new attempt by the drug cartels to rebuild their networks. Maybe it was more. Whatever their motivation, the men Judge Renwick was dealing with had demonstrated that they were ready to kill on American soil. And that they were skilled enough to reach inside a maximum security cell to do it.

From a pay phone in the Chuck Wagon, Kreeger dialed the number of an apartment in Bethesda.

"Collect from Mr. Galloway," he said when the operator came on the line. Galloway was one of Kreeger's numerous aliases. He had been carrying the pocket litter for it—driver's license, Social Security card, plastic—when he crossed the border, in place of his black diplomatic passport. It was a name he was sure Dorothy would remember.

"Jim? What's up? Where are you calling from?"

"I need a favor, Dot. I need you to have the Director authorize a quick trip to Washington to consult. I'll be there Monday."

"You got it. Is this good for a dinner?"

"You pick the restaurant. As long as they don't serve *mole.*"

Dorothy Hyslop was the CIA Director's secretary, but before that, she had worked for Kreeger in a succession of foreign postings, and a strong bond had developed between them. And a true friendship, as well.

Dorothy was a charter member of a league of similar Washington-based women that Kreeger thought of, lovingly, as the Mollycoddlers' Club—ladies of a certain age who had sacrificed their personal lives to the care and feeding of powerful men, and the preservation of the offices they held. Without the Mollies, by Kreeger's observation, the government of the United States would rapidly grind to a halt.

"You take care, Mr. Galloway."

As Kreeger hung up the phone, it struck him that "Mr. Cantwell," too, sounded the kind of name that belonged on CIA-issue pocket litter. Dorothy would be the ideal person to check that out. No Registry clerk would question an inquiry from the Director's suite.

SIX

□ □ □

1

On Monday morning, as Kreeger drove his rented car along Route 123 toward McLean, Virginia, he saw an Acura parked close by the exit for the CIA. In it sat two men in suits, one of them with a notepad in plain view. He marked them as novice spies from one of the new Central European services. From the old days, when he was first assigned to the Mausoleum, Kreeger remembered East European agents sitting out on the road, copying down the license tags of CIA employees on their way to work.

He logged in at the Mexico desk and rode the elevator up to the seventh floor. Dorothy gave him a friendly hug in Director Wagoner's outer office.

"He's not happy," she reported.

"This too shall pass," Kreeger intoned. Behind his broad grin, he wondered whether the Director had heard something about his sudden disappearance from Mexico Station.

Bill Wagoner, indeed, did not look happy. The Director gave Kreeger the briefest of handshakes and retreated behind the rampart of his desk. Seated, he could confront Kreeger at eye level. The Director was a small man, and to compensate, he had the seat of his swivel chair screwed up so high that his toes barely touched the ground. He favored assistants and security guards who were under five-eight.

"Where were you Friday?" he demanded in his Power Voice.

Kreeger said, "Montezuma's revenge."

Director Wagoner trained his excessively blue eyes on the Station Chief in an unblinking stare. There was an ugly rumor that Bill Wagoner had taken a course in executive hypnotism. The Director was a career man, but his life had been spent among form-fillers and paper-pushers. He had risen by punching the right tickets in Washington, and by keeping his copybook clean. Kreeger harbored profound suspicions about men who handled everything with such neatness. It suggested that they had never had the imagination or daring to do things otherwise.

"You know what's wrong with you, Kreeger?" the Director said after a weighty pause. "You're not a team player."

"I used to be a linebacker. Linebackers are team players."

The Director's lips formed a straight line. His game was tennis, and he was unsure whether to take Kreeger's riposte as a personal affront.

"Anyway," he pursued, "it's just as well you're here. I've been asked to brief President Butler on Mexico."

"I'm happy for you."

"The President has made Mexico a top priority. He's very concerned about the state of affairs down there. He thinks it's a disgrace that we've won the cold war and kicked ass in the Persian Gulf and are losing in our own backyard, and he wants to know what we propose to do about it. I must say, I can't disagree with him."

"Losing?" Kreeger picked up. "What is that supposed to mean? Mexico isn't ours to win or lose."

"Don't get smart with me, Jim. It's all in your own reports. In ten days, the Mexicans vote themselves a new President. The government candidate, whatsisname—"

"Paz Gallardo."

"Thank you. Paz Gallardo will lose, but they'll rig the count so he'll scrape in. In the *real* vote, the leftist candidate will win by a landslide, and everyone will know it, and his supporters will start blowing things up. Especially U.S. property. Have I got it about right?''

''Near enough. It's what happened last time, and the time before. But it will be more serious this time around, because a lot of people in Mexico are hurting, and the government's more unpopular than it's ever been, and the opposition can't understand why it's okay in world opinion to change the regime in East Germany or Chile, but not in Mexico.''

''We don't like it,'' the Director said flatly.

''*I* don't like it,'' Kreeger countered. ''But we can live with it.''

''Maybe you've been down there too long.''

''For Chrissake, I've been in Mexico eighteen months!''

''There's always a danger of fieldmen going native. Remember what happened in Iran? All we got from the Station was warmed-over piss from the Shah's secret police. Until we woke up and found the Embassy in the hands of a bunch of crazies who thought they heard Allah talking into their left earholes. And what about Iraq? Our guys in Baghdad were out to lunch.''

What the hell would you know about it? Kreeger thought. You've never been anywhere that didn't have working air conditioning. He refrained, however, from expressing these sentiments out loud.

''There is a certain concern in this Administration—'' the Director assumed his tutorial voice, ''—that the government candidate in Mexico is overly close to the Japanese.''

''He's been to Japan a couple of times,'' Kreeger commented.

''He's on the take, isn't he? I saw a figure of five hundred thousand dollars.''

''I believe it was two hundred thousand, and it was lecture honoraria.''

Director Wagoner snorted.

"I seem to remember a former U.S. President collected ten times as much," Kreeger observed.

"That was an *ex*-President. This is a gonnabe. Besides, this is a Mexican. Mexicans come cheap."

"If you want to build a scare about the number of sushi bars in Mexico, be my guest. But it's a red herring. The Japanese will find out what we already know. You can't buy a Mexican President; you can only rent him."

Kreeger was bemused by the Director's sustained, if erratic, attack. The Director was obviously looking for a Threat. If the Russians were perceived as less scary than they used to be, and the Agency had missed out on the war medals from Desert Storm, then pick on someone new—and do it fast, before the budget-cutters got out their choppers. Druglords were a perennial threat. So were the Japanese. Mexico had both, and it was close enough for U.S. voters to care. Was the Director trying to manufacture a Mexican crisis, or merely echoing opinions from higher up?

"It seems to me," Kreeger said, "that a lot of people are trying to stir the pot in Mexico. That's the reason I asked for this consultation."

"Ah, yes."

"I need to know if the Agency is involved in any secret operations in Mexico that I have not been informed about."

"Do you want to be more specific?"

"Are you aware of an operation called Safari?"

"Never heard of it."

"How about a case officer—or former case officer—called Cantwell?"

"There is no one by that name in the Agency."

The Director had excellent control of his facial muscles and they betrayed no hint of anything amiss, but he had responded too quickly to the query about Cantwell, and Kreeger noticed it. How could he *know*? Had he memorized the name of everyone on the CIA payroll?

Director Wagoner said, "I think you'd better tell me where you're coming from, Jim."

The lapse into colloquialism was another warning, Kreeger thought. "I picked up a few things from my sources. There's talk the Agency is mixed up in some half-assed plot to change the government in Mexico after the elections."

"Horseshit."

"That's what I figured. I just wanted to make sure, so I can check this out without getting any wires crossed."

"I may have missed something, Jim. Tell me again. Where's this coming from?" The Director leaned forward, the picture of cordiality.

"Just a few threads I stitched together."

"In Mexico City?"

Kreeger met his gaze. He had promised Hugh Renwick that he would not use his name. Even without the promise, an instinct for survival would have made him withhold vital details from the Director. For one thing, he had no intention of revealing his unauthorized role in the hostage trade. The Director had endeared himself to congressmen of both stripes—if not to his own fieldmen —by his insistence on doing things by the book.

"Here and there," said Kreeger. "I heard this Safari group held a get-together in south Texas. Mexicans and Americans. And this Cantwell guy."

"In Texas?"

"Yeah. Up at the YO Ranch."

"That's your neck of the woods, isn't it?"

"In a manner of speaking."

"Well, not any longer, Jim. I want you to listen very carefully. You're telling me about something that happened on U.S. territory. Right?"

Kreeger nodded.

"Fine. Then it's off-limits. Off-bounds. Do you read me? It's outside our domain. And it's sure as hell off yours."

"End of story?"

"Let me handle this. I'll ask around. If there's anything that needs a follow-up, I'll consult with the appropriate agencies."

The Director looked at his battery of telephones the instant before one of them rang on cue. He lifted the receiver and listened for a moment before he announced to Kreeger, "I'm needed over at the White House."

He stood up and gave Kreeger his hand. His nails were beautifully manicured. "Keep in touch, Jim. I'm here to help."

2

As soon as Kreeger had left his office, Director Wagoner scrabbled in the top drawer of his desk for his bottle of Novocain. He shook a couple of pills into the palm of his hand and gulped them down without water. He waited for relief from the shooting pains between his jaw and his cheekbone that had come from gritting his teeth, in the hollow of the night, these many weeks past. Relief had still not come when he felt impelled to pick up one of the phones and call Admiral Enright, the National Security Adviser, on his direct line.

"Bill?"

"Who's this?" the admiral's clipped, midlantic accent came back.

"It's me. Bill." Washington insiders called them the Two Bills.

"Are you on a secure line?"

"Jeez! I'm in my own fucking office!"

Admiral Enright was known as a stickler for security. "We're meeting in twenty minutes. What's up?"

"COS Mexico was just in my office. A guy called Kreeger."

"Yes?"

"He's onto Safari. Did you hear me? I told you we couldn't bypass Mexico Station." Alone in his office, Director Wagoner forgot appearances. His sweat glands opened up. He mopped his forehead with a Kleenex as he spoke into the phone.

"How much does he know?" Enright's voice was freshly ironed.

"Just a name. Cantwell."

"Okay. Tell me about Kreeger."

"What's to tell? He's a wild man."

"I heard that."

"A Texan."

"A Texan? Maybe the top man can talk to him, if there's really any problem. They're both Texans."

The top man, in this connection, was President Butler.

"I wouldn't risk it," said Wagoner. "I know Kreeger and I know his type. He's a maverick. He's no team player."

"Then we'll have to get rid of the bastard."

"Bill—you know, I was never happy about this whole deal. Maybe we should think about cutting our losses."

"I'll forget that you said that. I wouldn't want to have to report it to the rest of the team. We get rid of the SOB. Do you hear me, Bill?"

"I hear you."

3

KREEGER took Dorothy for dinner in the grill room at the Bethesda Hyatt, a two-minute drive from her apartment in a high-rise along the East-West Highway. He asked his big question between the oysters and the rack of lamb.

"Does the name Cantwell ring a bell?"

Her memory worked like a card index. She was famed for it. He watched her as she tracked methodically, back and forth. Dorothy's retrieval system might be slow but—unlike the computer terminals at the Mausoleum— it was never down.

When the waiter came with their salads, she was still sifting.

"Maybe you could check for me with Registry," Kreeger suggested.

Dorothy extracted an endive leaf from her plate and twirled it between thumb and forefinger. Then her pupils shot up into her head. For an instant, only the whites of her eyes were showing. It was a mannerism that alarmed strangers.

Dorothy blinked and said, "Clorox."

"Excuse me?"

"The salad made me remember. It was in Lima. Remember? We used a Clorox solution to disinfect fresh vegetables."

"Okay." Kreeger wasn't sure where she was leading, but he was content to follow.

"You had a bottle of Clorox solution in the refrigerator. It wasn't labeled, or the label had slipped off, or something. You were giving a party for some visitors. There was this gray man down from headquarters. You hated each other's guts. He wanted scotch and water, and you let him fix it himself. He got the wrong bottle out of the fridge, and after he took a swig he was gargling and puking in the bathroom for about half an hour. He was fit to be tied." She chuckled over the image she had summoned. "He swore you'd tried to poison him. He left in a tizzy, swearing to kick your ass out in the street."

Kreeger remembered the gray man with the clean, razor-cut neck, the tight muscles around the mouth. A bureaucrat who never used a positive if he could find a double negative.

"Jeez, I do remember," Kreeger laughed, "Paul Milnekoff sent me a copy of the memo that guy sent in.

Paul wrote on it, 'Nice try.' " Kreeger's laughter died in his throat. "Do you know who that was? That was Art Colgate."

"That was Cantwell." Dorothy skewered a piece of red cabbage and plopped it into her mouth.

"Are you sure?"

"Am I ever wrong?" Dorothy grinned at him.

"Would I dare to tell you if you were? But—shit!— Art Colgate! Didn't he have a different work-name on Company paper?"

"Kingsland. He was Kingsland in the correspondence. And there was always plenty of that."

"So how did you get the fix on Cantwell?"

Dorothy sipped her wine and put on an expression that was pure Mollycoddler. She looked at Kreeger like a schoolmistress contemplating a slow, or oversensitive, pupil, a boy who needed to have his hand held.

She said, "I think you're blocking something out. There was a time when you were living this stuff night and day. It was the last time we worked in the same office, at the CI shop. You asked me to pull Colgate's file, and all that stuff from Saigon. You didn't sleep, you didn't eat. Night and day, you were living with the ghosts of Vietnam. There were people who said you were cracking up. There were times *I* thought you were gone. You can't have forgotten everything."

"I haven't forgotten," Kreeger said quietly. How could he? There had been only one woman in his life, besides Karla, whom he had truly loved. And Art Colgate had killed her—or arranged to have her killed—when he was Station Chief in Saigon, a city that Kreeger had never seen, and which had lost even its name. This, at least, was what Kreeger believed. He had never been able to prove it, not even when he had commanded all the resources of the counterintelligence division. He had been able to establish only that, of all the fabricators and frauds and brown-nosers the Agency had spawned in the Vietnam era, Art Colgate was the very worst.

He said, "I still can't find Cantwell."

Dorothy sighed. "Too many manhattans. It incinerates the brain cells."

"I don't notice that booze has done any harm to *your* memory."

"I have the advantage of sex. Women weather better than men. We have to."

"I'm happy for you."

"Cantwell—" Dorothy gestured with her fork, "—was one of Art Colgate's cover names in Vietnam. When he came home, he reported that he had lost his pocket litter in the scramble to get on a chopper out of Saigon, ahead of the commie tanks. I thought it was worth another look, but you weren't too interested. I guess you had your mind on something else."

She gave him a wistful look, and for a moment she might have been thirty years younger. She did not speak the name of the woman Kreeger had lost, but it hung between them, no less present because unacknowledged. Val. Lover, teacher, friend. The woman whose last words to Kreeger before she had vanished into the jungles of Vietnam, had lived with him down the years. "Whatever happens, Jim, you have to stay in the Agency. If the good people leave, the bastards inherit everything."

Dorothy knew. Of course she did. Was there anything she ever forgot?

Kreeger, deeply disturbed, tried to haul himself back to the business at hand. The lamb was served nicely pink, garnished with rosemary and garlic. He ate out of habit, without savoring the taste.

"Why would Art Colgate—assuming he is Mr. Cantwell—be interested in Mexico?" he asked Dorothy, who was eating with her customary gusto.

"Let's see—" she spoke between mouthfuls, "—he's been out on the street for four, maybe five years. He has a consultancy outfit over in Arlington. He calls it Global Assistance Services. Something like that. GAS for short."

"That sounds about right for Art. He's always dealt in wind and piss."

"You haven't forgotten him, have you?"

"I don't harbor grudges, Dot."

"No. You do something that may be worse. You forget easily enough—you just demonstrated that. But you forget without forgiving. If something happens that reminds you of what made you mad before, you're as mad as ever. Maybe more so."

"Thank you, doctor."

"You're welcome. If it's any consolation, I feel about Art Colgate about the same way you do. I can't say the same for my boss. Colgate has the Director's private line."

Kreeger's head was pounding. Had Director Wagoner told him a direct lie? Or was "Mr. Cantwell"—aka Art Colgate—merely trading on high-level contacts to milk gullible clients? Colgate was a salesman, and the key to that trade is to convince the client you have something he needs. Access to the top, hard-to-get items, unusual expertise. Had Colgate, the entrepreneur, simply managed to flog his dubious assets to some good ol' boys and a bunch of Mexicans who—in the way of all Latin Americans—would never believe that a CIA man can be put out to grass? Or was Colgate back in harness?

Kreeger, the professional, reminded himself that he could not afford to indulge his personal feelings. He had to keep the lenses clean. He could not allow himself to be influenced by the fact that, of all the enemies he had encountered, there was no one he wanted to nail as badly as Art Colgate. He had to work this through, step by step, retaining his objectivity.

But he was going to need friends, especially since the Director had read him an explicit warning to Keep Off the Grass.

He inspected Dorothy, who was getting ready for dessert.

"Dot, I may need a back channel."

"That sounds sort of kinky."

"You handle Bill Wagoner's mail, don't you?"

"Only the sexy stuff."

"That's what I'm talking about. The ANTARCTICA channel."

She folded her arms, putting a barrier between them. To senior Agency people, the ANTARCTICA channel was especially sensitive. It referred to private communications from Station Chiefs to the Director. They were not supposed to be read—or even opened—by anyone except the Director of Central Intelligence in person. But Kreeger was quite confident that a senior secretary as savvy and as trusted as Dorothy was allowed to brandish a paper knife before the Director took a look at his secret mail.

"If I need to get a message through, I'll slip a note for you inside the outer envelope."

"Are you in trouble again, Jim?"

"Look, I played football. The most important thing I learned is there's a difference between pain and injury. I'm feeling a little pain. Just a little. If I'm injured, you may know it before I do."

4

BEFORE he flew back to Mexico City, Kreeger called Joe Cicero and asked him to lunch at the Thai restaurant near the old Soviet Embassy.

Joe Cicero was an old-style foreign correspondent. He had chased cannon fire around the world from the Seven Day War to the liberation of Kuwait. He was in Washington on the national defense beat, for the Baron-Ritter chain. Joe was one of the few reporters to whom Jim Kreeger would give the time of day.

They had done each other a few favors over the

years. But Kreeger never let his guard down completely, because he would never trust a reporter not to run with a story. Secrecy was anathema to Joe's profession, but it was the element in which Kreeger lived and breathed.

Still, Kreeger valued Joe as a sounding board, and an independent set of eyes and ears.

"So what's the score in Mexico?" Cicero demanded after his second drink.

"The government's going to steal the elections. There'll be a lot of heat from the opposition, and maybe complaints to the OAS and the UN. There'll be shoot-em-ups, and a million wetbacks trying to get over the border, and the bankers will be standing in a pool of sweat for a few weeks. Then I guess we'll be back to business as usual. Unless there's outside interference."

"From who? The Cubans? The Russians?"

Kreeger shook his head. "Not even in the bad old days. Mexico's too important to them. It's the best base they have for stealing our secrets."

"There's been talk about the Japanese moving in big."

"Sure, they're spreading some money around. They want a guaranteed flow of oil, and they want some new auto plants. If you believe that geo-economics has replaced geopolitics, that's something to watch. Frankly, I'm more concerned about people up here overreacting to the Mexico thing."

"We've got a Texas presidency," Cicero said casually, lighting a Marlboro between courses. "You Texans have always been kinda touchy about Mexico. And after Saddam Hussein shot his wad, I guess everybody's concerned about who controls major oil fields. Some of us went to a briefing on that over at the NSC. A lot of scary talk about checkpoints and Moslem fanatics. They really seem to believe in the reincarnation of Saddam."

"Was Bill Enright there?"

"Just his shadows. But the Admiral seems to have a bee in his bonnet about Mexico."

"You interviewed him in the early days, didn't you?"

"I've known Enright since Vietnam. Since he was running gunboats up the Mekong for your people. He's a charter member of the Saigon Society. You want to hear my theory about Admiral Enright?"

"I'm all ears."

"He's our answer to Saddam Hussein. He thinks history is a competition between the warriors and the softies. He doesn't know a thing about economics, and he can't stand all this trendy talk about an age of geo-economics. To a guy like Enright, that means we're going to end up letting the Germans and the Japanese drive all over us. He wants to use our military machine to keep us number one. He wants to rob the bank."

"I don't see what that's got to do with Mexico. Mexico's flat broke. It's a banker's nightmare."

"It's got oil," Joe Cicero reminded him. "And you don't have to fly through any time zones."

"You're making Enright sound like something out of *Doctor Strangelove.*"

"Well, he *is* pretty strange. He's not married, so he seems to work around the clock. And he missed out on Desert Storm. Pushing papers while Norman Schwarzkopf stole the ratings. He's spoiling for a fight. He thinks that Desert Storm is the model for dealing with restless natives. If it's not Mexico, it will be something else. I say, blame it on the Russians. If the Pentagon doesn't have the Soviet Threat, it has to find someone else to fight. Because if it doesn't fight, it runs out of moolah."

SEVEN

□ □ □

1

At Mexico Station, Kreeger stood in semidarkness in front of a bank of computer screens. Behind him, on a muted TV monitor, the news anchor for the state-run Mexican TV network was announcing the results in the presidential elections—a decisive victory for the government candidate, Rafael Paz Gallardo.

"This is how they're doing it," the Station's Mexico analyst said to Kreeger, indicating the names that were scrolling up on one of the screens.

Kreeger squinted to read them. He saw the names of a lot of people who all seemed to be called Maldonado.

"I don't get it. This looks like the telephone book."

"These are voters in a one-horse town in the state of Guerrero. Sixty-seven of them are called Maldonado. They all voted for Paz."

"So they believe in family discipline."

"It's better than that. They all have the same mother. And they were all born on the same day."

"Jeez." Kreeger looked again. Mexicans called Fernando Ramírez—the Minister of Government and the man responsible for electoral order—the Alchemist. He deserved an even better sobriquet. He had just performed a biological miracle. Minister Ramírez and his lieutenants had just delivered sixty-seven babies out of the same woman.

"They won't get away with it this time," said the analyst. "The shit is going to hit the fan."

"You're probably right. But I don't know that it's gonna change anything down here."

Mexico's ruling establishment, the wondrously named Institutional Revolutionary Party, or PRI, was not in the habit of losing elections. The Station's own soundings had confirmed the exit polling by independent groups: The government candidate had lost the election by a margin of two to one. By rights, the next President of Mexico would be the opposition candidate, Moctezuma Morelos, lampooned by his critics as Batman because he promised miracles. But there was no way the gang in power were going to bow out. They did not care about the much-heralded tide of democracy in Eastern Europe and South America. They allowed presidential elections to be held every six years on condition that their man always won. The next President of Mexico would be Paz Gallardo, a Harvard-trained technocrat. The analyst was right—the cheated opposition would make a noise, but eventually the noise would die away. That was the way things had worked in Mexico since the revolution at the turn of the century.

Kreeger's secretary stuck her head around the door. "Sorry to interrupt. There's a call you might want to take. It's Judge Renwick."

"Coming."

Kreeger took the call in his office.

"Hughie? How've you been? How's Donna?"

"She's back at school," the judge said curtly. "I've been expecting to hear from you, Jim."

"I'm sorry. I've been trying to chase down some of those names we discussed. But I got tied up with the election mess down here. It's like watching cats fight under a blanket."

"You hear anything I should know, Jim?"

"I ran down your friend Mr. Cantwell. He used to be in my business. He's been out for years. The official word is, he's still out in the cold. I know him. He's a flimflam artist. My guess is, you can discount ninety percent of anything he said.''

There was a long pause at the San Antonio end.

Then the judge said, ''It has to be drugs then, doesn't it? The whole Safari thing is a front for dopers. Hell, I knew John Halliwell was hurting. But I never thought he'd sink as low as pulling his friends into this kind of shithole.''

''I wouldn't jump to any conclusions,'' Kreeger cautioned. ''I'm gonna rattle some cages down here, see what I can get on your Mexican pals. What did the coroner say about Quintero?''

''Strychnine traces. You know what the Mexican press is saying? They're saying *we* killed the son of a bitch to keep him from naming U.S. government officials! I got Mexicans camped outside my courthouse. I got marshals watching TV in my front room. I'm pissed, Jim, and I don't mind who knows it. I got a mind to fly up to Washington and see Harry Butler. Seems to me the President ought to know what use is being made of his name in these parts.''

''That might not be such a bad idea.''

''Yeah, well I figure I gotta talk to Big John Halliwell first. I guess I owe him that much.''

''Hughie? I think you should play this long and slow. Don't tell Halliwell what I said about Cantwell.''

''You running scared, Jim?''

''Not for myself. For you.''

JUDGE Renwick decided to take a walk to clear his head. He lived in a leafy neighborhood, safe even at night. He shooed the marshals away when they tried to follow him out the door.

''Don't break up your game show, boys.''

A marshal followed him out onto the stoop anyway. The judge turned to offer some further discouragement, and saw that someone had spray-painted the word *asesino* in blood-red letters two feet high across the front of his house.

"I'm not taking this shit anymore!"

The judge stormed back inside and called John Halliwell's home number. A languid female voice responded at the other end.

"I'm real sorry, Mr. Halliwell is engaged right now." She sounded as if she was licking a popsicle.

"Well, honey, you locate Mr. Halliwell and you tell him for me that if he don't get on the horn right now he'll be engaged for about thirty years."

"I'll see if I can reach him."

When the oilman came on the line, sounding sulky, the judge's epithets flowed so fast and free that Halliwell had to ask him to stop and start over.

The judge's next comment was perfectly distinct. "You dragged me into this, John, and you've been using Harry Butler's name like a registered trademark. I don't know what you're playing at, but I've got a mind to talk to Harry before y'all cause him some real embarrassment."

The oilman could be silky when he put his mind to it. "I hear you, Hughie. Really I do. You're under a lot of stress. These threats, these lies in the papers. Those brown brothers squatting around the courthouse. Why don't you sleep on it? If you feel the same way tomorrow, I'll fly you down to Houston and we'll talk on it over lunch. If you still feel the same, I'll lend you my own pilot to take you up to Washington and bend Harry's ear. Now what could be fairer than that?"

"I don't need to sleep on it. My mind's made up."

"Okay. I respect that, Hughie. But let's talk it over face to face."

"I've got no problem with that."

"Fine. Here's what I'll do. I'll send my plane for you in the morning. I'll have you picked up at your own front door. Ten o'clock, okay?"

"Sure."

"Do me a favor though, Hughie. Keep this to yourself. You did say you wanted to save the President any embarrassment."

2

WHEN John Lee Halliwell relieved himself in the marbled bathroom of his Houston office suite, he generally talked to W. C. Fields, or rather to the picture of the legendary actor hung above the low-flush cistern.

John Halliwell was talking to him, late at night, about the phone call from the judge. "It's damned inconvenient, W.C. Me and Hugh Renwick go back a fair ways. Why'd Hughie have to go and get the jitters just when it's all coming together?"

He sucked in his gut, straightened the trouser cuffs over his ostrich-skin boots, and swaggered back into his office. The windows looked out over the black trapezoidal boxes of Pennzoil Towers, leaning into each other at crazy angles, as if the architect needed to get his glasses fixed. Beyond the Towers, Halliwell could see the stepped pyramid atop the Texaco building. It looked like a place of blood sacrifice.

His eyes traveled across to the Exxon Building, on Bell Street. The lights were still bright on the forty-third floor, the home of the Petroleum Club. He could picture the late drinkers setting odds on how long it would take for Hallow Petroleum to go belly up. The company stock had lost six points in the day's trading, since an item had appeared in the "Heard on the Street" column in that morning's *Wall Street Journal*, under the headline "Is Hallow Petroleum Heading South?"

If only he hadn't signed so many personal notes, like the one for that development on Padre Island the hurricane blew away, or the one for that fancy mall that was deserted except for an X-rated video store and a TV evangelist under indictment for having sex with minors. The paper value of his assets was well over a billion, but his debts totaled more than that, and the IRS was pursuing him for $423 million in unpaid taxes and penalties. And his high-ticket attorneys told him the case was not looking good.

He had decided to risk everything on the Safari Project. He had a scout he trusted, with an oil exploration crew in the northern Gulf. The scout had sworn to him that they were looking at the biggest find since Spindletop. The problem was, the oil lay under Mexican waters, and the Mexican government regarded petroleum as a sacred cow. No gringos wanted. Raúl Carvajal had promised to change all that. If Halliwell backed his revolution—and it succeeded—the new government in northern Mexico would give Hallow Petroleum exclusive rights to develop the oil fields. The papers were already drawn up. Halliwell had copies inside his safe. Who could tell what they were worth? Two billion? Five billion? Maybe more. *If* Safari prospered. Otherwise, Halliwell's contract was worth about as much as a Confederate bond.

Judge Renwick was an old friend, a straight shooter, a certified good ol' boy. How did that friendship weigh in the balance, against the promise of Safari?

The oilman hesitated for only a moment before he picked up the scrambler phone that the gray man who insisted on being called Mr. Cantwell had sold him.

He punched out a number in Dade County, Florida.

"Mr. Cantwell," a female voice responded promptly.

"Tell him to call John."

"Yessir."

Mr. Cantwell had suggested various exotic code names. Halliwell had refused to use them. John was his given name, and it was shared by about a quarter of the male population.

While he waited for Mr. Cantwell to return the call, Halliwell looked at the map of Mexico he had tacked to his bulletin board. It was a gift from Raúl. The six northern states had been colored blue. According to plans, he was looking at the embryo of a new republic. The politics weren't all that complicated, not from where Halliwell sat. Secession was in the air. The Québecois wanted to break away from Canada. Ukrainians wanted to secede from the Soviet Union. Why shouldn't the hard-driving businessmen and ranchers of northern Mexico go out on their own? The solution to all of Halliwell's problems lay here. Raúl could flaunt the presidential sash. Halliwell would settle for the oil fields off Tamaulipas.

The phone purred.

"Yes."

"This is Cantwell."

Halliwell had to admit that he got value for money with the scrambler phone. Cantwell's voice came through crystal clear. It was like talking inside a bell jar.

"Our taco-eaters have screwed up again," said Halliwell. "Now we have a problem with the judge. I want you to handle it. I want you to show me that you're good for something more than writing me ten-page letters."

"That's uncalled for, John."

"Suppose you prove it to me. Here's the deal. The judge is leaving in the morning. He's coming to Houston, then he's planning on flying up to D.C. to spill his gut to Cottongin."

"That's unfortunate. What do you suggest?"

"Goddamn, *you're* supposed to be the expert! Or did you suck those war stories out of your thumb?"

"I take it you are proposing a health adjustment."

"I don't want to know any details. I can't trust the Mexicans not to fuck up again. I need to know if you can take care of it."

"That's an affirmative. But it will cost."

"Send me a bill. Unless you're worried about my credit rating."

"That's a positive negative."

Halliwell hung up the phone and lounged in his padded swivel chair. He had climbed a long way since he had gotten his first job on an oil field as a mudder's assistant. There was nothing romantic about mudding. It was like working on a milk farm: no holidays, up to your ass in crap every day. He was on call twenty-four hours a day, to shoot drillers' mud, dosed with toxic chemicals—nobody cared what was in it back then—down into a hole where devil gas came spewing out of the earth's belly. If you were drunk or got lost on the road, that sucker could explode.

Now Halliwell sat on the thirty-fourth floor, behind an immense teakwood desk afloat on a sea of travertine marble.

He vaulted out of his seat and grabbed a hunting rifle from the rack beside an oil painting of a gusher. He trained the rifle on the picture window, taking aim at the Exxon Building through the cross-hairs of the sight.

He mentally rehearsed the verities of Mexican political life in which Raúl Carvajal had schooled him. Gringos weren't allowed in the oil business down there, except to do dirty and dangerous things, like poking the seabed in the middle of a blow. Under existing circumstances, a Mexican government that allowed the gringos back into the oil patch—the sacred treasure—would be committing political suicide.

Halliwell snapped the trigger of his gun, on an empty chamber.

Suicide can be assisted. If he had to break up a country, and start a war, to serve his purpose, John Halliwell was man enough—Texan enough—to do it. It was a shame about Hugh Renwick, but the law of the oil patch was eat or be eaten. Halliwell divided mankind into just two classes: those who got screwed and those who did the screwing. He knew where he belonged; too bad Renwick hadn't figured it out as well.

3

Judge Renwick did not go to the courthouse in the morning. He packed a little airline bag and smuggled it out into the back garden, where his wife Marion was sitting in the shade, drinking iced tea.

He kissed her cheek. "You tell those boys in the front room not to worry about me."

"Hughie? Where are you going?"

"I know what I'm doing, hon."

Marion Renwick frowned as she watched him slip into the neighbor's yard and vanish around the far side of the house.

A pearl-gray stretch limousine was idling at the corner of the street. The only person who saw the judge get into it was a retired Air Force colonel who was watering his lawn. The colonel was pretty sure that the driver was Mexican, but it was hard to see through the tinted glass. "I guess he could have been Oriental," the colonel told investigators later. "He definitely wasn't American. Not that I'm prejudiced, you hear?"

All the witness was certain about was that the judge had entered the limo of his own free will, and that he had been in a hurry.

4

THE Mexican government's theft of the presidential election set talking heads bobbing on American television, and sparked chain explosions from the border to the Isthmus. Along the Rio Grande, border crossings were blocked by bomb scares and lines of chanting protesters. An eighteen-wheeler was blown up on the bridge at Laredo, backing up traffic for twenty miles on either side. Down south, leftist unions closed down Pemex oil rigs and refineries, seized the city of Juchitán and proclaimed it a "liberated zone." In Mexico City, hundreds of thousands of angry demonstrators were converging on the Zocalo to demand justice for Batman.

Whenever foreign cameramen and news reporters were on the scene, the government played it studiously low-key. Different rules applied in the hinterland.

In the impoverished state of Hidalgo, northwest of the capital, peasants were marching under the white-and-red banners of the Movement for National Renovation. They started out from Pachuco. Their women and children walked with them. As they passed each village, their numbers increased. There were five or six thousand of them, straggling for a mile or more along Highway 57, halfway to the Altos Hornos steel mills on the outskirts of Mexico City, where they hoped that the union workers would join them. For a country tormented by *machismo*, there was a surprisingly large number of women in the front ranks of the column. The leaders were unknown outside their own district.

A big woman, part Otomi Indian, her broad features blackened by the sun, boomed to her neighbors, "We need a man with pants on, to defend us!"

A shriller woman's voice responded, "Miliano!"

Others took up the chorus. "Miliano! Miliano!"

Few, if any, of the marchers had ever laid eyes on this Miliano. He was not from their neighborhood. He lived among cotton-growers far to the north, in the Laguna district. He was not a national politician. He had never appeared on TV, in the commercials the government allowed the opposition to broadcast at strange hours of the night, sandwiched between dubbed American cartoons of the forties and fifties. For many of these marchers, Miliano was no less of a phantom than the Batman character, yet they chanted his name like a talisman.

"We need a man with *huevos!*"

"Miliano! Miliano!"

"We need a man of the people! A man like us!"

"MIL-I-ANO!"

They were still chanting when the shooting started. The state police had blocked the highway where the low hills, spiked by cactus scrub, provided natural cover on either side. The *Rurales*—a swaggering local militia—sighted their rifles between the bushes. They were reinforced by a few young thugs in black uniforms, members of a government-funded goon squad whose members called themselves *Los Zorros*. Rifles weren't good enough for them. They sported Uzis and Mac-10s.

No independent observer was present to verify who started the shooting. By the time it was over, however, a third of the marchers were dead or wounded. The woman who had called for a man who wore pants had thirty-seven bullets in her body. The vultures wheeled and tilted overhead.

Without blood sacrifice, the Aztecs believed, the sun will not rise. Without martyrs, revolutions languish. With its reflexive brutality, the government was supplying the revolution with martyrs in droves.

But so far, outside the villages where their families mourned, they were nameless.

5

THE janitor who unlocked the front doors of the San Antonio courthouse at 6 A.M. the next day swore at the trash
that had been dumped on the steps overnight. In addition to the debris from the latest protest rally—soiled
posters and leaflets, soda cans, and wine bottles—there
were outsize garbage bags, one of them apparently
stuffed full.

"Dirty motherfuckers." There, in the sight of the
Alamo, it seemed like an act of sacrilege.

"Hey, Abe!" A policeman slowed his cruiser to a
crawl. He was sipping coffee from a Styrofoam cup.
"Guess that doper's pals had themselves a real ball."

"Nobody got no goddamn respect."

The janitor tried to move the bigger sack. He gasped
at the weight of the thing. He flapped his hands in front
of his face, against the swarm of flies that flew at his
mouth and eyes.

What had they put in there? He tugged at the plastic
ties, and they ripped away from the sack, exposing the
contents.

"Oh, shit." He grabbed at his stomach, and staggered
down the steps, in the wake of the cop car. "Hey!" He
could not raise much volume, because he started retch-
ing, on an empty stomach. He doubled over, and a warm
trickle of bile ran down his chin, spattering his pants and
shoes.

The police cruiser made a circuit of the plaza.

"Hey, Abe! You sick or what?"

Wordless, the janitor pointed at the garbage sacks.
He was not going to look any closer.

The larger bag contained a headless torso. The legs
had been severed, above the knees, perhaps to make the
body fit into its container. The butchery had not been

done neatly. Each amputation had required several strokes, with an ax or a heavy knife. The forensic examiners entertained the theory that the cuts might have been inflicted while the victim was still alive.

The victim's hands were located in the second sack, together with his head.

The killers had sent a message.

Across Judge Renwick's forehead, they had carved the word *venganza*. Vengeance. On the judge's right cheek, they had incised the stylized head of a ram. It was one of the emblems of the Quintero drug family.

EIGHT

□ □ □

1

EDDIE O'Brien came into Kreeger's office with the news. "It's on CNN."

Kreeger stood motionless in front of the TV set. A reporter was interviewing the janitor who had found Judge Renwick's body on the steps of his courthouse. The man broke down, and hid his face from the camera, when he began to describe the condition of the corpse.

The scene shifted to Washington, to a White House correspondent in front of the familiar façade of 1600 Pennsylvania Avenue.

"High-level sources have told me that President Butler is heartbroken. He regarded Judge Renwick as a close personal friend, and a man of rare courage in fighting the war on drugs. The drug-style execution appears to have been the work of Mexico's notorious Quintero drug family. The President is expected to call on the Mexican government for full cooperation in hunting down the killers."

Kreeger stared mutely at the screen. A new but familiar face appeared on the screen. Rough-grained, saddle-brown, fleshier than Kreeger remembered. It belonged to John Halliwell. He was announcing that he would pay a $100,000 bounty to anyone who brought the judge's killers to justice. A newly formed organization, the Mexican-American League for Decency, had already offered to match the reward.

"Mexican gangsters have killed one American too many," said Halliwell. "If the Mexican government is too crooked to deal with the druglords, it's up to patriotic citizens, on both sides of the border, to put things to rights."

The oilman was asked if he was not afraid that he was making himself a candidate for assassination.

"We're used to taking risks down here in Texas," he said with a broad smile. "It's time to kick ass."

Kreeger thought John Halliwell looked surprisingly happy as he promised to kick ass in Mexico. Maybe the judge's brutal murder was more than it seemed, more than mere revenge for the death of a Mexican doper in his jail cell.

Kreeger gave Eddie the files of several rightist leaders up north. "I've been hearing some funny rumors about a northern conspiracy. I want you to fly up to Monterrey and check these guys out."

Eddie looked disappointed when he saw the subjects were Mexicans. "Fausto's people must be all over these jokers." Eddie mimicked the motions of a wiretapper putting a headset over his ears.

"Get me something Fausto doesn't know."

"What am I looking for?"

"Foreign visitors. Drug tie-ins. Arms deliveries. And an inside source."

When Eddie had left, Kreeger phoned Fausto García at SIN headquarters and invited him to bring his wife over for dinner. It was time for a frank exchange with Fausto, and Kreeger intended to conduct it on his own turf. It was a fair bet that anything said in the secret policeman's own environment was recorded for posterity. And the highest bidder.

FAUSTO arrived at the Kreegers' house in a convoy of black LTDs. Bookends took up menacing postures along the sidewalk. Drover, Kreeger's Australian shepherd, barked at them from behind the wall. Fausto entered the house minus his wife, which meant that he had a date later on with one of his mistresses, or an appointment at the bunker in Campo Militar Número Uno where he held intimate discussions with political prisoners.

Fausto wreathed Karla with embraces, and tried to slip her one of his little packages. They pushed it back and forth between them, like toddlers playing pat-a-cake, until Fausto laughingly conceded defeat. Either Fausto did not comprehend U.S. government restrictions on accepting gifts from foreigners, or he understood only too well, because he played this game every time he came to the Horseshoe Woods.

After dinner, the men sat in the courtyard, and Kreeger accepted one of the Mexican's Montecristo cigars. Light from the sconces behind them played on Fausto's diamond-studded Rolex, his gold bracelet, the silvery protozoa drifting down his Gucci tie.

"Worldly goods are no sin, my friend," Fausto told the station chief. "When the Indians invited me to New Delhi, I met a Parsi. A most enterprising businessman. He told me that, according to his religion, God created the material world as a joy for men, and a snare to entrap the devil. In itself, the material world is blessed. It is part of the eternal plan. Which includes drinking and fucking. But I embarrass you. You are not a *faldista*—a skirt-chaser —are you?"

"You never cease to amaze me, Fausto. Are you thinking of becoming a Zoroastrian?"

The Mexican chuckled. "Only if our next President fires me."

"Is there any danger of that?"

Fausto shrugged. "He's scared of Fernando." He was referring to his boss, Fernando Ramírez. "And Fernando handed him the election. That's the kind of present you are never forgiven for."

"You heard about Judge Renwick," Kreeger changed tack.

"I am sorry. He was your friend, wasn't he?"

"I'd be grateful for any leads you come up with. Off the record."

"It's not my department. This is a matter for the Attorney General."

"I understand that."

Fausto blew smoke toward the bougainvillea. Kreeger's dog lay with its head on his left shoe, watching the Mexican closely. "The Quinteros all have alibis," Fausto remarked.

"Naturally. Do you believe the Quinteros did it?"

"Who else? A life for a life. Biblical justice. It's obvious, isn't it?"

"I don't know. I've been getting some strange reports, involving some of your hotheads up north."

"Which ones?"

"Paco Carranza is one name."

Fausto blew out his cheeks, impersonating a bulbous fat man. "Carranza is nothing! I know when he farts, which is often!"

"He's mixed up with the drug cartels."

"Who knows? I told you before, Jim. Drugs are not a Mexican problem."

"Then there's the Monterrey crowd. Raúl's people."

"Raúl Carvajal?"

Kreeger nodded. He had tried various surnames with the first name the judge had given him, and Carvajal seemed to fit best. The Carvajals were a northern dynasty that had been warring with the central government for generations.

"Carvajal is a different animal," Fausto conceded, with grudging respect. "The hunting kind. Quick and dangerous. And with many gringo friends, I think. But his ideas are popular only with the business class in the north. He is no threat to us." Fausto watched Kreeger keenly, wondering why the CIA Station Chief was plying him with the names of rightist opponents of the regime.

Kreeger hesitated. He was about to break one of his own rules. It was not his practice to consult the Mexican secret police about U.S. citizens, especially former members of his own service. But he was angry and upset enough tonight to put aside his inhibitions.

"There are some Americans mixed up with this," he informed Fausto. "One of them is a former colleague of mine. Cantwell is one of his work-names. His real name is Arthur Colgate. I would be very interested in anything you might happen to hear about him."

Fausto took a leisurely sip from his brandy snifter. "I believe this is the first time you have volunteered the name of an American citizen. I am quite certain it is the first time you have brought me the name of a CIA agent —excuse me, a *former* CIA agent. This man must have done something very bad to you, Jim."

"We've had our problems."

"Colgate? He didn't serve in Mexico."

"No. He was in Saigon. Then Middle East division. Now he's a hired gun—or at least, a hired pen."

"What did he do to you, Jim? No, let me guess."

Kreeger began to feel slightly queasy. He had not drunk that much. At least, not yet. Was his nausea caused by renewed exposure to the Mexican capital, after a few days of clean air and clean ice cubes? Or perhaps by the sense that he had made a bad mistake by confiding in Fausto García?

"It was a woman," Fausto pronounced.

Damn you, thought Kreeger.

"I'm right!" crowed Fausto. "You're not the complete puritan! There was a woman!"

Kreeger puffed furiously on his cigar. *But that was in another country, and besides, the woman is dead.* Why not tell it all? Who remained to be hurt? Certainly not Val.

"You were down at Warrenton, weren't you?" he said to Fausto.

"Not me. You forget, Jim. You confine us third-worlders to cheap motels for our training courses. Your pretty white colonial houses are for people whose names don't end in a vowel."

"But you did take a CIA course in deception."

"I did."

"When was that? The late sixties?"

"I don't remember. I do remember a waitress. Honduran, flat-assed, but with tits like volcanoes. Very impressive on a small frame."

"I don't think I want to go on with this."

"Jim! I believe you're blushing! And I think it's altogether charming. I should tell Karla."

"You do, and I'll wring your goddamn neck."

Fausto seized the bottle and replenished their glasses. He was beginning to enjoy himself immensely. He had lived somewhat in awe of Kreeger—his physical presence, his skill and stamina, the immense power that he represented. He had finally located Kreeger's weak spot.

"You fucked her, didn't you?" Fausto lunged.

"What the hell are you talking about?"

"The woman you're going to tell me about."

Kreeger stood, his anger apparent. It was quickly dissipated, however, replaced by frustration.

"God knows," said Fausto, between drags on his double corona, "we Mexicans have our complexes. We most surely have complexes about sex. But never that it is wrong to indulge. On the contrary. The Mexican male —the *macho*—must be cock of the roost, even if it disgusts him. You must forgive my little lapses. Frankly, I am happy to discover your secret. There has been speculation. Karla is of course a lovely woman, but you have been married a long time."

"She's dead," Kreeger said dully. "It happened a long time ago. She was married to Colgate, but they broke up. She was a teacher."

"A teacher for the Agency?"

Kreeger folded his frame back into an armchair. "Her specialty was deception. I thought you might have come across her. That's why I asked. She used to tell the story of the assassination beetle."

"Ah yes, I remember. The assassination beetle mimics the mating signal of the female firefly. Horny males home in on the flashing lights, wanting to fuck. And they get devoured. It is the essence of deception—or rather, of provocation. The signal is real, but the results are not what you hoped for."

"So you did meet her."

"No, alas. I heard that story in bad Spanish, from a male translator who was reading from a spiral-bound manual. In my time, the Agency did not share its bed-dable women with third-worlders either. By the way, the whole course was a joke."

"It was?"

"What do you imagine men in seersucker suits can teach Latin Americans about deception? Or our Soviet friends, for that matter? We should be giving lectures to *you*. But you must forgive me. I have diverted you from your story. You were going to tell me what your Mr. Colgate—or is it Mr. Cantwell?—did to your woman."

"I don't know what he did," Kreeger said tersely. Now he was feeling decidedly unwell. "She disappeared. I could never get to the bottom of it. Look, I've been absurdly indiscreet."

"You've been personal, Jim. *Me alegro mucho.* Friends need to share personal things. It is the definition of friendship. So what do you want me to do about Mr. Colgate?"

"I would like you to keep me informed of anything you find out."

"It's done. But what do *you* think he might be doing in my country? How is he involved here? Do you think there is some connection with the judge?"

"That's what I intend to find out."

2

THE men who had butchered Judge Renwick were sitting in the first-class compartment of a Cathay Pacific airliner, bound for Hong Kong. Both had been born in Cholon, the Chinese quarter of what was now called Ho Chi Minh City. The elder man was a former Vietnamese Ranger, who had carried out executions of suspected communist leaders for Art Colgate when he was Chief of Station in Saigon. Colgate had the names of scores of similar men, inscribed in his personal cipher in the little black-bound address book he always carried on his person. They were nearly all members or associates of the Saigon Society, Colgate's personal network of old Vietnam hands.

Colgate was sitting in a soft-lit reception area on the thirty-fourth floor of Hallow Petroleum, contemplating a picture of an offshore oil rig being kicked sideways by a hurricane.

Everything about him was gray: his Brooks Brothers suit, his Turnbull & Asser tie, his neatly barbered hair. Even his skin was just this side of mortuary gray. Art Colgate was a man who would not attract a second glance in the street, and he liked it that way.

"Mr. Cantwell?" A bosomy secretary smiled at him from the doorway, displaying her profile. "Mr. Halliwell can see you now."

Halliwell was swigging cola from a pewter mug as Colgate entered the huge office. Silently, he passed the oilman a piece of paper. All that was written on it was a six-figure number.

"Hot damn! This is outrageous!"

"I'm not on retainer to make health adjustments," Colgate said evenly. "I am employed by you to provide consultancy services and specialized access in Washington. What you asked for was out of line. The price reflects that. I take it you are not questioning that we provided value for money?''

"I guess not," Halliwell said weakly. He had not been sleeping much since the judge was killed. "But Jesus, did your guys have to do it like *that?''*

"You left the methods to my discretion. I would not have accepted the assignment under any other conditions. I want the money wired to the Nassau account."

Halliwell did not dissent.

Colgate sat down on the sofa. "You're getting a bonus," he pointed out. "The psy-war aspects of this operation have proved to be entirely positive. People all over the country are mad about the drug violence coming out of Mexico. I understand the League for Decency has already pulled in over a million in contributions, and not just from Texas. We're building a grassroots constituency. I can assure you the White House and Congress are listening."

Halliwell's mood lifted a bit. He put his feet up on the coffee table, next to the Remington bronze. "You're the consultant. So consult. And don't give me that gobbledygook you put in your reports. This isn't one of your no-name committees up at Langley, where you can't see through the pipe smoke and the Ivy League fug. I've got a lot riding on this, and all we've managed to do so far is cover our ass. Is it gonna fly?"

"Frankly, when you called me in on this I had many reservations. I think the election fraud, however, has improved our prospects considerably. Mexico is becoming ungovernable. The bottom is dropping out of the economy. On Capitol Hill, both liberals and conservatives are demanding a change. They're writing a new National Intelligence Estimate in Washington. The majority view is that Mexico's political system is on the brink of collapse."

"I can get all that from the *Houston Chronicle.* Where do we go from here?"

"We play the Noriega card."

"Meaning?"

"We create a Mexican strongman that American voters will love to hate. It won't require much invention. We have Fernando Ramírez."

"The Minister of Government."

"Right. A traditional Latin strongman, probably the most hated man in Mexico. He's killed God knows how many opposition types—Raúl's father was one of them—and he stole the elections for the ruling party. He's up to his ears in every racket that's going. He's ripped off close to a billion dollars. He's not the *Presidente*, but he is the true source of power."

"Shee-et." Halliwell spoke with a sort of admiration. "Maybe we could work with that ol' boy."

"I doubt it. He's also a long-time pal of Fidel's."

"So what are you suggesting?"

"If we make enough noise about Ramírez, if we get the media interested in him, tie him in with the drug cartels—maybe even to the judge's death—the American people are going to get very angry. That could give the Administration a mandate to move on Mexico."

"I like it."

"That's the negative side," Colgate proceeded. "We have a problem on the positive front."

"Meaning?"

"If we're going to get Uncle Sam involved in Mexico, we need someone he can support. Raúl and his friends aren't enough. They're rich men, and they're too right wing. They might have a lot of appeal in River Oaks or Grosse Pointe and the businessmen's clubs in northern Mexico, but that's it. We need a front man with a more popular image. What, in Vietnam, we used to call a Third Force."

"Have you got anyone in mind?"

"We're looking into it. I hear there's a feisty little labor lawyer in the Laguna district called Miliano Rojas who's picking up quite a following. We could use someone like that."

Halliwell frowned. He wasn't interested in Mexican

politics—that was Raúl's bag. The oilman's sole interest was in getting his hands on the new oil field in the Gulf. He had learned just enough about Mexico to grasp that there were two conditions for doing that. First, they had to put a new government into power, one that took a friendly view of gringo oilmen and of John Halliwell in particular. The way Raúl had scripted it, this would be the government of a secessionist republic in the north, headed by himself, that would leave the rest of Mexico to go to hell in its own way. Second, they needed the full support of Uncle Sam, meaning U.S. troops on the ground. Halliwell couldn't see how a labor lawyer with radical friends was going to buy into any of this.

"He doesn't have to," said Colgate. "We'll tell him only what he needs to know, and we'll do it all through cutouts. If that doesn't work out, we make an adjustment."

Halliwell lit up a cigar and changed tack abruptly. "How's the mood in Washington?"

"Admiral Enright is with us all the way. I had dinner with him at The Haven the night after the elections. He's mad as hell about Mexico."

"Oh yeah? And why's that?" The oilman was suspicious of anyone who supported something without an apparent personal motive.

"Well, for one thing, Bill is concerned about the Japanese hold on the incoming Mexican President. He thinks the Japanese are getting ready to wage the economic version of World War Three, and that Mexico will be one of the front lines."

Halliwell shook his head. "There's gotta be more."

"I know the admiral quite well. He's a part of the Navy that never declared peace."

"You two were in Vietnam together, right?" the oilman suddenly remembered. "You got something on Bill Enright, don't you?"

Colgate's face closed up. "You don't need to know that."

3

THE Kreegers flew to San Antonio, en route to the judge's memorial service. Lucy was waiting for them at the airport with her old Volkswagen Golf. With great difficulty, Kreeger folded his large frame into the narrow space behind the wheel.

Lucy kept saying, "I'm fine," but she couldn't stop crying. Yes, she was doing fine at school. Nobody had bothered her. But she had recurring nightmares, about the boyfriend who had been killed on the Mexican side, and about Donna Renwick's father. "If there's a God," she protested, "how can he let those things happen to people?"

"I can't answer that," Kreeger said grimly. "But if I ever find the people responsible for Hughie's death, I guess I'll know what to do with them."

Their road led west on 410, past strip restaurants and new glass-walled office blocks. Fluffy cumulus clouds drifted overhead as Kreeger made the exit onto I-10 and sped between white, sandy foothills, climbing toward the Edwards Plateau. He pulled off onto the old Boerne Stage Road, and rolled down the window. Already, the air seemed cleaner and drier. The road wound up through cottonwoods, over low bridges across dry creek beds. A sign encouraged him to "Drive Friendly." The signs were all pure Texas. "Textured Pavement" meant there were bumps ahead.

When they reached the town of Comfort, Texas, Kreeger turned down High Street, into a scene from a previous century. The handsome storefronts were creamy limestone. The old Faust Hotel had been converted into a warren of fancy boutiques, but Ingenhuett's Grocery & Dry Goods Store was frozen in time; you could still buy anything from sherbet to shotgun shells in those cavernous rooms cooled by propeller fans.

Comfort was home ground for the Renwicks, just as nearby Boerne was for generations of Kreegers.

The memorial service was to be held at Immanuel Lutheran Church, and although they were more than an hour early, they could not park anywhere near the church. The street was cordoned off, and cars were double-parked along nearby roads. Television crews and news cameramen jostled for space outside the church, and at the edge of the cemetery across the road. There were police and Texas Rangers all over the scene, and serious-looking men wearing dark suits and sporting earpieces.

Kreeger recognized the lean, gnarled figure of Joe Strauss, a farmer of his father's vintage. Joe was evidently an usher; he was sporting a rosette in his buttonhole.

"Hey, Joe! What's up?"

"Jim! Glad you could make it!" He walked stiffly over to the car and leaned into the driver's window. "President Butler's coming. It's supposed to be a private service, but I guess the word is out. Still, I reckon it's mighty decent of the President to come down and pay his respects."

Kreeger finally found a parking space several blocks away, near the old railway tunnel. As he walked back to the church with his wife and daughter, in the fierce heat of the afternoon sun, he saw some of the TV people clustered around a tall blond man about his own age.

A network reporter jabbed a microphone into his face. "Mr. Culbertson, you must have heard that local businessmen have posted a bounty for Judge Renwick's killers. Do you have any plans to collect it?"

Kreeger did not catch the response; he was intent on his shepherding his family inside the church as quickly as possible. He did not want to attract any press curiosity, although it was unlikely he would anyway—he could count the number of American journalists who knew his face on the fingers of one hand.

There was standing room only, at the back of the church.

Several of the front pews had been reserved, presumably for the Renwick family and for President Butler and his retinue.

There was a stir in the church as Marion Renwick entered through a side door, dressed in black. The President was holding her arm. There were Donna Renwick and her brothers and some elderly female relations, one of them using a walker. They were followed by the usual contingent of presidential bodywatchers and aides.

Then Kreeger spotted another familiar face, one that seemed out of place. It belonged to the oilman, John Halliwell. Kreeger felt a surge of anger, seeing Halliwell walking with Marion Renwick and the President.

Kreeger barely heard the words of the service, and recalled only snatches of the eulogy that Harry Butler delivered, without notes, into the eyes of the TV cameras.

"Judge Renwick represented everything that was best in the state of Texas and the American legal system. . . . I will not rest until his death is punished. . . . He was the victim not just of individual criminals, but of a vicious international conspiracy whose main base in this hemisphere lies just across the Rio Grande."

When the President rose to leave, there was mayhem inside the church, as the media crowd jostled and elbowed to get to him before he disappeared along with his convoy of limousines.

Kreeger spread his powerful arms around his wife and daughter, shielding them from the surge.

"We have to speak to Marion," Karla said.

Kreeger suggested it might be easier to call on the widow at home, but outside the church, Karla saw Marion Renwick through a break in the crowd, and started pushing toward her. The White House cavalcade was already leaving.

The crowd closed behind Karla and Lucy, and Kreeger called to them, "I'll catch up to you!"

He slipped across the road to the simple limestone monument that stood at the edge of the cemetery like a broken sword. There was nothing else like it in Texas, or in any of the states that had fought for the rebel cause in the Civil War. It was a memorial to the hill country men who had fallen in 1862, in the cause of the Union.

"Treuer der Union"—"True to the Union"—was incised in big letters above their names. There had been sixty-eight of them, mostly German-Americans. In the heart of a fiercely pro-Confederate state, they had taken a stand on principle—for the Constitution, against the enslavement of their fellow men—against the odds, and against the ruling frenzy of their wider community. And just as they had banded together, they had died together. It had taken years for the wounds to heal; for some, they never had.

To Kreeger, this was more than a curious incident in the violent history of the Texas frontier; it was a blood memory. There, on the list of the fallen, was a Felsing, his great-great-grandfather on his mother's side. One of the pioneers who had settled the hill country, with the Kriegers who still spelled their name the German way, in the bold, bloody years when Texas had flown its own flag.

By the little obelisk in the Comfort cemetery, Jim Kreeger paid silent homage to his people, and checked his own bearings. The men who were honored by this monument had given their lives to do what they believed was right.

Hugh Renwick had done the same. Harry Butler, the politician, had promised that there would be an atonement. Jim Kreeger regarded it as his private duty to see that the promise was kept.

He looked up, and saw the blond man standing at his elbow.

"I guess you'd be Bob Culbertson."

"And you'd be Jim Kreeger."

"Have we met?"

"No, but the judge's daughter pointed you out. Said you'd helped her out of a tight spot."

"I'm afraid I can't talk about that."

"You're with the government, aren't you?"

"State Department."

Culbertson spat tobacco onto the dry grass at his feet. "I won't hold that against you, although I swear our government will be the death of us."

"Do you include the President in that remark?"

"No, I got time for Harry Butler. He's just an ol' boy on the make. I say good luck to him."

"You're the guy who brought Chocorrol Quintero out of Mexico, aren't you?"

"Yeah. I'm pissed about that. First they offed Quintero, then they got the judge. I knew Renwick. He helped me out some time back. I'd like to get the sucker who did it."

"Any ideas who's behind it?"

"The dopers. Who else?"

The two men looked at each other steadily. Then Culbertson said, "I'll tell you all I know. There's a lot of monkey business going on 'round the border. More than usual. We're talking automatic weapons, plastic explosives, gee-whiz stuff. Going south. I still got my sources, and I can move around a lot more easily now I don't have to ride on a government mule. You need anything 'round Del Rio, you give me a call."

He scrawled his number on a scrap of paper and winked at Kreeger. "What part of the State Department did you say you were with?"

4

Lightning crackled in the western sky as the presidential convoy swung off I-10, traveling in the opposite direction from the airfield. The horns of blackbuck and fallow deer formed a high arch over the entry gates to the Circle H Ranch, a spread which belonged to John Halliwell and several of his Houston business partners. The White House appointments secretary had been instructed to leave the rest of the day free. The press spokesman, left behind in Comfort, indicated to the reporters that the President was "consumed with grief" over the death of a friend, and needed time to himself to recover.

President Butler was feeling morose, confused, and thwarted, though he retained his photogenic smile as he shook hands with the Texans who were assembled in the ranch's vast living room. Their faces were all familiar. They had all been campaign contributors since Butler had made his first run for the Senate. After the ritual exchange of sympathies, they started plying him with questions. Nobody asked about riots in Amman, or the terrorism in Riyadh, or even the fight on Capitol Hill over new taxes. They wanted to know what the Butler Administration proposed to do about Mexico. Their business was hurting because of the violence along the border. People were worried about the tent cities of refugees that were springing up across the Sunbelt, with the new influx of illegal immigrants—"the biggest peacetime invasion in history," someone had called it.

As soon as he could gracefully free himself, Harry Butler walked out onto the porch, away from the din. John Halliwell followed him, glass in hand.

"I need some time to myself, John."

"I understand."

The President glanced at the Olympic-sized pool. It looked inviting.

"I might have a dip, if I can have a little privacy."

"You got it."

A few minutes later the President emerged from the pool house in a pair of borrowed madras trunks. He stepped out on the board and made a perfect dive, slipping cleanly into the water.

He felt slight cramps after six laps—he was getting out of condition, with all those state banquets—but he pushed himself on to the tenth.

When he turned for steps, at the deep end of the pool, he saw a pair of brown legs, then a hand with a champagne flute.

"Well done, Harry. You still swim like a fish."

"Raúl." The President was not amused by Carvajal's sudden appearance. "I didn't see you in church."

"I thought that might seem indiscreet."

"Why are you here?" The President climbed out of the pool, and the Mexican handed him a towel.

"To resume friendly relations. I hope we can forget our misunderstanding on the telephone. I admit some of our associates made mistakes. They have been corrected. Harry. You know my country is rapidly coming apart. Things are ready to explode. We have ten thousand men, armed and trained, ready for any contingency. There will be more tomorrow. You don't have to take my word. Send some of your military people to us. We will show them what we can do. You're going to need us, just as we need you."

"I don't want to hear this!" Butler glared down at Raúl, pushing his face quite close. "Do you know anything about Hugh Renwick's death?"

"What everyone knows. It was the work of the Quinteros. Or their partners. There are many people in Mexico with things to hide. If you want a name, I will give you one. Fernando Ramírez."

"The man who killed your father?"

"The man who is destroying my country."

"That's your family feud, Raúl. Not mine."

Raúl's eyes moved away. In the distance he saw thunderheads, slowly drifting in from the west. Almost on cue there was the sound of thunder, like a muffled drumroll.

"It must be strange for you," said the Mexican. "To be here at the pool, in hill country, with the storm on its way."

The remark would have sounded banal to any eavesdropper, but it stung the President. He flung his wet towel at Raúl. "Damn you!"

He turned on his heel, then thought better of it. "Damn you to hell! I want you to hear this, Raúl! I'm not going to go to war in Mexico for the sake of a country that doesn't even exist! This whole secession idea is crackpot! I'm the President of the United States, for Chrissake. Have you forgotten that the United States fought a war to *stop* a secession?"

"We read American history together," Raúl said evenly. "I think you've forgotten what side Texas was on."

"That may be clever talk, but I don't buy it. I won't back Safari unless I find a reason I can believe in."

"You'll have your reasons, Harry."

NINE

□ □ □

1

WHEN Kreeger got back to the Station, one of the first people through his door was Eddie O'Brien. Eddie had trawled about up north in the guise of an anthropologist looking for Tarahumara artifacts. He was still sporting part of his kit—snakeskin belt, bush shirt, Indian headband—when he came into Kreeger's office.

He showed his boss a series of pictures, shot through a telephoto lens, pictures showing columns of Mexicans dressed in desert fatigues, training on the Carvajal ranch and at several other points in the same area.

"Looks like they're loaded for bear," Kreeger commented, after inspecting photos that showed jeeps mounted with heavy machine guns and a couple of men toting portable rocket-launchers. "Do they know how to use that stuff?"

"Maybe better than the Mexican army. They have professional trainers. The usual suspects. A couple of Green Berets who used to be with the Contras in Honduras. I heard something about an Israeli, an ex-Mossad type, who was kicking around Panama a few years back."

"So what's the agenda?"

"Hard to read. Carvajal's building a private army. He's also got his finger into half a dozen independent political operations. The League for Decency, set up in Texas, is the one that's getting the news, but there's another one called the Division of the North, set up in the northern section of Mexico. That one hugs the shadows. They're putting out a lot of crap. Bumper stickers. T-shirts. I saw 'Liberate the North' on a few fenders. 'Death to Chilangos' is another slogan.''

"So there's a regional twist."

"Yeah. But Raúl seems to have his lines out to Mexico City as well. I ran into an old bush flier—he did a few jobs for the Agency, out of the Florida Keys. He told me he was hired to fly a couple of Mexican army generals up to the Carvajal ranch."

Kreeger shook his head, an expression of doubt on his face.

"I think my source was reliable," Eddie protested.

"It's not that. I just find it hard to believe that there's anything here our friend Fausto doesn't know already. You have any feel for that?"

"My guess is that SIN has got this crowd under round-the-clock surveillance. I bet Raúl doesn't make a phone call that isn't monitored at the telephone exchange."

"Exactly. So why is Fausto letting it run?"

"I remember, when I was a boy on Long Island, we would find wasps' nests about the place in the summer. My dad told us never to disturb them. If we left the nest where it was, then we knew where the wasps were. We got rid of them when the cold set in."

"Could be." Kreeger followed the analogy. It did not satisfy him, however. He felt there was something missing. "Did you get anything Fausto *doesn't* know?"

"I may have found us an inside source."

He produced the last photograph, the one he had been holding in his lap.

Kreeger glanced at it. He saw an antique Bentley convertible, painted cream and midnight blue. A uniformed chauffeur was holding the door open for a quite stunning blond woman wearing a rather revealing dress. She reminded Kreeger of Kathleen Turner.

"What do you think?" Eddie asked eagerly.

"It's hard to tell, with all the high-ticket props. Who is she?"

"She's Raúl Carvajal's mistress. I guess she gives good value. She has her own place in Colonia del Valle, a villa in fact. Raúl keeps her wrapped up pretty tight, but I got a look at her mail. There was a letter from San Diego addressed to a Shelley Hayes."

Kreeger jotted down the name.

"We could pitch her," Eddie suggested.

"Where?"

"She travels a lot. Houston, New York, Rio. Even to Paris. She seems to be something of an art collector."

"Does she ever get to Mexico City?"

"Raúl keeps a penthouse at the Presidente Chapultepec. Apparently she has been known to use it now and then."

"Shopping trips?"

"I guess."

Kreeger wondered what the other women in his life would make of Shelley Hayes. Maybe Karla would admire her, for exacting her pound of flesh.

He filled out a routine request for a background check on a Ms. Shelley Hayes, birth date unknown, stating that he required information for "development prior to recruitment." The clerks at Langley fielded tens of thousands of such requests every year. The low priority meant it could take weeks before the Station heard anything back on Shelley's employment, Social Security, and criminal records. There were faster ways of working things, but that would risk setting off alarm bells higher up. Kreeger wanted to avoid that until he had worked out just what kind of safari Art Colgate—and maybe Director Wagoner—were on.

"Miliano! Miliano!"

Emiliano Rojas—Miliano to thousands he had never met—sighed and rubbed his son's back. He was holding the two-month-old baby across his shoulder, supporting its head with his left hand.

The calls from the street seemed to grow louder. Out there was the sun's anvil. Between the cries, Miliano could almost hear it beat against the hard-baked earth of the dirt road, rutted like a dry arroyo.

"Miliano." His wife, Elena, moved, shy and graceful as a doe, through the obstacle course presented by their cluttered parlor, which was also their nursery and Miliano's study. "Give him to me. They're calling for you."

"Yes."

With loving care, he plucked the baby from his shoulder and delivered it into the arms of his wife.

He opened the door. The harsh sunlight fell into the room behind him.

"*Sí.*"

In this village, he was known as the man who could talk, but in fact, Miliano spoke few words that were not called for.

"Don Miliano."

He did not like to be called that. "Don"—it stank of the old ways, of the man on horseback, raising a whip to the men of the fields. But these were simple men looking up at him, wishing only to show respect. He must be patient. His country was a lesson in patience.

"*Sí.*"

"Don Miliano—he is coming. All the way from the south. He is coming on the train to Torreón! He is coming here, to Aguilas Negras!"

It was Huerta, the spokesman for the *ejido*—the collective farm down the road—who spoke.

"Who is coming?" Miliano said, with the patience he had struggled to master.

"Why, Moctezuma Morelos." Old Huerta scratched his stubbly thatch.

"Batman!" squealed a bare-footed urchin.

"Moctezuma Morelos is coming here?" Miliano said dully.

"He has heard of us! He knows we exist!"

"Batman *viene!*"

ELENA was pressing Miliano's black suit with a flat iron.

"What are you doing?" he demanded.

"You must look your best."

"I belong to the people. I will wear what they wear." He glanced down at his flapping white trousers, his open sandals.

"Miliano." She tilted the iron to the vertical plane, and inspected him with her almond eyes. "You are their lawyer, their *licenciado*. The one who went to university. They are proud of you. They want to show you off, to these big men who are coming to Aguilas Negras. They want you to appear as what you are. You do not have to playact, like a *chilango* from the capital."

Elena was right, of course. She so often was. The people of Aguilas Negras called her *La Profesora*, because she read books and taught school with more passion than anyone could recall.

She said, "Moctezuma Morelos is coming because he needs you. And because he wants to use you."

Miliano was shocked, both by the importance his wife attributed to him and by her disrespect for the leader of the opposition front, the man who was the rightful President of Mexico.

"There are a thousand Milianos," he objected. "There is only one Moctezuma Morelos."

"It is just the other way. Any child in the street can play Batman. Your Moctezuma Morelos played the games of the PRI for long enough, didn't he? He sat there in the capital, fattening himself on bribes like the rest of those thieves. When he knew they would never make him President, he joined the opposition. The people are nothing to him. Nothing! That is why he fears you. And why he needs you."

"I don't understand what you're talking about."

"Because somewhere—in between cocktail parties —Morelos has heard that in Mexico, revolutions begin in the north! Because you are one of those holy idiots who means what he says! Because you won't be scared off! Because, Miliano, you don't begin to understand what you mean to our people, do you? Do you understand why unarmed men—women with babies in their arms— face machine guns with your name on their lips? Do you?"

"No." Miliano stood abashed.

"God save us all!"

Elena was shaking violently. Miliano put his arms about her. He rocked her gently, as he had rocked the baby.

"If it were just a question of us—of the children—" she began.

"It is. You are my life. You know I would die for you."

"But it isn't just us, Miliano," she responded fiercely. Her breath came in dragging rasps. "If every good man says that—that all that matters is his family— then what hope is there for the downtrodden of this earth?"

Her intensity scared him a little.

"You will fight," she told him. "I will send you into battle. But you will fight on your own ground."

And for that moment, they both believed that he really might make a difference.

* * *

The town of Aguilas Negras straggled along Route 47, in the state of Chihuahua, sixty miles from Torreón. It was hard country, friendly only to Spanish bayonet, the murderous, spiked *espadas* that slit boot-leather and flesh to touch the bone, and the white scorpion, whose sting is usually fatal. To a driver lead-pedaling down from Ciudad Juárez, on the border, Miliano's town passed in a forgettable blur of low shacks along the highway—a couple of *vulcanizadoras,* or retread shops, a shabby restaurant whose sign read El Rey de Cabrito, a motel that hadn't seen a paying customer since Humphrey Bogart walked the Sierra Madre. Off the main drag was a scruffy town plaza with the church on one side and the Centro Comunal, with its pool tables, on the other. Six blocks from the plaza, where Miliano's two-bedroom house stood, the streets were unpaved, and street lights were few and far between. It was an old-fashioned town. Mothers and black-shrouded *dueñas,* or chaperones, kept a chilly watch over the Saturday night *paseos* in the plaza when the boys circled one way and the girls the other, signaling with their eyes. The government had never done much for Aguilas Negras. The PRI had never won a clean election there.

This was Pancho Villa country, and Miliano was reared on romantic tales of Villa and the Division del Norte. The stories came firsthand, from Miliano's grandfather; everyone in the town called him Colonel, a title that must have been handed out by the bushel when Villa ruled the north.

Drunk, the old colonel croaked the ballads of the revolutionary army. Sober, the colonel talked of battles and troop deployments. He talked wildly of burning out landowners, of capturing Mexico City. And of murder and treachery, promises betrayed. Then his face would darken, and he would lean in toward young Miliano.

Between the gusts of hot breath, his counsel was always the same: *"No floje!* Don't quit!"

Revolution was in Miliano's blood.

3

"I have something you really ought to see." It was Chuck Freeling, Kreeger's Mexico analyst, on the house phone. "Can you give me ten minutes, in my office?"

Freeling had a home video of a rally that had taken place a few days earlier, in the hippodrome outside the northern city of San Luís Potosí. The film was out of focus, and what looked like a dust-devil swirling around the race track didn't help the visibility.

Kreeger saw a huge banner advertising the Mexican-American League for Decency. Beneath it, the standards of a dozen or more political organizations and labor unions. They covered the spectrum from the radical left to the free-market right. On the platform, well-fed ranchers and lawyers sat beside sleek, cynical union bosses and wild-eyed student leaders.

"Nice operation," Kreeger remarked. In normal times, the men on the platform would be trying to cut each other's throats.

"That's the guy to watch." The camera zoomed in on a slight, sinewy Mexican with longish black hair and a droopy mustache who was taking the microphone. He was dressed in the white, baggy clothes of a farm laborer. To look at, he was nothing special. But as he spoke, the crowd grew unnaturally still, then erupted into a kind of religious frenzy when he said something that struck a nerve.

Through the roar of the crowd, the voice from the microphone was deep and compelling. The force of barely controlled emotion ran through it on high voltage wires.

"He's good," Kreeger conceded. "He doesn't say *como* this and *como* that, like your typical Mexican politician. He cuts to the chase."

"Watch the crowd. He's playing them like a stringed instrument."

"Who is he?"

"Emiliano Rojas. They call him Miliano. As in Zapata."

"What have we got on him?"

"Comes from a little town called Aguilas Negras, in the Laguna district. His granddaddy was an illiterate muleteer who fought with Pancho Villa. Miliano is the first member of his family who got any real education. He got a scholarship to UNAM. I guess those Marxist professors got to him. But he's an idealist, not an ideologue. He worked in the Ministry of Agrarian Reform for a while, until they sent him back home to screw the peasants. He's got a feud going with the local boss up in Chihuahua, name of Lobo Terrazzas. A few years back, the government decided to show it was democratic by allowing opposition people to capture a few municipalities. Miliano ran for mayor of his town, as an independent, and he won by a landslide. The electoral tribunal had orders to respect the voters' decision, but Lobo Terrazzas didn't like it. When Miliano started defending peasants' rights, Lobo sent *pistoleros* to shoot him out of the town hall. I hear this Lobo also raped Miliano's sister."

The story contained many tragedies, but in Mexico, that was almost commonplace. The man in the videotape was not. He had a presence—a charisma, even—that was rarely seen in national politics.

"Who owns him?" Kreeger demanded.

"Nobody owns him, so far as we know. He's also clean. Lives very modestly, sells his legal services for a chicken or the promise of one. His backing is mostly from the left, but this rally could mean he's reaching for a broader base."

"Or somebody's reaching for him. Okay, you got my attention. Let's keep an eye on Miliano."

Today, Miliano did what his wife told him. He wore his black suit and a black tie as well, a statement that he was in mourning for the campesinos machine-gunned in Hidalgo, and for a people cheated of its rightful leadership. Today, however, there would be no video cameras.

The plaza of Aguilas Negras was full of Miliano's neighbors and supporters. A few heavies who worked for Lobo Terrazzas, the local boss for the ruling party, lolled in the shade of the cantina. Some angry men—peasants whose land (or women) had been stolen—moved toward them, and the thugs retreated inside.

Miliano's attention was diverted by a gap-toothed kid who ran across the square screaming, "Batman! Batman! *Ya viene!*"

He was followed in short order by a truckload of straw-hatted men from the Campesinos for Moctezuma organization, who appeared to be posing for a bronze monument. Next came a lead car, full of bodyguards in dark glasses. Then the big car, with the white-red banner of the National Renovation fluttering over its prow.

Cabrón, Miliano swore inside his head. It was a Mercedes station wagon. The kids were more impressed by the fancy wheels than by the tall, loose-boned man in the back.

"Batman!"

Moctezuma Morelos waved his hand.

The crowd parted. The Mercedes nosed forward, to the very edge of the podium.

He was coming. As Moctezuma Morelos got out of the car, Miliano advanced to greet him. He nodded pleasantly at Miliano, and handed him his hat and his stick. Miliano stared at them in blank amazement as the rightful President of Mexico ascended the podium. He had been treated like a footman.

It is nothing, he reminded himself. Personal feelings are nothing. Great men are forgiven almost everything. This is our great man. This is our hope.

The kids were yelling: "Batman! Batman!"

The amplifiers were not working properly, and Moctezuma Morelos was having trouble raising the microphone to his mouth. He was very tall, and whiter than Miliano had expected. A real *gachupín*. How come he carried the name of an Aztec emperor? Miliano wondered.

No! Miliano rebuked himself. He must not think such things. The leader was talking. *His* leader. The speakers crackled and failed. Three rows back, the crowd could not hear him. Miliano walked briskly to one of the speakers. The wires at the back had been neatly severed.

He was calling to Fabio, who ran a retread shop and would know how to fix such things, when he heard the shots. Actually, he did not so much hear them as feel them, a sense of movement in the air, like a taut string released. He sensed, before he saw, Moctezuma Morelos grabbing at his throat, at his collarbone. He turned to see the chosen one arch up and then fall over backward.

Miliano's shouts were lost in the tide of voices.

He waded through them, up onto the podium. He held the lost leader in his arms. He saw, indistinctly, Moctezuma's bodyguards with their guns out, ranging the plaza for targets. Some of his own people had already raced into the cantina. Inside, there was gunplay. More men were dying.

Miliano felt for a pulse, and found none. He lowered his head and kissed the rightful President of Mexico on the cheek. He raised himself to his full height and took a part of the dead man's legacy into his hands.

One of the speakers still worked, and carried his message as he shouted into the microphone: "He lives! His spirit lives in all of us who will fight his assassin! They have taken only the life from his body! His spirit will make a true revolution!''

The last words were lost. The only working amplifier cut out.

''*No floje!*'' Miliano yelled at the seething crowd. ''Don't quit!''

TEN

□ □ □

1

Raúl Carvajal drove out into the foothills and called Houston on his scrambler phone.

"I never thought I'd thank Ramírez for anything," he told Halliwell. "But I thank him today. Fernando Ramírez has done half our job for us! There'll be no business as usual between Washington and Mexico after this! It's perfect! We are rid of one of the biggest communists in my country. And Ramírez will not be able to escape the blame."

"So who ordered the hit?"

"Ramírez. Or Fausto García. Who else?" The Mexican caught the undertow in the question, and chuckled. "I see Machiavelli lives in your soul, my friend. No, this is not a Safari affair. It is a gift."

"Hey, Raúl, you better watch your ass. If those clowns can do this to Batman, they can sure as hell do it to you."

"I've lived with that threat all my life," Raúl said with contempt. "I'll know if they're coming. Fausto García thinks he has ears everywhere. I have counted every one. My cook. One of my grooms. There are microphones in my bedroom. There's one beside the Jacuzzi. One of Cantwell's people went over the house with a fluoroscope."

"You mean we're on tape?"

"Don't be stupid. I left the bugs in place so the pigs don't put them somewhere we can't find them. Anyway, I own Fausto's man in Monterrey. There's very little money can't buy in Mexico. They won't dare to touch me, not with the world screaming for justice for the death of Batman. But there may be another problem.''

''Yeah?''

''The *Compañía*''—this was universal Latin slang for the CIA—''has been sniffing around. I understand that the Station Chief in Mexico may be taking a personal interest in our affairs.''

''I'll talk to Cantwell. He says he has a direct line to the top man. We'll see what it's worth. And, Raúl? Stay tuned to your TV. Mr. Cantwell has been courting somebody named Gail Armstrong, a producer on the *Twenty-four Hours* show. The way I hear it, the program has a segment coming up that will knock your socks off.''

2

IN Mexico, a corpse is often more popular than any live politician. Batman's supporters kept the body of their martyr on public display until long after it started to stink. The carcass was paraded through town after town in an open coffin. The ranks of the mourners had grown to more than a million by the time they converged on the Zocalo, in the heart of Mexico City.

The President of the Republic beat a prudent retreat from his capital to a fortified pleasure dome above the white sands of the Pacific Coast. Señor Paz, the President-to-be, flew off to Tokyo.

Fernando Ramírez, the Minister of Government, was left to hold the fort. His chief adviser, Fausto García, counseled caution in dealing with the swarms of angry demonstrators.

''Let them squat outside the National Palace until they get bored and hungry. Let the gringo reporters take their pictures. Passions like theirs don't last. And besides, the peasants will go home soon enough, to bring in their harvest before it rots in the fields.''

On a stand beside Batman's catafalque, garlanded with flowers, Miliano denounced Minister Ramírez, by name, as the "intellectual author" of the assassination.

Miliano's face did not appear on state-controlled Mexican television, and his charges were not reproduced in the Mexican daily papers. A progressive weekly attempted to turn him into a cover story, but leather-jacketed men from SIN took care of that. The night before publication, they wrecked the printing press and firebombed the editor out of his apartment.

But Mexicans all over the country tuned into the American networks. Their shows gave top billing to the furor over Batman's murder, especially after the news leaked that President Butler had sent a personal letter to the Mexican head of state demanding a thorough investigation of the death, and complaining, for good measure, that the Mexican government had stonewalled U.S. inquiries into the earlier murder of a federal judge in San Antonio.

"Find me the killers," Ramírez instructed Fausto García, keeping a straight face. Fausto undertook to carry out his charge within twenty-four hours.

He was as good as his word. In the city of Torreón, across the state line from Miliano's village, several off-duty members of the Judicial Police were machine-gunned by Fausto's agents while boozing in a low-grade dive.

Minister Ramírez appeared on state television. He read a sober statement announcing that the killers of Moctezuma Morelos had been shot while trying to escape—but apparently not before confessing that they had been hired for the job by Batman's rivals within his own movement. Ramírez congratulated the agents of SIN on a prompt action that served the honor and reputation of the republic.

At Mexico Station, Kreeger drafted a terse note to

the Director. "The episode in Torreón strongly suggests that Ramírez personally authorized the assassination in Aguilas Negras."

Fausto was right about the demonstrators. On the morning he telephoned Kreeger to complain about the state of American television, the great plaza in front of the palace was almost deserted, except for the usual crowd of hawkers and tourists.

"They're out to screw Fernando," Fausto complained.

"After your stunt in Torreón, that won't be a difficult maneuver," Kreeger said acidly. "If a TV show is all you've got to worry about, you're in good shape."

"This TV woman—Gail Armstrong—do you know her?"

"Not personally. I gather she's respected. And her show has quite a following."

"She looks like she needs to be fucked."

"I guess you're entitled to your opinion."

"You know what this *hembra* has done? She has made a special program about Fernando. People in your government have given her information. To have this show broadcast would be very bad for both of us, Jim. I think we have had a mutually beneficial relationship, no?"

"A professional relationship, yes." Kreeger thought of all the spools of tape Fausto had presented to the Station. Especially the Soviet material. He had been able to nail a mole in the supersecret National Security Agency thanks to SIN monitoring of a meeting in a Cuernavaca hotel room with a call boy employed by the KGB.

"I am sorry to say this, Jim, but our relationship may not survive this embarrassment."

"You're laying it on mighty thick."

"Fernando is my friend. He is also the best man we have. He is the one man who is holding this government together. I do not say he is perfect—that is not in the human plan—but we need him." Fausto used the plural as if it encompassed Kreeger. "You have to use your influence. This program must be stopped."

"Christ, Fausto. You talk like you've never been to the United States. You know the government doesn't control the media. If anything, it's the other way around."

"You once told me a favor demands a favor."

There was a pause, then Kreeger heard a click as Fausto hung up. Kreeger weighed the implications. What could he do? He needed Fausto, certainly more than Fausto needed him. Things were moving too fast, and too many things were happening at once. Somehow, all those events had to tie together. But how? Kreeger wondered. How?

3

HE mixed himself a pitcher of manhattans for fortification before settling in to watch the special edition of *24 Hours* on the Denver station.

The only company Kreeger had in the house was the Tarascan maid. She was singing in the kitchen in her native tongue. The notes came in a high, birdlike trilling, free of care.

Karla drove through the gate a few minutes before the hour. She had refused to give up her weekly anthropology class, although there had been riots at the university only the day before. She came in wearing a slinky new dress about ten years too young for her, and about two hundred dollars too rich for a college class. Kreeger thought perhaps she was making eyes at her instructor, a young guy with a ponytail and narrow hips.

"So what did you study today? Olmec mating rights?"

She stole a sip from his glass. "We heard about the Aztec ball game pelota."

"Riveting."

"I thought you'd be interested. You're a football buff."

"I'm interested, okay?"

"In pelota, you're not allowed to touch the ball with your hands. The Aztecs played with deflectors, strapped around their waists."

"I see."

"This is serious stuff. You win the game, you get sacrificed to the gods."

"If you *win?* Shit. You better call up the manager of the Cowboys. You'll make him feel a whole lot better. Maybe they've been teaching those rules to new recruits. It would explain a few things."

Kreeger pointed at the TV screen. The theme music for the *24 Hours* show was like the serenade to an invasion from another galaxy. An unseen computer punched out, in giant capitals, the title for the evening's special:

"MEXICO: NORIEGA NEXT DOOR."

Gail Armstrong, the anchorwoman, came on. She was a weathered blonde, dressed severely in a business suit, looking tough and shrewd. The way her eyes met the camera said plainly: I'm no cantaloupe from the breakfast shows.

Her face dissolved into a field of red. The voice-over ran: "This is the most powerful man in Mexico."

A black silhouette, like a paper cutout, turned into a black-and-white profile of Fernando Ramírez, the Minister of Government. It was replaced by a frontal shot. Ramírez's eyelids drooped. He seemed to be trying to duck the camera.

The mixer juxtaposed the profile with the frontal. Now Ramírez looked like an entry in a book of police mug shots. All that was lacking was an ID number along the bottom. They punched one out. Kreeger stared at it, in fascination. It was Ramírez's private line at the Ministry of Government.

"This man is wanted for murder," Gail Armstrong said as her face returned to the screen. "According to U.S. intelligence sources and Mexican civil rights activists, he ordered the assassination of Mexico's opposition leader, after orchestrating the theft of the Mexican elections. He is said to be the godfather of a vicious mafia with ties to the drug cartels, the Castro regime, and deposed Panamanian strongman Manuel Noriega. He has reportedly accepted bribes from the Quintero drug family and is believed responsible for the brutal slaying of Judge Hugh Renwick in San Antonio last June."

That was for openers.

The program was dense, crowded with facts and allegations, many of them plainly leaked by sources in the Butler Administration. Kreeger recognized material from his own reports, especially on Ramírez's long-standing friendship with Fidel, and understood why Fausto had sounded so badly rattled. Someone in Washington had decided to do a real number on Ramírez.

"Doesn't it make you feel sick, dealing with reptiles like that?" Karla demanded, during a break.

"I'm paid to go into snakepits," Kreeger observed. "It doesn't mean that I like it. I've been dealing with guys like Ramírez all my life."

"Is this going to finish him?"

"Maybe in the eyes of the American public. But it's gringo mud. Gringo mud doesn't stick to Mexican politicians. Ramírez can thumb his nose at Gail Armstrong— even at the White House—as long as he wants. Unless we send in the Marines."

Kreeger laughed, because the idea was truly laughable. That was where the TV producers had gotten it wrong. Mexico wasn't Panama. You couldn't send in the 82nd Airborne into a country of a hundred million people to remove a strongman you didn't like. Anyway,

Fausto's boss had not been indicted for anything by a U.S. court, and Kreeger was skeptical about the drug allegations—although anything was possible with a man like Ramírez.

Fausto's boss could weather the storm, he decided, unless the top guy found the courage to boot him. And a President who had run away to the beach at the sight of a pack of protesters was not likely to do that.

4

FAUSTO watched the TV show at his boss's mansion in Pedregal. By the end of it, Ramírez was shaking with fury.

"This is the work of the CIA! And that cowboy Butler! After all you've done for the CIA! No, don't deny it! I have my own sources."

Ramírez was contemplating a grand gesture, a real slap in the face for the gringos. That was always popular in Mexico.

"We can do better than that," Fausto interjected. "I know the people behind this business. They have just handed us the best opportunity we could ask for, and they don't even know it."

Ramírez did not understand. Fausto began to explain. The Minister of Government was a clever and devious man, but Fausto's plan was so complex, so multi-layered, that Ramírez failed to grasp it until deep in the hollow of the night. His reactions ranged from skepticism to rage to laughing incredulity. He bucked and kicked against the opening gambit. Fausto wanted his boss to resign, and to do it immediately, in time for the breakfast news programs.

"You're insane!" Ramírez shouted at 3 A.M. "If I resign, they'll fuck us over. They're waiting in line, with their flies already open!"

"If you don't resign," Fausto warned him, "our pretty-boy Paz Gallardo will fire you after December first. He promised the American Secretary of State. I have it on tape."

"Even so, we have nearly five months! Time to make arrangements. Time to provide for the future." The Minister did not need to say, "Time to sweep the government kitty; time to make bank transfers to Switzerland and the Caymans; time to make off with all movable items." All this was understood. These men had been in partnership for a long time.

"I'll take care of everything," Fausto reassured him. "I'm not going anywhere."

"You're crazy! Without me, you're naked."

"Not quite." Fausto reminded the Minister that El Señor—the departing head of state, drying out in the Pacific sun—would never dare to say boo to the head of SIN. Fausto knew every hole where the President had buried his money—he had stolen about a billion dollars, less than his predecessors. Fausto was secure, at least until December 1. Alas, the President-elect was too dull to have many interesting habits.

Ramírez was used to power. He was reluctant to relinquish it, even for a few months. He even confided, "The Old Man called me, to pledge his support. He thinks I should stand firm."

The Old Man, in this connection, was Fidel Castro, of whom Fausto neither approved nor disapproved. He thought of Fidel as an old-timer, as his nickname indicated. Fausto thought of no one in terms of ideology. Fidel called himself a communist, and now that seemed to irritate the Russians. Who cared? Only the gringos, who paid handsomely for any warmed-over gossip from Havana.

Fausto was finally obliged to disclose to Ramírez

more details of the game than he thought necessary, or desirable.

"The Americans believe," Fausto began, "that there is a serious conspiracy in the north. I was consulted on this by Kreeger, the chief of the CIA in Mexico."

Diplomatically, Fausto spoke as if his Minister had never heard the name before.

"There are Americans involved," Fausto proceeded. "Even elements from the CIA."

"And on our side?"

"Raúl Carvajal. Paco Carranza. The *ricos* of Monterrey."

"Scum! Fucking lice! Who cares about *them?*"

"There are Americans who believe in them. It is my opinion that we should do everything possible to encourage this belief."

"How can we gain?"

"This can make you President of the Republic, in such a way that the gringos will never dare to touch you."

Ramírez stared at him.

When Fausto had finished explaining the mechanics —and a curious quirk in his country's Constitution that they could use to their advantage—Ramírez sucked in his breath.

"You're a madman," Ramírez repeated.

"That's first cousin to a genius. You want it, don't you, Fernando? If you don't, please tell me, and I'll stop annoying you."

"*Cabrón!* You know I want it! What's in it for you?"

"Naturally, you would make me Minister of Government. I have always admired your offices."

"Naturally."

5

FAUSTO welcomed his guest with whiskey and cigars, enough to turn most stomachs at five in the morning, but his visitor seemed entirely comfortable. He belonged to the night. Despite the hour, he still wore his aviator sunglasses. Fausto had never seen him without them, except when he was having his picture taken for fake ID papers.

There was a stale, stomach-turning odor about the bunker. When the mood took him, Fausto conducted interrogations in the inner room, where the bloodstains were left on the walls. It seemed to encourage intimate revelations.

"You had no problem with the guards?" Fausto asked his visitor.

"No problem. The car I came in is a gift for you. Would you like to see it?"

Fausto leaped to his feet and led the way outside. In the distance, among the trees, tanks and armored cars squatted like beetles. Fausto patted the rump of the new-model Porsche that was parked on the grass in front of La Chiquita. In the thin moonlight, it was hard to determine the color.

"Champagne," Rico Sanchez told Fausto. "I believe it is the color you asked for."

"She's beautiful." Fausto caressed the sports car much as he would a woman, sticking his cigar between his teeth so he could use both hands. "Hard to get her across?"

"No problem," said Sanchez. He used the phrase a lot. "I got friends on both sides of the border. I drove her down myself."

"You're a good man, Rico." Fausto slapped him on the shoulder. "You bring exactly what you're asked for. How long have we been doing business?"

"Thirty-seven months."

"You see? Precise. No evasions! No excuses!" Fausto dropped his arm to his visitor's waist, and steered him back inside the bunker. "Let's eat! I've been going all night."

A SIN employee in an apron—more like a butcher's apron than a cook's—wheeled in platters of filet Dijon on a steel trolley.

Sanchez ate steadily and rapidly, like a soldier who did not know when he would get his next meal. He was a burly man, dressed—like Fausto—in a loose-hanging leather coat. At SIN headquarters, they called him the Colonel. In fact, he had been a colonel once, in the U.S. Army, before a messy affair in Salvador. He had been born and raised in the United States, but the blood of Mexico was in his veins, and he found Fausto García more *simpático,* and a damn sight more generous, than any of his superiors in the American military. Running hot cars down to Mexico—always luxury models, always on special order—had been a profitable sideline since he had entered the private sector. There were never any headaches on the Mexican side. SIN took care of that.

"I have something for you," Fausto told him, between mouthfuls. He reached into his pocket and pulled out a money clip, thick and heavy as a knuckle-duster. It was solid gold, garnished with diamonds and rubies. It coiled into the shape of a dollar sign. Not in the best taste, but worth at least five thousand, wholesale.

Sanchez accepted it without expressing his thanks, as though accustomed to such tribute.

"I have your money. Don't worry about it," said Fausto. "I could have a lot more money for you—more than you're used to—if I'm right about something."

"Right about what?"

"Why don't you take off those fucking shades? I need to look you in the eyes."

"To tell if I'm lying?"

"To tell how much I can expect from you."

Sanchez shrugged, and removed his dark glasses. His eyes gave back Fausto's own reflection.

"I seem to recall," said Fausto, "that when we first met you told me you'd done some jobs for the CIA in Vietnam. Is that right?"

"Correct."

"What was the name of the Station Chief in Saigon?"

"Colgate."

"That's what I thought. Are you still in touch with him?"

"Why do you want to know?"

"I might have something for you. Something highly profitable, assuming you can get alongside this Colgate. He's involved in something in Mexico. Do you know how to reach him?"

"I don't need to."

"I beg your pardon?"

"Art Colgate is looking for me. He called my office in San Antonio just this week, when I was out of town."

Fausto jumped up and patted his guest's pitted cheeks. "My friend, you have a face only a mother could love! But you're perfect! Absolutely perfect! Together, we can fuck the whole world!"

ELEVEN

□ □ □

1

PRESIDENT Butler paced the Oval Office, dressed in shirt-sleeves and suspenders. The others in the room, all members of his kitchen cabinet, had also removed their jackets, in deference to the chief executive's insistence on informality in closed sessions. All of them were Texans, apart from Admiral Enright, who was doing a lot of the talking.

"The Ramírez resignation is a ploy," the National Security Adviser averred. "The new Minister of Government is a Ramírez stooge. The boss of the secret police—an old Ramírez crony—is still sitting pretty. Ramírez is calling the shots from off-stage. The situation remains unchanged."

"Not from where I sit," the Secretary of State spoke up. He was an old-money Houstonian, schooled in the East, pinstriped and lean as a whippet. He resented the admiral's efforts to take charge of Administration policy toward Mexico. "You're forgetting that the President-elect gave me explicit assurances that he's going to clean up the government. I see no reason to disbelieve him. I think Mr. Paz is a man we can do business with. After he takes office, the Ramírez crowd will be out for good. That's the assessment of our Ambassador—and the CIA station—and I think we ought to listen to the opinions we pay them for."

He appealed to the President with his eyes.

Harry Butler said, "I'm here to listen to all opinions."

Phil Taylor, the Commissioner of Immigration, said, "We had a hundred thousand wetbacks, minimum, who came across the border last week."

Aaron Sturgiss, the White House Counselor, fussed with the long strands of hair that were plastered over his bald pate before adding, "We've had zero cooperation from the Mexicans on major drug cases, including the murder of the judge. A lot of the voters are fighting mad. It could be a big issue in the midterm elections."

The Energy Secretary, a native of Midland, Texas, chimed in, "As I see it, what it comes down to is oil. Since those ragheads shot the Saudi crown prince to avenge Saddam Hussein, consumers are paying fifty cents a gallon more at the pump, and they want to know what we're gonna do about it. Now we're looking at the potential of two million barrels a day, just south of Corpus. They could solve a lot of problems, assuming, of course, the area's in responsible hands."

The Chief of Staff avoided taking sides. He preferred to apply influence in less obvious ways, such as by screening visitors to the Oval Office and by controlling the flow of paper to the President's desk.

The Secretary of State spoke up again: "I think, Mr. President, that you ought to sit down with Paz. He's been asking for a meeting since the election."

"The election he stole," Admiral Enright interjected.

"He seems a reasonable guy. He went to Harvard, for Chrissake! A meeting would be common courtesy. And long-standing tradition."

"I wouldn't put too much faith in Paz," the National Security Adviser objected. "We have hard intelligence that he's sold out to Japan."

"That's extravagant." The Secretary of State picked lint off his trousers. "The Japanese have legitimate economic interests in Mexico. And they've treated the President-elect with more cordiality than we have."

"That's a nice way of putting it, Jim. I don't know whether I'm allowed to tell you this, but the NSA monitored some of Paz's luncheon conversations with the *zaibatsu* over in Tokyo. He's promised to sell them the farm. You can expect a lot more American voters out of work in Detroit, and in Silicon Valley."

"I'd need to see those transcripts," the Secretary said tersely. He was increasingly irritated by Admiral Enright's habit of preempting debate with some item of allegedly hot intelligence. "I do wish to say, Mr. President, that I take strong exception to any suggestion of precipitous action against Mexico. We are not dealing with a banana republic. And we risk jeopardizing our moral authority throughout the democratic world."

President Butler squeezed the bridge of his nose between thumb and forefinger. He said, "I agree with you, Jim. There won't be any precipitous action. But I remain open to all options."

"Including military options?" This was from Admiral Enright.

"I said *all* options. But I want it held tight. This goddamn town leaks like a worn-out boot. Each of you will be your own file clerk on this."

"Our contingency plans for a military insertion in Mexico are two years out of date," Admiral Enright observed. "I'd like your authorization to send some of our military people down there to do an update. Naturally, they'll be sheep-dipped."

"Sheep-dipped?" echoed the White House Counselor.

"They'll go in as civilians," Enright specified.

"Have we consulted the Joint Chiefs on this?" the Secretary of State demanded. "And why isn't the Secretary of Defense in on this meeting?"

"He's from Georgia," said Aaron Sturgiss. Nobody thought this was funny.

The President put up his hands. "We're a long way from any notion of using military force. You all know where I stand on this. I am not prepared to authorize U.S. military action, anywhere in the world, unless there is a clear and present danger to American lives."

2

A few hours later, over a lavish dinner at the Lion d'Or where he recounted this exchange, Admiral Enright remarked to Colgate, "Every President in modern American history has had to attend his blooding. It will be the same for Harry Butler."

"How's the President's mood?"

"He's cautious. He's doing everything by the numbers. I think he's going to sit down with Paz. He wants to be seen to be fair to all sides."

Over coffee and liqueurs, Colgate took pains to reassure the National Security Adviser that a plum job would be waiting for him at Global Assistance Services, Colgate's consulting firm in Arlington, when he retired from government service. "God knows, you deserve the chance to make some real money," Colgate told his guest. "I think it's a crying shame that a man of your caliber gives his body and soul for a piss-ant government salary and a goddamn parking space."

The remark about blooding lingered with Colgate. His paymasters had been momentarily stunned by the Ramírez resignation. Colgate flattered himself that this unexpected development had proved the success of his media operations, run out of a press office behind a discreet brass plaque on K Street. But Ramírez's hasty departure had also undermined the grand design of creating the bogey of a Mexican Noriega.

"We see it like this," Halliwell said, calling from Houston. "We gotta move into the action mode. Do you read me, Cantwell?"

"Perfectly."

"I want a professional in charge. No more screw-ups."

"I have the perfect man. He'll cost you twenty thousand a month." He did not add, ten for me, ten for him.

"Jeez, Cantwell! You'll be able to buy *me* out!"

"I have other clients."

Halliwell grunted his assent, and Colgate called San Antonio.

"Hispanic-American Marketing."

"I'm trying to reach Mr. Sanchez."

"I'm sorry, sir, Mr. Sanchez is still in Mexico. We expect him back any day now."

Colgate persisted. He finally ran down Rico Sanchez at his mistress's apartment two nights later.

"I may have something interesting for you. Want to make a little money for both of us?"

"Sure."

"This is sensitive, Rico. Why don't you fly up for the weekend?"

Sanchez did not hesitate, once Colgate said he would pay for the plane ticket. Colgate did not like Sanchez, but then he did not care much for most of the people he worked with. He had not misled Halliwell. He thought Rico Sanchez would be ideal for Safari. He was Mexican-American, which meant he could pass for a native down south. He knew more ways of killing than any human being Colgate had ever met. At Saigon Station, they had called him the Headhunter.

Rico Sanchez flew into Dulles Airport that Saturday; he found Colgate waiting with a stretch limo and a chauffeur. Colgate was a firm believer in symbols of rank and power. In the first years of Global Assistance, he had handed out silver medallions to favored clients and contractors, telling them that these were secret NSC badges that gave the holder immunity from police arrest. Colgate had abandoned the practice when someone cautioned him that Ed Wilson, the convicted death merchant who had hired himself to Qaddafi, had tried a similar stunt, and that the comparison could be rather bad for business.

Sanchez looked uncomfortable in his suit, although his cowboy boots improved his height by a couple of inches, giving him something of an ego boost. His weathered skin matched the color of the maduro cigar he lit up in the car. He was a nondescript man, one you wouldn't notice in the street. But when he removed his aviator sunglasses, there was something restless and avid about the eyes.

Colgate opened up the bar in the back of the limo and the two men sipped scotch on the ride out toward Culpeper. Sanchez claimed he had been down in Mexico on routine business, arranging a shipment of refrigerators.

"Refrigerators?" Colgate laughed. "Jeez, you must be bored out of your skin. You getting enough action these days?"

"I never get enough." Sanchez's voracious sexual appetite was part of his legend. He was said to have drilled his way through the entire ménage of the House of a Thousand Tits during two weeks' R & R in Bangkok, and Colgate did not wholly discount the story.

"You stick with me, buddy. I'll fix us a little action for tonight. If I remember correctly, you like them light, don't you?"

"What you get me up here for?" Hunger darted from Sanchez's eyes; Colgate wished he would replace his sunglasses.

"Later." Colgate nodded toward the chauffeur. "Tell me how you feel about the situation in Mexico. These killings. This guy Miliano Rojas."

"Miliano Rojas is a campesino. A poor dumb shit. The kind that always gets screwed."

"He seems to be building quite a following."

Sanchez shrugged. "I'm not interested in politics. I'm a technician."

"That's why I called you."

The limousine pulled off the Old Lee Highway and swept up a long, curving drive past ancient stands of oak to The Haven, a vast, modern brick house that appeared to be impersonating an English boarding school. Sanchez evinced total disinterest in his surroundings until he spotted a young whitetail buck and two does springing away across a distant field.

"Those deer on your place?"

"They sure are. I've got six hundred acres."

"I like killing deer."

Sanchez did not spare a second glance for Colgate's art collection, his boulle console tables, or the eighteenth-century sideboard that had been made for the Schuyler family in New York. He approved of the quadraphonic stereo system in the living room, and played loud music while they talked and continued their drinking.

"So what's the job?" Sanchez demanded.

"My principals are wealthy landowners in the north of Mexico," Colgate began carefully. "They are concerned about the present unrest in their country. They are obvious targets for kidnappers. Some of them are having trouble with squatters."

"Are these guys American, or Mexicans?"

"They're Mexican." Colgate saw no advantage in mentioning John Halliwell. If Sanchez knew the head of a major oil corporation was involved, he would start inflating his fee.

Sanchez blew smoke in Colgate's direction. "What area are we talking? Sonora? Chihuahua?"

"That general area."

"Hell, you don't need me. Those *hacendados* know how to take care of themselves. They've been shooting campesinos for generations."

"Let's say my principals feel the need to place their security on a more professional basis."

"I don't go around checking alarm systems, Art. You can go down to the FBI building and hire yourself a flatfoot off the street if that's all you need."

"I'm talking about something a little more ambitious. The mission will involve supplying state-of-the-art weaponry and equipment for a fighting force of say twenty thousand men. And training cadres and special units."

Sanchez stared at him. "That's enough to start a war! Or take over a country!"

Colgate said nothing.

"You'd better level with me, Art. Sonora, Chihuahua. That's dopers' territory. Don't get me wrong. I don't give a shit how many white boys—or black dudes—are frying their brains on crack. I just need to know what I'm getting into."

"Nothing to do with drugs. You have my word on that."

"So tell me. Is this a Company operation?"

It was the question Colgate had been waiting for, and welcomed. He was one of the rare people who habitually used the CIA as a cover. He spread his thumbs like propellers and said, "I'm not authorized to answer that question. You'll report to me. You'll be briefed on a need-to-know basis. You can take it or leave it."

"You haven't told me about the money."

"The money's good, Rico. Enough to support your bad habits. Ten thousand up front, ten thousand a month as long as the mission is operational. More if there are action requirements."

"It's the action requirements that interest me."

"We'll take this one step at a time, Rico. But I didn't pick you just to show Mexican boys how to punch holes in tin cans."

COLGATE wheeled in the hookers after dinner. They were supplied by a discreet escort agency in Fairfax with whom Global Assistance had a charge account. Predictably, Sanchez gravitated toward the peroxide blonde who was stacked like an adolescent's wet dream, but he pulled the redhead into the bedroom with him as well. Later, the redhead demanded extra money, saying Sanchez had slapped her around to make her do a couple of things that were not in her standard repertoire. Sanchez was not always gentle with women.

Sanchez came out of the bedroom, his shirt flapping open over his broad chest. The girls looked scared, and demanded to be driven home.

Sanchez, however, was ready to party. "After I fuck, I like to kill something. And the other way around." He grabbed at the tall blonde's breasts, and she squealed. "You got a truck, right?" he said to Colgate. "Every farmer's got a truck. Even a fucking country squire like you."

Colgate allowed that he had an old Ford pickup, out in the barn.

"Tell you what we do," said Sanchez. "We get the truck, we get a spotlight—you have a spotlight, don't you?"

Colgate, indeed, had a new halogen model that could hurl a beam of light for two miles.

"Okay. We'll rig up the spotlight and go jack us some of those pretty whitetail deer."

Colgate protested dully that the deer season had not officially opened, and that jacking deer was illegal at any time of year, throughout the United States.

"You want me to risk my ass in Mexico," Sanchez said angrily, "and you're too gutless to go hunting some dumb animal on your own turf."

Colgate's Vietnamese butler, drawn by the shouting, came and stood in the doorway. He was a former Ranger, doggedly loyal to his master, and could kill with a pair of nunchaku sticks as reliably as with a gun.

"We're fine, Chu." Colgate waved him away. He had decided to humor Sanchez. The Mexican-American was ripped, and Colgate did not want him shooting his mouth off any more in front of the hookers. Besides, he considered Sanchez's unabated passion for blood sport a healthy symptom, at least so long as it was harnessed to his larger plan. Colgate agreed to go out in the truck; he insisted, however, that the girls be sent home.

They bumped around in the pickup for half an hour, under a velvety, moonless sky. The spotlight stabbed across the fields and poked among the bushes. Colgate was glad he had no near neighbors.

"Gotcha!" Sanchez hissed.

Colgate followed his stare. Three hundred yards away, a ten-point stag and several does stood frozen in the glare of the spotlight. Safety lay at their shoulder, among a copse of trees, but the fierce light had paralyzed their instinct for survival.

"Dead meat," Sanchez pronounced, leaning out the window on the passenger side. He lifted Colgate's rifle.

Though he was not a man who cared about animals, Colgate felt an instant's sympathy for the deer. His last wife had accused him of psychological cruelty to her dog; it was one of the things her attorneys had cited in successive alimony suits. It got to the judge every time.

When Sanchez squeezed the trigger, the echo of the shot as it bounced back and forth inside the cab of the pickup was deafening. Colgate pressed his hands to his ears. He felt as if his eardrums had just been blown out.

Sanchez, seemingly impervious to the explosive sound, jumped out the door and loped across the grass to his fallen prey. The does scattered among the trees. His bullet had taken the stag between the shoulders; its blood fountained across the earth.

Colgate saw Sanchez stooping over the stag, the knife blade shining in his hand.

"Let's get out of here!" Colgate called to him. He reached up and snapped off the spotlight. He did not want to prolong the risk of drawing the attention of some passing highway cop.

In the darkness, Colgate could not see Sanchez clearly until he was next to the driver's window. He opened his mouth to speak, but the raw stench of hot blood floating in through the window made him gag.

"Oh, God . . ."

Sanchez laughed as he threw the stag's head into the back of the pickup.

"Did you have to do that?" Colgate complained, when Sanchez climbed back into the cab.

Sanchez was convulsed with laughter. "I thought for a minute you were going to faint. Like that guy Maury, Maury whatsisface. You remember?"

"Maury Atthowe."

"Yeah, Atthowe." He pronounced it Att-oo-ee. That had always pissed off Maury.

Colgate remembered. In Saigon, Colgate had put a price on the heads of the most-wanted Vietcong leaders and Sanchez had taken him literally. One night, he had come into the Station to claim his bounty. Maury Atthowe had been on duty and had made the mistake of opening the burlap sack that Sanchez dumped on his desk. When a Vietnamese head rolled out, Maury had fallen on the floor in a dead faint.

Colgate had not thought it was all that funny then, and he still didn't. As they drove up to the house, he said to Sanchez, "It wasn't just that one time. You always took the goddamn head."

Sanchez laughed.

"Why did you do that?"

"Tribal custom. *You* sent me up to the Montagnards. You should know."

"You're not a Montagnard."

"My people did it too. A while back. Ever hear about the Aztecs? They believed the same as the hill people in Nam. You take the head, you capture the spirit. You save yourself from a lot of bad nights. That scares you, doesn't it?"

"No." Abruptly, Colgate stopped the truck and turned off the ignition.

"Talk to me, Arthur. It scares the shit out of you, doesn't it?"

"*No!* I had to arrange something similar, just a few weeks back." As soon as he had said it, he realized his mistake.

The Headhunter narrowed his eyes. "Tell me about it," Sanchez urged. "Did you enjoy it?"

"I don't want to talk about it."

"Eating the heart is better."

"Shit. You never did that, did you, Rico?"

Sanchez laughed. It was a hollow sound. Colgate could not remember ever having felt more uncomfortable.

TWELVE

□ □ □

1

At a disused gravel pit on his own land, twenty miles from the villa, Raúl Carvajal watched the new instructor demonstrate the uses of a C-4 plastic explosive. The C-4 had been shipped from Houston in plastic bags, hidden inside drums labeled "drilling mud." Raúl tapped his earplugs. The roar was still impressive as a derelict bus exploded into whirling shrapnel.

The instructor was ready to demonstrate a new trick. He held up an unmarked bottle. He shouted at the Mexicans that it contained an additive that would turn the gasoline in the tank of a car into flaming napalm.

The man seemed to know his job. Still, Raúl did not care for him. He found the man cold and insinuating, continually seeking more information than he needed to know. He was a Mexican-American, and while his Spanish was fluent, Raúl thought his accent atrocious and his jokes unrepeatable. His skill with explosives, however, would be invaluable when the day came for the north to rise and claim its freedom. A few well-placed charges, at bridges and mountain passes and railroad lines, would isolate the north from any rapid land assault by the government forces. In the meantime, there were other uses for bombs.

With a thump and a WHOOOSH, a pillar of flame burst from an old farm truck and leaped a hundred feet into the air. The men of the Division of the North, fitted out in American-made fatigues and combat boots, applauded. Some of them fired their M-16s into the air, until the instructor barked at them, chastising them to save their ammunition for the *chilangos*.

Raúl climbed into his Land Cruiser. He felt nervous and on edge this morning. It wasn't because of his soldiers' lousy marksmanship, which he had witnessed earlier. They could shoot as well as Mexican army troops, and when the time came for military operations, some of them would be armed with the new laser-guided weapons Mr. Cantwell had been plugging so hard. With those things all you had to do was put the red dot on your mark and squeeze the trigger. Yes, the Division of the North would fight well enough, and they would last for as long as was needed, but they could not take on the Mexican air force. Of course, the Mexican air force was feeble, even by Latin American standards, but the fleet of Pipers and Learjets and Cessnas was more than a match for the Northern Force.

The requirement for victory, as Raúl saw it, was the involvement of the United States. But even in private, President Butler continued to withhold his endorsement. While the Administration debated option papers, the newspapers were full of reports that fences were being mended between Washington and Mexico City. The bankers were getting together to try to work out a new debt repayment schedule. The Mexican Attorney General had promised full cooperation with the DEA and the law enforcement agencies investigating Judge Renwick's death.

Raúl knew he could no longer rely on the diplomats and politicians. Too much was at stake, and there was not enough time. Other tactics were called for now.

Yes, it was time for Shelley to earn her keep.

2

CHUNKY men wearing white shirts and hearing aids prowled the hotel corridor, bunching together at the east end, where the first guests were arriving at the Lovell suite. The hotel advertised its discretion. Branch "Charlie" Lovell, ranking senator from Louisiana, had maintained a hospitality suite here since the last election, his monthly bills paid by a nonprofit organization whose principal supporter was Hallow Petroleum of Houston, Texas.

While a black butler in a white dinner jacket poured Chivas Regal and Stolichnaya for the senator's guests, a stretch limousine with shaded windows drew up to the hotel's side entrance on Washington's H Street. The vehicle was indistinguishable from a half dozen similar limos whose drivers were contending for space outside the hotel's front doors on 15th Street. A man leaped out of the limousine and vanished behind a protective wall of Secret Service agents.

No one, not even the inevitable streetwalker, had time to recognize President Harry Butler as he swept into the service elevator, held waiting by another man with an earpiece.

With him was Aaron Sturgiss, White House Counselor and the architect of the celebrated crusade to save Disneyland from the Japanese that had helped him win the election. They had been asshole buddies—or so Aaron would boast after enough bourbon—since they had voted the Mexicans for LBJ in the bad old, good old days down in Corpus. Washington insiders might dispute whether Harry Butler or Ann Travis Butler was the most powerful Texan in the White House. Nobody disputed that Aaron Sturgiss ranked third.

Aaron's clownish features and his down-home similes could be deceptive. He knew where power had gone in America—it had gone into the airwaves—and he had been instrumental in helping Harry Butler snatch it back from the other party. With Sturgiss's guidance, Harry had campaigned for the nomination, and then for the President's job, with the aid of his own video center: a mobile dream machine that transmitted to local TV stations across America via satellite hookup, armed with high-rent apex digital optics machines that could simulate 3-D, flip images on and off the tape, run simulations, or dazzle with arresting cut-ins at the flick of a switch.

Sturgiss had earned his position of power in the President's inner circle, and—right or wrong—Butler trusted him.

"What's Charlie Lovell want this time?" the President asked as the elevator rose to the top of the building.

"Well, he still wants to home-port the *Ulysses S. Grant* in Louisiana."

"He's drilling a dry duster. We're never going to build that carrier. We don't have the money. Charlie knows that, too. What else?"

"Mexico. I guess Charlie's banker friends are getting pretty scared."

"Aaron, I've got Mexico coming out of both ears. Jonah Pike wants me to resurrect Black Jack Pershing and the goddamn bankers want me to bail them out with taxpayers' money. It would be nice to spend an evening talking about something other than our brown brothers to the south."

"Charlie gives a good party," said Aaron mildly, as the elevator came to a stop.

It was a relevant observation, for in Washington, the influence of a dedicated party-giver can hardly be overstated. Public men need to let their hair down sometime. Harry Butler's campaign ads had touted him as "the President for the 21st Century," but he indulged in a very old-fashioned reverie: that the President of the United States could still conduct his private affairs without run-

ning into sightseers, terrorists—or reporters. In addition
to his official retreat at Camp David and his private ranch
on the Nueces River, two hours' drive from Corpus
Christi, the President, with Aaron's help, had established
a network of retreats within easy reach of the White
House. He called them his "safe houses." They were
places where he could relax, let off steam, and maybe
even talk Texas friendly to someone, maybe even an un-
attached young woman, without reading about it in the
paper. And without hearing about it from the First Lady
over the breakfast table or in one of the dawn ambushes
she liked to mount through the door that connected their
bedrooms on the second floor of the executive mansion.

Harry Butler's preferred hideaway was truly private:
a rambling old center-hall colonial on the Old Lee Highway, hidden from the road by spreading oaks and cherry
trees. Getting out there usually meant taking a chopper,
however, and that created a blizzard of activity all over
the White House lawn. Senator Lovell's hospitality suite
at least had the virtue of proximity. That he also served
good whiskey and passable jambalaya, and seemed to
know any number of good-looking women who didn't
talk to reporters, were pluses as well.

The Louisiana senator had no shortage of axes to
grind—he sat on both the Finance and Intelligence Committees—but President Butler felt on safe ground in the
senator's suite. Charlie Lovell had been the first man in
Congress, outside Texas, to back his run for the nomination; he represented the next-door oil state; they had a
lot of friends in common; and they had raked hell together down in New Orleans the week after Harry had
flunked his first try for the bar exams.

The lines of tension eased from the President's face
as he stepped into the Lovell suite. The party was the
right size: big enough so you could avoid anyone you
wanted to avoid; intimate enough for you to take in all
the faces. None of the men present had come with his
own wife.

From his earliest mentor, Lyndon Baines Johnson, Harry Butler had learned the principle that to succeed in politics, you have to be able to tell the minute you walk in a room who is for you and who is against you. The mature Harry Butler had observed, however, that people aren't generally for you or against you so much as they are for themselves.

He trained his practiced smile on what was clearly a Butler crowd—subject to the qualification mentioned above. The lobbyist for Black & Greenleaf, the giant construction and drilling consortium, had been putting together fund-raising activities for Harry Butler for more than twenty years. The leggy redhead was the socialite wife of a New York banker who never seemed to have time to accompany her to Washington.

In a corner above the bar, a muted TV set carried images from CNN. Or maybe it was C-Span, because there was Senator Jonah Pike, owlish behind his horn-rimmed glasses, resurrecting communists most people believed to be extinct.

"Hey, Charlie," the President spoke to his host. "Put on the sound for a minute, will you? I want to hear what that blowhard is saying about us."

The mute light went out, and Senator Pike, the right-wing tormentor of six administrations, was caught in mid-tremor:

". . . pimping for a bunch of dope-runners and corrupt officials who are turning Mexico over to the communists. Harry Butler makes out that because he's from Texas, he knows how to keep Mexicans in line. That might work on your ranch, Harry, or at Taco Bell, but it sure ain't working across the Rio Grande. The White House policy of cozying up to whoever stole the last election in Mexico is going to give us an Iran next door."

"That's a blivet, Jonah," Harry Butler addressed the TV. "Two pounds of shit in a one-pound sack." He motioned to the bartender to turn off the sound.

"I don't understand," the President said, turning to

Senator Lovell, "how a guy who enjoyed getting into bed with Marcos and Pinochet can sound off on Mexico like a long-haired radical. Is anybody out there listening?"

"They're listening, Harry," said Lovell. "Salomon Brothers is trading Mexican bonds for sixteen cents on the dollar. And falling. The Border Patrol caught six thousand wets in one bust last night down by Laredo. Six thousand!"

The lobbyist for Black & Greenleaf homed in. "Mr. President, I hope you're not going to let the Japanese take over down there."

Harry Butler bristled. "Who said the Japanese are taking over?" This was a sore point. Like it or not, his recent career was founded on thumbing his nose at the Japanese, and the President could not afford to be perceived as softening on the Japan issue now. One of the campaign ads the party was market-testing for the midterm election showed teams of flag-carrying Japanese businessmen closing down American factories and directing American workers to the welfare lines. The voice-over began: "You must remember this."

The lobbyist said something about the Canal Project. The plan to drive a canal across the isthmus of Tehuantepec was the stuff of daydreams for anyone in the construction business. If it were ever carried into effect, it would provide one of the biggest engineering and construction contracts in history—perhaps *the* biggest.

"There won't be a canal," Harry Butler said. "Who needs it, since we got rid of old Pineapple Face in Panama? And who's gonna pay? Those Mexicans are poorer than Job's turkey."

"The Japanese might put up the credit," said the man from Black & Greenleaf. "Big John Halliwell says if we let them get that canal, we better get ready to gas up the *Enola Gay*."

"Is Big John in with you boys on a canal deal?"

The lobbyist nodded his head.

"Well then," said the President, "you keep Aaron here posted."

Senator Lovell took his arm.

"There's a little lady here who came a pretty far piece to see you, Mr. President. Can't say I don't envy you."

Harry Butler squared his shoulders. He had a reputation in town as a lady-killer, but he had avoided public scandal. He was a beneficiary of the sour backwash from all the sex scandals of the previous decade, which had resulted in a tacit mutual truce between the two major parties. The media went their own way, of course, digging up dirt wherever possible, but Aaron Sturgiss had some clever ways of dealing with the gentlemen of the press. A few months into this Administration, a reporter had called to ask about the President's alleged tryst with a busty blond secretary. Aaron had phoned up the reporter's editor-in-chief and offered to send to a competing publication the credit-card receipts the reporter had signed for a call-girl service.

The President turned to meet his admirer.

She was wearing a basic black cocktail dress, and a double strand of pearls. The simplicity of her outfit enhanced the effect of her shimmering red-gold hair, her wide, gray-green eyes, her fine, glowing skin. Her face had a natural radiance; it seemed to be lit from within.

"Hello, Harry."

The President's smile froze on his face.

"You shouldn't show your teeth like that," Shelley told him. "You looked like that in the Sam Donaldson interview. People can see you're nervous."

Senator Lovell excused himself diplomatically, and drew Aaron Sturgiss away.

"I didn't expect to see you," Harry Butler said to Shelley, still wearing a forced grin. "You look well."

"Someone called me a *balzaciana* the other day."

"What in hell is that?"

"Something out of Balzac. Don't you read anything, Harry? Ann should set you a reading list."

The President's eyes slid sideways, then back. He gulped at his scotch and soda.

"How long have you been in Washington?"

"I flew up today. I started in Monterrey. Raúl asked me to talk to you."

"Not here," Butler said quickly.

Shelley's eyes flickered toward the door. What was back there? Oh Lord, the bedroom.

"I can't talk to you here," the President said. His smile slipped. She was wearing the same perfume—L'Air du Temps—and she looked so good. Seeing her like this brought back so many memories. It made him feel giddy, a little weak at the knees. She had put on a little weight, but it was all in the right places. He could almost imagine his hands fitting around her waist, pulling her toward him. Again.

"Then where, Harry?"

The words snapped him from his reverie. She seemed to take it for granted that he would not refuse her this time. Was it because she felt that he owed her, or because of Raúl? He was having trouble focusing. With all those eyes on him, it was hard to think. He knew he could not give in to old feelings. He had to keep their dealings formal. Private, but formal.

It came to him. "You know the Executive Office Building?"

"The old building LBJ wanted to tear down?"

"That's it. Room Three Forty-six. Ten o'clock tomorrow." He lowered his voice so she had to lean in toward him to catch the words. "Give the guard a different number."

Room 346 was an office used by Bill Wagoner, the Director of the Central Intelligence Agency, on the floor where Ollie North had shredded Iran-Contra papers. Harry Butler had marked Wagoner early on as a man who could be counted on to do the boss a favor, and he had never disappointed him.

The President turned his smile toward the socialite redhead, and then moved toward the bar. He was still feeling unsteady. It was disturbing that two years away from Shelley had not diminished his attraction for her. He almost felt like they had never been apart. If they had been alone, and he'd had a couple more jolts of Chivas, their affair could have begun all over. Shelley was different from the other women Harry Butler had known. It wasn't just a matter of looks, or that she had a quick, independent mind and was never scared to express it. She had more of a sense of life about her than the other women in Harry's experience. Suddenly the President felt very uncomfortable about the date he had just arranged.

3

SHELLEY watched the TV news over coffee and croissants in her penthouse at the Four Seasons in Georgetown. Again today, Mexico hogged the headlines. They were showing a tape of a news conference held by Mac Fitzgibbon, the President's press secretary.

"Will the White House comment on Senator Pike's statement that this Administration is—and I quote the senator's exact words—'a pimp and a whoremaster for a gang of dope-runners and crooked officials'?"

"I defer to the senator's superior knowledge of whoremongering," Mac countered, his voice steady but his face reddening.

"Will the White House respond to Senator Pike's demand that all U.S. loans to Mexico should be suspended until the Mexican government cleans up its act?"

"As I understand it, we're trying to get our loans back."

Shelley switched to another network morning show, but it was the same there. Mexico was inescapable. A horn-rimmed analyst from the Enterprise Institute was talking about rumors that the world banking consortium would reject Mexico's request to defer scheduled interest payments. The talking heads went off, and a mob of demonstrators came on. Mexican riot police were trying to break up the rally with tear gas.

American TV viewers were inured to scenes like this one. They had seen them in live footage from Teheran and Manila, Warsaw, and East Berlin. And Beijing. Sometimes revolt in the streets had brought freedom. Sometimes it had brought tanks and firing squads.

Shelley rummaged in her closet for the right clothes for a morning call on the President of the United States. She decided on a Prince of Wales check suit, fully aware that the skirt rode an inch higher than was altogether businesslike.

She took a taxi downtown, got off on 17th Street, and walked around the corner to the main entrance to the Old Executive Office Building on Pennsylvania Avenue, next to the west wing of the White House. The protestors in front of the White House were also captivated by the Mexican crisis. There were two rival groups, howling abuse at each other across the police lines: "Hands Off Mexico!" posters vied with "No More Noriega" signs. It struck Shelley that the two crowds looked remarkably alike. When it came to Mexico, left-wingers and right-wingers got hopelessly confused about where they were supposed to stand, and for two thirds of a century, Mexican governments had been assiduously working to spread this confusion at home and abroad.

Shelley walked up the steps, under the grand old wedding-cake façade of the Executive Office Building, and into the lobby, where the guard checked her driver's license and gave her a visitor's badge on a chain. She told him she was going to Room 302, Ollie North's old digs. They ran her pocketbook through an X-ray machine like the ones used at airports.

She took the stairs instead of the elevator, to give herself an extra minute or two to make sure she was fully composed. The columns of this building, running eighteen feet up to the ceiling on each floor, were cast iron. Some of the door frames were brass. The weight of all that metal had saved the place from destruction; it was just too expensive to pull down. On the third floor, the walls had been repainted a smoky beige, but the scuff marks on the black-and-white checkered floor remained —a memento of rougher times, when soldiers were quartered in these corridors during inaugurations.

Today, however, Shelley noticed nothing of this. Her mind was quickly canvassing a lot of memories, covering a lot of time. She was examining her motives, asking herself if she had been right to come here today. No one had made her. She wasn't doing it for Raúl and his dreams of power and revenge. She certainly wasn't doing it for Harry Butler.

Maybe she was doing it to settle accounts with *all* the men in her life. Maybe after this, she could get on with things, unburdened by the past.

Yes, this one's for *me*, she said inwardly.

Her eyes sparkled as she tapped on the door of the President's borrowed office.

"Say again?" Harry Butler responded.

He watched Shelley as she adjusted her skirt. She glanced at him mockingly from under her lowered lashes. He wondered briefly if she were flirting with him.

"Raúl says," she repeated, "that you should be prepared for a change of a dramatic kind in Mexico. You should be aware that the people who are involved are men of serious conviction who are friends of President

Butler and the United States. They count on your understanding. Their watchword is Safari."

Harry Butler felt his shoulders tense involuntarily. "That's *all?*" he demanded. "Nothing else?"

"He sent you this." Shelley gave him an envelope.

The President tore it open and glanced at the note inside. It contained just two words, hand-printed in block capitals: "HONEY HUNT."

President Butler flushed a dangerous shade of red. "Do you know what this means?"

"I didn't read it, Harry."

Butler tore the note into tiny pieces, letting them fall to the floor. Then, thinking better of it, he scooped them up and thrust them into his trouser pocket.

"Raúl is trying to hassle me. And he's using you."

"I'm a consenting adult, Harry."

"How much do you know? What do you know about Safari?"

"I know Raúl wants to be president of his own country. I know he's counting on you for help."

"Do you know the kind of people he's mixed up with?"

"I know he's a friend of John Halliwell's. I seem to remember Halliwell was one of your biggest supporters when you were on the Senate trail."

"Goddamn!" The President started pacing around the office, waving his arms. "You remember the first rule of Texas politics?"

"Always vote your constituency."

"Right. First, last, and always! John Halliwell doesn't speak for Texas, not the biggest part of it, anyway. People in Texas want peace along the border. They want to go back to doing business. They don't want trouble with Mexicans, on either side of the line. As for Raúl, I guess he doesn't speak for anyone but himself. Is he treating you okay?"

"I've got no complaints."

"I think you ought to get away from him, Shelley.

Get away from him fast. Otherwise, you're going to get hurt."

"I've been hurt already, Harry."

He paused to look at her. She crossed her legs. "You know . . ." He crouched beside her. She felt his breath on her neck. "You know I'm sick about what happened. I'd make it up to you if I could."

She responded with soft words, words that said she still believed in him, still believed in the good he could do for his country and others. For a moment, the space between them in the austere, impersonal office seemed to dissolve.

The President was standing over her, drawing her up to him, drinking in the comforting smell of her hair. She felt him stiffen against her. Instantly, she knew why she had come. She did not rebuff him.

Before she could respond, however, he jerked away, aghast at his lack of self-control. You have to get a hold of yourself, he thought. Here was the President of the United States, behaving like a teenager with raging hormones.

"I-I'm sorry," he stammered. "It's just, I guess I haven't gotten over you. I'll make it up to you somehow."

She watched his tense back as he retreated to the far side of the room. Yes, you will make it up to me, you son of a bitch, Shelley spoke to him with her mind. You bet you will.

4

"BREAKTHROUGH," Admiral Enright crowed to the Director of Central Intelligence. They were sitting in the same office in the Executive Office Building the President had used the day before. "The Commander-in-Chief has just authorized me to set up a special task force to work up some military options for Mexico."

Director Wagoner looked sullen. He had made it his policy to tack to the prevailing wind, but he did not want to find himself—or his Agency—at the short end of another Iran-Contra scandal.

"Lighten up, Bill," the National Security Adviser urged him. "We'll bury this deep in some basement over at the Pentagon. We'll give it some boring name, like the Office of Policy Adjustment. We'll give it cover inside the cover. If any smartass starts poking around, we'll make him think we're planning something against Cuba."

"Who's going to run the shop?"

"A Marine's Marine. A one-star general called Two Jacks Gilly."

"Two Jacks?"

"He's a Cajun. I worked with him on the Panama thing. He loves the smell of cordite, and he can run rings around those armchair warriors on the Joint Chiefs."

Director Wagoner voiced no objection. He had not been asked for any practical assistance, so thus far his neck was not too far out.

"How's that Mexico Estimate coming along?" Admiral Enright asked.

"It's a slow business. You know we have to take all views into account. The State Department is very cautious. So is our Chief of Station."

"Kreeger? I thought you were going to get rid of that bastard."

"I've looked into it. He's got a helluva record, and he's got a lot of friends in Operations."

"I might have a way to expedite things. The last thing we need is some jerk in Mexico City running interference."

"I hope you know what you're doing."

"Listen. If we can't sort out Mexico, we might as well stop pretending to be a world power. That's an exact quote from the man at the top. Oh, and Bill? I'm going to want a couple of million out of your slush fund.''

The Director checked the side pocket of his suit jacket for his bottle of pills.

THIRTEEN

□ □ □

1

At Mexico Station, Kreeger was fighting wars on paper. The Director had sent him a draft of the Special National Intelligence Estimate—pronounced Snee, like something from Gilbert and Sullivan, appropriately so, Kreeger thought—on Mexico. The tone, even filtered through committeemen's prose, was almost hysterical. A brisk survey of Mexico's turmoil (the usual: assassinations, political violence, drugs, corruption, economic chaos) was slanted to support recommendations for "active response" by the United States. The options for "active response" ranged from diplomatic chiding in the form of a State Department Travel Advisory (which would kill the tourist trade) through covert action all the way up to "military insertions in defense of U.S. citizens and assets."

Kreeger ran his fingers through his thinning hair. He saw Admiral Enright's hand in this. And while he was not inclined to question the National Security Adviser's motives, knowing full well Enright was a superpatriot, spoiling for a fight, what Kreeger found difficult to understand was how his own Director could sign off on such an alarmist appraisal. Director Wagoner had once called him a "cowboy" to his face, but now it was the desk jockeys, not the fieldmen, who were brandishing six-shooters.

Fueled by many mugs of coffee, Kreeger penned a response.

The amateur historian in him came to the fore as he wrote,

> In this century, Mexico has frequently endured similar problems. On two occasions, the United States overreacted with a physical invasion force. In both cases, we succeeded only in exacerbating tensions between our countries, and leaving a legacy of enmity and resentment.

He went on:

> I believe that a Mexican solution to the current malaise will be found. There is no evidence of significant foreign involvement in the crisis. Cuban activity is minor, and largely confined to traditional leftist groups they have long supported in the south. An active response on the part of the United States should therefore be confined to diplomatic and economic pressures that will assist in calming the situation. Any military action would create a fragmented Mexico, opening it to chaos, militant regionalism, and indeed a civil war that would endanger not only our economic interests but the lives of some 200,000 U.S. citizens living in this country.
>
> This office stands ready to execute any *positive* action required to enhance U.S. interests. You will understand that our relations with local liaison, despite recent disturbances, are such that we are able to press the views of the United States Government as forcibly as may be necessary.

When Peggy had typed his message, Kreeger sealed it in a white envelope and sent it to the Director through the eyes-only ANTARCTICA channel, together with a request that he be allowed to return to Washington to thrash out the Mexico Estimate in person with the other players.

2

SHELLEY was being stalked. It was dark and she stumbled through thorny scrub. It tore at her flimsy shift, at her exposed skin. Her mouth was parched. She couldn't swallow. She could hardly breathe.

The man who came panting after her was clumsy and misshapen—and enormous. There was no way she could fight him off. She had to keep running. Yet she felt that in a single bound, he could overtake her. She took a quick look back over her shoulder. She saw the huge knife, the gleaming blade.

She couldn't run anymore.

Exhausted, desperate, she turned on her pursuer. "All right, you bastard. Let's see what you've got."

She crouched like a cornered animal. Her long nails curved into claws. She would go for the eyes, for any vulnerable part.

The moment she turned to defend herself, the darkness began to lift. The whole scene lightened as if a switch had been thrown in a room. In fact, she was in a room, a formal dining room, where men in dinner jackets and women in designer ball gowns were sipping champagne under the sparkle of crystal chandeliers.

The man she had turned to confront was no disheveled brute, but a smooth, distinguished fellow in white tie and tails. The ribbon of some kind of decoration crossed his starched shirtfront.

She stared at the thing he was pushing toward her mouth.

It wasn't a knife at all. It was a fat asparagus spear, pale and soft.

The man resembled President Butler, but his features were unformed. They kept slipping and changing.

Now he looked more like another Texan she had known, bigger and cruder than Harry Butler.

"Bastard!"

She grabbed the spear of asparagus and whipped it across his face.

3

Shelley woke in a cold sweat, thinking about Harry Butler, and about a man who might or might not be her father. If she pushed them over the edge, it would not be for their greater glory. She was in the suite Raúl paid for at the Presidente Chapultepec, overlooking the park in Mexico City. She was further away from Raúl in the Mexican capital than in Houston or San Antonio—which were second homes to him—and often she felt the need for distance. A shopping expedition was always a good excuse, and there were still bargains to be had in the department stores along Insurgentes Sur, even in the smart boutiques of the Zona Rosa.

When Shelley returned to the hotel in the early evening, she was followed up to her room by a bellhop wheezing under the weight of her purchases, which included a rather good copy of a Claude Montana suit from the Paris show, ten pairs of shoes, and a Fendi briefcase for Raúl.

As soon as she unlocked the door of her suite, she sensed that something was wrong. The TV was on in the living room. Maybe the maids had been having a party while she was out.

She dropped her packages and walked quickly through to the bedroom. It hadn't been a party; it had been a riot.

Her clothes were all over the bed, on the floor. The

drawers of the dresser had been yanked open, the contents dumped out everywhere.

Of course, the money she kept under her pantyhose in the top drawer was gone. There had been only a couple of hundred dollars, no major loss. Unfortunately, she had stowed her passport in there too. She went through the drawer one more time. It was gone. Of course—someone had told her an American passport could fetch up to two thousand dollars on the black market. Now she would have to go into the consulate and waste time filling in forms.

Then she saw the jewelry case. She usually left it in her safe deposit box downstairs. How could she have forgotten?

She tried to remember what she had brought with her. Raúl was always giving her things. She put the most valuable items in a bank vault in Houston.

Oh, God. The diamond and ruby necklace. The one that had belonged to Raúl's mother. She had been planning to wear it to Placido Domingo's opening. How could she have left it in the room?

She called the hotel manager in a rage of anger and frustration, knowing that even though he promised to get his security men on the case, *ahorita*, it wouldn't do any good. She slammed down the phone, tears welling over her cheeks. Raúl was bound to notice that the necklace was gone. He would be angry and upset, but he would forgive her. It wasn't so much that. It was the sense of violation.

SHELLEY stopped by the American Embassy just before ten to see about getting a new passport. There were police barriers all around the building. The cops watched passively as a small crowd of demonstrators chanted anti-U.S. slogans.

"If a sparrow falls in Mexico," the woman in the

consular section commented, "the United States is blamed."

Lois Compton reached for a cigarette, and offered the pack to Shelley, who surprised herself by accepting one. She rarely smoked.

Shelley took one puff, and started coughing. "This is serious weed."

Lois chuckled. "Oh, yeah. Turkish. A bad habit I picked up in Westwood, in the fun times."

The chanting in the street was audible even in here.

"How long have the demonstrators been out there?" Shelley asked.

"Every day since Ramírez stepped down. They turn up at nine in the morning, like they were punching a time clock. Some of them are. Some of those guys are cops out of uniform."

"Really?"

"Oh, sure. The PRI hasn't stayed in power all this time without learning a few tricks. When people get riled up, you sic them onto the gringos."

For the first time in a very long while, Shelley found herself liking another woman. Lois's worldliness, her tart running commentary on Mexico, on men, on life in general, was all very refreshing. The two women had obvious things in common: They were no longer Girl Scouts, they had kept their looks, and they had been knocked around by men. From the minute she first stepped inside Lois's office, Shelley felt she had found a friend, something she needed very much right now.

Lois stacked papers. "This is no big deal. I can do it by this time tomorrow."

"Thank you, that's great." Shelley rose to leave, then asked impulsively, "May I treat you to dinner tonight? That is, unless you're already busy."

Kreeger's CI section chief said, "Why, I'd love to. Only I was thinking of asking you, so let's make it Dutch."

4

SHELLEY decided to have a long soak in the hotel tub before she dressed for dinner. She put the new Anita Baker CD in the player, and relaxed into the bubbles, a glass of champagne on the rim of the tub. She wondered why she felt so strongly drawn to this Embassy woman, as though she had found a soulmate. Shelley did not believe in chance. There was a reason for everything in life, however difficult—or unpalatable—it proved to be. She consoled herself with the thought that the theft of her valuables might have brought her a friend.

She was washing her hair when she heard the doorbell chime. She ignored it at first, but it went on ringing. Then came a persistent hammering, as if someone were trying to break the door down.

Shelley swore and rinsed her hair under the showerhead. Wrapped in a terrycloth robe, dripping water and suds over the living room carpet, she hurried to the door and squinted through the peephole. Several Mexicans in suits were standing around in the corridor. She recognized one as the hotel manager.

"What is it?" she called out.

"There is a gentleman who wishes to talk to you about the theft."

Shelley cursed them under her breath. The men with the manager were undoubtedly cops. In Mexico, if you have a problem, the worst place to take it is to the police. Shelley guessed that the cops in the hall had come to demand money up front before they made their investigation, which would result in the inevitable report that regrettably, the necklace could not be found. They could at least have had the decency to call up ahead.

"Just a minute!"

She pulled on a skirt and blouse, and wrapped her hair in a towel.

When she opened the door, the manager, who was all smiles and apologies, remained in the hallway. Only one of the men came in.

She noticed that his muted pinstripe suit fitted him very well, and she liked his Gucci tie: orchids blossoming in a field of scarlet. She did not, however, like the way his eyes walked over her.

"Who are you?" she asked curtly.

"My name is García. It is my privilege to be of assistance."

He did not produce a badge. He gave her an elegantly engraved card. It bore only his name, and a telephone number that had been added in pencil. He had one of those literary first names that Mexicans of all social classes inflict on their children.

"Are you some kind of cop?"

"Certainly."

"Well, are you doing anything about my necklace? I already gave the manager a description."

"It was an excellent description. You are a lady of rare perception."

He didn't talk like a Mexico City cop, or any other kind of cop she had encountered. Shelley wondered if she should pay him now so he would go away. She started to reach for her pocketbook, then hesitated.

"I don't suppose I'm going to see my jewels again, am I? The fact of the matter is—"

"Facts," he interrupted her, "are often the enemies of the truth."

She stared at him in unconcealed astonishment.

"That is my observation," he continued. "It was also the observation of Don Quixote de la Mancha. Now—" he removed a long buff envelope from an inside pocket "—I wonder if you would be so kind as to verify the contents, Señora Hayes?"

Shelley opened the envelope. The ruby and diamond necklace slid out into her hand.

She blushed. Her color deepened when she realized that, without makeup, her embarrassment was completely exposed to him. How could she have been so rude to him? But how could she have guessed that they would find the stolen necklace—and return it? The necklace was worth at least fifty thousand dollars. In Mexico, you could buy and sell whole police departments for that sort of money.

She opened her pocketbook. She mumbled something about wanting to show her appreciation, about the expenses of police work, the trouble she had caused Señor García.

He stopped her with a smile. "I think you mistake me, Señora. For me, duty is its own reward. I am happy to serve the public morals. There is just one little favor I would ask."

"Name it."

"If you will permit me." He took the necklace out of her hand, unclasped it, and draped it around her neck. She felt the brush of his hands against her shoulders.

"Ah." He stood away from her. "That is what I wanted to see. It is plain that the necklace belongs to you, Señora. Only an exceptional woman—a woman of extraordinary beauty and character—can dare to wear jewels like that. You have not disappointed me."

He inclined his head—it was a gesture somewhere between a nod and a bow—and seemed ready to leave.

"Wait," Shelley said. "Won't you tell me how you recovered the necklace?"

"Ah, that is a most intriguing story. But I am afraid that, for now, my business is pressing. If you would care to be my guest for dinner, we could discuss it."

"Dinner?" The unpredictable twists in this conversation made Shelley feel a touch light-headed. "No. I'm afraid that's not possible."

"A pity." He did not press. His eyes met hers briefly. He said, from the doorway, "I must hope for another opportunity."

5

SHELLEY took Lois Compton to Del Lago. As the name suggested, the fashionable restaurant was on the lake, in Chapultepec Park. Through the vast picture windows, Shelley could see her hotel on the far side of the pewter-gray water.

At nine-twenty, when the maître d' led them to a table by the water, Shelley and Lois were the only diners at the restaurant. By ten-thirty, when Lois was on her second manhattan—she shared her boss's tastes in cocktails—and her third or fourth story about her ex-husband's infidelities, Del Lago was starting to hum. The clientele was expensively dressed. The women's hair was either blond or silver, and even the bottle blondes had complexions fair enough to match their coiffures.

"They look like the people on Mexican TV commercials," Lois observed. Brunettes are rarely in television ads in Mexico. Whether the product is diet soda or a hemorrhoid treatment, the radiant people giving thanks for it are *güeros* and *güeras*—blondies. The implied message to the Mexican in the street—a dark-skinned mestizo—is not encouraging.

Lois, who had never been to Del Lago before, found the dinner crowd a fascinating study. An aspen-lean grande dame, dripping jewels, took her place at a booth above them. When she started gossiping with her female companion, her eyes darted like knitting needles.

"Look at him," Lois whispered. An elaborately tailored figure sailed past. "He looks like he's wearing a four-piece suit. I guess this is as close to old money as you get in Mexico.''

"No." Shelley was confident of her ground. "It's not. You'll have to visit the north."

"Tell me about him. About your—significant other."

The euphemism sounded so silly that they burst out laughing at the same moment. The arrival of the main course—red snapper in a red sauce—spared Shelley from having to make an instant decision on how much she should tell Lois Compton about Raúl.

She was still savoring the first mouthful when there was a stir in the dining room. Captains and waiters gathered by the entrance, like leaves blown along by a gust of wind. The man in the four-piece suit sailed back, his mouth distorted by an exaggerated grin.

All the commotion was over a man of middling height in a dark suit and a bold Gucci tie. The staff fawned over him as if he were a movie idol. He rewarded his reception committee with handshakes and backslaps, reserving a leisurely *abrazo* for the four-piece suit.

"I don't believe it," said Shelley. "It's him."

"Who do you mean?"

"It's the cop I told you about. The one who found my necklace and refused a tip."

Lois swiveled her head to see, then looked away quickly. The four-piece suit was conducting the new arrival to his usual table on the upper level, against the wall, where he had a commanding view over the whole restaurant.

"That's your cop?"

Shelley nodded.

Lois put her hand over her mouth.

"What's so funny?"

"I thought *you* were supposed to be the authority on Mexicans. You don't know who that is? My dear, that is Fausto García Medina."

This time, the name registered. Shelley had heard

Raúl mention Fausto in the same breath as his boss, Fernando Ramírez, the archenemy of all Carvajals.

"The head of SIN," Shelley said quietly.

"My dear," Lois said confidentially, "there are those who hold that Fausto is sin incarnate. But he got you your necklace back."

"Yes."

"By the way, did you figure out how Fausto pulled that off?"

"I've been thinking about that."

"Seems to me," Lois said as she rotated her wine glass, "that Fausto would never have found your necklace unless he arranged for it to be stolen in the first place."

Shelley felt a slight shiver run up her spine. Why was Fausto interested in her? Why had he arranged such a devious manner of introduction?

"Con permiso, señoras." The sommelier appeared, carrying a silver ice bucket and a bottle of Dom Pérignon. There was no note. The wine waiter merely said, "The gentleman insists."

Shelley glanced up at him.

Fausto raised his own glass, only a few inches, and gave a sardonic smile.

Shelley was unsure how to rank her emotions. Fear and anticipation were among them, but at that moment she could not say which was uppermost.

6

Lois was eager to tell her boss about the evening's encounter, though she was not aware that Kreeger was already making inquiries about Shelley Hayes.

In the morning, she found Kreeger in a foul temper. The Director had pitched a new demand. He wanted

Kreeger to revise his comments on the Mexico Estimate from his report. In fact, he wanted the report to reflect that Mexico was on the edge of revolution, and that the republic could break apart at any moment.

Lois had barely settled herself on Kreeger's club chair when Eddie O'Brien stuck his head around the door.

"Am I interrupting something?"

Lois blew smoke at him.

Kreeger said, "What have you got?"

"You remember Shelley Hayes? Raúl Carvajal's kept lady?"

Lois tilted her nose at a steep angle, plainly suggesting that she was fed up with the language of male chauvinism. She was also a little miffed that her new discovery was not news to the two men.

"Uh-huh," Kreeger grunted.

"We finally got a response from Washington."

"They sent it to *you*?" Kreeger stared at him. "How did you get your pawmarks on the request?"

"I've got a sister in document processing. A GS-7. That's where the power is."

"How many O'Briens are there?" asked Lois.

"Only eight of us, this time around. Strictly Police and Fire Department. Except for my sister and me. We're the black sheep of the family."

"Can we leave this ethnic crap and get to the point?" growled Kreeger.

"He's not in a good mood," Lois said to Eddie. "The Director wants to know when the revolution's coming."

"So who is she?" Kreeger demanded. "Don't tell me. Shelley Hayes is a hooker who picked up Carvajal on a slow night at the Golden Nugget."

"You don't think much of women, do you?" Lois was in a fighting mood. "Do you have a picture of this Shelley?" Some mischievous instinct was telling her to withhold the fact that she had met Shelley the day before.

Grudgingly, Kreeger retrieved the photo of the blonde with the Bentley. He had been keeping it in a locked drawer of his desk, which was so unlike his normal procedure that Lois raised her eyebrows.

"That's no hooker," she pronounced, after a quick look at the photograph. "Or if she is—I'm sorry to say this, Jim—she's way outside your league."

Kreeger glowered, and was about to say something highly profane when Eddie silenced him by commenting, "I guess President Butler agrees with Lois."

"*What* did you say?"

"Raúl's girlfriend was on Butler's staff for a few years, when he was the junior senator from Texas." Eddie now had Kreeger's full attention. "She was on Harry Butler's staff, listed as an administrative assistant."

"How long?"

"Four years, according to the employment records. She was pulling down nearly forty grand a year."

"On her back?"

Lois stubbed out her cigarette savagely and said, "I don't know how I can work with you guys."

"Look," Kreeger defended himself. "This woman is shacked up with Raúl Carvajal. A goddamn Mexican! She has a Jasper Johns on her fucking wall! She drives around in a Bentley! What does that make her? Carvajal's administrative assistant?"

"For an intelligent man—a professional—you miss one hell of a lot," Lois responded. "And by the way, I'm glad that your prejudice is not confined to women."

Kreeger ran his fingers through his hair. He felt under fire on all sides. The Director was telling him his reporting stank, and now Lois—one of his protégés—was in open mutiny.

"Why don't you fill in the gaps for me," he suggested to Lois, very quietly, sensing that she knew more about all this than he might have suspected.

"A man as rich as Carvajal—or as powerful as Harry Butler—doesn't keep a woman like that just so he can screw her when he feels like it. He keeps her because he needs brains and instinct and trust. Because he needs a confidante. Even a nursemaid."

"So you feel you know this Shelley Hayes?"

"I know her better than you guys. All you see is the boobs and the hair. How do you know she slept with the President, anyway? That's one hell of an assumption."

"I merely asked a question." Kreeger looked at Eddie. "What else do we know about Ms. Hayes?"

"She went to art school. Worked in a New York gallery for a couple of years. She was arrested twice. Once for driving while intoxicated, once for soliciting."

Kreeger avoided looking at Lois, but could feel her discomfort.

"The latter charge was quashed," Eddie proceeded. "It seems she picked up some Saudi prince in Dallas—or, excuse me, the other way around—who turned out not to be much of a prince. At least, his checks bounced."

"Interesting," Kreeger said mildly. "I think one of us should talk to this Shelley Hayes."

With a wicked grin, Eddie raised his hand to shoulder height. Lois, on seeing this, shot hers straight up into the air.

"Thanks for volunteering," said Kreeger. "I may just reserve this case for myself. Anyway, Lois, Shelley doesn't exactly come under the category of a CI subject."

"You'd be making a big mistake," said Lois. "Shelley has been through the wringer with men. She'll never trust a man the way she might trust a woman."

"You mean, like those hookers who turn lesbian?" asked Eddie, with genuine interest.

Lois turned, ready for attack.

"Before we start fighting over this one," Kreeger interrupted, "we have to decide how to make contact."

"That's not going to be much of a problem," said Lois. "As it happens, I had dinner with Shelley last night."

Both men stared at her.

"You've got a helluva problem with communication," Kreeger groused.

"You two seemed to need to share your hang-ups about women. I didn't want to interrupt."

Kreeger let the rebuke pass. He nodded at Lois and said, "Your case."

"There is one more thing I'd better tell you," Lois went on. "Fausto got there first."

FOURTEEN

□ □ □

1

KREEGER's survival instinct was not entirely dormant. He was fully aware that making a recruitment pitch to a former aide—and possibly a former mistress—to the President of the United States could set off a lot of alarm buzzers in Washington.

He was also conscious that to proceed without any paperwork could generate infinite complications. He therefore filed a standard request to headquarters for "provisional operational approval" for recruitment. Under this low-key procedure, he was not obliged to spell out specific details. He commented only that the proposed recruitment would assist the station in "improving coverage of business circles in northern Mexico."

Since thousands of similar requests flowed into the Mausoleum from stations around the world every year, Kreeger did not expect any adverse fallout.

2

LINDA Ronstadt, singing a *charro* ballad in flawless Spanish, flowed from the Kreegers' hi-fi. The room contained a mixed group of diplomats and Mexican officials, all accompanied by their wives. The occasion was Jim and Karla's wedding anniversary.

"How long has it been?" Nigel Yarrow, the Kreegers' friend from the British Embassy, asked Karla.

"Twenty-three years."

"Good God! You must have been a child bride!"

"Come off it, Nigel. I'm heading for the Big Five."

"I brought you a present. I'm sorry about the wrapping. Standard Yarrow issue."

She took the gift. It was a book, still in the store's paper bag. Karla looked at the title: *Coping with Difficult People.*

She glanced at her husband, who was methodically working the crowd.

"I think you're a saint," said Yarrow, pecking her cheek.

"I think you're right."

"Hello, here's Fausto. You *are* honored. He's brought his wife."

Karla glanced over toward the door. Indeed, there stood Fausto, resplendent in a violet Gucci tie, with a tiny, doll-like woman who might have stepped straight out of a Velázquez portrait.

Karla greeted Gabriela García as an old friend. Fausto's *abrazos* were so ardent Karla felt her ribs creak. He thrust packages into her arms, boxes wrapped in gold paper, and tied with red velvet ribbons. Karla added them to the pile of gifts that was rising from an old blanket chest by the door. In the swirl of the party, she forgot about the packages until the last guests had left and she went to inspect the loot.

Angie Yarrow had brought her a big box of Bendick's bittermints, for which Karla had developed a passion in London.

"You can have the book," she told Kreeger. "I'm putting these in the refrigerator, and I'm keeping track of every one."

Kreeger was not listening. Instead, he was brooding over something Fausto had whispered to him, information that earlier that day an American citizen using a passport in the name of Cantwell had checked into the Maria Cristina, a discreet hotel on the Calle Lerma, a short jog from the Embassy. Kreeger was debating whether to instruct Eddie O'Brien to assign a surveillance team, or to go over and confront Colgate in person. He was leaning toward the latter idea—he had a lot of unfinished business with Art Colgate.

Karla tore open another package, and gasped.

She tripped out into the hall, and Kreeger followed. He found her admiring herself in the mirror. She was holding a diamond and emerald necklace against her throat.

"Look, Jim. It's magnificent."

Kreeger did not need to look at the card. Only one of their guests handed out presents like that. Kreeger was no expert on jewelry, but he guessed that the necklace must be worth at least fifteen thousand dollars.

Karla asked him to help her with the clasp.

"Sorry," Kreeger said firmly. "It's beautiful, but it's going back. You know the rules."

"I know. But let's pretend, just for one night."

Kreeger sighed and fixed the catch. He had to give Fausto credit for trying. One day, a man like Kreeger—or his wife—might forget to return one of Fausto's gifts. Kreeger wondered if that had happened with any of the previous Station Chiefs.

"Fausto didn't forget you," said Karla. "You got two boxes."

He took them from her and tore off the paper. The first offering was vintage Fausto: a diamond-encrusted money clip. Kreeger could picture the chief of SIN handing them out to his favored lieutenants like Halloween candy. The second gift was more personal: a gold-plated Colt .45. It was like the one El Loco Quintero had been carrying that night at the Fantasma Club. Maybe it was the same one. Quite a souvenir.

Kreeger felt the beginnings of temptation, but resisted, shoving the gun back into the box. "Come on," he said to his wife, holding out his hand. "Showtime is over."

When Kreeger got into the office the following morning, his mind was fully focused on Art Colgate and his possible reasons for being in the Mexican capital. When Kreeger saw Maury Atthowe loitering by the water cooler in the hall, he was reminded that long before coming to work as deputy in the Mexico office, Atthowe had served under Colgate in the Saigon Station.

"In my office," Kreeger greeted him.

Atthowe trailed after him through the outer office, where Peggy was sifting mail.

Kreeger remembered Fausto's gifts. He dug into his briefcase and retrieved the packages, which he set on Peggy's desk.

His secretary inspected the fancy wrapping. "Gee, boss, you remembered my birthday. Only it was last month."

"Sorry. Get hold of George for me, will you, and have him walk this stuff over to Fausto's office before someone reports that I'm on the take."

Maury Atthowe fiddled with the knot of his bow tie.

Inside Kreeger's room, Atthowe arranged himself in a club chair that did not quite face Kreeger's desk.

Kreeger decided to dispense with formalities. "Did you know that Art Colgate's in town?" he demanded.

Maury steepled his fingers, apparently deliberating on the pros and cons of giving a straight answer. He finally said, "We had dinner last night. At the Hacienda de los Morales."

"Nice. Let me guess who was paying."

"Art is on assignment for the Foreign Intelligence Board," Maury sniffed.

"Really? I'm impressed. Especially by the acronym. FIB." It was almost as good as GAS, the initials of Colgate's Arlington-based consultancy firm. The committee that had preceded FIB was the President's Foreign Intelligence Advisory Board, or PFIAB. It had done some useful work in second-guessing the intelligence community—which was why it was closed down. FIB, by Kreeger's observation, was one of Admiral Enright's many fiefdoms, which suggested that whatever Colgate was up to, he had a backer in the National Security Adviser's corner of the West Wing.

"Tell me something, Maury. What do you know about Safari?"

"As in clothes, or big game hunts?"

The silly riposte had come too easily. Kreeger's instinct told him that Atthowe must have been briefed by Colgate, at least up to a point. Maybe that would explain some of the curious leaks of station material that kept surfacing in the American media.

"You and Art are asshole buddies, aren't you?" Kreeger pressed his assault. "What are you giving him?"

"I don't understand that question."

"What has Art promised you? Did he tell you he'd get you my job?"

From the rigid stare Maury Atthowe trained on the scruffy car park behind the Embassy, Kreeger guessed he was close to the mark.

He stood up and interposed his bulk between Maury and his view.

"If you're keeping something from me," Kreeger warned, "I'm gonna put your ass in a sling."

"I find your tone both unnecessary and offensive."

"Thank you. I'm going to ask you one more time. I want you to tell me what the fuck Colgate is doing on my turf. For Chrissake, he doesn't even talk enough Spanish to order ham and eggs."

Maury cleared his throat. "I'm not sure I can comment. This is being very tightly held."

"Don't give me that crap!"

"Well, let's say it's all a type of Team B exercise. I've cautioned you before on this. There is a measure of—uh

—dissatisfaction at the top with reporting from this Station."

"You miserable prick!" Kreeger exploded. "I guess I'll just have to screw it out of Colgate myself."

Kreeger grabbed his coat and headed for the door. As he passed through his secretary's room, Peggy was on the phone, apparently talking to George Camacho, the liaison man, about Fausto's gifts.

He was walking briskly down Calle Lerma, toward the Maria Cristina hotel, when Peggy went to the bathroom. When she returned, she noticed that the packages were gone, which surprised her a little, since George had said he would come up at lunchtime. She assumed that George's schedule had changed.

When George dropped by the office at one-thirty, both Peggy and her boss were out. Not finding the packages, George concluded that Kreeger had decided to take care of the errand himself.

3

KREEGER found Colgate breakfasting alone in the hotel dining room. Wordlessly, the Station Chief lowered his bulk into the chair on the other side of the table. Looking up from his paper, Colgate seemed nonplussed for only a moment.

Then he turned on a smile. "Jim. What a pleasant surprise. It's been a long time. How's your lovely lady?"

"Fine."

"Karla's a stand-up girl. Always was. How about the kids? Must be college age by now."

Kreeger was about to say that he was not making a social call, when he thought of an easier way to end Colgate's stream of sham-intimate comments.

"How's your boy?" he said.

Colgate looked vacant.

"I asked about your boy."

Colgate fussed with his tie. "He's a vegetable," he said with sudden viciousness, and mumbled something about a fancy clinic and useless treatments that cost an arm and a leg.

"I'm sorry," said Kreeger, somewhat chastened.

"It's the rest of the family that suffers. In a case like that, the kid ought to be put down."

"You haven't changed much, Art. You never did want to take responsibility for defects."

Colgate did not know how to take this. He started talking about the money he was making, his rolling acres in Virginia.

"I'm happy for you," said Kreeger. "Who takes care of the manse?"

"There's a small staff. Viets, mostly."

"No lady of the manor?"

"Nothing permanent. You know what old soldiers say. It's the third match gets you killed."

You bastard, Kreeger thought. You had your first wife killed. You drove the second one to booze and drugs.

"You must get lonely, walking those empty halls."

"Oh, there's plenty of action for them that want it. We throw parties like you wouldn't believe."

"So what are you doing in Mexico?"

"Oh, just a bread-and-butter job," Colgate said vaguely. "Standard country risk assessment. Nice binding. You know the drill."

"Who's paying?"

"A Fortune 500 company."

"Maury Atthowe said you're doing something for FIB."

"That too. Mostly because it impresses the hell out of a buttondown business type. Do you mind if I pick your brains?"

"Be my guest."

Colgate seemed to be well briefed. Kreeger quickly

realized from the series of questions on both rightists and leftists in Mexico that the visitor was trying to feel out the shape and extent of CIA coverage of the local opposition.

Kreeger played him along, diverting Colgate with a colorful account of peasant uprisings in the state of Guerrero, embarrassingly close to the lush resort town of Acapulco. Kreeger gave names and places. He talked about a dirt-poor village on a deforested mountain where the inhabitants stitched together soccer balls for a living. They had seized the municipal hall, burned down the PRI headquarters, and held off an assault by armed police, all in Miliano's name. Colgate jotted down notes. Kreeger did not inform him that he could have read a fuller account in the *Houston Chronicle*.

Colgate gave Kreeger a sly, patently false smile. "I guess you know Fausto García pretty well."

"I wouldn't call Fausto a personal friend."

"We got a handle on him, right?"

"I'm not going to answer a question like that," Kreeger snapped.

"Come on, Jim. We're both old hands. So when did we recruit Fausto? About the same time as Noriega?"

"Gail Armstrong's played that line already. On TV. It's getting tired."

"Okay, I won't push." Colgate raised his hands, palms outward. "Let me try a hypothetical. Mexico blows, U.S. lives are at risk, and you're asked to support a viable alternative. What do you do?"

"I don't deal in hypotheticals. But it sounds to me like your client is interested in a damn sight more than assembling a cheaper widget." Kreeger added carefully, "You seem to be embarked on quite a safari."

At the mention of the code word, Colgate froze for an instant.

Kreeger gave no indication that he had used it as more than a figure of speech, and Colgate made a brisk recovery. He gulped the last of his coffee and said something about a business meeting downtown.

A question bubbled up in Kreeger's mind. He gave it voice, though part of himself told him not to. "Art. Do you ever think of Val?"

Colgate's eyes went vacant, as if the tenant of the premises behind them had suddenly walked out.

Colgate finally said, "No. Do you?"

"I think of Val a lot. She was one of my first teachers, after I joined the Agency. Did you know that? You know what she told me? She said, unless good people stay on in the Agency—whatever pain it costs them—the bastards take over. She was right, don't you think?"

Colgate's eyes did not change. He opened his mouth and made a sound like a man trying to gargle noiselessly before leaving the room.

FIFTEEN

□ □ □

1

"I don't buy it," said Paul Milnekoff, the CIA's Deputy Director for Operations. The chief of the clandestine service was a gaunt, immensely tall man, who walked with a stoop, as if reluctant to impose his height on others. He was also totally bald, as a result of chemotherapy after a successful cancer operation.

"I've known Jim Kreeger since he joined the Agency," Milnekoff continued. "He's one of the most dedicated officers I have ever known. I don't believe he's done anything in his whole damn life for personal gain. Why would he risk blowing his career for that shit?" The DDO gestured at the objects on Director Wagoner's desk: a diamond-and-emerald necklace; a stunningly vulgar money clip, studded with diamonds; and a gold-plated .45.

"This shit, as you call it," Director Wagoner said, "is worth over twenty thousand dollars. We had it appraised."

"So it's expensive shit. It still stinks. If Kreeger was into smuggling jewelry out of Mexico, you can bet your ass he'd do it without leaving any fingerprints. This is a set-up, and you know it. The only question is, who's trying to frame Jim Kreeger?"

"And why?" the Inspector General chimed in. The IG was a Yalie, a New England patrician whose clothes never looked newly bought. He was generally respected in the Agency, even among fieldmen, because he was never intimidated by higher authority, and had been awarded a secret medal for conducting a successful exfiltration from China.

The packages had arrived in the pouch from Mexico Station. The pouch had been handled according to standard procedure, its manifest signed by Kreeger, with no reference to any personal effects. The pouch had left Mexico with the diplomatic bag, to conceal the CIA origin. It had been collected from the State Department mail room by a CIA courier who brought it out to Langley, where it had been opened at the Mexico desk. The problematic items had been accompanied by a typewritten note: "To be held for COS."

The use of the CIA pouch for smuggling was a very serious offense.

"Kreeger just isn't dumb enough to do something like this," the DDO insisted. "Even if he were corrupt, which he's not."

"I am inclined to the same view," said the IG, "but I think we are constrained to consider another scenario."

The Director was following this with keen attention. "Which is?"

"Let us assume, as a working hypothesis, that someone is trying to frame Mr. Kreeger. I would presume that person to be one of his colleagues at Mexico Station."

There was no dissent.

"Unless this person is deficient in intellect," the IG continued, "we must further presume that he—or she—will have anticipated the reasoning process we have followed thus far."

"Then why do it?" Paul Milnekoff demanded. "Why do it, if it's bound to be treated as a frame-up?"

"It is possible that whoever planted this—evidence—was trying to draw our attention to a problem. I believe the word for such a person is whistle-blower." The IG said this with evident distaste.

"That's a damn good point," the Director broke in. "Where did these items come from, anyhow?" He toyed with the Colt. "There are a helluva lot of questions we need answered."

Milnekoff squinted at the IG. "Blowing the whistle on what?"

"That's what we're going to find out!" exclaimed the Director. "Leland, I want you to put your best people on this."

"While Jim's away from the Station?" the DDO croaked, in disbelief. He ran his hand over his bald pate. It occurred to him that there was a simpler, and more disturbing reason why Kreeger might have been set up in such an obvious way: that whoever did it believed that the Director would accept the evidence at face value, because he wanted Kreeger out.

2

THE first person at Mexico Station to hear from the IG's chief investigator was Maury Atthowe. He arrived at Atthowe's home unannounced, and explained that, for obvious reasons—"morale in our outfit, not to mention the locals"—the noise had to be kept down. Was Mr. Atthowe aware, strictly off the record, of any improper dealings between his station chief and foreign nationals? Maury Atthowe kept the investigator scribbling in a shorthand notebook for three hours.

The next day, the same investigator intercepted Lois Compton, as she was on her way to a coffee break in the VIPS restaurant on the far side of the Paseo de la Reforma from the Embassy.

"Do I know you?" Lois said coolly, taking in the button-down shirt, the penny loafers, the tortoiseshell glasses.

He gave her his card.

"Your last name seems to be Esq," she observed.

"I graduated from Harvard Law School," he said, without false modesty. "Can we talk somewhere private? The IG wants to keep down the noise level on this."

She took him to VIPS, where the noise level suggested that a manic dishwasher was breaking the crockery, six pieces at a time.

"So what is it?" Lois demanded. "You looking into my love life? Has my ex ratted on me or what?"

"It's a somewhat larger problem. How do you feel about your boss?"

"I think he's a chauvinist pig. And I can't think of anyone I'd rather work for."

"Okay. Where were you between, say 0830 and 1000 hours on Thursday of last week?"

"0830? Were you in the military or something? Okay. I was down in the consular section, doing slave labor. What's it to you?"

His expression did not lighten. He did not tell her that his assistant had already grilled Peggy, Kreeger's secretary, who had recalled that her boss had left packages with her that were to be hand-carried over to SIN headquarters. The assistant should now be with George Camacho, the liaison man.

"Look." He took off his glasses and rubbed them with his thumbs. "The Station could be in a lot of trouble. You can help by talking frankly."

"I see. What kind of trouble?"

"That need not concern you. I can tell you that you are *not* under investigation."

"That's a relief." The waitress brought Lois a cappuccino, which she sipped calmly.

"Are you aware of any unauthorized operations involving the Station and SIN?"

"Are you posing a moral dilemma?"

"Listen, Ms. Compton. I didn't come down here to play games. This is serious business. I don't know if you've ever been involved in an IG investigation before, but they're not a laughing matter. Now. I want to get in and out of here fast, and I need you to help me. I'll say it one more time. Do you have cognizance of any unauthorized operations involving Jim Kreeger, or the Station, and the Mexican security service?"

"Are you telling me my boss is your target?"

"There have been allegations of irregularities."

"Define unauthorized."

"Not reported to headquarters. Not sanctioned."

Lois hesitated for a fatal second, partly because her tongue was numbed by the scalding coffee.

The investigator started talking as if he was reading her rights.

"We helped in a drug-related operation," Lois started, then faltered.

The investigator pounced. "What do you mean?"

"I don't remember that much about it."

"You're sure?" His face closed as if a visor had come down. "I don't want to bully you, Ms. Compton. You have an excellent reputation. I've seen your file. I'll talk to Jim about this. Then I may have to come back to you."

When Lois was sure he had left the restaurant, she ran for a pay phone and called Kreeger on his direct line.

"Don't worry," he cut through her hasty account. "And thanks. I'm glad I have a few friends left."

WHEN Kreeger was asked, point-blank, about a "drug-related operation" by the IG's full team of three men, plus a stenographer, he did the only thing possible, under the circumstances: He told the truth.

When he had finished his tale of the hostage swap, and of the help he had received from some of Fausto's people, there was silence in his office for a couple of minutes.

It was broken by the chief investigator. "Jim, I want you to know, in my book, you're a hero. If I'd been in your shoes, I hope I would have had the guts to do the same thing."

"I appreciate that."

"I'm afraid I'll have to file a full report."

"I understand. I trust that your report will contain the names of the guys who are out to screw me."

"We haven't been able to pin that down."

"That's just great." Kreeger had been going over everything in his mind. Maury Atthowe had been in his office the morning he came in with Fausto's gifts, and Atthowe had been out to dinner with Art Colgate the night before. Maury, he felt almost certain, was the man who had tried to frame him. He was not, however, going to lower himself to Maury's level—at least, not without proof. So where did this leave him?

Actually, he already knew the answer. He was going to be yanked back to headquarters, to face more questions, this time from Director Wagoner, who wanted him gone.

The summons arrived within twenty-four hours.

Lois and Eddie looked sick when they heard he was flying back to Washington.

"Hang in there," he told them. Then he misquoted the last words Val had spoken to him before she flew off to Saigon, the last time he ever saw her: "If good people don't hang on in the Agency, the bastards take over."

3

KREEGER was frayed and travel-stained on the morning he logged in at the Mexico desk at the Mausoleum. He rode the elevator up to the seventh floor. Dorothy gave him a friendly hug in the Director's outer office, but seemed flustered.

"I'm afraid the DCI is delayed at the White House," she told Kreeger. "He asked me to give you this."

Kreeger took the note. It contained a one-line order,

initialed by Director Wagoner: "Please report to Dr. Glass at 0940."

"A medical check-up? Before I see Bill Wagoner?" Kreeger glowered. "Whose bright idea was this?"

"I wouldn't worry about it," Dorothy reassured him. "You look in great shape to me."

"You're beautiful when you lie."

Kreeger walked down the hall and stopped in at the DDO's office. Paul Milnekoff was on his way out. He looked surprised to see Kreeger.

"Got a minute?"

"Sure."

They stepped into the DDO's private office. Milnekoff had put in his time in the trenches, and expressed the opinion that—for reasons incomprehensible to him—the Director had made Kreeger the target for a personal vendetta.

"There's more to it than that, Paul," Kreeger told him. "Sure, Bill and I never got along. But he's acting like he wants us to go to war with Mexico, and it's just not in his character to behave like that unless somebody higher up has told him to. You know Bill even better than I do. We're talking about a guy whose nose is permanently stained brown."

The DDO tried to suppress a broad grin. Kreeger's situation, after all, was no joking matter. He stood accused of breaking just about every rule in the book. He could be out the door tomorrow, a year shy of his pension. Milnekoff volunteered to go with Kreeger to confront the Director. He professed to be as startled as Kreeger by the peremptory summons to a medical check-up.

MEDICAL Services, the CIA's in-house clinic, was headed by Dr. Alvin Glass. He and Kreeger had been friends since they had served in the Army in Germany together—"in the time before the Flood," as Al Glass recalled.

The doctor moaned and tssked as he recorded Kreeger's weight and blood pressure.

"I usually go on the wagon for three days before I put myself through this," Kreeger observed. "I wasn't given fair warning."

"You're worse than borderline, Jim. I gotta be honest with you."

The nurse found a vein in Kreeger's left arm and drew two sets of blood samples.

When she left the room, Dr. Glass said, "She's not the only one who wants your blood."

"When did that occur to you?"

"Between us and these four walls, someone high up thinks you're going to flunk these tests. Now roll over and drop your shorts. That's a good boy."

"You're talking seventh floor."

"You said it, not me." Dr. Glass pulled on a pair of plastic gloves.

"Jeez, Al. Is that really necessary?" Kreeger grit his teeth.

After several moments of probing, Dr. Glass stood back. "We'll have to take a closer look. This won't take long. We're set up next door. I hope you didn't eat a big breakfast. Ever used one of these?" He produced a plastic bottle with a long proboscis.

To Kreeger's protests, Dr. Glass said firmly, "I can't help you unless we do this right. Someone took a pretty hard look at your file. Hell, they told *me* what to look for!"

"When?"

"When what?"

"When did they pull my file?"

"I don't know that."

"When did you get your instructions, then?"

"I got a call at home this morning."

Kreeger's face darkened, but he padded into the bathroom and did as he was told.

The nurse met him with a hospital gown and escorted him into a room hung with ominous black tubes armed with miniature scopes.

He found the process of a flexible sigmoidoscopy less humiliating than the preparations, and not especially painful until the last phase, when he felt his bowels swelling like a balloon about to burst.

It was eleven-thirty by the time all the tests were completed. Kreeger was glad Al Glass had checked his blood pressure at the beginning of the session rather than later on, because his reflections on what Director Wagoner was trying to pull weren't helping.

"What's the verdict?" Kreeger demanded of Al Glass.

"We'll have to wait on some lab results."

"Don't play with me, Al."

"And you gotta watch that liver."

"There's nothing wrong with my liver. I go on the wagon two weeks every spring. Livers grow back. That's why the ancients thought the liver was the seat of the life force."

"Uh-huh. Well, let's put it this way, Jim. You've got X number of manhattans in your future. It's a question of whether you drink them in ten years, or twenty, or longer."

"That depends on the shit coming down from the top floor. What are you going to tell the Director? Are things copacetic or what?"

Al Glass stroked his beard. "Buy me lunch?"

They squeezed into a corner booth at the Vienna Inn, down from the El Cid French Gourmet Restaurant on West Maple Avenue. Kreeger and Glass took a couple of belts of bourbon, and piled on crab cakes and chili dogs for ballast.

"So what are you going to tell the Director?"

The chief of Medical Services glanced around. The place was jammed with junior CIA personnel, but the noise level screened out conversations from as close as three feet away.

"Let's put it this way," said Dr. Glass. "You got high blood sugar, you're twenty pounds overweight, and your liver is less than A-1. Your heart's okay, but your blood pressure's worse than borderline, and you're gonna take medication for that. Which is to say, you eat wrong—" he belched deeply, "—and you don't exercise, you're probably stressed out. And you've mismanaged booze and cigars for longer than most of the kids in here have been out of diapers. You ought to change your life, but my bet is you won't."

Al Glass produced a pair of Bering cigars in aluminum tubes and offered one to Kreeger, who shook his head.

"Go ahead," Glass prodded. "It's too late to apply for sainthood. You fit a pretty shitty profile, Jim."

"I see." Kreeger felt a dead weight inside, pulling him down.

"It's the profile of a typical Station Chief. Here. Read it for yourself." He passed Kreeger a typed sheet.

"What's this?"

"It's my report to the Director. My report on you."

"You wrote it already? Jeez, that was quick. You were with me for all but ten minutes."

Al Glass dropped his voice to a whisper. "I wrote it after I got Wagoner's call. It could use some updating, I guess."

Kreeger skimmed through the report, which described him by his Agency work-name. He lingered over the last paragraph:

> Galloway's condition is similar to that of the majority of senior Chiefs of Station. Their state of health must be viewed in the context of their age, life styles, and the conditions of their employment. In my professional opinion, it is the role of Medical Services to ensure that the experience necessary to carry on our mission remains available to our operations staff. You may rest assured that my staff and I

will continue to maintain the health of such valued employees as Galloway. (signed) Alvin C. Glass, MSD.

Kreeger swallowed.

He passed the draft letter back to Glass and said, "I won't forget this, Al. But aren't you going out on a helluva limb for me?"

"No big deal, Jim. I can collect my pension and go fishing any time I choose. Now, buy me another drink and we'll see if you're right about the liver."

SIXTEEN

□ □ □

1

"I was trying to do you a favor," the Director told Kreeger. "To give you an easy out."

The Director had organized a lynch party. The only friend Kreeger could count on in Wagoner's office was Paul Milnekoff. The rest were people who had never been blooded in the field. To some of the younger ones, Kreeger seemed like a figure from a different age, embarrassingly larger than life.

"You used Agency personnel—case officers as well as contract employees—as your private army." The Director spoke as a prosecution attorney. "It's not acceptable. It won't be accepted."

Paul Milnekoff spoke up in praise of Kreeger's record. He suggested a compromise. With all the stresses in his life, Kreeger was obviously in need of a vacation from Mexico. "How long is it since you took a holiday, Jim?"

"I don't remember."

"That could be the problem," the Director chipped in, with feigned magnanimity. "A man needs some alternation in his life. Otherwise, he tends to lose his perspective. I'm going to recommend that you take two months' leave, while the IG winds up his investigation. Full salary, of course."

"It's not a bad offer, Jim," Milnekoff said. "Under the circumstances. If I were you, I'd grab it with both hands."

"I think the Director wants me out for longer than two months."

"*I* think you'd better explain yourself," said Director Wagoner.

"The whole object of this little game is to get me out of Mexico, isn't it? And the reason behind it is that some people in this room are involved with Art Colgate and a bunch of players who call themselves the Safari team. I'm putting everyone on notice that if you push me out of Mexico, I won't go quietly. It's come to my notice that a lot of people are playing funny games on my turf. Art Colgate is screwing around, giving out that he's working for you, and huddling with my deputy. You have a bunch of desk jockeys on the fourth floor writing a comic book to justify U.S. military action in Mexico, and the last guy they want to hear from is the man on the scene. And you've got a wildman over at the Pentagon who calls himself Two Jacks Gilly and makes Ollie North look like a simpering wimp."

The Director blanched. "That's highly classified. Who told you about Gilly?"

"I have a few sources. I'm trained to gather accurate information, and to put it to appropriate use. My point is that Mexico is drawing stuntmen and con artists like a screen door draws June bugs. It's about time you told them to butt out, and let the professionals do their job."

"Are you done?"

"Not quite. I'd like to know a little more about what that clown from the Big Easy—General Gilly—is up to over at the Pentagon. I gather some of his budget comes out of Agency slush funds."

"God damn!" the Director shouted. "Can't anyone keep his mouth shut in this town? That's off limits."

"You accused me of running a private army," Kreeger parried. "I'm starting to get the feeling that some people connected with the Agency are trying to start a private war, and I'd like to know why."

"I don't think I want to listen to any more of this."

"That's your call, Bill. J. Edgar Hoover didn't want to hear that the Japs were planning to attack Pearl Harbor.

Stalin didn't want to hear that Hitler was getting ready to invade Russia. I guess a few Houston good ol' boys didn't want to hear that Saddam Hussein was anything but a friend before he went into Kuwait."

"You're completely out of line!" Director Wagoner hissed.

Paul Milnekoff intervened, calmly recalling Kreeger's successes with agents and defectors over the years, his professionalism, his coolness under fire. He played character witness long enough—and well enough—for Bill Wagoner to reconsider the step he had been about to take, and for Kreeger to get his anger on a leash. Nothing was resolved regarding his status as head of Mexico Station, but Kreeger and Wagoner parted with a handshake.

Back in his own office, Milnekoff said to Kreeger, "You got him mad enough to fire you. I won't be able to save your ass next time, Jim. You're just one step ahead of the headsman."

WHEN Kreeger later got word the Director intended to ban him from returning to Mexico Station, and that Maury Atthowe was the hot favorite to replace him, he realized that he was obliged to do something that went against the grain. If Director Wagoner was going to allow politics to subvert the business of intelligence, then Kreeger was obliged to play politics too. He was well aware that in Washington, political battles are often won or lost by leak and counterleak. He had made a start. His information about Gilly's secret shop at the Pentagon had come from Joe Cicero, his reporter friend.

Now Kreeger needed some additional allies. He turned, once again, to the Mollycoddlers.

KREEGER took Dorothy to dinner at Il Vecchio. They laughed over old memories. Especially that of the fat girl at the Embassy in Lima who had gotten pregnant without anyone noticing, until her contractions started at the office. She had named the boy James Marcus, as in James Marcus Kreeger, and nobody showed mercy on Jim even after he tracked down the child's father, a Marine guard, and arranged a shotgun wedding.

"The Immaculate Conception," Dorothy giggled into her angel hair pasta.

Kreeger chose that relaxed moment to tell Dorothy that her present boss was doing his damnedest to fire him.

At first, Dorothy refused to believe him.

He gave her a couple of reasons, trying not to scare her, or to test her loyalty to the Director too far. Fairly soon, she shifted the conversation to a couple of her girlfriends, charter members of the Mollycoddlers' Club. This was not a diversion, and Kreeger did not mistake it for one. Dorothy's friends and occasional bridge partners were June Sergeant, the administrative assistant to the chairman of the Senate Intelligence Committee, and Roz Myers, the private secretary of the President of the United States.

Kreeger said he wanted to keep the line to Harry Butler in reserve, even if Harry was a fellow Texan. He would probably have only one chance to recruit the President, and when he went to the White House—he did say "when," not "if"—he wanted to go loaded for bear.

The line to the Senate chairman was another thing altogether. Kreeger, the man of secrets, had never regarded Congress as friendly ground, but he recognized that, in his present situation, a closed hearing might give him the chance to put a few things straight about Mexico, and about his chosen profession as well. It would have to be done right, of course. Kreeger must not be seen as the instigator. The invitation must come from the chairman.

Dorothy undertook to arrange it.

She did not tell Director Wagoner, so when the request to interview Kreeger came from the chairman of the Senate Intelligence Committee, the Director was both startled and alarmed—as Dorothy told Kreeger later. When Wagoner called Kreeger in to discuss it, he no longer spoke about vacations from Mexico. On the contrary, he urged Kreeger to get back on the job. He would explain to the committee that pressure of work prevented Kreeger from testifying.

"I'm happy to talk to Congress," Kreeger told him. "Unless you have some objection."

The Director could not think of one. But he was not at all happy.

KREEGER's second dinner with Dorothy took place at her apartment in Bethesda, the night before he was scheduled to testify, in closed hearings, to a joint session of the Senate and House Intelligence Committees. The evening did not begin auspiciously.

He had spent much of the afternoon in a suite at the Guest Quarters, being grilled by a bunch of congressional staffers. The principal was Joel Stein, the senior staffer on the Senate committee, a fire-hardened witch hunter from the inquisitions of the 1970s. June Sergeant had promised that Joel had mellowed since the days when he treated the CIA as a worse enemy than the KGB, but Kreeger did not see any signs of it.

He was asking himself whether he had made the right decision about the hearing when he pushed the key into the ignition of his rented car. The engine wheezed and died.

He got out and kicked the near-side front tire twice.

He was dog tired, his back ached, and Joel Stein had actually asked him, "How can I believe a word you say?" And now this—everything seemed to be going wrong.

He left the car on the curb, with a scrawled note under the windshield wiper, and rode the subway out to Bethesda.

Dorothy's apartment was a brisk ten-minute walk from the station, in a security-minded high-rise along East-West Highway. Kreeger stopped in at Crown Books to buy her a present, a new Dick Francis yarn. Dorothy loved horseflesh and English mysteries.

Leaving the bookstore, Kreeger sensed that he was being watched. He walked twenty yards before he looked. He found a short, sallow man in a cloth cap— possibly Hispanic, more probably Oriental—affecting to be absorbed in reading the morning headlines of the *Washington Times,* on display through the window of an orange vending machine.

Kreeger made a dogleg through the lobby of the Hyatt, across the main drag, to be sure.

The man in the cap did not follow him, but a trim man with a pencil mustache walked in and gave Kreeger a hard look before he sloped away toward the gift shop. This one looked Vietnamese.

Kreeger strolled to the phone booths and called Dorothy's number.

"Hey, honey. I'm running late. Don't let the meat loaf burn."

"Meat loaf!" Dorothy snorted.

"I don't want to bring any uninvited guests to dinner. Lima rules, I think. You remember?"

Dorothy did not hesitate. "Where do you want me?"

He told her. She was to park along a busy section of the highway, where there was a center island, pointing toward D.C.

"Opposite Dunkin Donuts," Kreeger specified. "Keep your engine running. I'll see you in ten."

There were plenty of cabs outside. As Kreeger boarded one, he saw a green Taurus pull out behind.

A quarter-mile short of the rendezvous, Kreeger told the driver, "You're going to drop me on the left side, next to the island. Maintain speed until I tell you to brake."

"I cannot stop here, gentleman." The cabbie sounded Afghani, or Iranian. "Is not permitted. Very dangerous."

Kreeger folded a twenty and slid it over the driver's right ear.

"Now hit the gas."

Over his shoulder, Kreeger saw the green Taurus switching lanes in heavy traffic, trying to keep pace.

The Dunkin Donuts sign loomed up on the right.

"Stop *now!*"

The driver slammed on the brakes, setting off a chorus of horns and squealing rubber. Kreeger hurled himself through the door, crossed the island in two strides, and sprang through an opening in the traffic.

"I think we're both a bit old for this," Dorothy remarked, as he slid into the backseat of her old blue Saab. Without need of instructions, she gunned the engine and sped along the shoulder, watching for a gap in the traffic. "Feels good, though."

Kreeger watched their rear. The Taurus was attempting a U-turn, in front of a Mobil station.

"Hang a right," he told Dorothy.

A few blocks on, he felt sure he had lost his watchers. "You done good, Dot. Now I'm ready for that meat loaf."

"I thought they were Orientals," Kreeger said of the men he had seen following him. "But I may have contracted the admiral's disease—galloping paranoia. I guess Bethesda is full of Latinos these days."

"I think we got half the population of El Salvador.

Will you do this?'' She gave Kreeger a bottle of wine and a corkscrew.

"I'm not sure why anyone would bother following me around Washington,'' Kreeger pursued. "Except to rattle me. Maybe Bill Wagoner wants to send me over to the shrinks, since Al Glass let him down.''

"Maybe someone's worried about you testifying tomorrow,'' Dorothy observed, after tasting the wine. "You know, you put a needle up Admiral Enright's rear end with those last comments you fired off on the Mexico Estimate. Not for the first time, either. He's not the type that forgives and forgets. He complained to the President about you.''

"He did?''

"Roz told me about it today, as a matter of fact. The Admiral did a real song-and-dance routine in the Oval Office about that SOB from Mexico,'' Dorothy went on. "He can be a real bitch. Did you hear that he's hired a male secretary?''

"Come on, Dot.''

"It's the living truth. Yeoman Phipps. Almost *too* pretty.''

The Mollies, fiercely loyal to their own bosses, were always good for gossip about other people's. The scuttlebutt about Admiral Enright's sexual leanings wasn't new to Kreeger. A bachelor of a certain age often attracted rumors of that sort. Kreeger doubted that Enright was an active homosexual, and if he was, what of it? One of the most capable Chiefs of Station Kreeger had ever known had kicked that way. Nonetheless, Kreeger wondered if perhaps Enright's own personal misgivings led him to push for brute force as a solution to America's problems abroad. It was as though he felt he had something to prove.

It also occurred to Kreeger that Admiral Enright could be vulnerable to the oldest kind of blackmail. Was this one of the keys Kreeger was missing?

When Dorothy had finished gossiping about Yeoman

Phipps, Kreeger said, "I don't see why the Director is going along with Enright on this Mexico thing. You know what I found out, Dot? They've set up an office over in the Pentagon headed by some hardline Cajun colonel, and it's being paid for out of the Director's slush fund. Has everyone in this town gone crazy? Or is it just me?"

Dorothy blushed, torn between two loyalties—to her former boss and her present one.

"The Director is under a lot of pressure," she said, treading the middle line. "The President is taking a personal interest in this whole situation."

"I've got another question for you, Dot. I've got a feeling that President Butler and the Director—and a lot of other equities—are going to get burned down in Mexico. Could be I can stop that. But I'll need an in with the White House. Outside channels."

"I already offered you Roz. Hell, Jim, you make me feel I'm still working for you."

"I'm grateful. I'll make it up to you sometime."

"You don't have to say that. I'll always be there for you. Just tell me what you need."

"I'll need access to Harry Butler. Quietly. At the proper time. This may have to be done on very short notice."

"Okay. Tell me how you want to do it."

"God, these men don't stand a chance, do they?"

Severely practical, Dorothy said, "How will you make contact?"

"I'll send you a covering note. With the ANTARC-TICA pouch out of Mexico City."

"I won't drop it, Jim."

It was nearly eleven-thirty when Kreeger jogged down a stalled escalator to the upper level of the Bethesda Metro complex. At night, almost deserted, the center had the look and feel of a futuristic movie. A lone bus was parked in the shadows beyond the concrete pylons to Kreeger's right. For a moment he regretted not taking up Dorothy's offer for a ride back to his hotel. But surely the men who had followed him earlier were long gone.

Ahead, the entrance to the main escalator leading down to the turnstiles and the trains yawned open like a gigantic storm drain. The escalator sloped down, for hundreds of feet, at a forty-five-degree angle. Kreeger had been told it was the longest—and maybe the steepest—in the world.

Kreeger wasn't inordinately fearful of heights, but tonight he felt distinctly unsteady on his pins as he boarded the escalator. He gripped the side for support. Maybe it was the wine at dinner, or a nervous flutter over the performance he would give on Capitol Hill in the morning, or just the fact that, empty of commuters, the escalator seemed even longer and steeper than he remembered. Below him the plaza was in darkness. Perched on this escalator he felt he was pitching forward into a bottomless well.

His grip on the handrail tightened.

Suddenly, without warning, the escalator came to a stop. Kreeger, however, continued to move forward, causing him to lose his footing. He stumbled down a few steps before regaining his balance.

A power cut? Or had someone pushed the emergency button?

He looked back. On the steps above him, silhouetted against the night sky, he saw a slim man in a trailing coat and a stockier man in a cap—the hoods he thought he had eluded earlier in the evening. They were moving down the escalator steps with enviable agility.

Kreeger didn't stop for an interview. He hurled himself down the stopped escalator. They were closing on him, so near now he could hear their breathing. If he could beat them to the bottom, he could handle one, maybe both. But not if they were armed. And they wouldn't come after him unless they were armed. His heart banged against his ribs. Why didn't they shoot?

It flashed through his mind that they might belong to the Quinteros, and the Mexican drug cartel. If they were hit men sent to get even with him for his role in the hostage swap, they might have been ordered to do something more colorful than putting a bullet between his shoulder blades.

He jumped the last steps. His shoes clacked against the paving. He wheeled, and went for them head down, working his elbows. He got one in the belly, but the other chopped at his neck with something cold and hard. He was down. A shooting pain stabbed through his kidneys like a red-hot poker.

He was flailing with fists and legs, yelling for help.

Something sawed across his windpipe, cutting his air. A chain, between hardwood sticks. A whirlpool swam behind his eyelids, red behind black. His jaws opened and closed, releasing only a dry gurgle. His tongue spilled out. Someone was tugging on it.

"You talk too much," a distant voice was saying. "We teach you better."

For an instant, this seemed remote from him. Then he bit down, and tasted his own blood.

A different voice floated through. "Hey, buddy! You need some help?"

Kreeger rolled and bucked. He was free. He saw his attackers running for the up escalator. Halfway down, on the other side, were five or six muscular teenagers. Their letter jackets were blue, with buff sleeves. The B was for Bethesda–Chevy Chase High, a few blocks away.

"Stop them!" Kreeger croaked. It took him two tries to get the words out, but he was relieved to find he still had the necessary equipment. "Those guys stole my wallet!"

Some of the kids started running back up the stopped escalator, yelling about blocking tackles. Kreeger's assailants made it to the top first, and got away in their waiting car.

But the kids were pretty quick. One of them got the license number, and offered to call the cops.

"Thanks," said Kreeger. "I'll take it from here." He looked at the boy who had taken the number. Big shoulders, legs like young oaks, a mop of straw-colored hair. "Linebacker?"

"Yup."

"Me too."

"Way to go, Pop." The kid looked doubtfully at Kreeger's ripped jacket and middle-aged spread. "Guess those guys caught you off-guard."

"They weren't playing ball."

4

WAS it a murder attempt, or just an effort to scare him off? Kreeger did not have an answer. He remembered the name of those whirling hardwood sticks, joined by a short chain. Nunchaku. An ancient weapon, invented by the peasant farmers of Okinawa, when they were first invaded by the Japanese. Its use had spread, like karate, to many other cultures. He thought of Art Colgate and Bill Enright. Men with Oriental pasts. He could prove nothing beyond a bungled attempt at a mugging. He did not bother to report it to the Maryland police. He could have someone check the license plate later, for curiosity's sake, although he suspected it would lead nowhere.

In the morning, he arrived at the Senate committee room with a bandage around his forehead and blood in his eye. His reporter friend, Joe Cicero, had called him in high excitement, almost before the sun came up, to feed him more information on the secret office that had been set up at the Pentagon under General Gilly. The staff were working up detailed plans for a military invasion of Mexico. General Gilly had sent U.S. militia advisers into Mexico. Kreeger had been able to glean more details from an old Army friend who blamed Gilly for shooting up his own side's position during the Panama operation. At least it was something to work with, and it gave Kreeger something he needed urgently at that juncture: leverage.

Despite his battered appearance, he turned a benign eye on Joel Stein.

"Jeez, what happened to you?" asked the Senate staffer.

"I guess somebody wasn't keen on hearing me testify."

"You've got damn near a full house. That doesn't happen often."

Kreeger had come with a prepared text, but he ignored it after a few minutes. His message was simple. Mexico was going through a period of traumatic upheaval, but the patient would survive. There was an obvious community of interests between Mexico and the United States. The PRI regime was corrupt and incompetent, but it was older than any communist system, and was likely to outlive them. Miliano Rojas was a formidable opponent, but if they were smart, the PRI party managers would co-opt him, or some of his key allies. The President-elect was no adversary of the United States; he was a Harvard man, after all. Certainly, Paz believed in keeping his options open, in terms of foreign policy and investment. But he had given Kreeger his personal guarantee that CIA equities in Mexico would be protected. Kreeger gave a few examples to remind his audience of how important Mexico was to the Agency's counterespionage efforts.

Senator Jonah Pike took the microphone before twenty minutes was up.

"Mr. Kreeger." He pronounced the name as though he were expectorating.

"Yes, sir."

"Seems to me you're out of step with the times. I'm glad that, for once, I can find common ground with the Administration on this. We got us a rigged election in Mexico. Agreed?"

"Yes, sir."

"We got a government that tramples on human rights, and is selling Japan, Inc., the wherewithal to flood U.S. markets with products that will put Americans out of work. And meanwhile, the US of A is being flooded with drugs and wetbacks out of Mexico. Seems a clear-cut situation to me. Either we make the Mexican government shape up, or we put a new one in there. Tell me this, Mr. Kreeger. Did you ever hear of a fellow by the name of Fernando Ramírez?"

"I assume you're talking about the former Minister of Government."

"Is this Ramírez on the payroll of the CIA?"

"You know I can't answer questions about sources and methods, Senator."

"Well, let me put it to you another way. Do you have—or did you have—a working relationship with Ramírez?"

"The Embassy had dealings with Mr. Ramírez when he was Minister of Government. If that answers your question."

"How about one Fausto García? Do you have a professional relationship with him?"

"I'm not sure where this is leading us, Senator."

"I'm trying to establish whether our CIA is supporting gangsters and drug dealers in the Mexican government. And whether that is why this Administration continues to tolerate a state of affairs in Mexico that is hurting our businessmen, our working people, and all lovers of democracy."

"That's uncalled for, Senator," interjected a liberal Representative from Illinois.

"I also want to examine the credentials of our expert witness," Senator Pike pursued. "Mr. Kreeger. Are you now, or have you ever been, a practicing homosexual?"

There was a commotion in the committee room. Someone cried out, "For shame!" The chairman of the Senate Intelligence Committee broke a pencil.

"Senator Pike," he rumbled, "you are doing a grave disservice to these hearings. And you are completely out of order."

"For the record," Kreeger interjected, "I think that I should state that I am not a homosexual. I have been happily married for nearly a quarter of a century."

"If you'll bear with me, Mr. Chairman," Senator Pike bulled on, "I have a question for this witness that may clarify this situation."

"Make it brief."

"Mr. Kreeger, is it not true that, some years ago, you underwent a special medical evaluation—a psychiatric evaluation, in point of fact?"

"Every CIA officer undergoes psychiatric evaluations from time to time," said Kreeger. "They are quite routine. Like medical check-ups."

"I'm not talking about routine. It is my understanding that this psychiatric evaluation was not voluntary. That it was requested by your superior officers because of allegations of a homosexual network within the CIA."

The din in the committee room drowned out the rest of Senator Pike's statement. Kreeger flushed damson-purple. Not just because of the lying insinuations, based on an incident buried twenty years in his past, but because he was quite sure that the senator's knowledge was based on his confidential CIA medical records. The only people authorized access to those were Director Wagoner and Dr. Alvin Glass, the Chief of Medical Services. And Kreeger was damn sure that Al Glass was not the source of the leak.

"Mr. Senator," Kreeger said, with such calm as he could muster when he could again make himself audible, "you are referring to an incident that took place twenty years ago. Since you seem to have gotten access to confidential files, you might have mentioned that there were four CIA officers, including myself, who were called in for evaluation. This was done at the insistence of a supervisor—a branch chief—with serious personal problems. Nothing adverse was recorded against any of the officers, including myself, who were tested. I hope I will not be accused of defaming homosexuals if I mention, for the record, that the supervisor in question resigned from the Agency after his own homosexual activities came to light. I believe that he was briefly employed by a member of your own Committee before committing suicide some years back."

"Thank you, Mr. Kreeger," the Senate chairman intervened. "I think we have spent more than enough time on this distasteful topic. I commend you for your patience, as well as your frankness."

"Mr. Chairman," Kreeger responded, "I have an additional statement I wish to make at this time. It is not part of my prepared deposition, and it has in no way been cleared by the Central Intelligence Agency. It concerns the illicit, immoral, and probably illegal involvement of a section of the U.S. intelligence community and of the military establishment, with a plot to destabilize a friendly country."

There was uproar in the committee room.

Senator Pike, red-faced, was bawling, "Traitor! Another goddamn bleeding heart!"

The senior CIA counsel rushed to the table, and

leaned over to whisper to the Chairman, who covered the microphone with his hand.

"In view of unexpected developments," the Chairman announced after hurried consultation, "we are going to take a brief adjournment."

Kreeger was sipping coffee and placing bets with himself on how long it would take the Director to get on the phone—and whether Bill Wagoner's reaction would be to bludgeon, to appeal to loyalty, or to trade.

It took less than ten minutes for the CIA counsel to reappear. He grabbed Kreeger's arm. "Quick. Director Wagoner's on the phone."

"Where?"

"In the hall."

Kreeger squeezed as much of his solid frame as was possible into the cramped booth, to shield his dialogue with the Director from the people milling about outside the committee room.

"Fuck you," Director Wagoner began.

"You try it, Bill, and I'll blow you wide open. The Safari operation. The payoffs. The drug connections. The theft of secret intelligence for Art Colgate and his paymasters."

Kreeger was bluffing, to a certain extent. He was certainly affecting to have exact information about relationships that he was still guessing about.

When he said, "Shelley Hayes," the Director shouted over him, *"Enough!* What do you want?"

"I want to go back to Mexico Station. I want to save the Agency—*my* Agency, the one you don't even know about—from being torn apart. I want a fishing license. I want your goddamn desk jockeys off my back."

Through the volleys of four-letter words that came over the line, Kreeger was given to understand that he had his deal: He had his station back.

After more consultations with the CIA counsel, the Chairman announced that Kreeger's personal statement would be postponed, *sine die*, for reasons of national security.

Joel Stein walked Kreeger to his car, and expressed both admiration and disappointment.

"You had my heart skipping a beat for a minute or two in there. I thought I'd gone into a time warp, that we were on the Church Committee hearings and you were about to unburden yourself at holy confession. Shit. That would have been great."

"You don't understand a damn thing, do you? I'm trying to save American Intelligence. Your guys in the seventies were trying to destroy it."

"I guess we are coming out into no-man's land from opposite trenches, aren't we? That's okay. It's kinda fun. Listen, I don't know why your Director is out to screw you, but I'll stand up for any guy who'll take on the Two Bills and can face down Jonah Pike. If there's anything you ever need, give me a call."

SEVENTEEN

□ □ □

1

MONTHS had slipped by since Shelley Hayes, unknown to Kreeger, had called on President Butler at the Executive Office Building. Mexico had returned to familiar patterns. The violence continued, especially in rural areas, but gradually the interest of the American media had shifted away. Overtly, cordial relations between Washington and the Mexican government had been restored, since Harry Butler had finally agreed to sit down with Paz Gallardo. But Kreeger knew, from the secret cable traffic —and from successive drafts of the much-delayed and much-debated Mexico Estimate—that the Two Bills and others in the Butler Administration were still praying, and planning, for a blow-up in Mexico.

Fausto gave every appearance of being entirely relaxed about the political situation inside Mexico, which was starting to look like *folie de grandeur*, or something more sinister, since Miliano Rojas's movement was continuing to gather support, from the border to the Isthmus. Kreeger wondered whether Fausto was falling into the secret policeman's trap of confusing omniscience with omnipotence. In the days of the tsars, he remembered, the head of the terrorist movement had been a tsarist agent; this had not prevented the terrorists from killing the tsar.

Most suggestive of all, Fausto had said not a single word about his relationship with Shelley Hayes, Carvajal's inamorata—and Harry Butler's former mistress.

Yet Kreeger knew, from Lois, that Fausto had taken Shelley to dinner at least once. According to Lois, the chief of SIN had "behaved like a perfect gentleman."

WE Mexicans are better at dying than at living," said Fausto García. He offered the silver brandy flask to Kreeger, who took a small mouthful. They were walking a dozen paces behind their wives, over the stony ground of a cemetery set high on a hillside, above Guanajuato. The night was held at bay by a thousand candles—heavy stumps of beeswax, cheap, evanescent paraffin tapers— burning among the tombstones. Below, in the city of the buried river, all the church bells were tolling. Not the measured, funereal knoll that announced the spirits of departed adults, but a happy, joyous ringing, to welcome the little ones. It was the night of the Little Angels, when dead children returned to their families.

"It is the one thing that binds us together," said Fausto, wiping his mouth. "Believer and nonbeliever. Mestizo and *gachupin*. We know that the dead come back. We honor our dead together. The Indians call it weeping the bone."

Karla and Gabriela García had stopped at a tiny headstone, no more than knee-high. The men watched while Fausto's wife, and her three surviving children, laid out a feast for the one that had been taken from them. Dead man's bread from the pastry shop, baked with corn and sugar and cinnamon. Candy skulls, with maraschino cherries for eyes. Ribs and thigh bones of chocolate and frosted sugar. Tasty sweets made from pumpkin seed.

The grave was already decked with gladioli and cornflowers, and vivid yellow bunches of *cempoalxuchitl*, brought all the way from Xochimilco.

Gabriela was on her knees, invoking the spirit of her lost child. "My beloved, I beseech you. Come to visit us this night."

Kreeger saw tears glistening on Karla's cheeks.

"Congenital heart disease," said Fausto. "My boy has it too."

Kreeger looked at Fausto's son. He was seven or eight, but he looked like an old man in miniature, with his high, bony forehead, his deep-set eyes, his sunken chest.

It was rare to glimpse Fausto like this, the father, the husband, in the midst of his official family. Kreeger couldn't decide if it made the man more human or more sinister.

"She is a good woman," said Fausto as he watched his wife. Gabriela García was like a porcelain doll, her jet-black hair accentuating the whiteness of her skin. She wore a gold cross at her throat. "But *muy mocha*. Excessively religious." He pushed the flask at Kreeger. "*Y ándale!* Let's get on with it!"

THE next morning, as the church bells tolled throughout the town, just before the Kreegers drove back to the capital, Fausto García presented them with a memento of Guanajuato. It was a walnut shell which opened on a tiny brass hinge.

"These are made by the convicts at our jail," Fausto explained. "I believe they are quite unique."

Inside the shell, carved in extraordinary detail, was a scene very like the one Kreeger had witnessed the night before, of Mexicans picnicking in a cemetery. One significant difference: the picnickers were skeletons.

Fausto watched as Kreeger admired the gift, clicking the walnut shell open and shut. "We are artists of death," he observed.

2

WHEN Kreeger got home from the office later that week, he felt his insides were ready to drop out. He was unsure whether to attribute his condition to overindulgence in pumpkin-seed snacks, maize atole, and stewed haws at Fausto's country table, or simply to renewed immersion in the fug of the Mexican capital.

By the time he emerged from the bathroom, Karla had gotten home from her class at the university.

"You up to making us a drink?" Karla asked as she gave Kreeger's neck a quick squeeze. He noticed that Karla was wearing what he called her sixties outfit— jeans and high boots and a loose mock turtleneck tunic, painted with bold designs, reminiscent of Aztec plumed serpents, inset with tiny mirrors. Karla maintained she was less conspicuous in gear like this when she drove across town once a week for her class at the university.

"Class go well?" he inquired.

"Wait till I tell you." There was suppressed excitement in her voice. Kreeger wondered what arcane gem of information she'd brought home this week.

He tasted his manhattan, pursed his lips, and dribbled in a little more dry vermouth. He walked through into the living room, where Karla had stretched out on the sofa.

She took a sip of her vodka. "Mmmm. That's good."

"Okay. What was it this week? Toltec methods of birth control?"

"I stayed after class."

"Yeah? That Pablo doing a number on you?" Pablo was her bearded instructor.

"I wish. I think Pablo's kinda cute."

Kreeger growled.

"Pablo took me to a Miliano rally."

"He did *what?*" Kreeger set his glass down on the coffee table so hard that the liquor sloshed over the cherrywood and onto the creamy rug. "I'll get it." He thumped out to the kitchen and returned with the soda siphon.

In between squirts at the rug, he said, "You must have been out of your mind."

"Don't yell at me, Jim!"

"I'm—not—yelling!" he said slowly, as if to convince himself.

"Jeez, Karla," he said when he thought he had his emotions on a leash. "Did you stop to consider what could have happened if someone knew who you were? If someone recognized you? You're a kidnap target."

"Hell, Jim. They just thought I was a good ol' girl looking for a pickup. I got a coupla offers, too. You can't bitch about it, honey. I don't know what you do in the middle of the night, but it sure ain't with me."

He told himself, I am a rock. I just let it roll over me. In a thousand years or so, it might wear me down, but not until then.

"You gonna tell me how I messed up your life again, or you gonna tell me about the rally?"

In response, Karla downed the vodka remaining in her glass and got up to fix herself a refill. Kreeger knew that if he wanted to get a clear picture of the rally, he had better get Karla talking now. Karla tended to get combustible after three or four drinks.

"Was Miliano at that rally?"

"He may be crazy, but he ain't dumb," said Karla, reentering the living room. "I reckon somebody told him if he came to Mexico City now, your friend Fausto would put him in a box next to Batman."

"Fausto's not stupid either," Kreeger said quietly.

"But he bumped off Moctezuma Morelos. Him and Fernando Ramírez."

"I think Fausto's smarter than Ramírez." He decided to spare himself a debate with Karla when she was in this kind of mood. "So how many people were at this meeting? Who were they?"

"Kids. Faculty. I guess there were a couple of thousand."

"Who spoke?"

"Miliano."

"Wait a minute. I thought you said Miliano wasn't there."

"They used a projector and a big screen. Just like at a movie house. It was a helluva show. Maybe better than a live performance."

"Color film?"

"You bet. It started with this train steaming straight at the audience, like the Pancho Villa express. The kids in the front row were screaming."

"You mean they used special effects."

"Uh-huh. And they had this scene of Miliano, dressed like a cotton picker, surrounded by children in white, like snowdrifts. It was a tender sight."

This was all new information to Kreeger. New, and utterly foreign. Since when had Mexican politicians—even the Mexican government—used sophisticated visual effects and state-of-the-art video techniques to get their messages across? The Safari crowd probably had that kind of money. But why would they invest in a socialist? Where had a small-town labor lawyer gotten the money and equipment and technical advice to put on a show like the one Karla described? Someone was clearly making a heavy investment in Miliano.

EIGHTEEN

□ □ □

1

INCIDENTS of violence throughout Mexico increased daily. Leaders of the Mexican Human Rights Committee were toppled like ninepins. In the south, there were reports the army and the landowners' *pistoleros* had shot squatters by the thousands, dumping their bodies in mass graves. In Tabasco, radical petroleum workers took revenge on their crooked union boss by hanging him from the chandelier in a restaurant where he was dining with visiting Japanese bigwigs.

Such Mexican-against-Mexican violence normally might rate a page-seven item in a Houston newspaper, and perhaps in Miami as well. In most other cities north of the border, however, such news would receive little notice, even when the shooting was going on a few miles outside Acapulco, a place dear to tourists everywhere. To the men behind the Safari Project, this situation presented a problem, since their success hinged on winning the right kind of news coverage—and above all, the right TV exposure—in Washington and New York.

Colgate was sitting in a private room at the Casino de Monterrey, making this point to a group of wealthy men presided over by Raúl Carvajal.

"So what will it take?" Carranza demanded of Colgate.

"We need visuals."

"So we blow up the bridges. We do it good this time. Everything stops. The businessmen are hurting. Everyone's screaming for Harry Butler to do something."

"We get hurt too," Raúl reminded him. "And we've done that before; it lacks novelty."

"So we hang a few PRI party bosses. I want to start with the Governor of Chihuahua. That *hijo de puta* has been shaking me down for years."

"They're Mexicans." Colgate developed a twitch in his right cheek. "I mean no offense, but we need impact. Mexican politicians get killed all the time, and in all sorts of ways—some of them truly ingenious. Still it doesn't matter. I bet already nobody up north even remembers who Moctezuma Morelos was."

"He was a fucking communist," spat Carranza. "That's one good thing Ramírez did, offing that piece of shit." Paco Carranza was still having some difficulty accepting one of the core elements in Colgate's plan: a tacit alliance with the left, necessary if they were to capitalize on Miliano's ability to mobilize mass support.

Fortunately, Raúl Carvajal had been smart enough, and strong enough, to ensure their cooperation. They were working on Miliano through a cutout, an editor of a Monterrey newspaper. Miliano was grateful for the unexpected flow of cash and video technology from obscurely identified sympathizers, but he would no doubt be more than a little disquieted if he found out his beneficiaries included *brutos* like Carranza.

"We are open to suggestion." Raúl spoke to Colgate.

"The way I see it, there are two hot issues in Mexico. I'm talking about media focus, not what people are talking about at Chase Manhattan or the National Security Council. To get TV coverage, it has to be simple, and visual. Sound bites. Footage. People have to be able to see it. One of the issues is drugs."

Paco Carranza's mouth turned down, and an ominous growl rose up from his belly.

"I guess we played that already, right?"

Carranza seemed slightly mollified.

"The second issue . . ." Here Colgate paused; his facial tic became more pronounced. He put a hand to his cheekbone. "Well, it comes down to this. Any threat to American citizens is a grabber. Hostages. Grieving families. Widows and orphans. It gets people mad. The media can't stay away from it." He removed his hand from his face and said, "It's what got us into Panama."

RICO Sanchez drove Colgate to the airport so they could talk in private. Colgate was to fly to Mexico City for a chat with Maury Atthowe. Kreeger had caused a helluva stink in Washington. Now, a Senate staffer named Joel Stein was snooping around the Global Assistance office, and he had recently dropped in at Two Jacks Gilly's shop over at the Pentagon.

"They liked the bit about widows and orphans," Sanchez commented on the meeting at the Casino de Monterrey. "Where did you find such a bunch of mean sons of bitches?"

"I'm sorry if you don't feel at home."

"I'm doing fine. Plenty of ass. But these fuckheads can't shoot for nuts."

"There won't have to be a lot of shooting, if we play things right."

Colgate was surprised that the Monterrey group had taken Sanchez into their inner circle so readily. Northerners like Raúl, with pedigrees as long as your arm, often looked down on Mexican-Americans, the way a Boston Brahmin might look down on a redneck from Appalachia. But if Raúl could work with Paco Carranza, maybe he could work with anyone.

Even more surprising for Colgate were Sanchez's thoughts about Miliano Rojas. Sanchez insisted that the Safari group should reach out and establish tighter control over Miliano and his inner circle. "Otherwise, Miliano's movement will get away from us completely. It will snap back and break our necks with its tail. We'll have Miliano's people and Carranza's shooting at each other from behind every cactus bush."

"So what do you suggest?"

"We have to put a man alongside Miliano, close enough to hear his heart beat." Sanchez had an idea about how this might be accomplished. Colgate listened, and liked it. The way would have to be carefully prepared. In the meantime, there was a job to be done that required the Headhunter's special talents.

2

IT was off-season at the plush resort hotels along the beach at Acapulco, but the season was year-round at the chic rejuvenation spa set on a knoll above the sand dunes a couple of miles along the seafront from Las Brisas. The clinic proclaimed itself, without false modesty, La Fuente de Juventud, the Fountain of Youth. Its owners had tried to copy the more celebrated Clinique La Prairie, in Switzerland. Their prices were cheaper, however, and their doctors' diplomas were on flimsier paper. Their clientele consisted, for the most part, of wealthy gringos of a certain age in quest of miracles the FDA had not acknowledged to be good for you: the exorcism of wrinkles, pouches, and spots; a magical reprieve from the aging process; the resurrection of the body.

That week, the clinic was playing host to a dozen Americans, including the wife of the Governor of Arizona, the ex-wife of a real estate tycoon, and Gary Winston, a Hollywood movie star of some renown in the 1960s, who was accompanied by his male secretary. The clientele at La Fuente might not be quite top drawer, but it included enough notables to make it a likely target for thieves. Or terrorists.

When the shooting began, the Governor's lady was sipping a mimosa on the terrace above the breakers, the developer's ex was practicing her backhand with a cute tennis pro called Angel, and Gary Winston was flat on his stomach on a steel table in a wellness room.

Then hooded men in black jumpsuits came racing across the terrace. One of them grabbed the Governor's lady by her ash-blond hair, twisting it into a knot. The others smashed through the French doors to the solarium, spraying everything breakable with bursts from their machine pistols.

When the first coherent reports reached the American Embassy in the capital, Kreeger learned that the casualty list was small. A couple of Mexican guards had been felled immediately. An elderly widow from Waco, Texas, had panicked and managed to break her neck jumping from a second-floor window. The list of wounded included Gary Winston, whose doctor's hand had slipped when the melee began, stabbing the movie idol with a three-inch needle. Also in bad condition was Winston's overpretty male secretary, who was gang-raped. He had evidently put up a fight, since his assailants had cut his thigh tendons to make penetration easier.

Sexual assault, the theft of money and valuables—the attack on La Fuente looked like the work of common criminals. Who might, of course, be members of the Mexican police. With mounting civil unrest had come a notable increase in banditry, all across the country. In Mexico, bandits and bad cops had something in common —they liked to bugger their victims, especially the males. In a relaxed moment, Kreeger had once asked Fausto to explain why this happened so frequently in a country where the *maricón*—the homosexual—was reviled. According to Fausto, the *chingón*—the man who did the screwing—asserted his manhood. "The rest is only female."

The assault on La Fuente, however, also had some unusual features. The hooded attackers littered the place with a crudely printed broadsheet announcing the birth of a new guerrilla organization, Los Héroes de la Pacífica, dedicated to armed resistance against "*yanqui* economic and cultural imperialism'' on behalf of the Mexican people and all ''the coming powers of the Pacific.'' The hit team carved ragged H's on the backs of their victims, including Gary Winston's lover, and daubed the same initial in blood on the whitewashed walls of the solarium. The organization sounded like a phony, but that left open the question of what the mask was intended to conceal.

There was a more urgent question, however—the Governor's lady was missing.

3

FOR three days, the hunt for the Governor's wife was the lead story on the nightly newscasts on the northern side of the border. The Governor of Texas appeared at a press conference to express his sympathy for his old friend in Arizona, and volunteered to send Texas Rangers to kick ass. Squads of FBI agents and police investigators flew into Acapulco from the United States. They were not impressed by the announcement from a *comandante* of the Guerrero state police that the crime had been solved within twenty-four hours of the assault on the clinic.

''The *Judiciales* just rounded up the usual suspects,'' the chief of the CIA's Guadalajara base reported to Kreeger. ''Political types the state governor doesn't like. A businessman who complained about being shaken down by the cops. Some of them were shot trying to escape.''

When Kreeger consulted the head of SIN, Fausto put it more pithily. ''The *Judiciales* are scum. They probably did this themselves, for the ransom.''

The White House asked the Embassy to determine whether there were possible Japanese links with the self-proclaimed Heroes of the Pacific.

American travel agents were swamped with vacation cancellations. Mexican resorts looked less and less like guaranteed fun in the sun.

By the fourth day, there was still no ransom demand, and no firm leads on the terrorist group with the improbable name.

4

AMBASSADOR Childs called Kreeger on the house phone. "Hey, Jim. You wearing socks?"

Kreeger found the Iowan's cultivated informality a welcome relief from the pinstripe brigade.

"What can I do for you, Mr. Ambassador?"

"I got an appointment at Los Pinos at noon. We got word the new guy—Paz Gallardo—is going to be sitting in. I want you to hold my hand. This might be a hairy one. Why don't you stop by my office and we'll talk about it."

In his private office, Ambassador Childs showed Kreeger the letter the Secretary of State had ordered him to present to Mexico's head of state. It was couched in the language of an ultimatum. Unless the Mexican government permitted U.S. law enforcement agencies to participate fully in the hunt for the Governor's wife and her captors, the State Department would issue a Travel Advisory, counseling all private American citizens—two hundred thousand residents as well as tourists—to leave Mexico. The issuing of a Travel Advisory would be a death knell for the tourist trade, and for the battered Mexican economy as a whole.

"I fought this one all the way, Jim," the Ambassador told Kreeger. "The Secretary fought it too. This comes straight from the White House. I don't know who Harry Butler is listening to these days, but he sure isn't listening to us."

Kreeger knew Shelley Hayes might have the answer to Childs's question. But if she were still in touch with President Butler—had truly been his mistress—she wasn't telling Lois, and Lois refused to push her faster than Shelley wanted to go. Kreeger recognized, in any event, that pursuing Shelley would in all likelihood lead nowhere. The United States did not conduct its foreign policy on the basis of the President's sexual interests. At least, Kreeger didn't *think* it did.

For the ride out to Los Pinos, Kreeger sat on the Ambassador's left, on the back seat of the armored black Cadillac limousine. Kreeger was accustomed to visiting *El Señor*—as the President's people called him—discreetly, after ten at night. The Station Chief felt distinctly uncomfortable riding in the big Embassy limo with the flags on the hood in the middle of a little parade. The procession was led by a black Ford occupied by two Embassy guards. Between it and the Cadillac was Fausto's contribution: an open jeep, packed with Mexicans armed with automatic weapons. A second jeep and a tail car followed behind.

Ambassador Childs coughed into his handkerchief—a dry, irritating little cough that left his throat raw.

"This is a helluva thing to do to Paz Gallardo the week before the inauguration," he complained. *"Damn!"*

A rock clanged against the armored hood of the Cadillac. Kreeger watched a boy dart away across the center lane of the Avenida Constitucional. He leaped among the cars with the defiant grace of a bullfighter making passes at a *corrida*.

The Ambassador spat into his handkerchief. "I don't understand these people. Don't they know we're their only hope? Who the hell else is going to bail them out? The Japanese? The Japs are strictly business. Only Uncle Sam gives something for nothing."

Kreeger wondered if this was remotely true. If it

was, he observed, it did not mean that anyone felt grateful. "It's like that with a lot of people. You save their ass, they hate you for it the rest of their lives."

"Sounds to me like you don't expect a whole lot of your fellow man."

"You spend enough time down here, sir, and you start believing in original sin."

The low-slung palace of Los Pinos was screened behind white pines and security walls from the gaze of casual passers-by in Chapultepec Park. The Americans were ushered into a dark, wood-paneled reception room on the right of the entrance hall. Twenty minutes later, they were escorted down the hall to the formal audience chamber. The furnishings were Spanish colonial. *El Señor* and his successor sat side by side on high-backed chairs, their faces smooth and oval as duck eggs. The Americans were placed on a low sofa, eliminating any differences of height.

They passed a very sticky hour. The Ambassador presented his letter. The Mexicans expressed their sympathy for "the honorable lady from Tucson" who had been abducted. They pointed out that terrorism knew no frontiers, that there was no proof even that the Acapulco group was composed of Mexicans, and that hostage situations are not readily solved overnight. Was it not true that there were Americans in Lebanon who had been held hostage for many years? Paz Gallardo, turning his gaze on Kreeger, professed his inability to comprehend why President Butler, who had seemed entirely reasonable during their meeting in Houston, could approve of an ultimatum that seemed calculated to shatter any chance of normal relations between Mexico and the United States.

"Surely President Butler, as a native of Texas, is alive to the fact that a Travel Advisory will be as ruinous for business in his own state as in our country."

Kreeger agreed with this statement. Even if Harry Butler had been swayed by the alarmists around him, he was a veteran Texas politician who could hardly have forgotten the cardinal principle: Always vote your district. The White House had to be bluffing. To what end? To get permission for visiting FBI agents to ride around in Mexican police cruisers, looking for a missing woman? The threat was completely disproportionate to the problem. It did not make any sense.

The Ambassador cleared his throat. "I have a personal message from President Butler. An oral communication. President Butler wishes it to be understood that the involvement of commercial interests from outside the hemisphere in projects of strategic significance in Mexico is unacceptable to the United States. Such projects would include the construction of a canal across the Isthmus of Tehuantepec."

The Ambassador bowed his head and waited for the storm to break.

"Blackmail" was one of the softer words used by Paz Gallardo, who represented the Mexican side of the discussion.

Ambassador Childs reminded him that he was only a messenger, and that he would continue to counsel strongly against the threatened Advisory, citing the Mexicans' assurances that no efforts would be spared to find the Governor's wife.

"We are not blind," Paz Gallardo snapped back. "We are well aware of a pattern of subversive provocations and inspired attacks from the American media. We know that the Butler Administration is no stranger to these provocations."

"May I speak, sir?" Kreeger, who had been acting as translator, took an active role in the conversation for the first time. "I am the servant of my President, and of the laws and interests of the United States," he told the Mexicans. "It is clear to me that we have a vested interest in the stability and prosperity of Mexico. I can assure you that the service I represent is not engaged in any activity hostile to the people or the government of the Republic of Mexico. Were it otherwise, I would no longer feel able to carry on my functions."

Kreeger proposed another personal meeting with President Butler, to be held on the earliest possible date after the Mexican inauguration. The other men agreed to this suggestion, yet the atmosphere in the room, when the Americans took their leave, was about as cheerful as a city morgue during the graveyard shift.

5

"You might have warned me you were going to hit them with the Japanese thing," Kreeger reproached the Ambassador, as their cavalcade moved past the soldiers at the barrier.

Norman Childs made some unconvincing excuses, and Kreeger wondered whether the Ambassador—an old pol, after all—had decided to slip in the canal question in order to secure brownie points with Harry Butler.

They swung out into the Constitucional. A little Volkswagen beetle in the inside lane rode level with the Ambassador's limo. Kreeger inspected the occupants. Two girls, Lucy's age or younger, laughing and tossing their hair. They looked like college kids.

Kreeger said to the driver, all the same, "Speed up or slow down."

The first rule of defensive driving, in Kreeger's book, was never to let anyone ride abreast of you. That was when you got shot.

The driver mumbled something about the traffic. They shot forward, then came to a shuddering stop, then jerked forward again. The Beetle in the next lane pulled ahead, then darted into a gap behind the lead jeep, forcing the driver to hit the brakes.

The Ambassador's driver responded too late and too

hard. A hammer blow slammed into Kreeger's sternum. It drove up his spine. His head smashed into the roof of the car. The next jolt sent Kreeger flying backward, as the Cadillac rammed into the back of the jeep. When he found his head, Kreeger saw that one of the Mexicans riding shotgun in the jeep had spilled over the side.

"Jeez!" He grabbed at the Ambassador. "You okay, sir?"

"I think so. Shit. I feel like I just broke my back."

Vehicles behind them concertinaed. Others were spinning and colliding like Dodg'em cars. Kreeger saw the yellow Beetle go fishtailing into the snout of a huge gasoline tanker, half a block ahead.

The Embassy driver was hunched over the wheel.

Kreeger tapped his shoulder. "Fred. You figure we can get out of this?"

The driver looked doubtfully at the chaos of stalled traffic.

"Maybe with a bulldozer."

"I'll take a look."

Kreeger opened the door, and nearly got sideswiped by another Beetle, trying to gouge a path along the center lane.

"*Cabrón!*" the driver swore, and shook his fist.

Kreeger knelt over the injured guard. He was losing a lot of blood, and only semiconscious. Kreeger helped the other Mexicans to load him into the back of the jeep, and walked on to the lead car. The Embassy bodyguards were trying to unlock their fender from that of a rusty old Kombi van.

"We need to get the Ambassador out of this," Kreeger said. "Can we play traffic cops?"

"I'll give it my best shot."

As Kreeger walked back to the Cadillac, he saw a motorbike zigzagging in and out of the stopped cars. Now *that* was the way to travel in Mexico City. Two kids in black leather, one riding pillion. The driver was wearing a fancy black-and-silver helmet with a smoked-glass visor. He was moving pretty fast.

A prickling at the back of his neck made Kreeger accelerate his stride. He leaped for the door, snapped the lock behind him, and yelled at Ambassador Childs, who had crawled back onto the seat, "Stay down!"

The windows of the armored limo were shatterproof glass, but no glass invented is guaranteed safe against slugs from an automatic shotgun pushed up to within an inch or two of the pane.

With the first burst, the window on Kreeger's side turned to cracked ice that blew inward, driving wicked splinters of glass at the two men in the back. The second burst, fired as the motorbike throttled clear of the limo, took out the windshield and tore off the front of the driver's face.

The Mexican guards and the Embassy men were shooting. Bullets ricocheted back and forth between the metal sides of the stalled cars. Kreeger struggled into the front seat, beside the dead man. The car phone was dead. He jumped out, wiping blood and powdered glass off his face.

"Damn!" One of the Embassy guards stamped his foot in frustration. "Those goddamn sons of bitches."

The men on the motorbike had gotten clean away.

"Your radio working?" Kreeger demanded. "Let me try."

He got through to Eddie O'Brien. "I need a chopper, and I need it yesterday."

"I'm on it."

The Ambassador was slightly dazed, bleeding from minor wounds on his neck and face.

"I've never been shot at before," he said, in a kind of wonderment. "Why did those jerks try to kill me?"

"Because you're there."

Kreeger wasn't happy with his answer, though Lord knew it was part of the truth. It seemed to be open season on gringos in Mexico. If a bunch of geriatrics at a cosme-

tology clinic were fair game, why not an Ambassador—
let alone the CIA Station Chief? But there was no doubt
in Kreeger's mind that this had been a professional hit,
carried out by hired guns, and not the work of political
zealots. The style was reminiscent of *moto-terroristas* of
Colombia's drug wars. The general effect would be to
signal Washington—and the tourist industry—that no
American citizen was safe in Mexico, up to and including
the Ambassador.

NINETEEN

☐ ☐ ☐

1

ON the day Paz Gallardo was sworn in as President of Mexico, the owner of a tire retread shop on Highway 15, a few miles south of Culiacán, left his coffee to investigate the yapping and snarling of hairless dogs in the back lot. He found the animals mauling an oversized garbage bag. When he kicked them away, he was unsure whether the body parts spilling out of the plastic were animal or human. Until he found what remained of the head.

Under normal circumstances, he would not have considered taking the matter to the police. The *Judiciales* were interested in quick payoffs, not lengthy investigations, and if they were in enough of a hurry, they might even arrest *him*. But he remembered the posters in town with the emblem of the League of Decency, promising a big reward for a woman who had been kidnapped in Acapulco, the wife of an important gringo. And the tire shop owner had a cousin in the state police in Culiacán.

Dental records confirmed that the mutilated carcass belonged to the wife of the Governor of Arizona. The Air National Guard sent a plane to bring her remains home for burial.

The discovery buried all other news from Mexico— including the presidential inauguration—in the American press. One of the weekly magazines ran a cover story, entitled "Mexico's Butchers," that dwelled on the horrific similarity between the treatment of the Governor's wife and that of Judge Renwick, whose murder remained unsolved.

At a televised press conference, President Butler was asked if he intended to meet with his Mexican counterpart any time soon. There had been talk of a ritual encounter on the border, at Ciudad Juárez or Laredo.

"I'm taking that under advisement," President Butler responded. "But when I do get together with President Paz, I can promise you that these killings of U.S. citizens will be at the top of our agenda."

"Mr. President!" Another correspondent claimed the President's attention. "Is it true that you have asked the State Department to issue a Travel Advisory, warning U.S. citizens to stay out of Mexico?"

"That's a matter for the experts," Butler replied gruffly. "I would remind you that we have a large community of American retirees living in Mexico. It's not just a question of tourists and business travelers."

"Mr. President! There are reports that the Administration has plans for a military invasion of Mexico." This came from a reporter for the Baron-Ritter chain.

"I haven't heard that report. If you're talking about contingency plans, I guess we have those for anything you can name. Including an invasion from Alpha Centauri."

This comment brought a crackle of laughter.

"I will say only," President Butler said, cutting the question period short, "that when it comes to Mexico, our options are wide open."

2

THE inauguration of Mexico's new President was celebrated along the U.S. border with car-bombings, bridge-blocking, attacks on government buildings, and a new surge of refugees. "Them brown brothers is rolling over us like an old eighteen-wheeler over a bunch of bullfrogs,'' Bob Culbertson remarked to a friend at Billybob's saloon.

In the capital, the chief representative of the Butler Administration present at the swearing-in of the new head of state was an undersecretary from the State Department—a calculated slight that was noticed by the opposition as well as the PRI. It was not forgotten, among those who knew some Mexican history, that one of the main triggers for the revolution of 1910 had been a signal from Washington that the United States no longer supported the status quo. Paz Gallardo remembered. He requested Kreeger to call on him discreetly at Los Pinos in the late evening of Inauguration Day. He asked Kreeger to press the Ambassador to confirm a personal meeting with President Butler, or to use his own channels if Childs proved unresponsive. He even suggested a time and place for the meeting. Gallardo had a long-standing invitation to speak to an international conference hosted by the Aspen Institute. Given the violence in the north of Mexico, the Colorado resort would be safer than one of the border towns where meetings between Mexican and U.S. leaders had often taken place. Kreeger promised that he would get the message to the White House. He did not tell the Mexican President about the lengths to which his adversaries had gone to try to prevent his other messages from getting through.

Raúl Carvajal remembered history too. He had studied the powder trail that had led to the explosion of 1910, and found many encouraging parallels with the situation that now prevailed in his country: widespread anger over a crude electoral fraud; hunger and suffering intensified to the point where people who lived from hand to mouth —people without leisure for politics—were ready for anything; violence flaring without warning, like bursting skyrockets; that tacit alliance of left and right, of all those opposed to a tottering regime of crooks and vain numbers-men, *científicos* then, *técnicos* today. The revolution of 1910 had not required national coordination and elaborate planning. All that had been necessary had been to raise the political temperature to the level of spontaneous combustion, and to have a man on horseback waiting to ride into the presidential palace. And, of course, to secure the neutrality—or active support—of the government of the United States.

Raúl had studied these things as a car mechanic studies an engine manual. He intended to do better than his ancestors who had made the first revolution of the twentieth century, better than poor Madero, punched full of bullets. He meant to seize power and hold it. He would do this in the name of democracy, since democracy was in fashion, but like the PRI, he would tolerate elections only on condition that he could determine the results. Miliano and his movement were allies of convenience for now. They would become an embarrassment, however, the day after the government fell. Raúl and his partners recognized this fact and had made contingency plans. Already there had been bloody clashes between some of Raúl's landowner friends and peasant squatters who carried the banners of the Frente Nacional de Campesinos.

Raúl had recognized, from the beginning, that it would never be possible to control the whole of a country so vast and divided. Under any scenario, the northern states would be his redoubt. If the United States stood behind him, the north could be held and defended against all comers. He could leave the *chilangos* of the capital to swim in the shit from their broken sewers.

That would suit John Halliwell and the Texas crowd just fine. They did not care what happened to Mexico. They wanted the oil fields. They would help Raúl get what he wanted, and then they would leave him alone.

The current of events was flowing toward their purpose—Raúl could feel it. He was a man of his times, more North American than Mexican; a man who trusted instinct more than logic, giving him a decisive edge over a mere logician like President Paz. From the ranks of the ruling party itself, important men were leaning toward Raúl, the coming power in the land. And not just local bosses like Lobo Terrazzas of Chihuahua, an old drinking buddy of Carranza's, but national figures, military men; leaders of the Ramírez faction who had lost their jobs—or feared losing them—since the head of their *camarilla* had fallen. Fausto García, the chief of the secret police, had sent friendly messages, hinting at his private sympathy with Raúl's cause. Fausto's man in Monterrey had turned a blind eye to the goings-on at the ranch. Fausto had invited Shelley to dinner in the capital during one of her shopping expeditions—an invitation Raúl had urged her to accept—and told her that necessity made amusing bedfellows. Raúl did not trust Fausto, of course, or anyone from the Ramírez clan—these were his family's blood enemies—but he rejoiced in the mounting evidence that the besieged regime was crumbling from within.

Raúl waited, watching from a distance as sporadic acts of terrorism and banditry kept the government off-balance and the Americans jittery. Sometimes Colonel Sanchez, the *chicano*, disappeared for days at a time, and the news reports brought word of new acts of terrorism carried out by phantom groups like Los Héroes de la Pacífica, or in the name of genuine organizations that usually disclaimed responsibility. Raúl wanted to maintain his distance; he did not want to know the details of Sanchez's work.

Nor did he want to know the man. Raúl was never at ease with Sanchez, this man of silences who laughed when others did not. A darkness traveled with Sanchez, something almost palpable, a clot of blackness in the air. Carranza, however, did not share Raúl's reservations. The two men went whoring and drinking together, and Carranza and his friends in the Quintero drug family loaned Sanchez soldiers for some of those special missions that Raúl preferred not to know about.

Still, Raúl had to concede that Sanchez had his uses.

He proved that admirably when Colgate called from the United States soon after the Paz inauguration to report that a Pentagon official named General Gilly wanted to make a confidential tour of northern Mexico. The general had been charged, *inter alia*, with U.S. contingency plans for military operations across the border.

"I know this general," Colgate told Raúl. "Two Jacks Gilly is a stand-up guy. One thousand percent on our side. I think it would help our case a lot if you people were able to demonstrate to him that you have serious capabilities down there."

Rico Sanchez volunteered to handle everything. "I've been handling guys like Gilly all my life," he explained to Raúl. "I know their mind-set. I know how to stroke them. You leave it to me. I'll give the general a tour he won't forget."

3

Two Jacks Gilly arrived at night, flying in from Houston on a private plane. Traveling out of uniform, he wore a brown turtleneck and a houndstooth check coat, tight about the armpits. Neither he nor his outfit looked comfortable.

Twenty men in camouflage fatigues snapped to attention as General Gilly climbed out of the Learjet. Two Jacks inspected his honor guard with appreciation, though he was supposed to be traveling under cover.

A short, heavy man in a black jumpsuit gave Gilly a snappy salute. He had an Uzi machine pistol clipped to his belt, though most of his men were armed with standard-issue M-16s.

"Colonel Sanchez, sir. I've been assigned as your temporary aide. It's an honor to serve under you, sir."

"Colonel? You Mexican military, Sanchez?"

"U.S. Army, retired, sir."

"Hell, it's good to have you with us. Does Washington know you're down here?"

"Not officially, sir. But you can check with Admiral Enright's office."

"That's okay, Colonel." Two Jacks slapped him on the back. "I guess I heard about you when you were down in Salvador. You don't take kindly to commies, is what I heard. Guess you and me are going to get along real fine. Now what have you got to show me?"

Sanchez took his visitor in a four-wheel drive to a more remote landing strip, where Gilly watched a landing drop worthy of one of his manuals. The incoming plane was guided in by the pulsing infrared lights from devices no bigger than Two Jacks's pack of Camels. They were powered by tiny six-volt batteries; their signal could be picked up with the aid of night-vision goggles.

Then Sanchez drove Gilly to a sprawling ranch house where the security guards were wide awake—there were two different exchanges of code words—and sat him down to a five-course dinner, washed down with whiskey and tequila. After the meal, they spent an hour with a series of charts prepared by the Defense Mapping agency—charts from the ONC XXH and ONC XXJ series—and Sanchez explained how, with a few lightning strikes, it would be possible to seize and hold all vital communications in the north, in the process isolating major population centers.

In daylight, Sanchez turned the charts into reality. He put General Gilly on board a Sikorsky-76 helicopter and whirled him around a series of sites where he inspected paramilitary detachments and secured landing strips. The chopper had been used, until recently, to transport drilling crews to offshore oil rigs. General Gilly observed that it could be converted, with minimal work, into a flying gunship.

"I bet you can do a whole lot better than that, General."

Two Jacks laughed and waxed rhapsodic about the Army's new Sikorsky MH-60K, the dream weapon of low-intensity warriors, with its infrared sensors, terrain avoidance radar, laser detector, and ALQ-136 pulse radar frequency jammer.

"Shit, the Messkins would never know what hit them. And that sucker's got self-deployment up to seven hundred nautical miles. There's a lot of brass hats sitting on their asses over at the Pentagon who'd sure like another chance to see it in action."

The general's remarks gave Sanchez a theme for the rest of the day's entertainment. In a time when the U.S. defense chiefs were scrambling to find new reasons why Congress should pay for new hardware, nothing appealed to a Pentagon man like a battlefield with room for his pet toys.

Sanchez did not forget, somewhere along the way, to suggest to the general that there would be an honorable role for the famed 22nd Marine amphibious unit—which Two Jacks had once commanded—in securing the Gulf oil fields.

Gilly was in an excellent mood when they arrived for a late *comida* at a low-slung hacienda in the state of Chihuahua. Their host was a loud-mouthed barrel called Lobo Terrazzas.

Sanchez explained to the general on the last leg of their flight that Terrazzas was the local PRI party boss, but was privately in league with Raúl Carvajal and the northern resistance. "Lobo promised to round up some of the local military, and maybe a couple of heavy hitters from Mexico City. I think this will show you the depth of support we got here for a decisive move by the United States. These guys will jump when Uncle Sam tells them to. You'll see."

Two Jacks saw, and he was impressed, though he expressed nervousness to Sanchez, before and after, about the holes that were being ripped in his cover. He was introduced at the dinner as "Mr. White," a private consultant, but the Mexican general who drew him aside, between cocktails and *carne asado*, addressed him as *mi general*.

The day had brought new outbreaks of violence, including a shootout on the outskirts of the Terrazzas ranch between Lobo's *pistoleros* and militant campesinos attempting to reclaim lands that had been stolen from a defunct *ejido*.

"This Miliano Rojas is pretty far to the left, isn't he?" Gilly observed. "Talks like a communist at a time when the pundits tell us communism has gone out of style."

There was enthusiastic agreement around Lobo's table.

"I know this Miliano has got quite a following," Two Jacks pursued, "but frankly, I don't see how you guys can live with him."

"You understand the problems of Mexico very deeply, Mr. White," said Paco Carranza, who had flown in on his own plane. "We have an archaic institution in my country called the *ejido*, the collective farm. It failed in Russia. It should be extinct here. We need modern farming, modern equipment, a free-market approach. The Chicago philosophy. It works. When we change the government, we will change everything on the land. We will break up the *ejidos* and sell them to private enterprise."

"Excuse me," said General Gilly. "I'm no expert on agriculture, or Mexican politics. But isn't Miliano's movement dedicated to strengthening the *ejidos*?"

"My friend," Paco Carranza leaned forward and clinked glasses, "I can assure you that Miliano Rojas is no problem for us, or for you." He picked up a tortilla chip and crumbled it between his fingers.

4

THE next day, General Gilly flew back to Washington to write up a gung-ho report on the depth of support inside the Mexican military establishment for a change of government and the ease with which a U.S. operation in Mexico could be mounted. That same day, Rico Sanchez volunteered to handle the problem of Miliano.

Raúl Carvajal and Paco Carranza were skeptical about his proposal. Through intermediaries, Miliano had accepted money and communications technology from the Safari group, but how could he possibly accept the services of a former U.S. Army colonel who had been employed for several months in arming and training a private army for the northern landowners?

"Don't underestimate me," Sanchez told them. "This old fox has learned a few tricks."

Art Colgate, who was consulted on the matter, endorsed Sanchez's plan, even though he had not been informed of its key element. None of them had. Carranza, who burned on a short fuse, might well have suffered apoplexy had he been told.

Miliano, as expected, received Sanchez at arm's length. Sanchez caught up with him in Michoacan, where Miliano had spoken at a series of rallies, and his supporters had occupied the municipal buildings in every town except the state capital.

"I have heard of you, Sanchez," Miliano spoke to him. Miliano was bone-tired. His feet ached. His wife, Elena, who had insisted on accompanying him on this tour, had made him soak them in a basin of hot water. She stood behind him, massaging his neck, while he talked with Sanchez. "Why do you come to me?"

"I come to you," Sanchez responded, "because only I can save you."

Sanchez took ten minutes or more to introduce himself. He spoke of his childhood in San Antonio. Of years of suffering and prejudice. Of the abuse and discrimination he and his fellow Mexican-Americans had suffered in the U.S. military. He said, "I am a warrior, a technician of warfare. But I still have a soul."

He told Miliano of the afternoon at the Terrazzas ranch, of the men who had vowed to break up the *ejidos*. He explained that Miliano had received money and help —perhaps without knowing it—from some of the same men who were bent on crushing his followers.

Miliano was assaulted by a migraine so fierce he swayed forward, close to fainting.

Elena gripped his shoulders. She said to Sanchez, "You must go now."

"No," Miliano gasped. "We must talk."

"You may talk tomorrow," Elena said firmly.

"Miliano," Sanchez said, ignoring the woman, "your enemies are armed. Your people are amateurs. You have survived assassination attempts. How many? Three? Four? Your luck won't last forever. I have come to bring you this warning, and to offer my services to protect you. I have skills that you need. I am the one who can save you. Look, I will show you."

Sanchez pulled a gun from beneath his leather jacket, and aimed at Miliano's chest.

Elena threw herself between Miliano and the pistol.

A beam of red light pulsed against her throat.

"You can't eat all the bullets meant for him," Sanchez said to her. "Do you know what this is?" He brandished the pistol. It was a 9mm Taurus 92, with a five-inch barrel and a laser sight. A Brazilian invention, now manufactured for the world market in Miami, where its retail price was less than nine hundred dollars. "Do you know how many of these have been sold to Mexicans? You don't even have to aim! You still don't know what you're up against, do you?"

"We will talk tomorrow." Miliano's voice came in a whispering rattle, a gust of wind through the corn husks.

Sanchez left, in search of food and a woman.

Elena made Miliano lie down, and helped him undress. She said, "How can you trust that man?"

"Can I afford not to?"

"He is a mercenary. A killer. He brought death into this room."

"He brought us a warning. He risked his life to do it. There are men who would cut his heart out because he told us what he did."

"You don't know that, Miliano. All you know for sure is that a gringo with a Mexican name pointed a gun at your heart. A gun from science fiction."

"Shh." He kissed her on the lips. "I'm sorry this man frightened you. But I must talk with him again. Because of the land." He could not speak of the land, of the *ejidos*, in ordinary language, because—for all his education—he was wedded to it, like any campesino tending his patch of corn. To Miliano Rojas, the land was the womb, and the sepulcher, of his people. It belonged to those who worked it, and conserved it. To those who returned thanks for its bounty. To defend the land, and those who loved it, he would deal with anyone. Even a man with a laser pistol.

In the morning, Miliano talked with Sanchez at greater length. He agreed to allow Sanchez to take charge of his personal security, and that of his family, in collaboration with the men who had journeyed with him from Aguilas Negras and the north.

Sanchez asked out loud what Miliano was asking himself silently. "Are you going to fight all those bastards alone? Or is it time to talk to President Paz?"

Miliano said, "I've been thinking about that. I believe that Paz Gallardo is not such a bad man. He has been in the hands of bad advisers. And perhaps bad genes. Our President does not know his own country. Perhaps I can help him to know it better."

Rico Sanchez astonished Miliano by suggesting that he might be able to arrange a personal meeting with Paz Gallardo.

"What am I to make of you, Sanchez? You come to me out of nowhere, and now you show yourself as a man of miracles."

"I am what you see, Miliano. A poor son of a bitch who lost his roots and found them again. A man who will take on the world for you and your cause."

As Miliano embraced him, the butt of Sanchez's Taurus 92 jabbed into his ribs.

TWENTY

□ □ □

1

THE jagged peaks of the Cañon Huasteca, outside Monterrey, loomed gray and forbidding. Shelley Hayes felt confined, even in the airy surroundings of her villa in the lush Colonia del Valle.

Sunday; she hated Sunday.

She generally felt this way, at least whenever she made the mistake of spending the whole weekend with Raúl. Sunday at 2 P.M., he turned, regular as a sundial, toward the Camino Real and abandoned her in order to play paterfamilias over champagne brunch to his official wife and his official family.

"If your wife gets you," Shelley announced to Raúl, "then I get the Porsche." The car was his favorite toy, at least for that month, and he had intended using it today.

Raúl hesitated between his desire to show off the Porsche and his need to placate his mistress.

He surrendered the keys, which mollified her a little.

"Where are you going?"

"Do I have the right to ask the same question?"

"I am a man."

"You mean you're a *macho*. Be one if you must. I am not an *hembra*." This was a coarse word for a female animal. It was the way a certain type of Mexican male—the type Raúl despised—referred to his women.

Raúl was sufficiently embarrassed to back off. Or at least, to advance from a different direction.

"You must not drive alone," he told her. "I will give you Rodrigo."

Shelley did not like Rodrigo, one of the new men from the ranch. He was skinny, with quick little black eyes that darted around, always restless, always prying. He was supposed to be a groom, but he spent little time mucking out stables or oiling tack. He was usually slinking about with a pistol in his belt, or squatting with his hat pulled low over his face. There were a lot of men like Rodrigo around the ranch these days. Some of them, Shelley knew, were on loan from Paco Carranza. They were florid and flatulent, like their master, and stole from the kitchen when the cook had retired to bed. She had even caught one of them trying to peep through her bedroom window. She had told Raúl about it, but he had insisted the man had been there for her protection. The man, however, had disappeared.

"I don't need a bodyguard," she told Raúl.

"I must insist. These are dangerous times."

"I'm just going for a spin, Raúl."

"You're going in my car," he pointed out. "Everything connected with me is a target. Those *putas* in Mexico City are growing desperate. They have killed Carvajals before."

"I don't like Rodrigo. I don't like his eyes."

He laughed. "You think you know a man's soul by his eyes?"

"Sometimes."

He kissed her lips. He smelled of leather and cologne. He had made love to her in the early hours before dawn, as he came out of a dream, aroused and ready. Lying under him, Shelley had not been sure whether he was still in the dream. Lovemaking had seemed of little actual interest to him since he had sent her to Washington. She credited his seeming distraction to the tension—and sometimes, the raw fear—in which he moved, but she could not help but wonder about other things. About whether, just conceivably, Raúl was a little jealous of Harry Butler, and what had been. She also wondered if the sands were running out for their arrangement.

When the time came, she had resolved, she would move on without looking back, without tears. She had learned how to handle these situations, and she would be the first to go.

Raúl said, "If you won't take Rodrigo, then take Felipe."

"What use is Felipe? He's fat and sloppy, like a worn-out retriever."

"He's a good man. His family has been with mine for generations. He would give his life for me."

"Are you trying to keep me prisoner?"

He put a finger to his lips. "I didn't tell you this. Someone tried to shoot me on Friday."

"Where?"

"Outside the Gran Hotel."

It was where *pistoleros*—gunmen sent by Ramírez—had killed his father.

"Why didn't you tell me?"

"Why alarm you to no purpose? As you see, the man was not a good shot. Rodrigo killed him. The police were actually quite helpful. I think maybe they are becoming a little scared of us. All in all, I'm rather glad it happened."

"How can you say that? Glad someone tried to kill you?"

"It has all been rather easy for us, don't you think? Your admirer Fausto García is no fool. The SIN is not asleep. The government has not evaporated. When there is trouble in the north, the government kills Carvajals. Or tries to kill them. If no one had tried to kill me, I would have been obliged to ask myself why my enemies have become so gentle. So. You will take Felipe."

SHE gunned the Porsche past one hundred mph, coming out of the smog of Santa Catarina, an industrial suburb in the lee of Saddleback Mountain. Placid, pudgy Felipe, strapped into the passenger seat, covered his eyes with his hand.

"You want me to drop you off?" she invited him.

Felipe gave her the look of a whipped puppy.

She drove up into the foothills, toward the caves. She wasn't fully aware, until she saw the tracks of the funicular climbing the steep slope, that this was where she had wanted to come all along.

The Grutas de García were a maze of limestone grottoes winding down into the bowels of the earth. The entrance was high up on the mountain face. Shelley told Felipe to watch the car while she rode up in the little train. There weren't many visitors about, but she bribed a guide at the top to take her through the caves alone, without commentary. She wasn't interested in the macabre names Mexicans obsessed with death had given to the weird conformations of stalagmites and stalactites— Dead Man's Finger, El Infierno, Coffin of the Undead. Descending into those cool depths, along slippery, broken paths, to the well of shadow where sea things from before the Flood crusted a whale-sized mother-rock, Shelley was responding to a private dare.

Shelley Hayes wasn't frightened of many things. She wasn't scared of heights: she had thrown herself down mountainsides at Aspen with the same abandon with which she had hurled the Porsche around tricky curves. She did not think she was afraid of death, so long as her daughter was provided for. Perhaps she feared the business of dying, but not of the exit itself, although she had no clear conception of what lay on the other side. One fear Shelley *was* aware of, however: She was terrified of caverns.

All caves reminded her of a nameless one, in a bone-dry desert in New Mexico. She had been ten years old. The big man who had said he was her father—a stranger with whiskey on his breath, a mudder from some hole in the oil patch—had come by her school in a Mustang. He had told her they were going away together, away from the Bitch. He never called her mother by any other name. She hadn't understood that this was a kidnapping. She hadn't heard that word until the police found her, abandoned across the state line. She had gone with the man who said he was her father because she deserved a daddy; she had been dreaming of him, waiting for him, all of her days. It had ended in a place of shadows, beneath a tunnel alive with bats and crawling, scurrying things.

Shelley's scream bounced and echoed through depths of darkness, multiplied on many chords.

The guide grabbed her by the elbows. She was swaying above a sheer drop.

"*Señora*. Are you unwell?"

She pulled away from him. "I'm all right, thank you. A dizzy spell, that's all." She leaned against the rock wall.

What had that shrink in Houston told her? That her addiction to older men—her acceptance of the tenuous life of a kept woman—was the product of a father fixation?

She had walked out of the psychiatrist's office. She had told him she didn't have a father. She knew this was God's own truth, because when she had asked her mother if the man in the cave was her father, her mother had said she didn't know.

The shrink had charged her for a full fifty-minute hour, and told her that nobody could help her until she was ready to re-enter her childhood and look her father in the face.

What the hell did he know?

She could not say, even now, just what had happened in that other cave. She had tried to please Daddy, so he wouldn't leave her again. Was she to be punished for that for the rest of her life?

"*Señora?*"

"I've seen enough," Shelley announced to the guide.

3

RAÚL was waiting for her back at the house. The fat *hacendado* she did not like, Paco Carranza, was with him. In the garden were armed men she had never seen before.

She was surprised to see them. "I thought the rule was, Never on Sunday. Isn't this your day for the Camino Real?"

Carranza laughed and popped a chunk of chorizo into his mouth.

Raúl looked strained. "Something has come up. I need to talk to you about it."

They went into the music room, so called in honor of the baby grand she had never learned to play.

"Things are moving faster than I anticipated," Raúl explained when he had closed the door. "We must be ready for all contingencies. I need you to go to Harry again."

"Why?"

"I think Harry is having second thoughts about our project. There are many people in Washington who cannot think beyond the status quo, in any situation. In Mexico or in China. The State Department. Even CIA. Harry has agreed to meet Paz Gallardo. There is talk of a new bailout of American loans in return for certain guarantees about human rights. The bankers are scared, and

Harry's business friends in the Sunbelt are hurting. They are trying to prop up a house whose foundations have collapsed. We need to keep reminding Harry that he has a better option."

"What do you want me to do?"

"Talk to him. The meeting with Paz will be held in Aspen. You told me you like Aspen. You can go skiing."

"Talk to him?" Shelley saw Raúl's mouth tighten.

"I think Harry misses you."

"I think you're a bastard."

"You're a clever woman, Shelley." His smile was too perfect. She knew she had stung him. "You know there is much more at stake here than . . ."

"Constancy?" It was Shelley's turn to smile. "It may be a Mexican custom for old buddies to share their women. But you don't own me, Raúl. I can walk out of here tomorrow and never look back. If you really want me to do this, you better give me some reasons."

"I'll give you a hundred thousand dollars."

The color rose in her cheeks. "You think you can buy *anything*, don't you?"

"I can buy a great many women for a great deal less."

Shelley paused, measuring the situation. Should she treat Raúl's remark as an insult, or a tribute? "I want the money up front, no conditions. Harry may not be missing me as much as you imagine."

"Agreed."

Raúl actually shook hands with her, as if they were concluding a routine business transaction. There were less pleasant names for it, Shelley knew. But nobody used them when the price was a hundred thousand dollars, and the john was the President of the United States.

4

MONEY makes some things easier. Shelley flew into Aspen's pocket-handkerchief airport in Raúl's private plane. The peaks shone like crystal under a flawless cerulean blue. A Range Rover was waiting, with a female driver dressed in a hip-hugging jumpsuit and wraparound shades. Her tiny waist gave Shelley just the faintest twinge of jealousy. The girl described herself as "a friend of Pete's," otherwise she didn't talk much on the drive across town. The Range Rover was fitted out with a miniaturized TV, a fax machine, and walnut drink holders.

Shelley knew Pete Conigliaro only vaguely. He was a Beverly Hills realtor, in with the Hollywood crowd, a little flashy for her taste. Raúl described him as a business partner and a particular friend of Paco Carranza, who spent a lot of time on the West Coast. Shelley had a fair idea what that meant. Carranza shipped dope for the Colombians and the Quintero family, which made Pete, in all likelihood, at least a part-time dealer. Not exactly suitable company for a President who had vowed to win final victory in the drug wars, but then, things like that could be overlooked since Pete had been a big contributor to the Butler campaign, and his Hollywood friends added glitz.

Pete's Aspen retreat was a polyglot mansion set high up on a ledge on Red Mountain, with a breathtaking view across the sweep of Roaring Fork Valley. Nobody seemed to be stirring in the house, apart from a maid who was emptying ashtrays in the vast, high-beamed living room.

"Pete crashed after dawn," the girl informed Shelley. "Guess he'll see you tonight. We had a crowd come in from D.C. It was a wild scene."

"I can imagine." She doubted that she would be seeing much of Pete. The connections had already been made by Raúl; he never seemed to have difficulty reaching Harry Butler. The President had said he would stop by for a nightcap after his private dinner with Paz Gallardo, over at the Aspen Institute. This time, Shelley's presence would not be a surprise. According to Raúl, Harry was anxious to talk with her.

There was a circular bed in Shelley's suite, with a circular goose-down duvet. Left alone to wash up, Shelley made a careful inspection of the TV, the audio equipment, the pop art on the walls, the lamp stands, the bathroom mirrors, wondering what Raúl and his cohorts had in mind, how they planned to use her, why she had been sent here. No. She knew *why*. But how . . . and to what end?

She thought of a spy film in which the bad guys, their flash cameras ready, burst into the bedroom and photographed their target, who was screwing around with a Mata Hari type. Raúl would never be as crude as that. Or would he?

She wasn't going to let it worry her. She ate lunch at Mezzaluna, drank several glasses of champagne, and received flattering glances from several men, a reassuring sign, especially considering the competition all around her. After lunch, she dropped two thousand dollars for a high-fashion ski ensemble, and stuck out her tongue at a gaggle of animal-rights activists outside the store who objected to her sable fur.

"These furs are Russian," she told them. "Don't you know sables eat better than people over there?"

She went up on Buttermilk in the mid-afternoon and reveled in wind and speed and the joy of making decisions without premeditation.

In the evening, the house on Red Mountain was deserted except for a movie star who blew her a kiss on his way out, and a familiar troupe of government men in dark suits with walkie-talkies who came in to check things out. They found Shelley curled up with a bottle of Dom Pérignon. She had been guided to it by a series of stick-on arrows starting in her bedroom and ending at the bar. On the bottle was a note: "My house is your house."

The chimes in the hall sounded ten o'clock. The Secret Service men vanished, and the President came into the living room alone.

Harry Butler looked awful. He had lost a lot of weight; there was a gap between his neck and his collar. He wore his perennial tan, but the skin around his eyes was yellowed and puffy.

He said, "Thank you for coming," as if he had issued the invitation.

He declined the champagne and poured himself a long scotch. Then he sat down on a sofa facing Shelley. The firelight left half his face in shadow.

"How were the Mexicans?" she asked, after a dragging pause.

"Shit, I got Mexicans coming out of my ears. How can I run this damn country when all I get is Mexico? I come out of a summit meeting, and all the press want to ask is what are we doing about Mexico. I announce a plan that will save our Social Security system, and the same goddamn reporters want to know how we're gonna pay for these wetbacks."

She let him talk, a monologue fueled by another jolt of whiskey, a stiffer one.

He complained about Paz Gallardo, who seemed to be asking the United States to finance a Marshall Plan for Mexico, as if he had never heard of the U.S. deficit.

After a while, he said, "I wish we could just sit a while and relax, Shelley. Like the old days."

"So do I." She rearranged herself on the sofa. For the first time, he let his eyes drop below her neck, then looked quickly away.

"There's something I have to talk to you about."

"I'm here, Harry."

"Raúl is really on my case. I feel throttled. When Raúl first came to me with this . . . this Safari Project, I told him he was out of his mind. But I said I'd cover for him, up to a point, because we go back a long way. Now I'm very much afraid the shit's gonna hit the fan, and I don't plan to be anywhere close if it does."

"He won't be happy to hear that."

"It's not my job to keep Raúl Carvajal happy. He's got you, hasn't he?" The President looked wistful for a moment.

"He doesn't own me, Harry. Right now, there's nowhere I'd rather be than right here with you."

The President didn't know how to respond. He made himself another drink. Butler held his liquor well, and Shelley had only rarely seen him turn violent, or mopey, after too much whiskey. She had heard, however, that recently his mood swings had become sudden and unpredictable.

Tonight his tiredness seemed to be edged with anger. "You understand what Raúl is trying to do, don't you?" He was on his feet, glass in hand, pacing in front of the fire. "He wants to break up a whole goddamn country and set up his own fucking state!"

"It's been done before."

"Yeah. And what did the world get? Bangladesh! Or how about Azerbaijan? Or Biafra? That was a great one."

"Mexico is collapsing under its own rotten weight. It's a seismic event. Raúl didn't invent the problem." Shelley paused to congratulate herself. She had learned well.

They had debated like this in the old days, in Washington, when Senator Butler had relied on her—more than all his staffers—as a faithful sounding board. The familiarity of the moment, and perhaps the stream of Chivas Regal, made him relax. Soon he was sitting next to her on the sofa, unselfconsciously touching her hand as he talked. She massaged his neck, as she used to do.

"God, I'm so tired," he groaned. "If only . . ."

"You want to take a shower?"

It had been one of his favorite things: to hold her close to him under the hard spray, their bodies slippery with soap, the rest of the world obscured by steam. The promise of sex was not always fulfilled. It was the intimacy that he needed. Shelley suspected that this kind of intimacy, skin to skin, was something the President never found with Ann Travis Butler.

The President tensed, shifting his body away from Shelley.

"Nobody's going to see us," she said. "Nothing's going to happen unless you make it."

"Oh, Lord, I wish . . ."

Shelley got up. She announced that *she* needed a hot shower, because she'd been using some muscles she'd forgotten about out on the Buttermilk ski slopes. He could join her if he liked, and that was the full extent of the invitation.

She had been running the shower for at least five minutes before he came into the bathroom. He was as coy, to begin with, as a young boy. When he stepped into the stall he even covered himself with his hands. Shelley gradually worked the shyness out of him. She gave him the soap, and guided his hand, then tussled him for it, touching every part of his body. She drew his face down to her lips, to the valley between her breasts. When he became aroused, he still said, "I'm sorry."

He said it again on the goose-down duvet, when he rolled away from her, leaving both of them unsatisfied. "I must be overtired. Too many drinks. Too many bureaucrats."

She smoothed his hurt away. She cradled him, rocked him, crooned a wordless lullaby over him. She gave the President what he needed, wondering all the while who was watching.

AFTER lovemaking, the President seemed more rejuvenated than tired.

"Why don't you come back to Washington?" he asked Shelley. "I can find you a job someplace. How about State Department protocol? I'll talk to Jim."

"I don't think the First Lady would go for it, Harry. And I seem to remember you telling me once we couldn't trust ourselves if we lived in the same town."

"That's water under the bridge. I want you where we can be together. Just to talk would be fine. And I want you away from Raúl. He's bad for both of us."

"Isn't he supposed to be your oldest friend?"

"I don't know who he is. He's been pushing me too hard. We were close once, but I'm not a college senior on an allowance anymore. I'm the President of the greatest country on earth. And I'm going to do the right thing, whether it's what Raúl wants or not."

"I'm never sure I know what you mean when you say that, Harry."

"I talked to Paz. He seems to be on the level. He gave me his solemn word he won't enter into any deals with the Japanese that will harm American interests. And he promised to clean out the snakepit in Mexico City."

"And you believe him?"

"I do."

"Sounds pretty thin to me."

"Look, when a frog's in a pan of water, he can boil or he can jump. Paz is gonna jump. And he's jumping the right way. You know this guy Miliano Rojas? The liberals in Congress think he's the best thing since sliced bread. Well, Paz told me he's going to sit down with Miliano and cut a deal. Some kind of national coalition. I think he's sincere. I told him we'd back him all the way, if he delivers."

Butler suddenly seemed to remember where he was and to whom he was speaking. Then he realized the extent of his indiscretion: "I wouldn't want you talking about this to Raúl."

"He doesn't own me, Harry."

THE next day Shelley recounted her pillow talk, word for word, to Raúl. She was surprised that she got less pleasure from the betrayal than from Raúl's anger, which was extreme.

Shelley did not bring Raúl the film from the videocamera which had been concealed in the bedside lamp in the room in Aspen. That was flown down on a private plane, hand-delivered by one of Raúl's employees.

Raúl understood perfectly that the Safari Project had reached another crossroads. Urgent measures were required to abort a possible deal between the Mexican government and Miliano—and to raise the pressure on Harry Butler a notch or two higher.

The instruments were at hand. Sanchez was in position, stationed at Miliano's elbow. And there was the videotape of President Butler having sex, very limply, with a woman who was not his wife.

The Mexican dispatched an envoy to Sanchez, with a coded message whose content was extremely simple. If Miliano entered into any deals with the government, he was to be terminated.

TWENTY-ONE

☐ ☐ ☐

1

MILIANO came to the city of Dolores Hidalgo. He came to the high, sun-baked terrace in front of the famous church where Father Hidalgo had raised his cry for Mexican independence. He looked out over a sea of faces, filling the shady alameda below, jamming the windows of the posada. Faces full of hope. The people wanted to touch him, as if he were a miracle worker, or a holy relic from the deserted church behind him. His bodyguards held them back.

More than a hundred armed men traveled with him now. They were all volunteers, tough men from the ranches and *ejidos* of Chihuahua and Durango. Sun-bronzed faces, black mustaches, here and there a bright bandanna. They knew how to use their weapons. The new man, Rico Sanchez, had worked them hour after hour, shooting at cans and bottles. With his army training, he had licked some of the wildness out of the steer-ropers and charros who rode shotgun on Miliano's odd convoy of asthmatic buses, farm trucks and pickups, and Volkswagen beetles. Rico, because of his U.S. background, was also living proof that Miliano's cause had spread even beyond the border. Miliano was glad to have him.

THE gringo reporter was squatting on the stone head of a feathered serpent, installed in front of the church by a government embarrassed by the Christian symbolism of the most important shrine of Mexican independence. The gringo was taking photographs. He lined up four or five of the most colorful members of Miliano's escort in one frame. The cocky, swaggering fellow nearest the camera could have been Pancho Villa's brother.

Villa had had his John Reed. Miliano had Joe Cicero.

Miliano had been followed around by flocks of U.S. reporters in the early days of his movement. Then they had dropped away. Mexico had become last week's story. The press corps had gladly fled from *turista*, back-country roads and unspeakable doss houses to trouble spots with five-star hotels.

Joe Cicero had stayed on. He had decided that he liked Miliano, and the feeling must have been mutual, because Joe Cicero was the only foreign pressman who had been included in this surprise jaunt through the old Spanish towns of the *Bajío*. Something was definitely up. Joe could smell it. Miliano's itinerary was being kept very tight; the newsman felt sure this wasn't just because of fears of another assassination attempt.

Cicero had tried to pump Rico Sanchez. "Can you tell me where we're heading?"

"*Ni modo*. No way."

When Joe had persisted, Sanchez's lips disappeared. "Mind your own fucking business."

Joe Cicero didn't care for the bullethead chicano with the dayround shades. Sanchez reminded him of shadow warriors he had brushed up against in Honduras, at one of the contra camps. And in Vietnam back in the heyday of the Phoenix program. And in shady bars from Kinshasa to Rosslyn, Virginia. Rico Sanchez had Agency written over him in Day-Glo colors, Joe thought. He wondered how on earth the CIA had managed to con Miliano into putting an obvious spook on his team.

He had even asked Miliano, in a quiet moment on the campaign bus on the road from Querétaro, "Don't you think there's something funny about Rico Sanchez?"

"I know what you're saying." Miliano looked at him

warily. "Don't worry about it. Sanchez is a professional. Such men resemble each other. But Rico is playing on my team."

"I'm glad to hear it. Will you tell me what's on the rest of the tour?"

"Who knows? Maybe Mexico City. Be patient, Joe. I won't disappoint you. When we reach Guanajuato, you will see. You'll get your story, all across page one. When the time is ripe."

This had not relieved Joe's confusion. But the happy word *exclusive* began to dance in his head. So long as no other U.S. reporters showed up. Cicero was suddenly thankful for the treacherous mountain roads, and the fact that the nearest commercial airport was at León, a good two hours' drive away.

THE crowd in Dolores Hidalgo was especially enthusiastic.

"Miliano! Miliano!" they shouted.

"Miliano—*al poder!*"

Miliano raised his hand, and the clamor of the crowd fell away. He spoke to their wounds, to their fears. He told them of the crooks in Mexico City who were selling off their birthright to foreign corporations. He talked of starving in the ruins of their homes while the government stole the food and money the outside world had rushed to their relief.

Miliano's voice shook with emotion, but his voice was thinner than usual. He seemed deathly tired, almost somber.

He spoke of looming catastrophe, of the shadow of a civil war that would set father against son, brother against brother. Of a Mexico in flames.

The hotheads in the audience misinterpreted his language.

They called for the war he was begging them to avoid.

They called for blood.

"Muerto al PRI! Death to the PRI! Death to the assassins! Death to the robbers who steal bread from the mouths of our children!"

2

In the late sun, Miliano's cavalcade wound down Route 110, into the shadowed valley of Guanajuato, the city of the buried river. As was his wont, Miliano made camp in a *colonia* of the poor, upon a hillside overlooking the spires and narrow, crooked streets of the Spanish colonial town.

Joe Cicero went downtown in search of a drink, a shower, and a bed without bugs. He found all three at the Posada Santa Fe, the old hotel on the Jardín Unión that had once been home to the Prussian consul. He relaxed at the sidewalk café, sipping beer and watching the strikingly pretty doe-eyed Spanish girls making their ritual *paseo* around the tiny triangular plaza, while ten-year-old mariachis plied the table.

He was outside again in the morning, getting a shoe shine, when he saw Rico Sanchez come out of the hotel. Sanchez made a sharp right, and walked briskly down toward the Four Frogs restaurant, moving, Cicero thought, as if he had a date.

Tipping the shoe-shine man, the reporter took off after Sanchez, one shoe mirror-bright, the other still scuffed.

There were cars parked at the curb, and roving taxis, but Sanchez took neither. He marched down the narrow street. Cutting and ducking, Cicero shadowed his mark up the steep street that led past the former Jesuit college and the university. The cobbled road narrowed so sharply that the sidewalk vanished and Joe had to flatten himself against a wall to avoid the car that came barreling through behind him. He thought he had lost Sanchez, but when he rounded the bend, he spotted him passing an old house that proved to be the birthplace of Diego Rivera.

Now the path was downhill. The reporter held back, nervous of being spotted. He saw Sanchez hurry down into bustling Calle Hidalgo, stopping in front of a restaurant that advertised *comida económica*. Its name belonged in one of those South American works of magical realism that Joe Cicero found unreadable: La Gallina Aristotélica.

In front of the Aristotelian Hen, Sanchez boarded a taxi.

Cicero looked about frantically for another taxi, but there were none in sight. He trailed along Hidalgo after the cab, wondering what Sanchez was up to. A break came when the taxi was stalled in traffic and Joe spotted another one idling in front of the grand façade of the Mercado Hidalgo.

"*Siga, no más,*" Cicero instructed the driver.

They rattled up a sharp ascent.

"What is this street?"

"Calzada del Panteón." The driver swiveled around to expose an imperfect set of teeth, stained tobacco-brown. "Where five go up and four go down."

"Excuse me?"

The driver laughed. "Four on their legs. One on their backs. In a coffin."

This response left Cicero totally mystified. And distinctly uneasy.

"You go to see *las momias,* no? This road only goes to the mummies."

His meaning only became clear to Cicero half a mile on, beyond a few meager hill farms where goats foraged among the rocks and chickens straggled across the road.

The end of the road was a parking lot in front of a building tunneled into the hillside. There were a few touristy gift shops off to one side. All but one were shuttered.

"Está temprano," the driver observed. "It's early."

There were only two other cars in the lot: the taxi Sanchez had arrived in, and a black Ford LTD. The initials DF were on the plates. *Distrito Federal.* Mexico City. A thickset man in a suit stood by the LTD, puffing on a cigarette and giving Cicero the once-over.

Joe Cicero draped his camera strap around his neck. Thank God for the camera. A gringo with a camera had natural cover.

The sign over the main building read Museo de Momias. Museum of the Mummies.

Cicero told his driver to wait and strolled over to the entrance. A heavyset Mexican in a dark suit who looked like the twin of the hood in the parking lot emerged from behind the turnstiles and told Cicero in Spanish that the museum was closed.

Playing the tourist, Cicero pretended not to understand.

He started pushing through the stile, flourishing a five-dollar bill.

A powerful hand closed, viselike, over his forearm.

The Mexican banged his other fist against a wall sign with the heading, "Horario." Opening time was 10 A.M. Cicero glanced at his watch. It was barely 9:20.

"Okay?" said the man.

"Okay," Cicero agreed.

FAUSTO García enjoyed the mummies of Guanajuato. The museum—a considerable domestic tourist attraction in a country that revels in the rituals of death—was attached to the municipal cemetery. The singular dryness of the air in these mountains, assisted by the vapors of the earth, had the effect of mummifying the corpses laid to rest in the graveyard, without the aid of naphtha or other embalmers' solutions. The cemetery was grossly overcrowded, and the poor could not afford the price of a permanent grave. When it became necessary to create room for new burials, older corpses were exhumed. The grislier specimens were placed here, in the Museo de Momias, to feed the inexhaustible public appetite for the macabre.

"As a people," Fausto remarked, "we are better prepared to face death than to cope with life. That is the problem of Mexico."

He strolled the narrow rooms, hands clasped behind his back, with Rico Sanchez in tow, pointing out favorite exhibits.

The mummies stood erect, their skin creased and yellowed like parchment, their hands folded across their rib cages, as their relative—or the undertakers—had arranged them. Their jaws hung open, the triumph of bone over rotted flesh. The cause of death, in many cases, was startlingly obvious. Here was a woman killed by cancer of the stomach. The tumor swelled out of her shrunken body like a monstrous gourd. Here was a man with a gaping hole in his chest, hacked out by a knife. Here a Chinaman, with the mark of the strangler's garotte around his throat.

Fausto walked past the child mummies without comment. The bodies of the infants were decked out like porcelain dolls.

He paused in front of an elderly woman who had her right arm raised in front of her face. Her eyes were wide. She seemed to be trying to gnaw through her wrist. Her face—her whole contorted body—was a soundless scream.

"This one was buried alive," Fausto reported. "She suffered, I believe, from what the physicians call catalepsy. After her last attack, she displayed no signs of bodily life—no pulse, no breathing—for twenty-four hours. So they put her in the ground. You see what she woke into. One begins to understand the character in Poe's story who is obsessed with the fear of being buried alive. As I recall, his fear was self-fulfilling."

Rico Sanchez said nothing. His eyes were hidden. He

examined everything in the murky room through his dark glasses.

"We are agreed then," said Fausto. "Your man will arrive at five precisely. Naturally, the streets will be secured. You may bring six men."

"It is not enough," Sanchez protested. "Miliano's people will never allow it."

"It is sufficient," Fausto said firmly. "Here are the passes." He produced a thin sheaf of official forms, each bearing the presidential seal. "Miliano will accept it."

"Miliano is too trusting."

Fausto looked at him quizzically. "I trust you're not getting too fond of your Miliano."

Sanchez shrugged. "He is *un hombre recto*. An honest man. I have not encountered many."

"I never expected to find you sentimental, Rico."

Sanchez waited. A vein throbbed, pulsing like a trapped serpent, burrowing along the edge of his forehead.

"Six men for the escort," Fausto specified again. "And you, Rico. You and two others may enter the Alhóndiga. The others will remain outside."

"I don't like it."

"It is how it will be. Look, you can bring some of Miliano's supporters into the amphitheater. No more than two hundred. You know how small it is. They must come unarmed. You must make that perfectly clear. There will be searches. There must be no incidents before the meeting. Do we understand each other?"

"My job is to protect Miliano. I cannot be seen to fail in that."

"I understand you. And my job is to protect the President of the Republic. Would you ask me to shirk my duty?" Fausto patted Sanchez on the shoulder. "Come. We both have work to do, among the living. It will be a great day."

* * *

Fausto left the museum first. He noticed the second taxi, and the sloppy-looking gringo who was haggling with a concessionaire over the price of his knickknacks.

Fausto thought nothing of it. Guanajuato was slightly off the beaten track for *yanqui* tourists, but there was a sizable resident population of expatriates, and many foreign students at the university—and a growing number of Americans who had realized that there was more to see in Mexico than Acapulco and Cancún and the border dives.

But as he got into his car, Fausto saw the tourist taking his photograph. He snapped his fingers. One of his men jumped out, sprinted across the parking lot, and made a grab for Joe Cicero's camera.

Joe had been obliged to give up many things in life— a wife, an apartment. However, he drew the line at that camera.

He was still struggling when Fausto breezed over, slipped the strap up over his head, and neatly ejected the film.

"My apologies," Fausto said to the reporter, as he returned the camera. "Perhaps you will permit me to compensate you for your film." He produced a roll of bills.

"I want to know who the hell you think you are," Cicero erupted, ignoring the money.

"Just one of the natives. Perhaps your travel agent did not tell you, Mr.—ah—"

"Cicero."

"Cicero. A name that carries responsibilities! Surely a man called Cicero can understand that it is highly discourteous to photograph the natives without asking their permission."

Joe coughed up a feeble excuse, something about wanting to photograph the entrance to the museum, but Fausto was not interested in prolonging the discussion. As he walked quickly back to his car, he did, however, make a mental note of the number of Cicero's taxi.

3

JOE Cicero rode the taxi back through town and up to the hillside *colonia* where Miliano had spent the night. He found him in a circle of campesinos, doing something rare for a politician—listening instead of talking. As the people told him of their hardship, Miliano jotted notes in a little spiral-bound notebook.

Joe joined the group, and after a few minutes, slipped Miliano a note: "We have to talk."

Eventually, when Miliano excused himself to answer a call of nature, Joe Cicero followed him out. He told Miliano about Sanchez, and his secret meeting with a man from the capital, a man with bodyguards, who was scared of being photographed. He was, Joe told him, obviously a man from the government.

"I fear for you, Miliano."

"I am grateful for your concern, Joe. But I think you worry too much. You see plots everywhere. I know about this meeting. Rico Sanchez was acting under my instructions."

"Will you level with me, Miliano? Will you tell me what the fuck is going on?"

"At five in the afternoon, you will come to the Alhóndiga."

"The what?"

"Ask anyone. It is the most famous building in Guanajuato. It is our Bastille. It is also the place where the Spanish governor displayed the head of Father Hidalgo, and other heroes of independence, when they fell into the hands of his soldiers. They hung the heads at the four corners of the Alhóndiga, in wooden cages. They hung there for years, until they were skulls."

"Charming. May I ask why you are going there?"

"There will be a meeting. I believe we will make a peace."

"With the government?"

"With the government."

"There are a lot of your supporters who won't like it. They'll say you are selling out."

"I know. I tried to explain to them in front of Father Hidalgo's church. I am going to make a peace that will respect the rights of the people."

"With Paz Gallardo."

"He is my President."

"Can you trust him?"

"I believe so. There have been certain discussions—I regret it was impossible to tell you anything of this, Joe. I think that Paz Gallardo is not a man of violence. He is not a Ramírez. I know there are many people in my camp, and in his, who will fight this agreement. Paz must deal with the PRI in his own way. I must try to reassure those who have risked everything in this struggle that I am still their defender. I know only one way to do that."

"Which is?"

"To give myself as a hostage."

Cicero's heart skipped a beat. The images of the morning—the museum, the hoods with the black LTD, the place of severed heads—streamed together.

Miliano laughed at his expression. "It is not as bad as you think. I am going to join the government. I know, I know. You are right. There are some who will say I sold myself. I will prove them wrong. I will do something that has never been accomplished in Mexico. I will make the Ministry of Agrarian Reform live up to its name. If the *dinos* try to stop me, my protest will carry to all of the thirty-three states of Mexico. And these troubles in the north—the kidnappings, the murders—these are not our people, and they are not of the government. Something is afoot there which must be stopped. We can do that only through unity, through strength."

Miliano stopped abruptly. He glanced around, taking

in the peasants who stood waiting at a respectful distance, the bodyguards who stood watch along the road, at the edge of a vertiginous drop to the valley where the city backed up against the mountains.

"After five," he said sternly to Cicero, "you may write these things. Until then, you are voiceless. *Me entiende?*"

"Yes," Joe Cicero agreed. "I understand you."

"You will not be permitted to enter the Alhóndiga. But after the meeting, there will be a ceremony. There is a small outdoor auditorium. You will see."

"Will the Mexican press be there?" Joe was less nervous now about Miliano's safety than about his exclusive.

"No reporters," said Miliano. "That is part of our arrangement. But Paz Gallardo will bring his publicity men, and his photographers. So I can bring mine."

He fished in his pockets and produced a card with the logo of the Frente Nacional de Campesinos.

He borrowed Cicero's felt pen, and scribbled his name in the blank space. He added the phrase *"Servicio de Relaciones Publicas,"* and handed the card to the reporter.

"Now, my friend, you are *legítimo*. How do you say that in American?"

"I think the word is kosher."

4

Miliano was the first to arrive at the Alhóndiga, anxious for the meeting that would spare his country from civil war and *yanqui* invasion. The streets around the huge square building had been cordoned off by policemen and soldiers. Paratroops of the Presidential Guard walked the roof of the Alhóndiga itself. It was strange to recall that this building had been constructed by the Spaniards for a modest purpose, to store grain and flour. Inside, it was grand enough for a viceregal palace. Double galleries overlooked a tiled courtyard, open to the sun and wind. Now the place was a museum. Miliano walked up the stairs, under elongated frescoes of bleeding heroes and flying skeletons. Rico Sanchez walked behind him, counting the guards on the rooftop, checking that his own guards—one above, one below, outside the Recinto de los Héroes, where the meeting would take place— were alert.

Miliano's eyes slid over the swords and uniforms of dead armies, the photographs of the flood of 1905 that had turned the Jardín Unión into a drowning pool. He lingered in a narrow room that contained a few pre-Columbian artifacts. He studied the inch-high letters of a placard on the wall. His lips moved as he recited them silently. Then he read them out loud.

> Solo venimos a dormir,
> solo venimos a soñar.
> No es verdad, no es verdad
> que venimos a vivir en la tierra.

> We only come to sleep,
> we only come to dream.
> It is not true, it is not true
> that we come to live on the earth.

The author was anonymous. The attribution said simply, *Poesía indígena*. Native poetry.

Miliano said to Sanchez, "Is that not extraordinary? For a simple people, a people who live so close to this earth, to grasp so clearly that man is here for a higher purpose. To quest higher, always higher. To dream. Look how they say it twice. *No es verdad. No es verdad.* The wisdom of these people! It is the hope of our country! The *ricos,* in their palaces, they do not know these things."

Rico Sanchez said nothing, nor did his face hint at a

response, his eyes rendered expressionless behind the green-black lenses of his glasses.

They heard a noise from outside, as of a swarm of bees.

Rico Sanchez walked out among the columns. Miliano followed. Overhead, they saw four Bell helicopters, flying in tight formation. Three of them were painted in the colors of Mexico—green, white, and red. The fourth was khaki.

President Paz had flown from the capital to the private airfield at Silao, on the road to León. Now he was coming by chopper to the soccer field at Campo Nieto Piñar.

Miliano said, "It begins."

THE meeting between Rafael Paz Gallardo, the chosen son of the PRI, and the man the PRI most feared took place behind closed doors, in a room that resembled a shrine. A solitary candle burned in front of the greenish copper head of Father Hidalgo, suspended on a wall. Hidalgo's hair streamed off his head. His lips were pursed. The copper head of Father Morelos hung in the connecting room to the right; that of Captain Ignacio Allende in the room on the left. All heroes of the struggle for independence; all butchered and beheaded.

Paz Gallardo and Miliano sat alone, facing each other, on straight-backed chairs brought in for the occasion.

The general terms of their agreement had been settled by intermediaries, but Miliano had to be sure. He ran, point by point, through his list of conditions. It closely followed the public program of the Frente Nacional de Campesinos.

The collective farms would be defended. The lands stolen under the existing government would be restored. The government would provide money for irrigation, for schools, for medical assistance. The mines that had been sold off to private interests and foreigners would be reclaimed by the state. There would be cast-iron guarantees that the national patrimony—the oil fields, the beach resorts, the earth itself—would be reserved for the people of Mexico.

An independent investigator would be appointed to inquire into the assassination of Moctezuma Morelos.

Paz Gallardo pinched the bridge of his nose between his thumb and his forefinger. He felt a migraine coming on, and Miliano's list was very long.

"Enough!" said the President. "Do you realize how many men would be willing to kill both of us to prevent this agreement from being consummated?"

The door to the Ignacio Allende room swung open. Paz Gallardo turned, in annoyance, to identify the source of this interruption.

A man in dark glasses stood in the doorway. The silencer attached to his 9mm automatic, distorting the instrument's sleek lines, added to the men's immediate sense of disorientation.

Miliano, half-rising, said, "Sanchez!"

Rico Sanchez squeezed the trigger once. He was an excellent marksman. Any more shots would have been purely for show.

5

JOE Cicero was bored with hanging about in the little outdoor auditorium below the Alhóndiga. Every seat was taken—the front rows occupied by local notables, the bleachers at the back filled with Miliano's people. Some of the campesinos had come in their work clothes, but mostly they were rigged out in their Sunday best. The soldiers weren't letting any more through the checkpoints, but beyond the wire fence, there were thousands of them, passing around *gaseosas,* trying to quiet squalling babies, or just squatting, waiting for something to happen.

Joe Cicero walked up the road, past the auditorium entrance to the corner of the skinny Calle Mendízabal, which fell down the slope to the town's main street and the Mercado Hidalgo on the far side. The market had been closed on government orders, but a few persistent vendors sat outside, with little displays of purple cactus fruit—*tuna*—or cool, peppery slices of jicama root in paper cups.

A dog growled at Cicero from the flat roof of the house on his left. Orange flowers spilled over its whitewashed walls. Almost too pretty, Cicero thought. He took off his lens cap and checked his exposure.

He dropped the camera when he heard the first shots. It bounced against his chest, supported by the strap around his neck. A sharp burst from a single automatic was followed by the sputter of machine-gun fire, the crack of rifles, the yells of *"Asesinos!"*

The guards on the roof were shooting down into the courtyard of the Alhóndiga. Uniformed men were running in all directions. Cicero started moving toward the steps of the main entrance, but backed off when he heard the click as one of the soldiers on guard released his safety catch.

He found himself stumbling down Calle Mendízabal, in front of a student hostel. He had no clear idea of what he was doing.

He thought, the bastards did it; they killed Miliano.

He studied the back side of the colonial granary. Maybe there was a way in. Maybe he could get inside, and get the evidence to disprove whatever lies the government would tell the public. He still had his camera.

It was madness, of course. There was a balcony, above Calle Mendízabal, but it was blocked by soldiers in olive drab. The doors around the corner must be bolted from the inside.

Wait. One of them was opening.

Joe Cicero stumbled back, into the pool of shadow under the sign of the student hostel. A man in dark glasses slipped out of the Alhóndiga and started walking downhill, without evident haste.

Rico Sanchez.

Cicero looked at the men on the roof. Didn't they see Sanchez? What was going on?

"Hey!" Cicero tried to shout, but all that came out was a dry croak.

He aimed his camera at Sanchez's retreating back and tried again. "Hey!" he shouted.

One of the guards on the roof craned around. His rifle cracked, and a puff of dust came out of the wall next to Cicero's cheek.

Hell. They were shooting at *him*.

He darted across the street, hugging the wall beside the Escuela Luís Obregón, where he was out of the line of fire.

Sanchez was running now, past the lime-green façade of Local 54 of the Miners' Union. Cicero ran after him.

Sanchez slid between the parked military trucks on Hidalgo.

Where had he gone?

Breathless—too confused even to wonder what had happened to the security men he had seen posted earlier at the bottom of this street—Cicero stared around. He saw the solid faces of the women selling cactus fruit, the cast-iron brackets of the lamps that flanked the massive portico of the Mercado Hidalgo, the shuttered doors. Sanchez was not there.

Behind him, the shooting had not stopped. Women's voices keened above the bullets.

He glanced up and down the Calle Hidalgo. Nothing.

Then he saw the steps leading down under the market. He hurled himself down them, losing his balance. His heels clattered, then went skating. He broke his fall by grabbing the stone balustrade.

The air down there, in the underground street, was fetid. It carried the breath of sewage, the revenge of the buried river.

Cicero heard, as if close at hand, the clatter of running feet. The sound was echoed and magnified by the stone walls.

He panted after it. Ahead he saw Sanchez, running where the street widened and sunlight fell through a hole above. There was a parked car waiting for him, with its lights on and the engine idling. A black LTD. It looked like the car Joe Cicero had seen outside the Museo de Momias, except the plates were local: GTO in place of DF.

Sanchez did not even look back. He jumped into the back seat, and the car immediately pulled away, accelerating before Sanchez could even close the car door.

Cicero thudded after it, following until it squealed right into the Tunel de los Angeles. Straining for air, he admitted defeat and crawled up the nearest flight of steps.

The sign read *Callejón de Besos,* Little Street of Kisses.

Joe couldn't make it. His calf muscles seized up, his stomach mutinied. He folded onto a middle step, and his lunch bubbled between his knees.

It took him twenty minutes more to haul himself back to the Posada Santa Fe, where he would be able to dial long-distance direct.

His first call was to the American Embassy in Mexico City.

"Get me Kreeger."

He listened to the clicks and crackling on the line until a cool female voice said, "May I tell him who's calling?"

"Yeah. Tell him it's Joe. And it's big."

She put him on hold.

She came back and said, in a satisfied way, "Mr. Kreeger is not available."

"Listen, tell him I'm doing him a favor. We're talking assassination here."

"Where are you calling from?"

"I don't know if you'll be able to call me back. I've been shot at already."

"Hold the line, please."

Kreeger came on. "I'm listening."

"They got Miliano."

"Who's 'they'?"

"A guy called Rico Sanchez. I got a nice photo of his rear end."

"Uh-huh."

"Jim, I gotta know. Was he one of yours?"

"No."

"But you'd say the same if he was, right?"

"Don't lose your cool, Joe. Hang in there."

"You're telling me to hang in there? The same guys that nailed Miliano are on my case. Bye, Jim. I gotta file my story."

"Just a second, Joe. How do you know they got Miliano?"

"What do you mean?"

"All I'm saying is, you better check it out before you file your story. You might look pretty silly otherwise. And thanks, Joe."

"Yeah."

Joe Cicero pressed his forehead against the cool surface of the telephone box. The throbbing was intense. It felt as if someone was exploring his frontal lobe with a Black & Decker drill.

JIM Kreeger did not feel much better. When he hung up, he looked at the case officers who were sitting in his room—Lois, Eddie, and George Camacho.

He said, "That was a reporter I know. We owe each other a drink or two. He says Miliano got hit in Guanajuato. I guess he got it wrong."

This last statement was directed at George.

The liaison officer said, "They're bringing Miliano to Mexico City in leg fetters. If he survives the trip."

"You're sure we got this right, George?"

"Fausto's deputy made the call. He was pretty emotional. Why would he lie about something like this?"

"I agree with you," said Kreeger.

Ten minutes before Joe Cicero's call, the Station had received word from the deputy director of SIN, through official channels, that President Paz Gallardo had been assassinated in Guanajuato. Miliano had been arrested as the intellectual author of the crime, although it was unclear who had actually pulled the trigger.

"My reporter friend may have given us something," Kreeger continued. "He says a guy called Rico Sanchez was involved. Does that name mean anything to any of you?"

Eddie and Lois shook their heads.

George Camacho frowned. He knew the name, but could not yet summon the images.

"By the way, where's Fausto?" Kreeger added at once, "No, don't tell me."

They said it almost in unison. "He's in Guanajuato." Protecting President Paz.

TWENTY-TWO

□ □ □

1

RAÚL Carvajal was out riding when Carranza telephoned and demanded that he be found at once. Carranza was brusque and surly with Shelley, something she was accustomed to. Carranza was a brute. Today, however, she detected a new note in his voice, something like fear.

She sent Felipe after Raúl. "Go toward the Cerro del Aguilar." She knew that this was where he would be—on his eagle mountain, his secret place of power.

Raúl had few words for her when he returned. He strode through the house, unsmiling, his spurs jangling as he crossed the parquet floor. He sealed himself up in his study, behind the heavy oak door.

Still she was able to hear his rough shout, a strangled cry of either anger or disbelief. Then she heard a heavy fall, so sharp that it rattled the floor lamp at her left hand. Suddenly she feared for him.

She ran to the study door; it was not locked.

Inside, Raúl had knocked over the heavy lectern in front of the bay window, the one that held the Carvajal family Bible. Foxed, watermarked pages had torn loose from the binding and lay scattered about the floor. Raúl did not seem even to have noticed this sacrilege. He was still on the telephone.

Shelley bent to pick up the Bible, its loose pages.

"Get out!"

She began to ask him what was wrong.

He yelled at her, "Get out! Get away from me!"

She would have stood her ground, but his voice contained a menace she had never heard before, more animal than human, like something trapped, all fury and fear. His eyes, too, were those of an animal with no place to flee, a thing of teeth and claws.

As she closed the door, she heard him say, "He killed the wrong man."

2

AT the inn on the Jardín Unión, in Guanajuato, Joe Cicero was also working the phone when he learned, from the shouts outside his window, that he had indeed gotten the story wrong. The man who had been shot inside the Alhóndiga was not Miliano. It was President Paz.

Cicero was possessed by an overwhelming sense of disorientation.

He wrestled his way through the narrow, crowded streets, back to the scene of the shooting. He had to find out about Miliano, and about Sanchez.

The whole area around the Alhóndiga had been sealed tight. An edgy soldier jabbed his rifle in Cicero's guts when he demanded to see the officer in charge. The reporter called to a dark suit behind the cordon, "Where is Miliano Rojas?"

The suit pointed upward. Joe Cicero craned his neck and saw a flight of helicopters, headed east. The authorities had wasted no time getting Miliano away from Guanajuato—and away from his caravan of supporters. They must be taking him to the capital, Joe thought. He resolved to follow him there, to confront Kreeger, to get some answers.

He looked for familiar faces on the street, for men from the Frente Nacional de Campesinos. Some of the organizers had been arrested. Only a few hundred of

Miliano's followers were still milling around downtown. They seemed dazed.

Joe Cicero walked among them, demanding *"Qué pasó?"*

An old man with wrinkled, sun-blackened skin gave him an answer. The *policía* said that Miliano's bodyguards had murdered President Paz, that Miliano would have to stand trial. Knowing this had to be a lie, Miliano's followers had tried to break through the lines of soldiers, to reclaim their leader. There had been fighting. Some were killed. Then the President's men had come out the main door of the Alhóndiga, holding up the corpse of President Paz for all to see.

This death was a fact.

There were some who had applauded, who had shouted that the time to make the revolution was now, with Miliano at its head. They proved no match for the machine guns of the soldiers.

Joe Cicero searched for other facts. What had happened to Miliano's bodyguards, the ones who had gone with him inside the Alhóndiga? They had all been killed by the President's men, so far as anyone knew. Only Miliano had been brought from the building alive.

Cicero, of course, knew more. Did any of them know Sanchez? Had anyone seen Sanchez leave the Alhóndiga?

They could tell him nothing.

As Joe Cicero dragged himself back to the hotel, his earlier sickness returned, his stomach overwhelmed by uncommon exertion and stress, as well as too much bad food. It was at least half an hour before he was able to get on his feet, his legs still weak and rubbery.

He knew that he needed to drive to Mexico City that night. He needed to tell Kreeger all that he knew about Sanchez and the men he had seen at the mummy house, but his head was swimming, his balance was gone. He had to use both hands to hold a glass. There was no way he was going to be able to make that drive tonight.

He had half a bottle of bourbon left. Maybe a couple of drinks would help. Then he remembered he had to call in his story, which he did only sketchily, giving them the bare bones. He had trouble getting the words out. He repeated himself a few times.

"Hey, Joe," the subeditor interrupted, "you been drinking or what?"

"I'm sick, is all. You getting this stuff down? It's an exclusive. I was the only reporter on the spot."

"Yeah? Well, you're not the fastest. Cable news and wire services have already put out the Mexican government version. They say the assassination was part of a plot to pull down the government."

"I don't know. There's something more. Something I haven't got a handle on yet."

"You got something you haven't told us yet?"

"It's gut instinct."

The sub observed that Joe's gut didn't seem to be very reliable.

Cicero found the words came more easily as his anger increased. "There's an American mixed up in this." Cicero was about to give the name, but then it occurred to him that his phone might be bugged. *"I can't say any more about it."*

"An American? What kind of American? You telling me CIA, or what?"

"I can't talk on an open line."

"You playing spook down there, Joe?" Cicero's intelligence sources were a standing joke around the news bureau's headquarters. And a cause of occasional resentment, because he didn't share them.

"I got cramps. I'll call in tomorrow."

It occurred to Joe that the Sanchez thing might just turn out to be the story of a lifetime. He weighed the risks of trying to run a trace on Sanchez over a phone that might be tapped, against the possible reward of a Pulitzer.

He decided to cut the risk by dragging himself down

to the pay phone in the hotel lobby, where he used his credit card to call a number in Chevy Chase.

Joe had put out saucers of milk for his Washington sources for a good many years. They were working stiffs, the kind of people fancy reporters on the White House beat didn't bother with. These people didn't forget. The one he was calling tonight was a major in the Defense Intelligence Agency.

A female voice told him the major was out for dinner.

Joe felt his head spinning again. "Just tell him Joe called. No, I'm kinda hard to reach. Tell him I'll catch him later."

He did not make any more phone calls that night. Instead, he lay on his queen-sized bed, swathed in every blanket and covering he could find, trying to sweat the sickness out of his system.

In the morning, he felt a little stronger. Or perhaps, he acknowledged, it was just the smell of a story that was carrying him along. He decided not to waste time on the phone. He would get to Kreeger in Mexico City. He was certain he had enough to make Kreeger listen, and maybe to level with him.

When he checked out, he was told at the desk that the rental car he had ordered wasn't ready yet. The agency spun him a line about a problem with the transmission, assuring him they would have another car—a larger model, for the same rate—ready in no time.

"How long?"

"*Ahorita.*" The word meant anything you wanted it to mean.

Cicero decided it would be a smart move to take on a little ballast before hitting the road, but the sight of hotel guests digging into scrambled eggs made his stomach heave. He walked out into the Jardín Unión, past the shoeshine stands, and claimed a table with a parasol near the door of the Café del Sol.

The waiter who came seemed a bit flustered. He said something about how they didn't serve breakfast.

"You serve beer, don't you? I'll take a Carta Blanca."

The waiter vanished into the cavernous interior of the bar. A few minutes later a different man brought the beer.

It was in a fancy black bottle with gold lettering on the label, which made Joe conscious at once that it wasn't the beer he had ordered. He was going to complain about it, but changed his mind. Why not try a new brand, especially when the name was Simpático? They were probably trying to sock the gringo for a few pesos more, but what did he care about that? It would all go into the expense account. Besides, the waiter had already gone back inside.

The bottle was sealed, and it wasn't a screw-top. The man had left an opener on the table, next to the glass.

Some service, Joe thought. Well, he'd take it out of the tip.

As Joe reached for the bottle, he began to compose a toast, to the Pulitzer the Sanchez story must surely bring. He did not complete the toast, however, because as he touched the cap, the fancy black bottle blew up in his hand, exploding with such force that it left a crater in the flagstones of the terrace, and nothing of Joe Cicero that was recognizable above the waist.

3

KREEGER had spent the night at the Station, able to catch only a few minutes' sleep on the office sofa. The reports flooding in were murky and often contradictory. By one account, Miliano had been shot attempting to escape—always a distinct possibility in Mexico. Another posited that he had died in a helicopter crash. The one that proved to be true was that he had been brought to the capital in fetters and confined in a cell at the grim Reclusorio del Norte. Kreeger believed this last report only after George Camacho visited the jail and bribed the governor for a glimpse of the prisoner.

After Joe Cicero's phone call, Kreeger had sent head-quarters a cable requesting an all-sources trace on a former U.S. military officer called Sanchez, FNU, nicknamed "Rico." He had flagged this message "Immediate," which meant that a reply was expected within eight hours. He had hesitated for a moment before sending the request, because he knew it would rattle cages all over Washington. It would be circulated to every government agency —from FBI to Treasury—that had possible information on Sanchez, or any other Sanchez who fitted the vague profile, producing a probable torrent of paper. It also would alert interested parties that the Station was looking for the man.

Kreeger had a visceral aversion to this scattershot approach, but if an ex-U.S. Army officer called Sanchez had played a part in the assassination, then a lot of people must be looking for him. If so, Kreeger wanted to get to him first, and to the truth of what had happened in Guanajuato. If a U.S. citizen had been working as Miliano's security adviser, it was curious that Fausto had never mentioned the fact, let alone complained about it. And it was inconceivable to Kreeger that Fausto had simply been unaware of the existence of Rico Sanchez. It was also irritating that Kreeger had not known it.

Assuming the SIN commander did know of Sanchez, it seemed to Kreeger there were two likely explanations for Fausto's silence. Either Fausto believed that Sanchez was working for an agency of the U.S. government, or he had a private relationship with the Mexican-American. Kreeger had an uneasy feeling that, either way, it came to the same thing: Sanchez was part of a game Fausto was playing.

An assassination game? Kreeger hated even pursuing that line of thought. Fausto was capable of many things. But the murder of his own President? To what end? It did not seem possible.

Morning brought the first tide of paper from Washington: the Vietnam service record of one Enrique M. Sanchez, Customs receipts for cotton and papayas shipped by the same individual across the border, copies of end-user certificates for the legal export of arms from a warehouse in Alexandria, a bunch of old news clippings about the dirty war in El Salvador. The promise of more to come.

George Camacho came in with a steaming mug of coffee, to report that Miliano was alive and as well as could be expected, given the welts across his face and the fact that he was charged with treason and murder.

Kreeger waved a sheaf of paper at his liaison officer.

"Remember the other day I mentioned a guy named Sanchez? Well, I got more information. His name is Rico Sanchez. Mexican-American out of San Antone. Army officer in Vietnam. Does that ring any bells?"

Camacho thought for a bit. He grimaced when he made the connection. "Hell, yes, I know that SOB. I knew him in Saigon. Haven't seen him for years."

"And?"

"He had a chip on his shoulder the size of a giant redwood. You know the kind, thought the establishment was out to get guys like him. I suppose he wasn't altogether wrong. I mean, people like Sanchez got the dirty jobs in Vietnam. But he enjoyed it, too."

"Enjoyed it?"

"Oh, yeah. Some of the guys had a name for him. The Headhunter. He liked to go out at night and kill Cong, almost for sport. Sometimes he went by himself, or with a few Rangers or Montagnards from the hills. Sometimes he brought back mementos, if you catch my drift."

"I see. So Sanchez worked for the Station?"

"I could never quite figure that out. He was assigned to Army intelligence, but he was always waltzing in and out of Art Colgate's office like he owned the place. I guess he and Colgate had some deal running. It made some of us pretty nervous."

It came back to Kreeger now. In her last letter from Saigon, Val had complained about a man she described only as The Headhunter. A man who frightened her. One of those she called the lost soldiers.

"I want you to look around for me," said Kreeger. "See if any of your contacts over at SIN know about Sanchez. Don't make it official."

"Gotcha." Camacho's sole mission in life—so far as the Station was concerned—was to live with SIN. He handled the care and feeding of a number of CIA agents in the Mexican service that Fausto was not supposed to know about. "Are you going to tell me what this is about?"

"It all goes back to the phone call I got from the reporter. He told me he saw Sanchez leaving the Alhóndiga by the back door, after President Paz was killed."

Camacho gave a soundless whistle. "I'm on it."

Kreeger's secretary came in with a fresh pile of cables. Kreeger sifted through them until he came to a confidential report from the chief of the U.S. advisory team in El Salvador that explained Sanchez's retirement from the Army five years before.

Kreeger had visited El Salvador once or twice on special assignments for Paul Milnekoff. It was a little country, where warfare had the intimacy—and the raw terror—of hand-to-hand fighting in the Middle Ages. From the windows of the luxury hotels in the capital, you could see rival forces slogging it out on the slopes of the volcano. Rico Sanchez had been assigned to Chalatenango, a few weeks after the guerrillas had seized the command post of the Fourth Brigade and stripped it bare. He had taught the Salvadoran army the lessons he learned in Vietnam, means of achieving pacification through terror. He had warned the army death squads to wear peasant rags, or guerrilla fatigues, when they went

out at night to shoot up a village suspected of rebel sympathies. Purification. Cleansing. Rape the women and the
boys. The men in one of the death squads forgot their
trainer's advice. They wore their military uniforms when
they butchered Jesuit priests whose crime was to imagine
that the teachings of Christ applied to the relations between men as well as the relation between man and God.
They were caught, but not before Sanchez had been
flown home and given an honorable discharge and the
pension of a lieutenant-colonel.

He had set up his own business in San Antonio, trading on his military contacts and his command of the
Spanish language. Brokering deals. Selling guns. Front-
ing for crooked Mexican politicians who wanted to stash
their money away north of the border. What else?

So Rico Sanchez had been Colgate's man. Just the
man for a killing. Who was paying him now? Where was
he?

Eddie O'Brien stepped through the open door, and
cleared his throat.

Kreeger said, "Spit it out."

"It's about Joe Cicero."

"Yes?"

"Somebody spattered his face all over the Jardín
Unión."

4

THE next twenty-four hours were among the toughest
Kreeger had endured. George Camacho came back from
a trawl around SIN headquarters and a private chat with
Cuco Salazar, Fausto's official liaison with CIA. And the
Agency's most useful agent inside SIN.

"I may have something," George reported. "I mentioned Sanchez to Salazar; he didn't miss a beat. He said it

was a helluva common name. I gave him a bit more, about a Mex-American colonel. He remembered that a while back he couldn't get into the boss's office because an American military type called Sanchez was in there. He figured they were cooking up a business deal. Hot autos, the usual stuff.''

Kreeger waited. A dull ache of dread moved through his body. Sanchez and Fausto. Colgate and Sanchez. A dead President, and a man in Guanajuato with his head blown off. Joe Cicero was a friend, even if he did work for the media.

"I asked Salazar to check around," Camacho pursued. "He met me at a bar after lunch. Now it's *harto poco.*'' It was a Bolivian expression meaning, roughly, a lot of nothing. "He was scared. The guy was sweating so hard he was standing in a puddle. He said he couldn't find out anything. He'd made a mistake about the colonel in Fausto's office. Nobody in SIN has ever heard of an American colonel called Sanchez.''

"He's lying."

"How do you want me to handle this?"

"Keep on him. How much are we paying Salazar?"

"A thousand a month." It wasn't peanuts, since Salazar's official salary came to about two hundred dollars a month, at least at last week's exchange rate.

"Give him whatever it takes. There are no limits on this one, George."

5

Kreeger spent a sleepless night. Figures from his past laid siege to him, hallucinations larger than life. He saw Val— lover, teacher, soulmate—with a narrow red line about her neck, like the mark of a piano wire. Joe Cicero stumbled by, headless, a portable typewriter in his hand.

Kreeger rolled from bed, groggy, unable to focus his eyes. He nicked himself three times shaving, and came out of the bathroom with toilet paper glued to his face.

"What's the matter?" Karla demanded. She began in a chord of loving concern, but dropped back into a tone more familiar in recent years, something close to accusation.

"Must be the shrimp I ate last night. I haven't felt this bad since I took part in Sy Gottschalk's experiments as a trainee." He broke off, realizing that he had never told Karla about this. Sy had been the off-center genius the Agency had employed to research parapsychology and various means of mind control—grist for many congressional showmen a decade later. Kreeger had volunteered to take part in his tests. He had been fed shellfish toxin as part of an experiment to establish whether it could be used in interrogations. He had ended up groggy and incoherent, after a bout of lurid hallucinations, sexual and otherwise. Ready to confess to anything, but quite unable to make a usable statement.

He said, "Shellfish toxin. Bad dreams. It happens."

"Try conscience," Karla challenged him. "You ought to listen to your dreams. You might hear from the parts of yourself you've been shutting out."

Kreeger groaned and lumbered toward the coffee pot. He did not give much credence to dreams, to night visitations. He believed in the power of the rational mind, not telephone calls from the dead. *Los racionales*. That was the name a Venezuelan tribe, the Yanomana—the Fierce People—gave to non-Indians. To the ones who had forgotten how to dream.

Kreeger sucked on his coffee cup, his mind a jumble of memories—Val, saying good-bye; Val, warning him to be careful; Val, dead and gone—none of them rational, none of them productive.

"Jim." Karla's voice cut through the tumult of his thoughts. "You haven't listened to a word I've said."

"Sorry."

"Are we going to end up like those retired couples we see in restaurants back home, sitting out the meal without speaking to each other? Chewing, fixing their dentures, picking their gums? Finding life only at other tables?"

"I don't know what you're talking about."

"I'm telling you to get out of the Agency while you still have a marriage."

"You might pick a better time."

"You never have time, Jim. Not for me. Talk to me next week, I have to save the Western world."

"I don't believe you're doing this."

"You screwed up, Jim. You dropped the ball. Why else is Joe Cicero dead? He was here for dinner, for Chrissake. He was a decent man. He had heart. He listened to me once in a while."

"You've no right to use Joe."

"Why is he dead then?"

Why *was* Joe dead? The question pulsed inside Kreeger's skull. Was it because Cicero had seen Sanchez? Because someone was covering up? And who—Colgate or Fausto? What game was Fausto playing now?

6

KREEGER sat inside the Bubble with Lois Compton, talking constitutional law. It wasn't his subject, but Lois had a law degree and an eye for a wrinkle. Kreeger wanted her to tell him he was wrong.

The political section said that the bosses of the PRI had been up half the night, poring over the same fat white document Lois was studying. The Mexican Constitution. Whoever wrote it was no admirer of Jeffersonian prose.

The only thing that was simple about the succession

to President Paz was that there was no precedent. Not since the blood-and-guts days of the Mexican Revolution, before this Constitution was written, when the succession was decided by whose *pistoleros* were quickest on the draw.

Under Mexico's Constitution, there was no automatic line of succession. No Vice-President waiting in the wings. No House Speaker in reserve. The President had no official heir.

"It's like a medieval kingdom," Lois observed. "Kings rule or barons rule, all that good stuff. Knock off the top guy, and the barons of the party start sizing each other up. The way I read it, the presidency is up for grabs. I guess they wrote the rules this way so the number two wouldn't be tempted to bump off the number one."

"I've been trying to think this through," Kreeger said. "Let me run through it again. Tell me if I've got it right."

"Shoot."

"Step one." Kreeger held up a forefinger. "Since the Mexican Congress is not in session, this rump group—"

"The permanent commission."

"Right. The permanent commission picks a provisional head of state. And we know—or think we know—that they are going to put in Eduardo Arroyo, because he's a fat-ass crook everyone knows and detests and is not a serious bidder to take over on a long-term basis."

Lois made a face. Sloppy, jowly Eduardo Arroyo was one of the more primeval members of the PRI regime.

"Step two." Kreeger raised the social finger. "The Constitution requires the *provisional* President—that's Arroyo—to call an emergency session of the full Congress within eighteen days. Congress elects an *interim* President. He gets to run the country for a maximum of eighteen months. Then he is required to call national elections."

"Which he—or his nominee—will win, short of an act of God or a revolution."

"That's step three," Kreeger agreed. "Now, the interesting stuff is all in Article Eighty-two. Let's go through the fine print."

Lois read the article out loud, clause by clause. It listed the basic qualifications for a President of Mexico. He had to be a Mexican citizen by birth, born on the territory of the republic. The same was required of both his parents. He had to be at least thirty-five years of age. Clergymen and ministers of "any cult" were banned from office.

Clause 6 stated that in order to be President "it is necessary not to be a secretary or undersecretary of state, the chief or secretary-general of an administrative department, the Attorney General of the Republic, or the governor of any state for a period of six months prior to election day."

Lois yawned.

Kreeger said, "Don't give up now. You just read the good bit."

"I don't get it."

"The six-months exclusion. Don't you see? Government ministers and state governors aren't eligible to take over the presidency unless they've been out of office for six months or more."

Lois stared at him. The leadership of the PRI—and the country—was in the hands of five or six political families. Under normal circumstances, the President would be chosen from among the chiefs and favorite sons of these rival *camarillas.* But the circumstances were not normal, and a little snag had just bobbed up. The leading candidates to inherit the presidency were all ministers, and therefore excluded under the six-months rule.

"So who gets to be President?" Lois looked at Kreeger's face. "No, don't tell me."

They said it in unison. "Ramírez."

"I checked the dates," Kreeger told her. "Ramírez resigned six months and eleven days before President Paz met his maker."

They went through it again, looking for a flaw. They worried at the phrase "six months prior to election day." If that meant the date of the national elections—and not the election of an interim President by Congress—then Ramírez lost his advantage. They called on the political section for a second reading. The political section said the meaning was in doubt. There were no precedents. The caretaker chief of state, Arroyo, would decide. And he had been breakfasting with Fernando Ramírez.

"It's quite brilliant," said Lois.

"Quite."

"Do you think Ramírez was looking this far ahead when he resigned? I mean, everyone thought he was forced out by the scandal. Is Ramírez smart enough, ruthless enough, to have planned all of this?"

"Ruthless enough, perhaps, but Ramírez couldn't have planned it alone." Kreeger didn't respond to Lois's raised eyebrows. He did not say, Fausto has been calling the shots, from beginning to end. He said, "Thanks, Lois. I'll take it from here."

"You just wanted a sounding board?"

"I wanted confirmation. A cold eye."

He went back to his office, drank his eighth or ninth mug of coffee. He could see the pattern now, or some of it, anyway. The weave of events: the corner of a rug rolled back, exposing a section of another underneath it. If Sanchez had been working for Fausto all along, it meant that SIN had been monitoring the rebellion, perhaps even encouraging it, in order to flush out and destroy hidden opponents of the regime. A classic provocation. If Fausto had ordered Sanchez to kill President Paz, he must have been aiming for a double target: to capture the presidency for Ramírez, his old patron, while framing their common enemies.

It *was* brilliant, and it suggested qualities of ruthlessness and ambition in Fausto beyond anything that Kreeger had glimpsed. Kreeger felt sickened by the deaths, the betrayals. Most especially by his own failure of instinct.

His mind reeled back to the late-night drinking session at which he had first alerted Fausto to the existence of something called the Safari Project, and the involvement of a CIA veteran called Colgate. He remembered how they had even talked about the rules of deception that night, and Fausto had bragged that gringos were too clean-cut, too naive, to play the game as well as Latinos.

Had Fausto hatched his master plan that same night: to hijack the Safari plot and turn it to his own ends? Had he persuaded Ramírez to step down, with the assurance of strutting into the presidential palace over a dead man's body? Had Fausto moved all of them—Raúl Carvajal, Art Colgate, even Kreeger himself—like pawns on his chessboard? Had Kreeger's indiscretion, in addition to the ravening greed of the Safari crowd, opened the way to the tragedy of Guanajuato?

Now Ramírez, who had proven himself to be a political butcher and a world-class criminal, was in place to become the next President of Mexico.

Joe Cicero's headless body was being flown home for burial.

And Jim Kreeger had proof of nothing—unless he could reach out and pluck The Headhunter from whatever dark hole he was hiding in.

TWENTY-THREE

□ □ □

1

THE rat-poison vendor walked through Colonia Roma, past Cuco Salazar's apartment building, which canted a little to one side, like a man worn out by swinging a pickax. The rat-poison man dangled a dead rodent by the tail. Since the drought, the rats had multiplied, infesting the homes of the middle class and the *ricos* as well as the shanties of the poor.

Across the street from Salazar's apartment was the hole where a six-story building had folded on itself in the last earthquake like a collapsible silk hat. The rubble had been left where it fell. Squatters were camped in it. A bright new poster had sprouted overnight on the eyeless wall above them. It depicted Fernando Ramírez. He seemed to be striding on a mountaintop, or gliding above it, poised on a cloud of light. The artist had performed liposuction with a brush, stroking the familiar, coarse-grained face into a mask of purpose and nobility, weirdly reminiscent of the cheap portraits of Catholic saints that were sold outside the churches. Bold capitals spelled the message: *"Mexico encuentra su destino."*

"What is your destiny, *cuate?*" George Camacho glanced around Salazar's cramped living room, taking in the soiled covers, the mess of children's toys, the baby sucking its fist, the wide-beamed wife negotiating the narrow galley behind the kitchen counter.

The bottle from which Salazar was drinking was a gift from George. So was the new mobile for the baby's crib, and the toy spaceship for his older son. And so was the envelope in his pocket, containing money which would pay for the apartment he rented for his mistress, a tawny, light-boned girl from Oaxaca.

"Is this the farthest you can go?" A sweep of George's hand took in the shabby room, the cracked plaster. "You're a very capable man. You can do a lot better for yourself. I think we can help."

Salazar stared at him with hungry eyes. Camacho reminded Salazar of how Fausto had passed him over when a plum job—chief of SIN in the Federal District—had fallen vacant. "Your hat was never even in the ring. I checked around. Some reward for loyalty."

The CIA man had touched a raw nerve. In the big reshuffle a few months back, Salazar had pushed Fausto as hard as he dared to give him a promotion, to district chief or head of a division—to a job that brought a bigger share of the widows' and orphans' fund. The district chief in Nuevo León or Jalisco grossed millions in an average year. Fausto had told Salazar he was too valuable to be moved.

Salazar sat, wordless, listening very carefully to what George Camacho was saying.

"If Fausto moves upstairs," Camacho pursued, "he won't be doing you any favors."

Salazar concurred. It was common knowledge at SIN headquarters that if Ramírez became President, he would make Fausto his Minister of Government. And it was generally believed that if Fausto went upstairs, he would bequeath his present job to a longtime member of his personal *camarilla,* a man who had been district chief in Monterrey and who had accompanied Fausto to Guanajuato. More to the point, there was no love lost between him and Salazar.

"A man's reach should exceed his grasp," Camacho quoted.

"Yes, but that's how a tree-climber gets his neck broken," Salazar objected, speaking at last.

"Let me put it to you like this. You get me Sanchez,

and I'll make you a very wealthy man. Maybe I'll be in a position to do a lot more for you. You're a capable man. You could go a lot higher in the service. We don't forget our friends.''

Camacho had studied his subject closely. Salazar lacked Fausto's grace and quickness, operating instead on a more primordial level. He could be stirred into action by greed and envy—these were the triggers Camacho had used to recruit him—and by Camacho's observation, he possessed no moral scruples whatsoever. He was a dark, heavy creature, slow to move, but when his appetite was aroused, capable of swallowing his prey whole.

Salazar's thoughts coiled in silence. The truth of Guanajuato was hidden from him, as from the Americans. He did not know whether the gringos wanted Sanchez so badly in order to conceal their own actions or to prove something against Fausto García. His chief had made this business with Sanchez his personal affair, and it was not easy to find anything out at SIN headquarters. But Salazar had discovered a private channel. His sister had telephoned, anxious for news of her husband, Abelardo, who was also employed by SIN. Abelardo had gone with the SIN detail that had accompanied President Paz to Guanajuato. Salazar's brother-in-law had not yet returned. Did Salazar know where he was?

Salazar did not, but he had certain suspicions. They could be parlayed into big money—to judge by Camacho's urgency—and perhaps a great deal more, but it was necessary to play this out carefully. Above all, he must not set a price too soon.

It occurred to Salazar that Sanchez might be dead, his body abandoned in a garbage bag at the side of a road or concealed in a shallow grave for coyotes to scratch at. It would be necessary to extract a serious advance, because the gringos might balk at paying for a dead man. Numbers drifted through Salazar's mind, ballooning into six figures.

The Mexican silently sipped some more Johnny

Walker, savoring the warmth of the good scotch as it glided down his throat, savoring as well the headiness of making the CIA wait on his pleasure.

2

Fausto García asked Kreeger to call on him at SIN headquarters. The tone of the invitation was coldly formal. Kreeger asked George Camacho to accompany him, so he would have a witness.

"You want me to wear a wire?" asked George.

"Things can't be *that* bad," said Kreeger, instantly doubting his own words. The tone of the cable traffic from Washington had bordered on the hysterical since he had reported that Ramírez was the man most likely to succeed as Mexican head of state. Yesterday, the Threat in Mexico had been seen as the Yellow Peril, in the persons of Paz Gallardo and his Japanese business friends. Today, it was a more familiar bogey: ruthless dictatorship with hints of ties to Cuba, in the unlovely shape of Ramírez.

"Anyway," Kreeger remarked, "Fausto will be happy to record everything we say. You can't pick lint off your suit in that office without being heard in stereo."

That morning, Fausto omitted the ritual *abrazos*, instead greeting his visitors with curt handshakes. He also did not offer drinks from the bar, or even coffee.

He said, "We have long been aware that an aggressive faction in the American government has been involved in a campaign to destabilize the Mexican political system. We know that the same elements who regarded our late President as an enemy are likely to turn, with even greater viciousness, on his successor."

"You refer, of course, to Fernando Ramírez.."

"That will be decided in accordance with the democratic process."

"I am delighted to hear it."

"I asked you here," Fausto proceeded, "to offer a few words of caution and advice. I would ask you to convey them to your Director, and to Admiral Enright in particular."

"I'm all ears."

"In the event of any further attempt by the American government to intervene in the domestic affairs of my country, we will feel obliged to make public certain information that could be highly damaging to your employers, and indeed to your President. We have assembled a quite lengthy dossier, documenting the illegal activities of agents of the CIA and the Pentagon on Mexican soil."

Fausto ran through some of the highlights, most of which were familiar to Kreeger. They included various trips to Mexico by Colgate—whom Fausto insisted on describing as a "notorious CIA operative, expert in psychological warfare and wet operations"—and by General Two Jacks Gilly.

"Fausto," Kreeger interjected, "you're coming out of left field. Haven't you forgotten who first told you about Colgate?"

"That could be interpreted in various ways," Fausto observed, with a smile that contained no warmth. "But I see that I have not succeeded in dramatizing my point, something I expect to be able to do within a matter of days. We are already in possession of incontrovertible evidence that the assassination of our President in my native city was the work of CIA operatives, in league with fascist conspirators in the north."

"This is madness!" Kreeger exploded. "Who the hell do you expect to believe that crap?"

"I think our Japanese friends might be very interested to learn the lengths to which your people will apparently go, Jim, to prevent an elected government from doing business with commercial rivals of the United States."

Kreeger thought for a moment about the nature—and the magnitude—of this threat. In essence, Fausto was threatening to spark a political war between the United States and Japan. It would, of course, generate an uproar from Congress and among the American media. Fausto's dossier would be believed by many, and maybe even by some people inside the intelligence community, who would simply refuse to accept the possibility that a "taco team" south of the border had outfoxed and outmaneuvered some of the most powerful men in Washington.

"I assume you are suggesting an alternative," said Kreeger, "to all this—embarrassment."

"We know each other very well, my friend. Nothing has truly changed between us. All I am asking is for understanding, for tolerance. Fernando is the best man we have. He is a man your President Butler can do business with. There is no need for further dramas."

"And you'll be here to keep an eye on President Ramírez. As Minister of Government."

"That would be his decision," said Fausto modestly. "The arrangement could only lead to closer cooperation between our services, Jim."

Kreeger gripped the arms of his chair. He said, as mildly as he could manage, "You won't get away with it."

"Get away with it? Get away with what? I did not invent the Safari Project, Jim. I did not employ Mr. Colgate and his mercenaries to terrorize civilians, including American citizens."

"What about Sanchez?" Kreeger hurled the name like a javelin.

"Sanchez." Fausto's eyes went vague. "It is a very common name. To whom do you refer? I believe there is even a book by one of your sociologists—*The Children of Sanchez.* Is that the Sanchez you mean?"

DESPITE his revulsion, despite his professional sympathy for a fellow chief of state, Harry Butler *was* relieved by the assassination of Mexico's head of state. He was confident that with the death of Paz Gallardo, the Safari Project would collapse. The opposition party was being blamed for the murder, and its populist leader, Miliano something—a heartthrob to young liberals in Harry Butler's party—was in jail. There were reports of mass arrests. If Raúl Carvajal was smart, he would jump over the border, or seek sanctuary on some tropical island, before the goon squads came after him. The Japan Scare that Admiral Enright was forever banging on about had also gone down the tubes.

President Butler could relax, and wait for the dust to settle.

And such was the policy he had determined to adopt. But then he received two phone calls.

The first was from his National Security Adviser.

"We just got word out of Mexico Station."

"I thought you said their reporting wasn't worth spit."

"For once, they may be on track. The next boss-man down in Mexico is going to be our pal Ramírez. He's a bona-fide Cuban agent. We've put together a file on him about three feet thick."

President Butler groaned. He was fed up with being asked to play God in Mexico, and he said so to Admiral Enright.

"May I say something, sir?"

"I'm listening."

"You remember that TV show on Ramírez, before he stepped down last summer?"

"Something about Mexico's Noriega, right?"

"Right. If you sit by and let Ramírez take over the rackets, you'll be in for more flak than Bush had to face before he decided to take out Pineapple Face down in Panama. I'd like permission to go to an active phase on Operation Safety Net."

"I gotta think this over," President Butler said, alarmed at the speed with which events seemed to be moving.

"Don't take too long, sir. Ramírez has a way of offing anybody who disagrees with him. We drag our heels over this, and we'll find we've nobody left to greet us at the landing strip."

"I said I'll think about it," the President snarled.

The second call came late at night, when he had escaped the White House and the First Lady for some serious drinking down at his colonial retreat in Fauquier County. He kept changing the numbers of his personal lines, but the man he least wanted to hear from always seemed to be up to date.

"Comanche Moon," the man said when Harry Butler lifted the receiver. There were only five or six men left alive who had known Butler long enough—and well enough—to use the old signal. All of them were Texans, except this one.

The President did not speak.

"We are still in business," said the caller from Monterrey. "Did you hear me, Harry? There is a certain symmetry to what has happened. Almost like poetry. I prefer an enemy like Ramírez. A killer. He is more of a challenge. And he has many lives to answer for. There are many people in your country—in your *government*—who think as we do. We are on safari together, Harry. Nobody leaves until it is over. Do you hear me, Mr. President?"

"I hear you, you goddamn son of a bitch."

Harry Butler slammed down the receiver and proceeded to drink a whole fifth of scotch before he had stunned himself sufficiently to drop into bed. He dreamed of a tawny blonde who used her mouth like a milking machine. He woke with a cry that brought one of his bodyguards into the room, with his pistol out.

"Are you okay, Mr. President?"

"Yes," Butler replied after a moment to orient himself. He lied, of course—he was *not* all right.

It would not be seemly to ask for another drink. And how could he tell the Secret Service agent that he had roused from the dream because he had realized that the woman was servicing him inside a coffin?

4

AMONG the American reporters drawn to Mexico after the assassination was Gail Armstrong, who arrived there with a full-fledged production crew from her TV network. Eddie O'Brien spotted her in the lobby of the Maria Isabel, and told Kreeger she looked better without the pancake makeup she wore for the cameras.

"Why don't you ask her to dinner?" Kreeger suggested.

"Are you serious?"

"Why not? You're in the consular section, aren't you? Tell her we're concerned about a missing U.S. citizen called Rico Sanchez, who vanished the day Paz got shot."

Eddie waited for his boss to crack a smile. He didn't.

"You're serious, aren't you?"

O'Brien knew that Kreeger was frustrated. The days were slipping by, Ramírez and his advance men were buying up votes in the Congress, and still there were no leads on Sanchez. Kreeger was even thinking very seriously about leaking the fact that a lot of people wanted to talk to a former U.S. colonel named Sanchez. So far there had been no mention of Sanchez in the papers. Maybe Kreeger owed it to Joe Cicero to get the story out. Maybe that would help to flush Sanchez out of hiding, if he was still alive, or to flush out the truth, if he was not. This was not the way to do it, however.

Kreeger looked at Eddie and smiled. "Forget it. I just wanted to see how much you liked Gail Armstrong."

"I could like her enough."

Kreeger told Eddie to get over to the Station's observation post across the street from the Soviet Embassy and see who was calling on General Fomin. The bread-and-butter work of the station did not stop because Mexicans were shooting each other.

Eddie expressed mild disappointment. "I always wanted to turn an anchorwoman."

Kreeger, the professional, was not about to expose one of his best case officers to Gail Armstrong or anyone else from the press. If a contact needed to be made, he would handle it himself. Furthermore, it would be better if the story seemed to come from somewhere other than Mexico City. He needed to find a suitable channel.

Joel Stein gave it to him.

Along with the reporters came a crowd of visiting firemen, including two congressional delegations. Joel Stein, senior staffer for the Senate Intelligence Committee, came with one of them. Kreeger took his call, because he remembered what Stein had said to him after he had run the gauntlet Senator Pike had arranged for him at the closed hearing in Washington: "Anything I can do."

They lunched at Bellinghausen, at a table under a striped awning in the garden. Margaritas in tiny glasses that tasted like daiquiris. Slabs of meat with little dishes of green salsa.

Joel Stein had a pale, round face. His cheeks puffed out like a baby's when he dropped his chin. He had lost maybe thirty pounds since Kreeger had last seen him, but he moved like a larger man, in an envelope of fatty tissue. His lost dimensions were almost palpable, like an aura.

The Senate staffer wanted to know if Ramírez was going to become President, and if he was as bad as everyone said.

"He's dirty," Kreeger conceded.

"This thing with the Cubans, is it for real, or is it hype from the NSC?"

"What have you heard?"

Stein told him of a confidential briefing. Admiral Enright and a battery of experts. Maps and pointers. Electronic aids. Further proof that Ramírez for decades had been a friend and crony—some said even a business partner—of Fidel Castro and his bagmen. Plus there were new charges about drug connections.

"Some of it's true," Kreeger commented. "The Cuban thing, with Ramírez, goes pretty deep."

"Jonah Pike is riding his hobbyhorse again. He says the Agency's been protecting Ramírez and Fausto García the way it protected Noriega."

Kreeger complained that the Panama episode seemed to be burned into Washington's collective psyche. "Panama was a disaster. We had quiet options. We forgot how to use them."

"You're missing the point, Jim."

"Which is?"

"Noriega was, in some measure, the Agency's creation. Its Frankenstein monster. Have we done the same thing here?"

"Noriega never had a decent case handler."

"I'm talking about the shit and you're talking about the toilet paper."

Kreeger did not laugh, but he did not protest either. Stein's crack ran too close to questions that had been haunting him since Joe Cicero died. Questions about his relationship with Fausto.

"So how do we block Ramírez?" Stein demanded.

"You know enough about the real world to understand that Uncle Sam does not make and break Mexican Presidents."

"I also understand that the fate of this country is in the hands of the United States."

"Now you sound like Admiral Enright."

"It's a direct quote. You know, I believe they really could send in the Eighty-second Airborne."

"The President isn't crazy. He won't let it happen."

"I'm not so sure."

"On what pretext?"

"American lives at risk. A felon in power. The damnedest thing is, I believe that in its present mood, Congress would back an invasion. It worked like a charm in Kuwait, to begin with, anyway. And Enright was pretty convincing on the Hill. *And* there are a lot of angry constituents out there."

"If a U.S. combat soldier takes one step across the line, you know what we'll accomplish? We'll turn Ramírez into a popular hero. We'll isolate the United States from the whole damn hemisphere. We'll give the Soviets a propaganda victory big enough to blow up NATO—if anything's left to blow up. And we'll watch the Eighty-second Airborne fly home in body bags."

"So what do we do?"

"We get smart. We look for quiet options."

Kreeger ordered a beer. Joel Stein stuck to the high-octane margaritas, so different from the Tex-Mex version.

"There's something I need you to do," Kreeger told the Senate staffer. Both men relished the irony of these words, crossing the table between old adversaries. In a low voice, Kreeger recounted Joe Cicero's tale of the man fleeing from the back door of the Alhóndiga, tossing in details from his own research on Rico Sanchez and his network. He concluded by saying something that surprised him, despite his resolve: "I don't mind if this gets into the newspapers."

SHELLEY felt like a caged animal. It seemed she could not even venture down the hall to the bathroom without running into an armed man. She told Raúl she needed to get away from the ranch, from the feeling of being under siege. He begged her to be patient, just for a few days, until the situation was clarified. He, of course, never explained what that meant.

Paco Carranza was encamped in the guesthouse. The man made her nervous—and curious, arriving as he had with a large collection of pigskin suitcases. Late one night she had eavesdropped on an angry conversation between Carranza and Raúl; she heard talk of money and vengeance.

Carranza traveled with large sums in cash—only natural in his business. Shelley knew Raúl was loath to acknowledge it, but Carranza was one of the biggest transshippers of cocaine in Mexico, something which, if publicized, would be a major embarrassment to some of Raúl's American friends.

When Raúl was out of the house, Shelley stole a look inside his office safe. He had opened it a few times in her presence, in their free-and-easy early days, and she had listened to the tumblers roll, memorizing the combination. A businesslike precaution, she told herself, nothing more.

Today she found neat packages of hundreds and fifties. She did not need the practiced eye of a bank teller to guess that there were several million dollars in the safe. Was it drug money en route to a cooperative bank across the border, to be laundered beyond recognition by electronic transfers back and forth between New York, the Bahamas, the Isle of Man? Or money to buy more guns and men and politicians? Or was it simply there in case it was needed in a hurry, perhaps for a getaway?

She heard padding footsteps in the hall. She recognized them as belonging to Rodrigo, Raúl's answer to a pit bull. She had the safe sealed up tight and was lounging with the telephone, pretending to talk to her daughter in California, when Rodrigo stuck his lean face into the room.

Shelley tolerated captive status only until Raúl announced that he was going to Houston on urgent business.

"I'm coming too," she announced.

"I'm sorry. It's not possible."

"Then I'm going away by myself. You can't keep me chained up like a pet indefinitely. Besides, I won't stay here with that pig Carranza." She made up a story about how Carranza had propositioned her, pressing his leg between her thighs when she was alone in the stables.

Color drained from Raúl's face. He knew Carranza well enough to regard this story as plausible. Reluctantly, he agreed to let her go away for a few days, so long as she did not leave the country. Crossing the border—even by plane—might prove to be increasingly difficult.

"Where will you go?" he asked.

She told him she was going to Mexico City. It just popped out, but she saw the logic in it. She needed to talk things over with a person she could trust. A woman. With Lois Compton, from the consulate. Of course, she did not say this to Raúl.

Carvajal frowned and said, "Fausto García is in Mexico City."

"I'm not going to see him. I'm going to spend some of your money."

"García may want to see you."

"He has no hold over me. I'm an American citizen."

Raúl thought about it, and his mood seemed to brighten. "If Fausto García calls on you, tell him it's finished. That I'm planning to leave the country. That he's won."

"Is it true?"

"That depends on Harry."

Shelley had watched Harry Butler on TV, reading a statement of condolence to the Mexican people on the loss of their President, vowing to join in the fight against political terrorism. Harry had seemed to speak from the heart, sounding almost like the old Harry, the one who had stood up for ordinary people as a fighting attorney in Corpus. Like the man she had once loved.

Raúl said, "You must promise to come back to me within two days. I need you."

Shelley had nodded wordlessly.

Later, she watched Raúl fly off toward Houston. Then Felipe drove her to the Monterrey airport.

When Felipe did not return to the ranch, Paco Carranza sent men to look for him. They found the Mercedes in the airport parking lot. The windshield wipers, the radio, and the hubcaps were missing, along with the hood ornament.

6

Fausto García dressed for occasions—a *guayabera* for a sultry evening at Mazatlán; jodhpurs for the ranch; a double-breasted dinner jacket with silk revers for a state banquet or a museum ball.

That night, Fausto sported a belted black leather jacket, with matching pants and gloves; underneath the jacket he wore a black cotton turtleneck. He was at La Chiquita, a soundproofed bunker hidden away among the pines behind the high wire and machine-gun posts of Campo Militar Numero Uno. He was ready to entertain.

The prisoner slumped between two guards, who

supported him by the shoulders. His eyes were vacant, his expression stunned. He did not appear to focus on the bloodstains that patterned the whitewashed walls.

He blinked under the halogen lamp. Sagging jowls, crooked teeth. Hairs sprouted from his nostrils, from his ears. His stubble was almost white. The man was a poor specimen, hardly worthy of Fausto's attention. An insignificant man. Gomez. Felipe Gomez. An insignificant name, appropriate for a man who mucked out stables and drove automobiles badly.

Fausto pronounced the short syllables with distaste. "Felipe Gomez. You are employed by Raúl Carvajal."

The Bookends had to jab the man in the kidneys before he responded. A poor specimen, stupidly loyal, like a gelded dog.

"You have a woman—" Fausto used the coarse word, *hembra,* so there would be no misunderstanding, " —and daughters and grandchildren. If you wish to see them again, you will cooperate to the fullest extent."

Felipe's head lolled on his shoulders.

"Foto de pasaporte," Fausto instructed his men. A passport photo. A small beating. Nothing that would show on the face. Just to remind.

"We will understand one another," Fausto informed the groom. "I know this is hard for you. Your family has worked for the Carvajal family for generations. I understand the habits of feudalism die hard. You have been duped. You have been victimized. I will liberate you from all of this. Do you follow me?"

Felipe's jaw slumped to his chest. It might have been a nod.

"Bring this poor fellow a chair."

They sat him down on a straight-backed chair, offering him a cigarette and a *gaseosa.* Felipe puffed on the harsh tobacco, and coughed.

"I want you to search your memory. You drove Raúl Carvajal, your master, to Dolores Hidalgo."

"I have never been to Dolores Hidalgo. I have never been to the capital. I am a simple man, not a traveler."

Fausto was surprised by this rush of speech from between cracked lips. He suggested to the Bookends that they should give Felipe the *gaseosa*, to enliven his memory cells. They laced the soda with flaming chili sauce before they shoved the bottle up his nose. An old technique, crude but effective. Fausto had studied many techniques of interrogation. He knew about parapsychology and hypnosis, about psychedelic drugs and electrodes. Perhaps they had their use, but he believed that the best methods are simple—loss of sleep, repetitive noises, when there was time. Raw terror and the *gaseosa*, when there was not.

He began to assist Felipe to remember. How he had overheard Raúl Carvajal conspire with Miliano Rojas in Dolores Hidalgo to arrange the assassination of President Paz. How, prior to this, he had witnessed the traitor Paco Carranza contribute money from his drug deals to a plot to overthrow the legitimate government of Mexico.

How, as Carvajal's loyal chauffeur, he had waited in an underground street behind the Alhóndiga in Guanajuato, to provide an escape for the gunman who had murdered the President. This information would be recorded in a second confession, to be held in reserve in case of need. Fausto García was a provident man.

Fausto consulted the typed documents on the table. He had covered the basic points. There was more. It was a waste of time to read it all to the man who would sign it.

"Can you write?" Fausto asked the prisoner.

Drool on his face, blood streaming from his nose, the fool affected dignity. Of course he could write.

His hand was so shaky—or so untutored—he could barely scratch out his name. He did not read what he was signing.

Fausto called for the attorney of Felipe Gomez to witness the confession. The prisoner and his lawyer had not been introduced, and they parted without exchanging a single phrase.

Felipe signed yet another statement, acknowledging that he had not been abused in captivity. This document was witnessed by an independent physician, who did not inspect the prisoner.

Fausto wrinkled his nose. The prisoner stank. Who would contest his confessions? Not the attorney-general, a political survivor accused by the gringos of assisting the members of the drug cartel in Guadalajara who had butchered a DEA agent. Not the acting President, Eduardo Arroyo, whose penchant for little boys had been fully monitored by SIN. Not the man who was certain to become head of state, or the next Minister of Government.

Certainly not Felipe.

There were rules at La Chiquita, as at any club. One rule was that those who signed confessions never recanted. They joined the ranks of *los desaparecidos*—the disappeared—in the lime pit behind the bunker.

TWENTY-FOUR

□ □ □

1

MAINTAINING cover was the part of Kreeger's job that was cruelest to the liver and the waistline. That evening, it meant cocktails at the Bosnian Mission, which occupied a townhouse around the corner from the British Embassy and the Bristol Hotel.

Karla was wearing her basic black, which left her shoulders fetchingly bare. She wanted to know where Bosnia was.

"It's where the First World War started."

"It's hard to keep up with all these new ministates. Some of them sound like they ought to be run by archdukes with funny mustaches."

There actually was an archduke at the reception, or a pretender, at the least. He did not have a funny mustache, but he told everyone who would listen that he was expecting a summons at any moment to return to Budapest and save the Magyars.

Nigel Yarrow kissed Karla at the base of the neck, letting her feel his teeth. "Angie's here," he announced. "Let's have dinner later on. I need to talk to you, Jim."

Across the room, Kreeger saw Angie Yarrow, compact and kittenish in her cocktail dress, chatting with Shin Yamada, the Japanese spy.

"I see Angie has the Japanese covered."

"Poor Shin," said Yarrow. "Not a bad chap, really. I wonder what he makes of it all. Terrible loss of face for the Japs, losing Paz after they spent so much money courting him."

Kreeger lifted a scotch and soda from a waiter's tray. Karla took a glass of white wine and drifted off to talk to Angie.

Yarrow dipped his chin, and Kreeger glanced over toward the bar table. Peter Fomin, elegant in a charcoal pinstripe, was chatting with the Bosnian Minister. The KGB chief smiled at Kreeger and raised his glass.

"Marvelous scene, don't you think?" said Yarrow. "The spies' quadrille. Tell me honestly, did you imagine it was going to be quite so much fun when you signed on? You Americans were so terribly earnest in those days. Plotting cold wars in cold, leaky shacks in front of the Lincoln Memorial. Binary thinking. Zero-one. Good guys and bad guys. Them and us. It's so much more amusing now everybody has their own team, and nobody wastes their breath trying to explain what they do with an Ism. Back to the good old game of nations. Changing dance partners when it pleases us. It's what we're all about, isn't it? It's what we were always about. Like native witch doctors, guiding their tribe on the great hunt. I do hope you're not going to spoil it."

"What the hell does that mean?"

"You're not going to let old Harry Butler play cowboys and Indians in Mexico, are you? It would really spoil the party. Look at our friend Fomin. He's positively beaming at you. I believe he's actually coming our way. I'm going to chat up the girls. It's you he wants to talk to."

Fomin made no attempt at indirection. The KGB *rezident* and the CIA Station Chief were on open ground. They had exchanged a few curt civilities at social functions of this sort, but their real dialogue was conducted in different ways, through hidden cameras, listening devices, agent debriefings. And through intuition: the ability to crawl inside the other man's skin. There was an exact symmetry in their relationship. It was that of two marksmen viewing each other through the cross hairs of their rifle sights.

Fomin said what Yarrow had said, in an Oxbridge accent that would have been fully at home in Yarrow's club on Pall Mall: "I need to talk with you."

"I'm all ears."

"What I have to say requires a different environment."

"Your place or mine?"

"Neutral ground."

Kreeger hesitated for a moment. A direct approach from Fomin meant, in all likelihood, a trap of some kind. But there were other possibilities: Perhaps the Russians wanted to pass on a message, or there was even the long shot that Fomin had screwed up an operation, fallen out of favor with Moscow Center, and wanted to jump. There had been no shortage of East European spies throwing themselves at the Americans since the Soviet empire broke out in shingles.

Kreeger, searching for leverage on the Mexican government and his own, also did not rule out the chance that he might learn something of use from the KGB, if only by reading the pattern of its deception.

"Okay," he said to Fomin, "I too would like to talk."

They gravitated toward the bay window, away from curious ears. Kreeger mentioned that he had promised to take his wife on a Saturday outing to Cuernavaca. He did not mention that this promise had hung in suspended animation for several months.

"I am fond of Cuernavaca," said the Russian. The city of flowers, with its steep, broken streets and sudden *barrancas* had been a playground for Soviet secret agents for three quarters of a century. The Russian Embassy maintained a large residence in the town. Fomin said that it was high time that he made an inspection.

Kreeger knew then that part of his weekend would have to be reserved for writing a very detailed contact report. He was a fieldman, body and soul, and felt that he was suffocating in the paperwork Washington demanded, however much he diverted to his deputy's office. But you did not sit down with Fomin without covering your rear end.

2

Mexico's Congress would assemble on Monday to elect the interim President. Over a suspiciously yellow Caesar salad at the Calesa de Londres, Kreeger and Yarrow discreetly compared notes on the numbers. The Station's sources gave Ramírez a narrow lead—ten or twelve votes. Yarrow's friend in the PRI gave him a more comfortable margin. Their contacts agreed that Ramírez was probably unstoppable.

Yarrow leaned in closer. "You must have something on him, don't you?"

"For Chrissake, his record's all over the fucking newspapers!"

Karla complained about the language.

Yarrow's question was one that Kreeger had put to himself many times in recent days. How do you blackmail a Mexican President? He is expected to have mistresses; without them, he is held to be less than *macho,* maybe even a *maricón,* so there was no mileage in that. A President is presumed to be on the take—a previous Mexican head of state and his gang had stolen no less than five billion dollars and no one had ever complained. Accusations of drug-dealing upset the gringos, but narcotics were perceived as a North American, not a Mexican issue. The murder of political opponents was commonplace, and the crimes were solved only when it suited those in power. Nobody doubted that Ramírez had ordered the assassination of Paz Gallardo after stealing the elections, but it would never be proven unless Fernando's enemies took control of the government. His crooked deals, his rip-offs, his ballot-rigging—even the Cuban connection and the drug allegations—were all over the American press. But only a tiny left-wing magazine had attempted to repeat those stories in Mexico City, and its plant had been fire-bombed. Fausto owned some of the newspaper editors. True, Fausto could not prevent Mexicans from tuning in to American TV, but it did not seem to make much difference. The whole political class knew what Ramírez was. And with Fausto at his elbow, he could still sign up enough deputies to have himself made President.

How do you blackmail a Mexican President?

Kreeger had to admit he was stumped.

3

On Saturday, Kreeger negotiated the road winding down from the high plateau, southward to Cuernavaca. Karla lazed behind sunglasses, pleasantly surprised by the outing. She watched the passing scenery—handmade haystacks, gathered in at the top like enormous straw brooms; comic-book burros; wordless road signs, one of which showed a mountainside falling on top of a car. They arrived in Cuernavaca in time for a quick visit to the cathedral and the palace of Cortés, followed by a beer at a sidewalk café on the plaza. A boy hawker came up, trilling "Papayas! Papayas!" and offered Kreeger a Popeye doll with a corncob pipe.

Just after two, they strolled through the cool lobby of Las Mañanitas, the restaurant Karla had been talking about since they arrived in Mexico. They were followed in by a busload of Japanese tourists, marching in orderly fashion behind a leader with a company pennant. The only other American in evidence was a weather-beaten man in a *guayabera,* seated at the bar. He was obviously a local; the season had not been kind to the tourist trade.

They had drinks in the gardens, under a spreading banyan tree. The captain planted a green wooden flag with a number in front of their table.

"It's like being on a golf course," Karla observed. "Are we the nineteenth hole, or a sand trap?"

They lunched indoors, away from the Japanese tourists. Karla was disappointed with her appetizer. She had ordered tamales, and complained that they had no taste.

Kreeger informed her that people did not come to a place like this to eat peasant food, a comment which led to a brief, discreet food fight. It was an uncommonly carefree moment for them. Tensions outside their home had taken their toll inside, and Kreeger welcomed this precious time.

Around three-thirty, Kreeger consulted his watch and reluctantly called for the bill.

"Why don't you look around the shops," he proposed. "That silver place across from the cathedral looked interesting."

"Aren't you coming?"

"There's something I have to do. I'll meet you back here in a couple of hours."

"I thought this outing was for *me.*"

The air of adventure, the sense of sharing—it all faded. Once again, it was business as usual.

"You don't change, do you? Your mistress always comes first."

4

KREEGER spent half an hour watching his back, out of habit more than necessity, since he assumed Fomin's people would have both of them covered. He was pleased to see that Eddie O'Brien was keeping a low profile. In his loud shirt and straw hat, Eddie looked the picture of a gringo tourist, even if that breed was something of a rarity just now. Kreeger did not spot any other surveillance. Either Fomin's people were very good, or this truly was an unofficial rendezvous.

At four, Kreeger paid a few pesos for an entry ticket and walked into the Italianate gatehouse of the Jardín Borda. Two dignified old men in dark suits were playing chess in the inner courtyard. Above the checkered tables, words from a Borges poem unfurled in a flowing, cursive script. Kreeger paused to read:

> *Cuando los jugadores se han ido,*
> *cuando el tiempo los haya consomido,*
> *ciertamente no habrán cesado el rito.*

> When the players are gone,
> when time has consumed them,
> the rites will continue.

He wondered whether Peter Fomin had stopped, as he had, to study these lines. He was confident that Fausto García knew them by heart.

He followed an eccentric flagstone path down to a dead pool, choked by fallen leaves. Fomin was waiting. Without a formal greeting, the Russian started walking beside him, adjusting to Kreeger's longer stride without falling in step.

Kreeger said, "I'm listening."

"This conversation is completely unofficial."

"I see."

"If you report this meeting, and the details are transmitted to Moscow Center—we both know this can happen—I will deny everything. I will say it is an American provocation."

You slippery son of a bitch, Kreeger thought. I wouldn't put it past you to come here wearing a wire.

"I requested this meeting," Fomin continued, "because I believe we have common interests in Mexico. Service interests. Governments sometimes forget these things."

"I'd love to hear about them."

"Let me attempt to build a foundation. I would like you to understand how we view the state of affairs."

"We? You said this was an unofficial conversation."

"Let us say that I speak for the more enlightened members of my service."

Kreeger thought he had heard this theme before. Hawks versus doves in the Kremlin, and at Moscow Center—a standard Soviet deception ploy, although not necessarily a gesture. The KGB might change its name, but it did not forget its old tricks. Soviet intelligence agents were taught that at the core of every successful deception is a *kanva,* a kernel, of truth.

"Our world has changed, quite profoundly, since you and I entered the service," Fomin pursued, speaking as if KGB and CIA were sections of some supranational agency. "My country, in particular, has changed. We have adopted a more pragmatic view of our interests. We are not in the business of exporting violence and instability. We have quite enough to contend with at home. We are not interested in propping up client states that cannot pay their own bills. We have different priorities.

"This has brought our countries much closer together. We have common concerns. For example, the money weapon of Japan. And the German problem. Has it occurred to you that the game of nations is coming to resemble the game of the nineteen-thirties, when Germany and Japan were on the rise?"

"It's an idea with a following, but I think it's awfully superficial. And frankly, I don't see where this is leading us." Mildly irritated, Kreeger thought that Fomin was starting to sound like one of the talking heads on the *MacNeil/Lehrer Newshour*.

"I am trying to establish a certain perspective. So we can discuss the Mexican problem within the correct focus."

"You mentioned service interests."

"You are pressing me a little. Very well, I accept. Let me come at it a different way. Mexico is a sympathetic environment for both our services. Do you agree?"

"It may be more sympathetic to you than to us."

"You are jesting, of course."

"If you say so."

"From our perspective, it would be most regrettable if the status quo in Mexico were disrupted."

Indeed, Kreeger thought. Mexico was the Soviets' favorite operating center, second only—if at all—to the United Nations. For that matter, if the Soviet Disunion vanished off the map, Mexico would continue to be the main espionage base for anyone who wanted to steal American secrets.

"We are well aware," Fomin said, "that there are powerful interests in Washington, and in Houston, who wish to change the rules of the game in Mexico. If they succeed, they may draw the United States into an irresponsible course of action that would profoundly damage our interests and, if I may say so, yours as well. Mexico, in this hemisphere, is like Vienna. Or Geneva. A neutral zone. It is our common interest, as professionals, to keep it this way."

"I assume you are about to make a proposition."

Fomin took an exaggerated time to light a cigarette, turning his shoulder to the wind. His hands were perfectly steady. He said, "I propose a friendly collaboration."

"I'm not entirely comfortable with that word."

"Then shall we say, a coordination of effort. You know, we still have some influence with the left in Mexico."

"You're talking about Miliano's movement."

"Not with Miliano Rojas. But there are other leaders. We can help to restrain certain elements on the left, to maintain a temperate government in Mexico."

"A temperate government under Fernando Ramírez."

Fomin looked at him. "Ramírez will become President. It is not our doing. And Ramírez is not our property."

"Maybe you should talk to your Cuban friends."

"I would not call them such good friends. When history accelerates, there are people who cannot keep up. They become anachronisms."

Kreeger said, "Talk to me about Fernando."

They sat side by side on a stone bench. A eucalyptus tree threw a lattice of sun and shadow over the flagstones. The Russian spoke of his posting to New York, many years before. He had targeted a high-living Mexican diplomat called Ramírez, a man who had collected more unpaid parking tickets than anyone outside the Nigerian delegation. Fomin had asked his chief for a hunting license. The request was sent up to Moscow Center, and the reply had come back promptly: Hands off Ramírez. He belongs to *los puros,* which in this context was a reference to Havana cigars rather than moral virtue.

Fomin talked of other encounters. Of a private party at a luxury villa, on Varadero Beach, near Havana, where the seafront was closed to ordinary swimmers and sunbathers. Fidel and his brother Raúl had both been there. And Ramírez.

Fomin shook a cigarette from the pack and tapped

the end against the back of his hand. He said, "But you know all this."

Kreeger said, "Where does this leave us?"

"I give you Ramírez. At least, the key to Ramírez."

"Which is?"

"Ramírez had a father."

"I'm happy for him."

"Forgive me. Sometimes my English slips."

"I haven't noticed that yet."

"The father of Fernando Ramírez was born in the United States. In south Texas. I believe you are familiar with this region." Fomin paused. "Do you know what I have given you?"

Kreeger thought back to a tedious conference with Lois, poring over the fine print of the Mexican Constitution. He tried to summon up the image of the page that contained Article 82, the one dealing with the qualifications of a candidate for the presidency. He did not capture it all, but he captured enough. Both parents of a Mexican President had to have been born on Mexican soil. The requirement reflected the fear of foreign influence—especially from the north—that was comprehensible in the only country in the world that had a museum entirely devoted to the history of its various occupations, dismemberments, and defeats.

If Ramírez Senior had been born on the wrong side of the Rio Grande—in this connection, if no other, the American side—then Fernando was automatically disqualified from seeking or holding the presidency.

Kreeger said, "How do you know this?"

"Cubans can be rather indiscreet."

"Is there proof?"

"Texas is your territory, not mine. I imagine it would be easier for you to find records than for me."

"Texas is also a helluva big place. Do you have anything more specific?"

"A name and a date. Cotulla. The year was 1922."

Kreeger had driven through Cotulla. It was a dried-up railroad town, sixty miles north of the border.

"Why have you given me this?"

"I told you already. We have service interests in common. I give you Ramírez. You call off the dogs of war in Washington. We have more interesting games to play than these buffooneries."

Kreeger left the park five minutes after Fomin, his mood compounded by elation and nervous tension. Was Fomin sending him off on a wild goose chase? If Fomin had told him the truth, could he document it? Could he find out anything in time to avert a disaster?

The questions assailed him with fixed bayonets.

He did not mind that Karla had bought herself a chunky silver necklace, studded with turquoise, though the thing felt like it weighed a couple of pounds. She showed it to him when he rejoined her at Las Mañanitas. He was fully preoccupied with the most difficult question of all—whether to take the ball Fomin had tossed him and just run with it, up to Cotulla or wherever.

If he ran with it, what did he risk? Being out of town when the balloon went up. Making a fool of himself. Giving the Admiral—and the Director—the excuse they needed to kick him out. All of the above.

On the other hand, if he could prove that Ramírez Senior was born in the United States, he would be able to answer the question that had stumped him at the dinner with Nigel Yarrow. How do you blackmail a Mexican President?

And he could give the Butler Administration a better option than shooting itself in the gut over Mexico.

A quiet but very powerful option.

WHEN Kreeger awoke on Sunday, his mind was fully resolved. He would mete out the things that needed to be done at headquarters between the people who could handle them, leaving as little room as possible for Maury Atthowe to foul up. He would send Director Wagoner a request for emergency leave, for family reasons. A request of this type had never been refused, in Kreeger's experience, and no doubt the Director would be glad, in any case, to have him out of the way.

He would file a report on his meeting with Fomin in the Station registry, to be kept under wraps until he gave further instructions.

He drove into the Embassy to send the ANTARCTICA message. He enclosed a note for Dorothy with the package. In their agreed code, he told her that he expected to be in Washington during the coming week, and would need her to set up a private visit with President Butler.

He was still in the communications room when George Camacho came in, his face flushed, his tie askew.

"I tried you at home," George reported.

"What's up?"

"I think we got him."

In his preoccupation with Fomin and the possible handle on Ramírez, Kreeger was momentarily at a loss.

"Sanchez," his liaison officer prodded him.

"Let's have it."

George Camacho gave it to him in a few terse sentences. He had suspected that Salazar had been stalling him, trying to puff the money. So George had resorted to a squeeze maneuver, making it clear to the SIN agent that unless he produced the goods, and quickly, there were ways of letting Fausto García know about his private dealings with the CIA. Salazar had become notably more efficient. Specifically, he had gleaned from his sister the information that her husband Abelardo was holed up in Matehuala, at a safe house. The sister was evidently a formidable woman; Abelardo had phoned to reassure her he was not with a mistress.

"I figure that Sanchez must be there," George concluded.

They studied a road map. Matehuala was several hundred miles north, on Highway 57, which ran all the way to Eagle Pass and, eventually, to San Antonio. Kreeger had once sped through the town with El Loco Quintero, en route to the hostage swap that had freed Donna Renwick. It was also on Kreeger's way home, if he decided to drive up to Texas instead of taking a plane. And he had already put in his request for a leave of absence.

"It never rains—" Kreeger began.

Camacho waited in vain for the rest.

Kreeger rapped out instructions. "Get some wheels. Get Salazar. We'll need him. Get him to bring some of those license plates Fausto's people use. We'll need some firepower."

George Camacho was grinning from ear to ear. He had joined the Agency for the action, before it went out of style. He had just been given his second youth.

TWENTY-FIVE

□ □ □

1

FIFTEEN miles north of the Tropic of Cancer, Rico Sanchez slept with his ghosts, and with two flat-faced brown women provided by SIN. He did not ask the names of the women. He knew the names of his ghosts.

Sanchez was lodged in a four-room stucco house that turned its back on a dirt road. It was a typical SIN safe house, mostly used for drinking binges and shacking up with whores. It was tended by taciturn Indian maids who asked no questions. Sanchez had been there since he shot President Paz, his constant companions men from the security detail that Fausto had selected for the President. They barbecued steaks over a bottled gas burner in the yard, emptied cases of beer and tequila and cheap Don Pedro brandy, and played the TV, day and night. One of the men was called Abelardo. The nail of the little finger on his left hand protruded an inch from the tip, lending him a slightly effeminate air. That fingernail told Sanchez a great deal about Abelardo. It told him that the man came from a poor family that had never risen above manual labor, or worse. Now he wore his fingernail as long as a Chinese tart to prove to the world that he had climbed above his own people, and would never sink back. Sanchez understood. He knew what it meant to be poor. He had seen his father, a Mexican refugee from the time of the civil war, used up in the cotton mills outside Corpus. He remembered the evenings when his family had sat down to rice without beans, or a meager fistful of tortillas.

One of the girls in bed with Sanchez fingered his Rolex. He felt it slipping down his wrist, and slapped her hand away. Then, on reflection, he pushed both the women out of bed, watching with rapidly increased interest as their buttocks jiggled when they reached for their clothes. Without preliminaries, he mounted one of them from behind, pushing her down on all fours, forcing her sphincter with hard, brutal strokes. She cried out in pain, but not as loudly as Sanchez when he came inside her. He felt as if molten lead was shooting through his urethra. It had been this way since he had picked up a low-grade venereal disease, resistant to penicillin. Because the pain was excruciating, it should have reduced his sexual appetite; instead, it seemed to have the reverse effect. Perhaps to compensate, Sanchez generally managed to ensure that he meted out as much pain as he experienced.

When he finally kicked the women out of the room, Sanchez drew back a corner of the heavy drapes, and stuck a finger between the slats of the Venetian blinds underneath. It was full daylight. How long had he been there? Ten days? Twelve? He had lost count.

There were bars on the outside of the windows, confirming what Sanchez had known since Fausto's men had brought him up here: He was a prisoner. He had been a fool to let them take his gun away, though any ballistics expert could prove that it had fired the shot that entered the President's brain. He looked at his callused hands, hard-grained as wood. These, too, were killing tools. If necessary, he would use them. The men watching TV outside his room were spoiled and sloppy. They would never be his match. He had been places none of them had dreamed. He had been tempered by fire. He carried the strength of the warriors he had killed, though they rebelled against him in nightmares. He had learned ancient skills in the highlands of Vietnam. He could make himself invisible. A Mexican ninja. Sanchez smiled at the phrase.

He was safe for now. He felt confident that Fausto would not abandon him, for the time being, at least. Fausto had proved this already—by killing the only witness who had seen him leave the Alhóndiga. His pact with Fausto dated back more than three years, long before Art Colgate had approached him with the Safari Project. They were two of a kind, Sanchez and Fausto; they would prosper together. Fausto had already paid him half a million dollars, held securely in a Miami bank. More had been promised.

Fausto telephoned every day, reassuring Sanchez that everything was proceeding according to plan. He inquired after Sanchez's creature comforts. He counseled patience. He affirmed his enduring friendship.

And Sanchez trusted him, though he was not a trusting man.

The choice of a safe house midway between the capital and the Texas border—and the nest of conspirators at Monterrey—suggested that Fausto had further uses for him.

If Sanchez's instinct told him to go, the men who were fondling the bought women in the outer room would not be able to stop him. He had survived the tunnels of Cu Chi. He had escaped the Vietcong. He was invisible.

2

SANCHEZ was shaving with a disposable razor when he heard one of the guards shout *"Chinga!"* and the TV set was switched off.

The shout, and the absence of the omnipresent blare from the TV, was so unusual that Sanchez rushed out of the bathroom, lather on his cheeks, to see what was going on.

The women had left. A guard was positioned by the door. Abelardo looked scared. His eyes flitted nervously from Sanchez to the darkened TV.

"Que pasó?" Sanchez demanded. "Did you break a nail, pretty boy?"

He switched on the TV and caught the tail end of a news report on an American network.

He saw his own face, in an old black-and-white photograph. Army fatigues. Cropped hair. He had not changed very much. His hair was still black, but the skin had tightened over the bones.

The voice-over began in midsentence. ". . . known among GIs in Vietnam as the Headhunter. Sanchez carried out assassinations of Vietcong leaders, and is alleged to have trained right-wing Salvadoran death squads in similar methods. He is now being sought by authorities on both sides of the Mexican border in connection with the murder of President Paz."

The guard by the door opened his jacket, exposing the butt of the heavy pistol stuck in his waistband. Abelardo snatched up a pump shotgun, his hands shaking.

It dawned on Sanchez that he was no longer invisible.

The guard told him to sit down in the corner, and stationed himself next to the telephone.

They waited for the phone to ring.

3

THERE had still been no word from Fausto when a black LTD pulled up outside the house. Sanchez had never seen the blocky, dark-skinned man who walked into the living room, but he recognized him as immediate danger.

The guard addressed the stranger deferentially, calling him *comandante*. Abelardo appeared to be his relation, because the big man caught him up in a hearty *abrazo*.

Sanchez chose that moment to make his leap. From his squatting position, he pushed off the balls of his feet. He broke Abelardo's neck with a single, slicing blow, and grabbed for the shotgun with his free hand.

The *comandante* was faster than Sanchez had expected, however, and he had the advantage of weight. He landed a hard right punch that broke Sanchez's nose, and dropped him to his knees. He jerked Sanchez's head back by the hair and drove thick fingers into his throat on either side of the windpipe, cutting off his air. Breathing hard, he swung his pistol by the barrel and slammed the butt down against Sanchez's skull.

When Sanchez came around, he was bound hand and foot with mean straps of rawhide that bit into his skin.

"Help me take him to the car," said the *comandante*.

The security man was edgy. He looked at the telephone, and muttered something about waiting for orders.

"I already have my orders," the *comandante* told him.

The phone rang. The *comandante* picked up the receiver and listened, speaking only just before hanging up. "*Entendido*," he said. "Understood."

He turned to the guard, saying with apparent satisfaction, "Time to feed *la paloma*." In the vocabulary of SIN, doves are always victims.

SANCHEZ was put in the trunk of the LTD, where a pair of small holes had been drilled in the metal for ventilation. He was driven for half an hour or more along smooth roads before the car made a sharp turn and bumped along a rutted, spine-jarring surface. Then the car wheezed to a halt. Sanchez heard the driver's door slam shut, then footsteps, diminishing to silence.

He brought his knees up to his chest and tried to

force the trunk with his feet. The metal bulged outward, but the lock held.

The *comandante* came back and opened the trunk. He cut the cords around Sanchez's ankles and helped him out of the trunk.

Sanchez found himself in the parking lot next to a low, L-shaped building, a motel that obviously had not seen paying guests in a long time. The sign hung down at a crazy angle, letters missing. Dust swirled in front of boarded-up windows. A pair of buzzards tilted overhead.

Two men were standing next to a big American car. Neither looked Mexican, although one was Hispanic. An Argentine, maybe, or a Cuban. The other, solid and wide as a linebacker, could only be an American.

The *comandante* stood behind Sanchez while he tried to make out his situation. "You are going with these men," he spoke into Sanchez's ear.

"Who are they?"

"They will explain everything to you. You will explain everything to them, my friend."

Without warning, Sanchez's captor grabbed his right hand—the one with the pinkie ring—and sawed into it with a hunting knife. Sanchez squirmed violently as he was shoved flat on his face in the gravel, his wrists still bound behind his back. Through the entire ordeal, however, he did not cry out. He would never do that—not in front of these men.

"Salazar!" the American yelled. "What the fuck are you doing?"

Salazar kept sawing away. It took several slashes to completely sever the finger.

He heard the American grumbling. "Have you taken leave of your senses, Salazar?"

"It was Fausto García's order," said the *comandante*. "He requires proof that the job was done. He will have it."

Jim Kreeger assisted Sanchez to his feet, and bound

his own handkerchief around the last knuckle of Sanchez's right hand to staunch the bleeding.

"You should be grateful that Fausto did not ask for your head," Salazar said to the captive. "You are a dead man missing only a finger."

4

KREEGER drove up Route 57 all the way to Piedras Negras, stopping only once, at Monclova, for gasoline and for disinfectant and proper bandages for Rico Sanchez. There were a dozen roadblocks along the highway, manned by state and federal police and, at one point, by soldiers with armed vehicles. They saw the familiar first digits—333—of the SIN license plates on the car and waved it through.

Kreeger changed the plates at Piedras Negras. The Customs man on the U.S. side of the bridge looked at the Texas plates, and at Kreeger, and said, "Welcome home."

THEY took two rooms at the Alamo Hotel, on the outskirts of Eagle Pass. Kreeger drove back into town and purchased a camcorder, a VCR, and half a dozen blank videocassettes. For what he intended to do, video beat out audio every time. Besides, President Butler watched TV a lot. It was his mastery of the visual medium, after all, that had helped him win the election.

Kreeger was perfectly aware that what he was going to do was probably illegal, under the laws of the United States. The interrogation of a U.S. citizen, on U.S. soil, was not within the purview of the Central Intelligence Agency. He had given some thought to alternative options, but they were not very alluring. He could have turned Sanchez over to the *Judiciales*—sworn enemies of Fausto's service—or the Attorney General's office down in Mexico. But, judging by past experience, Sanchez would have disappeared without trace. Then again, he could have called in a U.S. agency with an interest in the matter. Perhaps the FBI, or the Bureau of Alcohol, Tobacco, and Firearms. But Sanchez was not under indictment in the United States, and time was of the essence.

Kreeger knew he was sticking his neck out, but the situation demanded decisive action. George Camacho was also putting his job on the line, and Kreeger had told him he would not forget. Beyond his connection with Comandante Salazar, George was the ideal man for the work at hand. He was a specialist in interrogation, and he knew Rico Sanchez.

As it turned out, they did not need to use any exotic techniques on Sanchez. The missing finger had accomplished more than several days of grilling.

"I'll talk," said Sanchez in the motel room. "That is, when I know the deal."

"I don't have the authority to make any deals," Kreeger told him. It was the right answer. Sanchez had worked for the U.S. government long enough to know the rules.

"What I can do for you is this," Kreeger continued. "I can recommend to the higher-ups that the Agency should fit you out with a new identity, a safe haven, whatever. I can guarantee you your life, in any event. I guess you can pay your own bills."

"What's your recommendation worth?"

"It depends on how much you give. Tell you what. If you don't like the deal, we drive you back across the border and call up Fausto García. Or maybe Raúl Carvajal. Your call."

Sanchez thought it over.

George Camacho said, "I hear things rattling around in your head."

Sanchez said, "I want to relocate in Florida."

"Agreed," said Kreeger. "If I get approval. If you

give me enough reason. It's doable, Rico, I promise you that. How about your family?"

"I don't need them. They don't need me."

"If you say so. Now, why don't you start by telling us about the first time you met Fausto García?"

Kreeger motioned to George, and he pressed the button of the camcorder. Naturally, it was Japanese-made.

Sanchez was a gifted storyteller, once he warmed up.

"I was doing a little cross-border business," he began.

"On whose account?"

"On my own account. I got my own company."

"When was this?"

"Three or four years back, after I left the Army. I was down in Coahuila, bringing in a couple of truckloads. TVs, VCRs. Nothing major."

"You're sure it wasn't drugs?"

"I don't need that shit. I don't hold with it."

"I'm glad to hear you sometimes draw the line. Go on."

"We got picked up. By SIN, not the *Judiciales*. It seemed to be a routine shakedown, but there was more. Fausto García turned up in person. He said we could do a lot of business together. Fausto said he had friends who needed to make deposits in U.S. banks. Big deposits. And I happened to know a few hungry bankers in Texas and south Florida. That's how it began."

"Laundering money for Fausto and his friends. Drug money?"

"I didn't ask where it came from."

"Where does Art Colgate come in?"

"That miserable prick." Sanchez laughed. "I remember when he first came to Saigon. Colgate wanted results. Quotas, body counts. You know how it worked. Colgate wanted to go one better. There was some adviser passing through, a Brit who was also a big wheel with the Nixon White House. He told how the British had gotten results in Malaya by putting a price on the heads of CT's—Communist Terrorists. That's the way people talked back then."

"I remember."

"So Colgate put out word he wanted their heads."

"And you killed Judge Renwick the same way."

"That wasn't my bag."

"You'll have to convince me."

"I don't know anything about that."

"I don't believe you." Kreeger's instinct told him that Sanchez was telling the truth, but he felt compelled to keep pushing. He owed it to his boyhood friend.

"You ought to ask Colgate," Sanchez said. "We were out hunting. It was the night he signed me on for this stunt. He said something about having a man killed, the way we used to do it for the Station in Nam."

The interview lasted more than six hours. By the end of it, Kreeger had proof that the Safari plotters had orchestrated the murder of U.S. citizens in Mexico, and that they had been able to co-opt key members of the Butler Administration. He also had proof that Fausto García had planted a mole—a mole who, by his own confession, had assassinated President Paz.

"You're going to look after me, right?" Sanchez demanded.

"I ought to bury you." Kreeger stared at the man with disgust. He still had one last question, a personal one. "Let's go back to Saigon. There was a woman at the Station. Blonde, quite attractive. Her name was Val. You must have run into her."

"No."

Sanchez's eyes clouded. For the first time in the conversation, Kreeger was quite sure he was lying.

Sanchez confirmed it when he added, "Ask Colgate. She was his fucking wife."

5

"SAY the word"—George Camacho was talking; they had fed Sanchez enough sleeping pills to make sure he was out for a few hours. "I'll make the adjustment."

Kreeger hated that euphemism for killing; it smacked of Colgate.

"I promised I'd do my best to get him a deal," said Kreeger. "I generally keep my word."

"There are times I don't understand you at all," Camacho complained. "We've got the videotapes. What more can he give us? None of this is going to hold up in a U.S. court of law. You want the son of a bitch to retire in the Florida sun after all he's done?"

"No. But I want Art Colgate. And before I'm done, Sanchez is going to help me."

TWENTY-SIX

□ □ □

1

As expected, Fernando Ramírez was sworn in as Mexico's interim President. Protest rallies were dispersed by riot police and troops firing live bullets. The U.S. Secretary of State recalled Ambassador Childs for consultations, setting off rumors around the Embassy that he would not be coming back. There were scare reports in the Mexican press that U.S. military maneuvers being conducted in the deserts of New Mexico were camouflage for a projected invasion. In the U.S. Congress, Senator Pike called openly for a "surgical strike" to oust Ramírez and bring him to the United States for trial. After an attack on the U.S. consul in Guadalajara, Embassy staff were advised to send their families home on the earliest available flights.

The *Washington Post* came out with a front-page story on covert U.S. operations against Mexico, allegedly run from General Gilly's office at the Pentagon. The principal source of this story was Joel Stein, who had been following up Kreeger's leads in Washington. A testy White House spokesman refused comment. Admiral Enright counseled "accelerated action."

Late that night, President Butler sat on the Truman balcony at the executive mansion, staring off in the direction of the Washington Monument, much to the dismay of the Secret Service man on duty, who pointed out that the President was making himself vulnerable to a sniper with a high-powered rifle.

Actually, Harry Butler felt vulnerable to many things

that night. In the *Post* report, he had read things none of his close advisers on Mexico had told him. The men he had covered for in Houston and Monterrey were playing a rougher game than he had expected, and details were beginning to spill out. These were the same men—with independent support from Bill Enright and some of the Pentagon brass—who had been pushing for U.S. intervention. Harry Butler had had doubts all along, and now they were turning into certainties.

It was the President's habit, on nights when he could not sleep, to watch movies on the VCR in his private quarters. He had asked one of the Filipino servants to bring up an old favorite, a William Holden film. When the giant, high-definition TV screen came alive, the President was startled by a scene that certainly was not in the original cut. He saw himself sitting on the edge of a circular bed. He was buck-naked. Shelley Hayes was crouched between his knees. The camera angle left nothing to the imagination.

Caught between horror and fascination, Harry Butler stared at the screen, stunned by the realization of what he saw. Suddenly aware that his wife had walked in from the bedroom, the President grabbed for the remote —almost in time. Ann Travis Butler had caught only a fading glimpse of a woman's heart-shaped buttocks as she went down on a man whose face was hidden from view.

"You dirty son of a bitch," she shouted in fury, assuming that the President had been watching a porno flick. It would not have been the first time. She turned in fury and stormed from the room.

As soon as he was alone, Harry Butler ripped the tape from inside the shell of the videocassette and threw it on the fire. When he sent for the Filipino servant who had brought up the video, he was informed that the man had left the White House before the end of the shift, complaining of stomach pains.

No verbal message had come with the tape, but

Harry Butler did not doubt for a moment that the signal had come from Raúl—a reminder that he was on the hook. Now, because of a single, stupid lapse in Aspen, when he was bone-tired and lonely, they were pushing him toward a military adventure that, in his heart, he did not want.

The President did not like to be herded, although the political resurrection of Ramírez had made confrontation with Mexico almost unavoidable. In Florida, a belligerent Federal attorney was again urging the case for Ramírez's indictment before a sympathetic grand jury. Harry Butler did not know where to turn.

2

AT the CIA Station in Mexico City, Maury Atthowe, who despite Kreeger's efforts to minimize his role, had assumed the position of acting chief, seemed to be enjoying the crisis. He went about with an I-know-something-you-don't smirk on his face. He took personal calls from Washington. He made time for tennis with the Army and Navy attachés. He read files. He demanded to see CI material that belonged to Lois Compton.

"You're not cleared for that," Lois told him.

"I can get any clearance I want. I can go to the Director on this."

"Then go. I'll need a written directive, and if you get one, I'm still going to fight it."

"Listen to me, Lois. I'm going to give you a word of advice. You're a damn good officer. You've earned a lot of respect. But signing on with a personality cult could bring on an early frost."

"What is that supposed to mean?"

"You're overcommitted to Kreeger. Jim is making a lot of mistakes. Frankly, I'd hate to see him pull you down. You could wind up sorting papers at the Central Registry."

Lois left Atthowe's office with a drumming behind her temples.

She took Maury's threats seriously enough to know that she needed to get a warning to Jim. She was not privy to Kreeger's travel plans, although she knew he had gone to Texas. Maybe she could reach him at his parents' place, in the hill country behind Kerrville. If anyone at the Station knew how to reach him, it would be Eddie O'Brien.

She rode the elevator back down to the consular section. There were many telephone messages on her desk, mostly from scared U.S. citizens who wanted to know whether they should leave the country. One message, however, was from Shelley Hayes. She was back in town, and had left word she would wait at her hotel for Lois's call.

When Lois reached her, Shelley sounded edgy, maybe a little tight. She wanted Lois to meet her for dinner at her favorite place, Del Lago. Although it seemed to her an odd time for Raúl Carvajal's mistress to visit Mexico City, Lois agreed to meet her around nine-thirty.

Next, Lois sought out Eddie, asking him to join her for coffee. Together they strolled across the Reforma and took a booth at the VIPS restaurant on the edge of the Zona Rosa.

"Maury's an undersized prick," Eddie commented when she told him about her talk with Atthowe. "He doesn't know an operation from a hole in the ground. He only got this far by losing tennis games to the right partners."

Eddie did agree, however, that they needed to talk with Kreeger. "Jim called me at home this morning. He said he'll be at his parents' place tonight. Why don't we have dinner and make it a conference call?"

"Sorry. I've got a date."

"Who's the lucky guy?"

"Not that kind of date." It struck her that it might be useful to have Eddie around. He had a way with the ladies, and he was nonthreatening.

Lois proposed to Eddie that he show up at Del Lago. He could have a drink at the bar. If Shelley seemed in the right mood, they could bump into Eddie, as if by chance, and make it a threesome.

Eddie asked, "What's she *really* like?"

"She's not exactly your girl-next-door type. I doubt you'll find you have much in common."

"You'd be surprised. I've lived in some fairly exotic neighborhoods."

3

WHEN Lois walked into Del Lago, the band was in full swing. Several couples were dancing to an old Roberto Carlos number. She found Shelley at their regular table, by the window, sipping a vodka martini.

Shelley got up and embraced her, swaying a little. "Before we talk—hell, before we eat—I want to see you down at least two of these." She held up her martini glass. "I don't like drinking alone."

Lois held up two fingers to the waiter. "But make them manhattans."

Shelley watched Lois drain the first of the manhattans before she spoke: "I want you to tell me the worst thing a man ever did to you."

"Well, after I broke up with my husband, there was this guy I met in L.A. He was a fitness freak. You know, weight lifting, gyms. He had these violent mood swings. Steroids, I guess. One time he started slapping me around."

"Bastard. What did you do?"

"I gave him this." Lois held up her clenched fist. "I

come from a pretty tough neighborhood. Czechs on one block, Slovaks on the next. I generally know how to take care of myself."

"Good for you. How about the man?"

"I dislocated his jaw. The asshole sent me the hospital bill, if you can believe it."

"How about your father?"

"He was a decent man. Worked himself to death for his kids, I guess."

"Did you ever go with an older man?"

"How much older?"

"Old enough to be your father."

"I had a crush on one of my law professors. What are we doing here? Group therapy?"

"I've always gravitated to older men. I suppose it's my insecurity. I never seem to have time for men my own age."

"I don't see that age has much to do with it."

"Tell it to *them*." Shelley's eyes swept the candle-lit dining room. A number of well-heeled older men were sitting with women half their age. "Look at them! Those vampires! They imagine that young blood will give them back their youth! Doesn't it disgust you?"

"Actually, I think it's sort of funny. By the time a woman reaches her prime, a man is coasting downhill. Or should I say, pointing downhill? Mature women deserve younger lovers. We have so much more to teach them!"

They clinked glasses, and Shelley said, "Thank you for that."

"You never married?" Lois asked, after a pause.

"I was married for two years. To a homosexual. A friend. It was his suggestion. He thought my daughter should have a father's name on her birth certificate. Who knows? Maybe he wanted cover at that point in his life. He died a couple of years ago. One of life's victims."

"And the real father?"

"Not somebody I want to talk about," Shelley replied, looking away, out through the window.

Lois wondered how many tragedies there were in this woman's life, lurking behind the surface glamour. "You never wanted a real marriage?"

"No. I suppose I never trusted a man that far. Except once. And he was already married, of course."

The captain came for their order. Shelley asked for crepes and patzcuaro fish; Lois said she would have the same.

"I don't want to burden you with my problems," Shelley said, trying to sound dismissive.

"Hey, what are friends for?" Lois sensed that far from ending, the real discussion was just about to begin.

"I don't know how I got in so deep. I have these . . . these terrible dreams," Shelley said. "My mother screaming at me. She's been dead for twenty years." She was trembling. As she continued, her words spilled over each other. She spoke of Raúl, then of other men—Lois found it difficult to follow. Her monologue ended only when the waiter arrived with the first course. When he had left she spoke again, but with less urgency.

"There's a mystery about you, Lois. I think you do more for the Embassy than stamp visas."

"I'm flattered. And if it were true?"

"I need help. Raúl has become a madman. You know what I am."

"I know you're a woman with a lot of heart."

"A kept woman. It is almost a vocation. It has its rules, its silences. I don't expect wives to understand. Ann Butler called me a whore."

Lois gripped her fork very tightly, to prevent it from rattling against the plate. Shelley had just told her what she had not dared to ask directly: that she had been the mistress of the President of the United States.

Shelley veered away from the subject of the First Family. "I had an arrangement with Raúl. A civilized arrangement. It pleases a man like Raúl to pay for his pleasures. It reassures him of their value. But he has used me for something so . . . vile, so shameful, I feel I could shower in acid and the stain wouldn't wash off.''

After a pause while the waiter cleared the first set of plates, Shelley asked, ''Have you ever hated a man? Hated him enough to set out to destroy him?''

''I wanted to take my ex to the cleaners. He thinks I did.''

''Beyond that. Has a man ever hurt you enough to make you want to kill him?''

''I've never let a man hurt me that bad.''

''I'm glad. It took me a while to learn something, Lois. We can't afford to hate. You try to injure another human soul, and it comes back on you.''

Lois took the plunge. ''Is all this to do with Harry?''

Shelley paused, looking directly at her dinner companion. ''How long have you known?'' she asked, with reasonable composure.

''You just told me. If you want to tell me something more, I'm here for you. If you ask me to keep it to myself, I'll do that too.''

''You're CIA, aren't you?''

Lois took a deep breath. ''If I was, I'd tell you no.''

''I don't think there's anything you can do, whoever you're with. It's too late. It was all a game until people started getting killed. I wasn't prepared. Raúl never told me it would come to that.''

''Look, Shelley, you're scaring me. If you need help, I know how to get it. No matter what you've done. Nothing in life is irreversible.''

''I'd love to believe that,'' Shelley said, staring at the empty glass in her hand.

''Would you excuse me?'' Lois stood up. ''I need to make a pit stop.''

On her way to the rest room, she took a swing through the bar. Eddie was sitting at the far end, with a view across the lake. He was drinking ginger ale.

''Good boy.''

"How's your dinner date?"

"She's in the orphan mode."

"I beg your pardon?"

"Drinking to kill the pain, bitching about men in her life, waiting for a gallant knight to rescue her."

"I'm ready."

"I don't want to rush her. We'll catch you on the way out. Maybe a nightcap."

"Anything else I should know?"

"She slept with President Butler. And her friend in Monterrey knows that. It might explain a few things."

Open-mouthed, Eddie watched Lois walk away, around the edge of the tiny dance floor. He was distinctly looking forward to making Shelley's acquaintance. Reflexively, he pushed his cowlick back off his forehead. A couple of dyed blondes, drinking at a table by the wall, gave him hopeful glances.

Eddie swiveled on his stool to face the huge picture windows. The shadows on the lake were deep indigo. Lights winked from the high-rise buildings across Chapultepec Park. It was a mild, soft evening, and there were lots of pleasure boats out on the water. Lovers in dinghies, trailing their oars. Speedboats, darting like fireflies.

Some Mexican *júnior* was showing off in a powerboat, zipping dangerously close to the water's edge. The pointed prow of his boat stabbed straight toward the restaurant. One of the blondes let out an involuntary scream, which fractured into embarrassed giggles as the powerboat swerved away.

Eddie caught a glimpse of the man at the wheel. Not a *júnior* at all. The leather and grease and gold chains looked doper-chic. As the speedboat came around, Eddie saw a second man, propped against the rail for support as he shouldered a dark, tubular object.

The next instant, O'Brien was on his feet, racing toward the dining area. He barreled his way through the dancers, pushing them aside, turning the dance floor into a bowling alley. One angry man threw a punch at Eddie.

He missed his mark, slipped, and skated into the percussion section of the band.

The maître d' and several captains or waiters lined up across Eddie's path like a firing squad.

He shouted to Lois.

He saw her face change, saw her jerk forward toward Shelley, rocking their table. As she moved, the huge picture window blew inward, hurling knives of glass across the restaurant. The diners abandoned their tables and fled for the exits, a stampeding, leaderless mob. Eddie fought his way through them.

Out on the lake, the powerboat churned water, whipping around again. Eddie dove for the floor as the man on the rail fired another burst into the restaurant. When he came up, he had a pistol in his hand. He fired after the retreating boat. Others joined in. It was amazing how Mexicans packed firearms.

Soon the powerboat was only a smudge in the distance. Eddie stumbled to Lois's table through the debris of broken glass and china.

"Lois . . ."

The woman who crawled from beneath the overturned table was a stranger. Tawny-gold hair. Her watered silk dress splotched with food and wine. Her necklace broken, bouncing and scattering pearls across the floor.

Eddie helped her to her feet. Even in disarray, pale beneath her makeup, a row of false eyelashes crawling over her cheekbone like a caterpillar, she was quite lovely. He saw this, but knew that gallantries would have to wait, because he saw another woman lying under the ferns, spackled with blood.

His heart in his throat, Eddie reached for her, lifting her by the shoulders. His nausea at what he saw contended with his sense of relief, because she was not Lois.

He felt breath on his neck and stood, turning directly into Lois.

"Thank God. How in heaven's name—"
For the first time, she kissed him.
Lois said, "I come from a tough neighborhood."

4

As they drove back to Lois's apartment, Shelley kept saying she was sorry. "Those men came for me."

"Did you know them?"

"They work for Paco Carranza. Or the Quintero family."

"The drug cartel?"

"It is all the same."

Lois made hot cocoa while Shelley curled up, like a little girl, under an afghan on the sofa, enjoying its warmth. Eddie sat on the floor beside her.

Lois said, "You can talk to Eddie. He's not bad, as men go. He can help."

She left them alone for a few minutes. When she returned, Eddie was cradling Shelley's head in his arms, stroking her hair.

In the hollow of the night, fueled by more cocoa, plus black coffee, Shelley told her story, a tale worth killing for. By the time Lois remembered, it was far too late to call Jim Kreeger at his parents' house. That would have to wait until morning.

After a few hours' sleep, Shelley said she had to make a phone call. To Raúl. Afterward, she announced that she was going straight to the airport. She was going to fly back to Monterrey.

"You can't be serious," said Eddie. "After what happened? By your own account, Raúl's friend tried to kill you."

"I will be safe with Raúl," Shelley said with quiet determination. "Raúl still needs me. And there is something I have to do."

TWENTY-SEVEN

□ □ □

1

KREEGER's route from Eagle Pass to San Antonio ran for two and a half hours along Highway 57, through the mesquite flats. He drove the whole way. George Camacho sat in the back with the prisoner Sanchez, who had become uncharacteristically passive since they had made his life story into a home movie. Kreeger stopped in town just long enough to drop off George with Sanchez at a motel and to confirm that Judge Renwick's mother was still living up in Kendall County. Then he headed for hill country. The Sanchez tapes were dynamite. But Kreeger would need more than conventional explosives for the mission that lay ahead of him in Washington.

He was allowing himself two days, at the outside, to find what he needed. Otherwise, he'd have to go on without it. He had watched President Butler declare, on a morning TV show, that Fernando Ramírez was "unacceptable" to the United States, even as interim head of state in Mexico.

What Kreeger did not know was that the Secretaries of State and Defense, together with Director Wagoner and the Chairman of the Joint Chiefs of Staff, were now sitting with the National Security Adviser to approve General Gilly's plan to place fifty thousand combat troops —mostly airborne units, scattered between Fort Benning, Georgia, and Fort Lewis, Washington—on Delta One Alert. Only the Secretary of State demurred from Admiral Enright's forcefully expressed view that it was the duty of the United States to intervene on behalf of the "friends of democracy" across the border, if a request for assistance was made by "credible parties." There was unanimous agreement that in the event of new acts of violence against American citizens in Mexico, the Administration must make an effective demonstration of its ability and its readiness to protect American lives and property. The Butler Administration was sitting on a hair trigger. The time for Kreeger's "quiet options" was fast running out.

2

COMING into his hometown, Kreeger passed a new Wal-Mart, one of the chains that were eating up the old-time family stores. Give it a few more years, Kreeger thought, and Boerne would be a suburb of San Antonio. The plaza, at least, was as he remembered it, except that the Dienger house, on the corner of Blanco and Main, had been turned into the town library.

It was well past lunchtime—nearly one-thirty—when he stopped at the Inn for a bite to eat and a quick dose of nostalgia. The Kendall Inn occupied a southern-style mansion with wide verandahs. There were still no Mexicans in the dining room, decorated with old Burma-Shave advertising signs that used to be spaced out along the road when young Jim Kreeger had gotten his driver's license.

No Mexicans to wait on tables—the waitresses were springy, yellow-haired Texas girls—but the menu offered fajita burgers, along with cowboy soup and blueberry pie. Kreeger glanced through the Boerne *Star* while he chewed his meat. The lead item was about the big win the Boerne Hounds had scored over the Kerrville Antlers. Below it was a story about a woman who had caught a freshwater prawn in the Guadalupe River. The shrimp was twenty-five inches long. A different world.

After lunch, Kreeger drove on through Kerrville. The thought for the day on the board outside the Church of Christ read: "If you don't want others to know about it, don't do it."

The drive-in where Kreeger had enjoyed his first memorable date with Karla was still there, and looked like it was still showing movies, *de vez en cuando*. A couple of pickups were parked outside a new eatery, José's Cowboy Yacht Club. On the far side of town, along Route 16, the Neighbors' Vaudeville Dancehall was still in business. At eighteen, after too many beers, Kreeger had once broken one guy's nose and another guy's ribs in that joint in a fight over a girl whose name he couldn't remember.

He nearly missed the turn-off to his parents' place. He remembered goats grazing in the scrappy pasture along the bend, but now a trailer camp had sprouted there. Along the rutted dirt road leading down to the creek, the pecan grove was still intact, but there was a squatters' encampment under the trees. Wetbacks. Through the open window, Kreeger could smell kerosene and charcoal fires.

Buzz, his mother's superannuated schnauzer, came hopping and yapping at the unfamiliar car.

"Hi, Buzz." Kreeger opened the door, and the schnauzer, recognizing his scent, hurled itself into his lap. Kreeger stroked its chest with his forefinger, and found the spot Buzz especially liked.

He looked up to see his mother coming out of the house, surrounded by a multitude of cats. She was a gentle being, full of love for all God's creatures, but she wouldn't admit to it. Hill country people, bred to a hard, merciless land, affected its manners.

His mother was not demonstrative. She did not kiss or hug him. She merely said, as if he had returned from a ball game in San Antonio, "Your room's a bit leaky, Jim. There's a bucket beside the bed in case it rains."

Kreeger's father came padding behind. He was moving slower now. His greeting was slurred, because of his stroke, and his face reddened with anger and frustration as he tried to express himself.

Kreeger put his arm around his father. "I've missed you too, Dad."

They did not ply him with questions. They had never asked him about his work. It was enough for them to know that he was in government service. For his father, a veteran of two wars, that was still a source of pride. If he wanted to tell them more, they would listen with avid attention, but it was his call. In the hill country, a man was not required to justify himself.

He sat with them in the big kitchen overlooking the creek; they talked about old times and old friends. His father drank endless cups of coffee—the doctor had banned alcohol—and his mother drank bourbon and water out of a thimble-sized cup.

He told them, "I've run up against a few problems."

His father said, "You still have a home, Jim. You know where you belong. I live for the day you'll come back to us."

"It may be soon." His pronouncement was accepted without question.

The talk followed an aimless course. They told him about the hailstorm, only the week before, when pellets came down the size of oranges. That was why the roof over his bedroom leaked. They brought him up to date on people he knew and some he didn't.

He asked, finally, about old Lottie Renwick.

"Lottie?" his mother echoed. "Why, she said you'd never amount to anything. I guess you showed her. She's full of beans, as always. Goes about like a painted woman, at eighty-four."

"Eighty-nine," Kreeger's father corrected her.

"I need to visit with her. Where's she at?" Kreeger asked, dropping unconsciously into the rhythms of his native territory.

"I guess she's still up in Comfort," said his mother. "Still drinking the sheriff under the table."

It was a three-cigar night for Kreeger, and his father had two, in defiance of all medical practitioners.

"You sleep well now," said his mother, when he was the first to call it a night.

The rain came, in the hours before dawn, and Kreeger woke to the sound of water slapping the plastic sides of the bucket beside the bed. A calico cat—one of his mother's strays—was in the bed with him. Kreeger felt warm and at home.

He rose in high spirits, and scampered along the creek like a kid, throwing a ball for Buzz. It was good to be here, among his own folks, among people who did not ask him for reasons.

3

LOTTIE Renwick lived in a small frame house set among pecan and plum trees. She was sitting on the porch, with a rug over her knees, when Kreeger turned up the drive.

"I know why you came to see me, Jim Kreeger. You want to hear about me and Sam Houston. I have to tell you, Sam was a pretty poor lover."

Lottie was always cracking jokes about her age, but she never let on just how old she was. She said she aimed to hang on until the funny fat man announced her hundredth birthday on the *Today* show.

There was a milky cast to her eyes. Her hands were liver-spotted. The skin was creased and dry to the touch, like old parchment. Lottie had rigged herself out in a ruffled white dress with a high collar. Her head was crowned by a set of tight brown curls that were obviously not her own. But she had kept her trim figure, and there was a firm set to her jaw.

She sat Kreeger down in the dining alcove, with the good china.

She rattled on about three generations of Kreegers and Renwicks, about her teaching days at the Boerne grade school, about the times she had sent young Jim Kreeger to the headmaster for fighting in the hall.

"I was always less scared of him than of you," Kreeger recalled.

"You and Hugh. You were right scalawags. The two of you. I don't know which of you was worse." She stopped abruptly, remembering that her son was gone.

"So come on, tell me! What does the Army want with an old teacher?"

Kreeger wasn't about to try to set her straight about his employment.

"I wanted to ask you about the old days, when you were down in Cotulla with LBJ."

"There never was anything between Lyndon and me," Lottie informed him. "His ears were too big. Anyway, Lyndon was only interested in rich girls back then. He was all right, though. He treated us gals like his mother. And he wouldn't stand for Mexican talk around the school. He'd whip a boy who said *buenos días*. He made those Mexican kids greet him with a song. It went, 'How do you do, Mr. Johnson? How do you do?' "

Gently, Kreeger guided her back to the redbrick schoolhouse in the hot, dusty south Texas town. They called it the Mexican School, because most of the kids belonged to the Mexican families who lived on the wrong side of the Missouri-Pacific Railroad tracks. They had come up to work for slave labor rates on the ranches that hugged the narrow river bottoms. The Depression had come early to Cotulla.

"To anyone but a Mexican," Lottie recalled, "that town was the end of the earth. Those were hard times, and that was just about the hardest place."

"Do you remember any of the Mexican kids?" Kreeger asked, easing into his search.

"Those kids were okay. Lyndon kept them in line. But the cheeky ones used to follow him around, aping the way he walked behind his back. You know how Lyndon walked." She flapped her arms and chuckled. "I recollect one day Lyndon caught them at it. He told them to remember to copy him when they grew up, because he was going to be President of the United States. I guess he did it, too."

"A kid called Ramírez," Kreeger prodded. "I guess he must have been seven or eight when you were down there at the Mexican School. Ring any bells?"

"Ramírez, Rodriguez. They all sound the same to me, Jim. They all looked the same, too." She spooned more sugar into her coffee. "I guess they all went home when the war came, anyway. When word got 'round the government was fixing to draft the wets, they knocked the water out of the Rio Grande getting back down to Mexico."

Her mind slid away from Cotulla. She started up on how the Kreegers had always been tight. "Your mother was real bad. She used to holler, 'Cut out that light! You're burning a hole in the ceiling!' "

Kreeger tried to ease her back to the schoolhouse. She remembered scraps, bits and pieces of the place and the time. She remembered a bright boy with a funny first name, more confident with English than the others. The one LBJ stood up on a plank to recite "Oh Captain, My Captain" at the school concert.

Kreeger asked, "What was funny about his name?"

"His folks called that poor boy Saragossa."

"Zaragoza?"

"Maybe. Didn't mean anything to me."

"It's the name of a town in Spain." Kreeger's interest quickened. A Ramírez had come from Spain around the turn of the century. The name of Fernando Ramírez's father, according to his CIA file, was quite ordinary: Guillermo. But Zaragoza might have been a nickname, or an embarrassment he had dropped as soon as he was old enough to choose for himself. "You're sure the last name wasn't Ramírez?"

She was sure of nothing, apart from the funny first name.

Kreeger's spirits dipped. He was going to have to slog it out. He had checked into the steps he would have to take with the man from INS at the Embassy in Mexico City. The courthouse in Cotulla was one place to look. Maybe there would be a record of a birth in the Ramírez family. Kreeger had already made the call. There wasn't.

The state archives in Austin were another possibility. Kreeger had called his daughter and asked her to do some digging, although he was not optimistic about what Lucy would find.

Under the 1917 act, which had been in force when the Ramírez family were at Cotulla, all aliens were supposed to register with the Attorney General. There was a slight chance that the parents could be traced. There might be something in an A file at the INS district office at San Antonio, or on microfilm at the center in Dallas. Or in Washington, among the millions of scattered files that were sitting in banana crates out in the halls.

Another option for Kreeger was to file a multimanifold G-135. It would bring seven government agencies in on the search, including CIA, FBI, and Social Security. If there were paper records of the Ramírez family in the United States, they would turn up eventually.

These checks, however, would take a lot more time than Kreeger had, and they would alert anyone who had a vested interest in Fernando Ramírez.

Kreeger felt an ache in his lower back. Whatever youthful rejuvenation he had felt upon exploring childhood memories was rapidly fading.

The trail Fomin had opened seemed to be running into the sand. Was that what Fomin had intended?

"I'm sorry to pester you," Kreeger said to his old schoolteacher, "but this Ramírez thing is important. Can you think of anyone who might remember?"

"They'd all be dead."

"I guess the Mexican School didn't have a yearbook, or anything like that."

"Hell, we were lucky to have a blackboard. Though things got better the year Lyndon was there. He charmed that superintendent up in Houston. Lyndon always was good at getting his nose up the right ass."

She cackled at Kreeger's shocked expression at her irreverence.

"You sure got a burr under your tail about that kid, don't you, Jim? You sit right there. Maybe I've got something that will freshen up the old memory cells, if I can think where I put it."

She walked stiffly into the parlor and rummaged around in the blanket chest that doubled as a coffee table. She brought back an old album and a bunch of photographs of all shapes and sizes.

She showed Kreeger a snapshot of herself with a gangling, jug-eared LBJ. Part of the photograph had been snipped away.

"Where's the rest of it?" Kreeger asked.

"Oh, we didn't need *her.*"

There was a signed portrait of LBJ as a candidate for the Senate, taken by a professional photographer, and some holiday snapshots of Renwicks and Kreegers on the river together. Lottie held them up one by one, delivering rambling commentaries.

"May I?" Kreeger reached down and pulled an old eight-by-ten out of the pile. It wasn't what he wanted. The boys and girls were all Anglos, lined up in front of the Boerne grade school. Kreeger recognized himself in the back row.

Then he saw something more interesting. It was another group photograph, less formally posed. The long-boned young man standing up on the platform between two women was LBJ. His eyes were trained on a black-haired kid whose hand was pressed to his heart as he recited the Pledge of Allegiance.

"Who's that?"

Lottie peered over.

"That's him. The one with the funny name."

"Zaragoza?"

"I knew I had something."

Kreeger looked more closely at the picture. There was a vague resemblance to Fernando Ramírez, especially in the aquiline curve of the Mexican kid's nose, as well as in the high, bony forehead and the calculating eyes. Not close enough to be sure. Certainly not enough to sustain a bluff.

Kreeger turned over the photograph.

Lottie heard his sharp intake of breath and said, "Something wrong?"

LBJ had signed the back in his bold hand. So had Lottie, and the other teacher, and the county judge who was sitting up there with them. In a show of good fellowship, they must have invited the Mexican boy who spouted poems in such good English to sign along with them. He had written, "Z. G. Ramírez."

Kreeger let out his breath. "Mind if I borrow this?"

"Hell, I haven't looked at that old thing in years. Sorry I couldn't give you what you wanted."

"You just gave me everything I need."

TWENTY-EIGHT

□ □ □

1

WHEN Kreeger returned to his parents' house by the creek, his mother told him about a phone call he had gotten. Long distance, she thought. A woman's voice. She would not leave a message, but had said she would try again at noon. Kreeger waited for the call. When it came, he immediately recognized Lois's voice, husky from all those cigarettes. She spoke without using proper names, but he understood her message well enough. And he felt finally that he comprehended the erratic behavior of the Butler White House in relation to Mexico. He told his folks good-bye, and drove to the San Antonio airport and bought a ticket for the first flight to Washington.

2

WHILE Kreeger was waiting for his plane, Gail Armstrong and a TV camera crew were following the shadow of their chartered Bell helicopter over the amoeboid sprawl of Mexico City. The chargé d'affaires at the American Embassy was sufficiently alarmed about Gail Armstrong's safety—after her notorious televised indictment of Ramírez—to have placed a personal call to the director of news programming at her network, warning of possible danger.

The network executive wanted to know if the call

was an indication that the Butler Administration was backing away from the Ramírez problem.

"Look, there's a State Department Advisory in force. One American reporter has already been killed in Mexico. Isn't that enough?"

"We care about Gail too. She's a helluva reporter. And she would not tolerate any backing away from a story."

The chargé decided that he had more than discharged his obligations.

Gail Armstrong had told her American pilot—a bush flyer who would ferry anything, except drugs, for a buck —to make a pass over the jail where Miliano was being held.

The pilot followed her request, shouting against the storm of the rotors to tell Gail tales of other celebrated inmates of the Reclusorio del Norte. These included union bosses and dopers, whose money bought them luxury suites, hot-and-cold running women, and meals from five-star restaurants, and had their visitors sign guest books.

"That's enough," Gail Armstrong said after the second pass. "Now I want you to take us over Campo Militar Número Uno. You know where that is, don't you? I want to see where they dump the bodies."

The bush pilot was not at all happy at this request. He tried to explain the Mexican rules, that airspace over military installations was strictly off-limits. It was the same in any country.

"We fly over the Campo Militar, they're likely to start shooting at us."

"I'll give you a bonus."

The pilot looked hard at his passenger. She was quite sexy, with her straw-blond hair floating free.

"How about dinner?" he asked.

"How about five hundred dollars?"

"Then I'll pay for dinner."

"I'll think about it."

The pilot agreed to make one quick pass. He had worked long enough in Mexico to have heard something about Campo Militar Número Uno. It wasn't just the home of some armored battalions that garrisoned the capital. It was the place where SIN performed vanishing tricks. Critics of the government claimed that thousands of *desaparecidos* were buried among the pines.

As he dipped low over the huge enclosure, the cameraman leaned out the door. The pilot saw uniformed troops racing in all directions, as if he had chopped the top off a hornet's nest. Their reflexes were faster than he had allowed for. He tilted sideways, out of a spray of heavy machine-gun bullets. He wasn't joining this party, even for five hundred extra dollars and a dinner with a sexy TV celebrity.

He veered away from the nest of gunners near the main checkpoint, dipping low to throw off their aim.

He did not see the high-tension wires until the moment before the rotors collided with them. The chopper swirled like a top before it exploded into a fireball and took the roof off one of the fancy houses near the Avenida del Conscripto.

3

THE news reached Washington while Jim Kreeger was in the air, bound for Dulles Airport.

President Butler postponed a scheduled meeting with the French premier for forty-five minutes while he conferred with Admiral Enright and his kitchen cabinet.

Aaron Sturgiss, the White House Counselor, reminded the President that there was no proof that the Mexicans had shot down the helicopter.

"Mr. President," Admiral Enright spoke up, "it is my considered opinion that we have to move now. If we let

Ramírez get away with this, the world will conclude that the government of the United States is a patsy. American reporters are dead. American lives are at risk. The country is screaming for action."

"The polls are with us," intoned Sturgiss. "At least for this week. But we could lose a damn sight more than we stand to gain."

Harry Butler wavered, poised on the edge of decision. He wondered whether any of the men in the Oval Office had the faintest conception of how much he had at stake—personally—in Mexico. For reasons he could not explain to anyone in Washington, he had covered for Raúl Carvajal and the group who called themselves the Safari team. Now he was being pushed—by events, by public opinion, by Bill Enright—to commit U.S. forces to their enterprise. He was being invited to a blooding. Such situations had been a rite of passage, he knew, for every President in recent memory. But what had gone before did not give Harry Butler a great deal of comfort. He did not live for the history books, and ultimately he would have to live for himself. Could he be sure, in his own heart, that he would be acting in the best interests of his country if he approved what Bill Enright was urging?

"Let's go over it again," said the President.

Admiral Enright was in his element. In broad strokes, he reminded the President of the key elements in Operation Safety Net, the euphemistic code name for a limited military invasion of Mexico. He stressed the ingredient of surprise. There would be no visible troop movements near the border. The U.S. units committed to the operation, totaling some fifty thousand men, would be airlifted from bases far afield. They would seek to avoid inflicting significant civilian casualties by targeting strategic and economic targets—including the Mexican oil fields—and communications, rather than major population centers. They did not anticipate serious resistance from the Mexican armed forces, many of whose officers were secretly opposed to the Ramírez regime. In any event, the U.S. strike force would go in with the best eyes and ears known to modern technology. The highly classified Lacrosse satellite, launched by the space shuttle Atlantis at the end of 1988, would survey the ground for them. Unlike the KH series, the Lacrosse was based not on optical imaging, but on microwaves beamed to the earth, bouncing back accurate signals that could identify and target objects as small as three feet across. It had worked like a charm over the *other* gulf. It was the pride and joy of the National Reconnaissance Office, which had the largest budget in the entire intelligence community.

"It will be slicker than Desert Storm," argued Enright, "and a damn sight cheaper."

"We were invited to the Persian Gulf," the President reminded him, "and we had the world community on our side. I won't do this without an invitation."

"If I may say so, sir, that's a formality."

"Not to me. I want to see the dance card."

"You'll have it, Mr. President."

4

Despite his desire to keep up the semblance of normalcy, the President canceled two further meetings that afternoon. After an exchange of calls over scrambler phones between Admiral Enright and Art Colgate in Monterrey, it was established that the "friends of democracy" in the north of Mexico were fully prepared to declare a Provisional Liberation Government. They were confident, despite recent reverses, that with U.S. support, they could control the six northern states of Mexico. In the course of a few days, they insisted, U.S. pressure would bring the fall of the Ramírez government in Mexico City. And if Ramírez persisted in power nonetheless, they were ready to announce a formal secession of the northern states. Their personal envoys were already en route to Washington.

After a meeting of the Joint Chiefs of Staff, President Butler reluctantly approved the implementation of Operation Safety Net. The assigned units were already on Delta One alert. Admiral Enright circulated a prepared document identifying tasks and aerial movements to be conducted between 6 P.M. and 3 A.M., which was H-hour. American units, organized in three independent task forces, would launch a three-pronged incursion against targets identified by General Gilly.

The President also approved a draft statement to be released after that phase of the operation had been successfully accomplished. It read, in part:

> The President this morning has directed U.S. forces to execute a preplanned mission in Mexico to protect American lives and restore the democratic process. Democratic opposition forces have been recognized by the United States Government as legitimately defending the interests of all Mexicans in protecting the values of their nation. The U.S. Administration will aid these forces in restoring normalcy to Mexico.

Harry Butler initialed this statement and gave it to Roz Myers, his trusted secretary, to send through channels. It had been argued that, in order to minimize the possibility of leaks, the President would devote the latter part of the day to scheduled commitments. These included a White House banquet for the French premier to which the First Lady had invited many of her socialite friends.

The President was startled, and initially testy, when Roz asked him to make room in his program for an unscheduled visitor—Jim Kreeger.

"As a favor to me," she added.

"We've been together for a while, Roz."

"We have, Mr. President."

"I hope you're not taking advantage of it."

"I'm just trying to protect you, Harry. You're father and son to me."

"Dammit, you do have a way of getting around a man. I hope you're not making a mistake. I'd hate to have to let you go."

Roz said nothing.

"The way I heard it," the President went on, "this Kreeger is a maverick."

"Of course. He's a Texan," Roz pointed out.

"Okay. I guess I can spare a few minutes for a Texas boy."

TWENTY-NINE

□ □ □

1

When he emerged from the PMI parking lot between 17th and 18th Streets, Kreeger turned up the collar of his raincoat against the blustery wind that shoved dead leaves and sandwich wrappers along Pennsylvania Avenue. Rush hour was long over; the streets were almost deserted. As he waited for the light to change, Kreeger was accosted by a well-dressed woman in her early thirties. She didn't look like a hooker, and she wasn't.

She said, in an educated voice, "Can you let me have a dollar? I'm in an extenuating circumstance."

Kreeger paid for the line. He had never come across a panhandler who talked quite like that. And he felt a degree of sympathy for persons caught in extenuating circumstances.

He crossed Pennsylvania Avenue and walked past the Executive Office Building to the manned gate in front of the West Wing of the White House. He gave his name to the guard and asked for Roz Myers. Within five minutes, the President's secretary came out to escort him in.

Roz looked a lot like Dorothy. A little wider, perhaps, and a little grayer, but she possessed the same brisk composure, the same air of competence. She gave him a sharp look that said: I've carried out Harry Butler's bedpans. You let him down, and I'll scratch your eyes out.

What she said out loud, as they walked together, was, "The President is looking forward to meeting you, Mr. Kreeger. He's heard a lot about you. I've heard a lot about you, too. From Dorothy. She says you're the man the President needs."

"I hope so."

"I kept you off the appointments schedule. Dorothy said that was important."

"Thank you. Are you from Texas, Roz?"

"Columbus, Ohio. But I've been with the President since he ran for the Senate. I guess I picked up the twang."

"You must know Shelley Hayes."

"Oh, yeah. We all know Shelley." From the way her face clouded, Kreeger could see that the President's personal life was not a secret to Roz Myers.

Behind the gauzy drapes of the National Security Adviser's office, at the corner of the West Wing, Kreeger saw the silhouettes of several men huddled in conversation.

He said, "I guess Admiral Enright works late."

"Never leaves before eight." Roz's curled lip suggested an additional, unspoken comment: And he makes sure we all know it.

They paused in the West Lobby, where a uniformed guard gave a reasonable impression of a Cyborg terminator, checking Kreeger's attaché case for the second time.

"How long have I got?" Kreeger asked as they passed the Norman Rockwell cartoons in the hall.

"Fifteen." Kreeger must have looked crestfallen, because she added at once, "It's the best I could do. He's got a state banquet at eight. And there's a lot going down tonight. I guess you know that."

Kreeger nodded. He had risked a call to Dorothy at the office, and had gleaned what she could not tell him over the phone from an old friend in the Defense Intelligence Agency. Harry Butler was really going to do it. Within a few hours, a fleet of C-130s, Hercules, and A-141 Galaxies would be airborne, heading south. Kreeger had been allotted fifteen minutes to give the

President the reasons why he must abort a scheduled disaster.

President Butler received Kreeger in the Oval Office. Butler prowled the room, like a large predator confined in a cage, sniffing his visitor out.

"Does Director Wagoner know you're here?" the President demanded.

"No, sir."

"Then I guess you're putting your ass on the line."

"I'm willing to do that, Mr. President, if I can prevent my government from making an irreparable mistake in Mexico."

"Those are strong words, Mr. Kreeger. I hope you can justify them."

"Mr. President, I think I can prove to you that some of your senior officials have fallen for a sting operation that any street hustler would have known for what it is. You are about to commit U.S. military forces to a situation where such involvement is completely inappropriate. I think I can offer you some better options, if I can have a little of your time."

Harry Butler gave him a sidelong look as he went on pacing, hands clenched behind his back. "You talk kinda funny. What part of Texas are you from, anyway?"

"Hill country. A place called Boerne."

"Hell, I know Boerne. I got me some trophies stuffed down there. You a hunting man, Jim?"

"My daddy used to take me out when I was a kid. Jackrabbits, mostly."

"You been up to the YO Ranch?"

"Sure."

"Best hunting I ever had, including the Travis spread. You play football?"

"Texas U."

"Me too. What position did you play?"

"Linebacker."

"Was old Buck Cousins still the coach in your day?"

"Yeah. Buck was quite a character. He could teach a Marine Corps drill sergeant how to chew a guy's butt."

They both chuckled at the memory of the foul-mouthed, tobacco-spitting coach. The ice had been broken. The President said, "Seems to me we got a lot to talk about, Jim," and buzzed Roz Myers to ask her to cancel his next appointment.

Butler strode to the door of Aaron Sturgiss's office. Aaron had his feet up on his desk. Four TV monitors were tuned to different channels.

"Shit, Aaron," the President said to the White House Counselor. "You'll go cross-eyed with all that TV. You just go get yourself a hamburger or something. I got an ol' boy from Boerne here that needs a drink."

"We got the results of that new poll," Aaron reported. "Sixty-seven percent favor military action if it will save the lives of U.S. citizens."

"I'll look at it later."

Aaron put on his coat, shook hands with Kreeger, and forfeited his office with relatively good grace.

Harry Butler reached for the box files on the shelf. They were labeled "Scotland," "France," and "Kentucky."

"What's your pleasure?"

"Kentucky is fine."

Out came the bottle of Early Times.

The President slipped off his jacket and sat behind the desk in the Counselor's chair. "Let's get to it."

Kreeger had crafted an elaborate presentation, using the Sanchez tape. Now, alone with the President, he abandoned his prepared speech. He had been warned he had fifteen minutes, and Harry Butler had already consumed five of them with social amenities. The thing to do was to hit the President between the eyes.

"You and I had a mutual friend," Kreeger told him. "Hugh Renwick. I went to school with him. I also got his daughter away from some Mexican dopers. Director Wagoner wanted to fire me over that."

"I did hear it said that you're a wild man, Jim. That's no criticism, not from me."

"I have reason to believe that Judge Renwick was murdered because he was planning to come to you. To blow the whistle on the Safari operation."

The President raised his glass to his lips, maybe in an effort to mask his expression. Kreeger watched the eyes —they were hard, but frightened too.

Harry Butler said, "What is Safari?"

"Safari, Mr. President," Kreeger's eyes did not move from Butler's face, "is a plot to drag your Administration into a war with Mexico in support of a secessionist state. A sort of Baja Texas. If you let it succeed, the new state will be run by your college friend Raúl Carvajal and a bunch of dopers and right-wing landowners, and the oil will be milked by your campaign contributor, John Halliwell. By the way, I saw Halliwell with your party at the judge's memorial service. Down in Comfort. It was a touching scene. Especially since Halliwell issued the contract for the judge's murder."

"You're throwing a helluva lot of names around, Kreeger." The President glowered at him. "You better have some damn good evidence to back up what you're saying, because I can put you out in the street quicker than you can say Boerne Hounds."

"I have a videotape I think you should watch."

The President grimaced. He had had his fill of video entertainment in recent days.

"The subject is a man called Sanchez," Kreeger pursued. "Former U.S. military. A mercenary hired by the Safari crowd to help get the United States into Mexico. His immediate employer, I'm sorry to say, is a former colleague of mine. It's all on the tape."

"Hold it right there!" The President was on his feet, telephone receiver in hand. "I want Admiral Enright in on this."

"I strongly advise against that, sir."

"Goddamn, I'll call in whoever I like!"

"Admiral Enright is a close friend of the man who hired Sanchez. His name is Colgate. They served together in Vietnam. I have reason to believe that Colgate covered for Enright when he was caught smuggling drugs out of the Golden Triangle. The evidence disappeared. I don't know whether that entirely explains Enright's actions in relation to Mexico, but I do think you need to acknowledge that your National Security Adviser is deeply compromised with the people who have been doing all these killings."

The President subsided into his chair. He looked physically depleted.

"You mean *they* carried out all these murders? Hugh Renwick? The Governor's wife? President Paz? I can't believe it."

Kreeger noted that Butler had given up feigning ignorance of who "they" were.

"The Sanchez tape will answer some of your questions. Maybe not all of them. Sanchez killed President Paz, but he didn't do it for Safari. You see, he was serving two masters. All the time he was taking money from the Safari crowd, he was reporting back to Fausto García, the head of the Mexican secret police. Fausto is smart, and he's slippery. He put his own penetration agent inside Safari in order to use the plot for his own purposes. If you'll let me roll the tape . . ."

"I don't need to see the goddamn tape! *You* tell me!"

"Very well, Mr. President. Fausto mounted what in my business we would call a classic provocation. The object was to put his pal Ramírez in power, with himself as number two. He could have put Safari out of business months ago. Instead, he let it run so he'd have a convenient scapegoat. The usual suspect—Uncle Sam."

The President pressed the knuckles of his right hand against his temples. His anger was evident. He brought his fist down hard on the desk, scattering Aaron Sturgiss's opinion polls. "Well, your Mexico friend miscalculated!" he roared. "You're giving me prehistory!

The whole thing stinks, but what we're facing now is Ramírez! The worst crook in this hemisphere, and a certified Cuban agent! I've got no damn choice in the matter. We have to act.''

''I think you should reconsider,'' Kreeger interjected. ''If I understand the situation, you are about to commit U.S. forces in support of people who have terrorized and murdered Americans, including Judge Renwick.''

''I'm talking about Ramírez! You've just told me he —or his people—had his own President knocked off! This guy is as bad as Saddam Hussein! I'm not going to sit on my hands while he takes over our southern border.''

''I share your concern, Mr. President. I think I can give you a better option. A quiet option.''

Kreeger then proceeded to explain the quirk in the Mexican constitution that disqualified Ramírez from serving as President.

Harry Butler was puzzled. ''I don't get it. You're telling me that we have a handle on Ramírez because his daddy was born in Texas? What if he was? That's not going to stop a man who just had his President bumped off.''

''I think it could. Unless Ramírez wants to drop any pretense that Mexico is still a democracy, unless he is prepared to rule as an outright dictator. If that happened''—he looked at Butler—''then, yes, I would hold other options open. But for now I think we should give this one our best try before anyone else gets killed.''

Harry Butler turned away from Kreeger's stare. The President was obviously confused, and scared. He had just heard a lot of things he had never wanted—or expected—to hear, and it was hard for him to accept them all at once. There was also the matter of his discarded mistress, the hateful videotape, and the threat hanging over him.

He said, ''Are you sure about Hugh Renwick?''

"I couldn't prove it in a court of law. But I'm sure. If I ever catch up with Colgate, I think I'll have it all."

There was a light tap on the door, and Roz Myers's moon-round face appeared.

"Mr. President, the First Lady wants you to know the guests have arrived."

"Tell her I'm tied up. I'll join them for dessert and coffee."

"And Admiral Enright is waiting to see you. He says it's an emergency."

"Tell him to wait."

"Very well, sir." Roz pulled the door shut behind her.

"You can stop it," Kreeger told the President. "Let me deal with Ramírez. Then we can concentrate on putting some of this Safari gang where they belong."

"I wonder if you know what you're saying."

"I have a pretty good notion, sir. I also have a friend who may be able to help us out. Would you mind if I brought this person in on this conversation?"

Harry Butler looked more confused than before.

"This will only take a few minutes," Kreeger said. "If I could use the phone."

The President responded by waving his hand, as if to say, Go ahead, I don't have the strength to resist.

Kreeger called a number that Dorothy had given him.

No more than ten minutes had elapsed—time in which Kreeger patiently explained more details of the Mexican situation—when Roz tapped on the door again. She ushered in a new visitor, swathed in Blackglama mink from her neck to her calves. The visitor was Shelley Hayes.

Harry Butler leaped to his feet, turning on Kreeger like a cornered wolf. "What the fuck is going on here?"

Roz beat a hasty retreat.

"Nice reception, Harry," said Shelley.

Kreeger helped Shelley to remove her coat. She was

wearing a red silk dress that flattered her bosom and hips, and a serene smile that did not waver when the President yelled at her, "Who are you whoring for now?"

Shelley silently arranged herself in a club chair.

The idea for this encounter had been seeded in Kreeger's mind by a guarded telephone conversation with Lois, after Lois had indicated the depth of Shelley's feelings of guilt and fear over her knowledge of what was going on in Mexico. Plus, he knew that Raúl Carvajal had ordered her to carry a personal letter to Washington. Kreeger had been obliged to leave it to Lois and the indispensable Dorothy to coordinate things to get Shelley out of Mexico and into D.C. He had not been sure that it would all come together until he had called Dorothy's contact number, in the presence of the President. Watching Harry Butler struggling with bitter fury, Kreeger worried that his efforts might have misfired.

"I'm sorry to take you by surprise, sir," said Kreeger.

"You!" The President's forefinger trembled as he pointed it at the Station Chief. "As of tomorrow, you're gone! You have your marching papers! You're in the street!"

"That's your call, Mr. President. But I hope you'll hear us out before you make any rash moves."

"How's your blood pressure, Harry?" said Shelley.

The President collapsed into Aaron's swivel seat.

"Miss Hayes agreed to come," said Kreeger, "because she and a friend of ours—one of my best case officers—came damn close to getting their heads blown off in Mexico City. The would-be killers work for the Quintero drug family. They are friends of a man called Paco Carranza. Maybe you've heard of him? No? Well, Carranza is up to his neck in the Safari Project. He's currently staying with Raúl Carvajal, outside Monterrey. I know that you are familiar with *him.*"

"Does Raúl know you're here?" Harry Butler glowered at Shelley.

She glanced at Kreeger. He nodded to her.

"Raúl gave me a letter for you." She put the envelope on the desk.

President Butler tore it open, scanned the contents, and sucked in his breath. With a mumbled apology, he stuffed the letter in his pocket and crossed the room, hurriedly entering the private bathroom and slamming the door. Through the surge of running water, Kreeger thought he heard Harry Butler throwing up.

He said to Shelley, "I'm glad you made it."

"Didn't you trust me?"

"I couldn't be sure. Did you have trouble persuading Raúl to let you go?"

"The funny thing is, Raúl thinks this trip is his idea."

"No problems with Carranza?"

"He never saw me leave."

They listened to Harry Butler banging around in the bathroom. There was a crash of glass. Kreeger jumped up and walked halfway to the door.

"Mr. President? Anything you need?"

Through the closed door, Harry Butler called him several choice names.

Kreeger walked back to Shelley. "Guess Raúl doesn't trust his old college buddy too much. Did you read the letter?"

"I have a fair idea what's in it."

"You know Harry. How's he going to jump?"

"I don't know. Harry likes easy options. I guess he just doesn't have any right now."

There was no time for more, because the President returned from the bathroom, outwardly composed but a shade or two paler.

Kreeger immediately turned to him. "Mr. President, let Shelley tell you all she knows about what's going on in Northern Mexico. At least let her tell you about Raúl's plans for—"

"No. It's not necessary," Butler interrupted.

He sat down and killed his drink.

"You might have heard there's a law in Texas elections,'' he said to Kreeger. "Always vote your safe precincts last. That way, if the other guy's ahead on numbers, you got ways to fix it. I guess you learned that real good, Jim. Hell, you ought to be running for something.''

"Not me, sir."

"Not me, either. Not when this gets out." He rounded on Shelley. "What happened to you? I thought you were supposed to be Raúl's woman!"

"I'm my own woman, Harry," she said evenly. "You taught me. Remember? And I don't like Raúl's business associates. They tried to kill me."

Butler did not meet her eyes. Instead, he looked up at the chandelier. "I guess I'm screwed if I do and screwed if I don't. What in hell am I supposed to do?"

Kreeger said, "You could do the right thing."

The lights kept flashing on Aaron Sturgiss's battery of multiline telephones. Harry Butler sat at the desk, one hand hovering over the phones, the other grafted to a cut-glass tumbler of whiskey.

"Jim," the President's voice was low and gravelly, "I guess you're asking yourself how we could get to this point just because I once shared bed sheets with a woman who is not the First Lady." He avoided looking at Shelley.

"It had crossed my mind," said Kreeger.

"Listen to me, Jim. Seems to me you and I could both go along with a lot of the objectives of the Safari crowd. A free-market country in northern Mexico, one hundred percent on our side, policing the border for us. Makes a lot of sense. I'll tell you, there are some very able men in this Administration—and in Congress—who would buy it."

"How about the methods? Terrorism, sabotage, lying to the press. Cozying up to drug-runners."

"That's why I tried to back off." The President

ucked at his glass. "I tried to turn off the water. They
wouldn't let me."

"Because of Shelley."

They both looked at the woman, who sat very still,
her arms folded across her chest.

"Not only because of her." Now the President's
voice was little more than a croak. "There was another
girl. Raúl is the only one who knows." He hesitated. His
eyes turned back to Shelley. "Do *you* know?"

Shelley shrugged. It could have meant either yes or
no.

"I guess you really get off on seeing me dragged
down like this," Harry Butler accused her. "You brought
me that note from Raúl."

"I told you, I didn't read it."

"What did it say?" Kreeger interjected.

The President mumbled, almost inaudibly, "Honey
hunt." Then anger flared up. "I don't need to tell you
any more. It's none of your damned business."

"I'm afraid it is, sir."

The fight seemed to drain out of the President. He
said wearily, almost abstractedly, "It was a long time
back. Before I ran for the Senate. There was a crowd of us
up to a guest ranch in hill country. A lot of rich boys.
Raúl was there. Somebody arranged some female entertainment. It turned into a honey hunt. You know how it
works." He appealed to Kreeger.

"I'd like to hear about it, Harry," said Shelley.
"What did you do? Bring some hookers up from San
Antonio? Doesn't the rule book say, you fuck the one
you grab? I can just picture you, running around bare-
assed under the cedars."

The President flushed deep red. "I ended up with
this little blonde. It's the damnedest thing. I can't even
recollect her name. She had this frizzy hairdo, like she'd
touched a live wire. We went skinny-dipping in the pool,
late at night. I guess we'd both had a few drinks. She
must have cracked her head on the pool. Raúl says I

threw her in the shallow end. The truth of the matter is, I don't recall.''

''What happened to her?'' Shelley demanded.

''I guess she concussed and drowned. Raúl tried to get her out. It was too late. Raúl was the only witness. We told the sheriff we found her there in the morning, and he bought it.''

Silence grew between them. There were legal terms for what Harry Butler could be held accountable for. Manslaughter. Concealment of a crime. Maybe worse.

Shelley said, ''I guess I was lucky. When you dumped me, it wasn't in the pool. You left me sleeping pills. Remember?''

Kreeger's glance traveled between their faces. He was thinking about the idiocy of politics. A guilty man, nailed to his past, was on the point of committing the United States to the worst foreign policy blunder since the Bay of Pigs, and of wrecking the presidency in the process. And there were men in Butler's Administration, stupider still—idiots like Admiral Enright and Two Jacks Gilly—who would push him all the way, in the belief that they were demonstrating to the world that the United States was still number one.

The President appealed to Kreeger with his eyes.

''Raúl is the only witness,'' he repeated. ''Can't you Agency people fix that son of a bitch?''

''Give it a little time, and Fausto García may do that,'' Kreeger began. He broke off, because the door burst open and Ann Travis Butler swept into the room. She was wearing a stunning Claude Montana ensemble, identical to Shelley's, except that the First Lady's was cut three sizes smaller—and was no doubt an original, rather than a Mexican knockoff. The mirror effect did not improve Ann Butler's humor.

''You!'' she wheeled from Shelley to her husband and back again. ''You shame me under my own roof! You even steal the clothes off my back!''

She had evidently been drinking. She advanced on

Shelley with deliberation, as if she meant to slap her. Shelley stood up, gripping the arms of the chair.

The President pushed his bulk between the two women.

Ann Butler slapped him instead.

Then the First Lady burst into tears and fled the room. Harry Butler started after her. Kreeger stood silent. Shelley couldn't help herself. She put her hand over her mouth, but the laughter seeped through it.

The President paused in the doorway. "You see what you've done?"

"What are *you* going to do, Harry?" Shelley demanded.

"Watch me on TV," Butler snapped at her. "That's where I saw you last."

PRESIDENT Butler picked up one of the phones and called Admiral Enright, in his corner of the West Wing.

The President said, "Stand down the troops. Operation Safety Net is postponed."

There was a storm of protest on the other end of the line.

"I don't care if there are goddamn planes in the air," Butler stormed. "You can tell them to turn the hell around! No, I don't know what I intend to do tomorrow. I'm going to take some quiet time, and I suggest you do the same."

2

It was a few minutes past ten when Kreeger and Shelley reached the PMI lot, a block away from the White House. The gates were down; the lot wouldn't reopen until breakfast time. There was an edge of winter in the air and no cabs in sight.

Kreeger swore under his breath.

Shelley took his arm. "Let's walk down to the Hay Adams," she proposed. "We'll get a taxi there. Easy."

There were no cabs at the door, and no doorman, so they went inside to talk to the concierge.

"Let's have a bite to eat first," said Shelley. "I don' know about you, but I'm starved."

They ordered club sandwiches from the bar. Shelley drank Chardonnay, while Kreeger nursed a manhattan.

He said, "I'm grateful to you."

"However it turns out?"

"However. You've taken one hell of a risk. Are you going to be okay?"

"Sure. If nothing else, I've learned to look out for myself."

"Listen. If you need expense money. Or anything . . ."

"I'm fine, Jim. Dinner's on me. Okay?"

"Anything you say."

She smiled. She found him quite attractive. He was strong, yet so awkward, sitting alone with a single woman. She found that refreshing.

"Why did you do it?" Kreeger asked suddenly.

"Why did I allow myself to be used this way?"

Kreeger nodded.

"What if I told you it was very profitable?"

"I don't think you're that mercenary. Or that hard-bitten. Though I'll bet you can put on a good show."

"Why thank you, Mr. CIA. Then you tell me. Why *did* I do it?"

"Because you wanted to even the score with Harry. Because you wanted to see him sweat."

"My mama told me only losers hold grudges. I'm not a loser. And you're wrong—it wasn't just because of Harry."

"What else then?"

"John Halliwell. And his cronies. And all the men like them."

"What's he to you?"

"It's too complicated, Jim. Let's just say he hurt me —worse than even *you* can imagine. For one thing, he was the first man who ever knew me. In the biblical sense. He was not bothered by the fact that I was too young. Nor were his friends. It's not something I want to remember. But I did want to get it out of my dreams, and I couldn't. Until I started fighting back." She shivered, remembering a cave in the desert.

"Then you *wanted* Safari to fall apart. Is that why you talked to Fausto?"

She laughed. "Fausto got nothing from me, except a blonde to show off at Del Lago. But he's a charming host. And a woman my age should keep her options open."

The waiter brought the check, and Shelley waved him over to her side of the table.

"I think I should do this," Kreeger objected.

"You have a problem with a woman paying for your dinner? Look, you already said I could treat, so bug off."

He took it with good grace. She wondered what he would say if she told him that she was several million dollars richer than she had been before she left Monterrey. In her profession—and she had come to accept, in her own mind, that it *was* a profession—there were no pension benefits, no tax deductions for Keogh contributions. She had simply collected her own retirement money, in a nice lump sum. Paco Carranza, no doubt, would not view her action quite the same way. But he wasn't going to report her to the Feds or the IRS.

After carefully counting her change, Shelley said to Kreeger, "Take me home."

"Where are you staying?"

"The Four Seasons."

"Under your own name?"

"You think I'm crazy?"

So they shared a taxi out to Georgetown, and

Kreeger agreed to come inside the hotel, just to check that her suite was clean. In the lobby bar, the pianist was singing Billie Holiday favorites.

"You could have a nightcap," Shelley suggested when she had entered her suite and kicked off her shoes.

"I could," Kreeger agreed, "but I won't. You're a glorious woman. But we both have our dreams, and I don't feel like rousing any of them right now."

THIRTY

□ □ □

1

"WE got us a gusher," John Halliwell said to the picture of W. C. Fields which hung over the toilet in the marble bathroom of his penthouse suite at Hallow Petroleum. "This is the big one."

After all the zigzag turns, Halliwell was glad that he had held to his course. Raúl had promised that Harry Butler would back them to the bitter end, and the Mexican had delivered, at least to judge by the gung-ho, if guarded, call the oilman had just received from Monterrey. "It's a go," Colgate had reported. "A definite go."

Halliwell knew the broad outlines of what the Pentagon termed Operation Safety Net. The U.S. military would make three "insertions" into Mexico. The one Halliwell would enjoy most, of course, was designed to secure the Gulf oil fields. There had been an unexplained last-minute delay, but his sources said it was only to guarantee a coordinated effort. The troops had been scheduled to go in before dawn, but that hadn't happened. Whatever, the oilman was told not to worry about it. "Harry wants everything open and aboveboard. Watch him at noon on TV. You won't be disappointed."

Halliwell told his secretary to reserve the Vintage Room at the Petroleum Club for an early lunch, and to rustle up a select group of guests. Several of them, including Sam Newman, the Governor's fixer, had been in on the meeting at the YO Ranch the day the Safari Project had caught fire. He wanted them to be there for the celebration.

Among the fine old wines on the racks in the Vintage Room, the showpiece was a jeroboam of 1971 Château le Caillou Pomerol, price-listed at $1,850. It had been a good few years—despite recovering spot market prices for crude—since Houston oilmen had thought nothing of springing for a treat like this wine.

With his guests assembled at a quarter before the hour, Halliwell said, "My friends, we've been on the backside of a bubble, and it's been a bitch. Well, we will remember today as the day we got back on top. It calls for a rare celebration."

He waved at the sommelier. "Bring me that jerry."

While the wine waiter was uncorking the huge bottle with the reverence it deserved, Harry Butler's face appeared on the TV. He was speaking from the Oval Office. Despite a touch of makeup, the President looked like he had not had much sleep.

"My fellow Americans," the President said, speaking straight to the cameras, "you all know we are facing a crisis on our southern border. The lives of U.S. citizens have been placed in jeopardy. Some of our countrymen have already been viciously killed or maimed. This cannot go on. The Government of the United States cannot tolerate a continued state of lawlessness in Mexico."

"Right on, Harry!" one of the bankers cheered.

"The acting President of Mexico, Fernando Ramírez," Butler continued, "is no friend of our country. He currently faces indictment in Federal court on charges of criminal activity including arms smuggling and racketeering. We further have hard intelligence information that the relationship between President Ramírez and the Cuban secret service extends beyond the bounds of propriety."

"Way to go, Harry! Remember Desert Storm!"

The sommelier placed the jeroboam of Pomerol on the table near John Halliwell's elbow, and carefully decanted a small amount into a wine glass for his approval.

His attention riveted to the screen, Halliwell left the wine untouched.

"However," the President continued, "it has come to the attention of this Administration that persons outside the Mexican government have been seeking to exploit the tribulations of our neighbors, to use this time of crisis for their own private gain. These persons, it saddens me to report, include U.S. citizens who have committed probable violations of the Neutrality Act. In essence, they have attempted to draw the United States into the reckless exercise of military power against a friendly country. I wish to say to all of you out there who are concerned for your country and the values it embodies, that Harry Butler cannot and will not allow the functions of government to be usurped by private greed and ambition."

Halliwell stared aghast at the screen. The sommelier hovered at his right hand.

"May I pour the wine, sir?"

Halliwell said, "It's corked."

The sommelier pointed out that he hadn't even sniffed the cork.

Halliwell tossed off his taste, and spat over the tablecloth. "I tell you, it's fucking vinegar!"

The sommelier begged to differ.

Halliwell rounded on him in fury. His thick forearm connected with the jeroboam and sent it crashing to the floor.

Halliwell did not hear the rest of the President's telecast. He did hear Sam Newman say to him, as he headed for the nearest phone, "You're still going to have to pay for it, John."

2

At the Carvajal ranch outside Monterrey, Raúl, Paco Carranza, and Art Colgate were tuned in to the same television broadcast from the Oval Office. They had a private army deployed around the property. A small fleet of planes and helicopters was gassed up against the need for a sudden strike—or a quick getaway. Raúl had drafted his own statement for the airwaves announcing the creation of a provisional government in the north. He was planning to read it over Radio XEG, "La Ranchera de Monterrey," as soon as the city had been secured with the aid of Harry Butler's paratroopers.

"*Hijo de puta!*" Carranza exploded, when it had become plain that Harry Butler had decided to jettison his old friends in the north. At first he cursed the screen, but Carranza's anger quickly focused on Raúl. "You swore the bitch could be trusted! I warned you against her! I told you she was a spy!"

"I don't know what happened. She probably had nothing to do with this." Raúl was very pale, his expression stunned. It was at his suggestion that Shelley had flown to Washington to meet President Butler this final time, the third such trip since they had hatched the Safari Project. She was sent to make sure Harry Butler remembered his obligations. Shelley had called the ranch that very morning to confirm—with a two-word code—that everything had proceeded according to expectations. What could have gone wrong?

Art Colgate excused himself, mumbling something about taking a leak.

Carranza, oblivious to Colgate, was pounding the floor like a caged beast.

"I'm getting out," he announced. "Without the Americans, we are screwed. I want my money. Now."

One speaks gently to a man who holds a .357 magnum in his fist, and whose face speaks only of rage. Raúl said, very calmly, "You can have your money any time you want. Do you take me for a thief?"

"Now!" Carranza repeated.

Raúl walked into his study ahead of Carranza, conscious of the gun aimed between his shoulder blades. In his mind, he was making his own dispositions. He could fly across the border in his own plane. And afterward? Perhaps a different meridian, a different life. He would miss his barren ranges, and their dreaming. But his people had been wanderers before.

He spun the combination lock of his safe.

He saw, before Carranza, that the crisp stacks of hundred-dollar bills had been removed. Raúl had given no one the combination of his safe, but he had no doubt, in that instant, that Shelley was the thief. She had had opportunity enough to watch him. What a fool he had been! Had she at least left him his gun?

He scrabbled for it, among the legal papers on the lower shelf.

He felt the heat of Carranza's breath close against his head, and the cold snout of the magnum, rammed into the back of his neck. Raúl mouthed words to a God he hardly knew.

Carranza fired only once.

He left Raúl with his head inside the safe, leaking blood and viscous matter. Then he remembered the gringo who had hired Rico Sanchez. The living room was deserted. He heard an angry drone from outside, like a swarm of hornets. Carranza lumbered to the door, into a storm of dust and bullets.

He saw a four-wheel drive, swerving away from the pickets, Colgate at the wheel. He yelled into the dust and noise, "Kill the gringo!"

Nobody heard him, in the hailstorm of fire from the helicopter gunships that were assaulting the ranch. There were so many of them that Carranza thought, for a moment, that it must be the Americans who were attacking. When he was flushed out of his last hiding place—Raúl's wine cellar—by Mexicans uniformed entirely in black, from their boots to their baseball caps, he knew that Fausto García had won.

3

PRESIDENT Ramírez watched the Sanchez tapes in his private study, deep inside Los Pinos. Two walls of the room were covered by photographs of Ramírez with other world leaders. As he watched, Ramírez affected to have difficulty following some of the English. Each time Kreeger hit the pause button to make sure there was no room for misunderstanding.

On the tape, Sanchez recounted, step by step, how he had assisted Fausto to convert the greed and power-lust of a group of Texan businessmen and Mexican right-wingers into a mantrap on a giant scale. President Ramírez laughed. "That Fausto is a real *chingón.* Carvajal, Carranza. Those people are finished. Even now, we are hunting them down." He bit into a serrano pepper, then doused the fire with mineral water.

Ramírez seemed in excellent spirits. He snorted when Sanchez told the tale of Two Jacks Gilly's underground tour of the Mexican resistance.

His face darkened when Sanchez described how Fausto had paid him half a million dollars to assassinate President Paz, and arranged his getaway in a car provided by SIN.

Ramírez shouted, "This man is lying!"

Sanchez was holding up the stub of his finger.

"I think most people will find his performance highly convincing," Kreeger observed. "It is entirely possible that these tapes could find their way into the public domain.''

"Are you threatening me?"

"I am pointing out certain risks."

Ramírez thought about it, while Kreeger turned off the video machine, extracted the tape, and put it in his case.

"It is such a waste," Ramírez mused after a moment. "Fausto is a man of unusual talent. But I see he will have to go."

"I think so too."

"His resignation will be announced tomorrow, when the counterterrorist operation in the north is complete. He has assumed personal command."

Kreeger had no strong views about the timing.

"Is that it?" Ramírez asked.

"No. There is more."

"Yes."

"I have been reading the Mexican Constitution." Kreeger looked into Ramírez's eyes.

"I find you are a man of many parts."

"I think it will come as a surprise to the leaders of your party that you are disqualified from holding the presidency under Article Eighty-two."

"I have no idea what you are talking about."

"I am talking about the fact that your father was born in the United States."

"You jest with me."

"I don't think many Mexicans will find it a joking matter. One of the failings of our country's bureaucracy, and one of its strengths, is that it loves to hoard paper. I have read a lot of paper about you, Fernando. But the most interesting I read is that your father was born in Cotulla in 1922. He was born a U.S. citizen, in my part of Texas. Here he is, practicing to be a loyal little gringo." Kreeger produced the old snapshot Lottie Renwick had dug out of her trunk. He held onto the corner tightly as Ramírez stared at his father, costumed for the Cotulla school concert, reciting the U.S. Pledge of Allegiance with his hand to his heart.

"You see that teacher standing next to him?" Kreeger pushed his bluff all the way. "That's LBJ. They don't come much more American than that."

Ramírez lost his bravura for a moment. He released the photograph and slumped down into his seat, deflated as if the air had been let out of him.

He made a quick recovery, however. To Kreeger's astonishment, he thrust out his open palms and said, with a lopsided smile, "I'm yours."

"What about your Cuban friends?"

"They are yours too. I'll feed them to you." That was only the beginning of it, according to Ramírez. He could deliver a ring of agents who were operating in the United States. The coordinates of the most wanted drug felons in the hemisphere.

Ramírez's rough-grained face shone dully. He was ready to barter all allegiances, all friendships, for his survival in power.

"You are a professional, Jim. You know how to work with discretion. We will talk about all of this carefully. But first, we will have a drink."

For Kreeger, the professional, this was a stunning opportunity. The spymaster in him wanted to reach out and seize it with both hands. It is not every day of the week that the head of state of a serious country offered himself to the Agency—as an unconditional agent. He stared at the man. This was tempting.

"No, Ramírez, I want you out," Kreeger said.

Fernando Ramírez did not believe it. He worked on sweetening his offer. He even hinted that Kreeger could become a very wealthy man. He pointed out there were worse places to retire than a forty-room villa overlooking the Pacific.

"I want you out, Fernando," Kreeger repeated. "I don't care what reason you give. There won't be a lot of folks in mourning. And I want Miliano Rojas out of jail, with proper security."

"Miliano Rojas?" Ramírez was openly incredulous. "What is he to you, or the United States?"

"He's a man who cares about his people. After all the killing, this country deserves a government that will at least try to heal the wounds. Miliano must be given a fair chance."

4

"You have disappointed me, Jim. I never took you for a moralist. We could have done business together. We are both professionals."

Fausto looked around his office. A stuffed tiger's head protruded from a packing crate. The big glass-fronted cabinet was already gone, along with the wall clock. Fausto seemed determined to leave nothing behind for his successor.

"Now you will have to talk to Salazar." Fausto gave him an upside-down smile. "Do you imagine you can trust him? That one will pick his own pocket, just to keep in practice."

Kreeger resisted the urge to light a cigar. "Why did you do it?"

"It was politics. Family politics. The only kind that are interesting."

"That doesn't satisfy me. You were one of the most powerful men in the country. The strings were all in your hands."

Fausto shrugged. "I could not have survived with Fernando out. There were twenty men waiting in line, each one wanting to fuck me over."

"You're still not telling me the whole of it," Kreeger objected.

"Love of the game, then. What do you want me to say? That I couldn't resist the chance to show the almighty CIA that a bean-eater—that's what your instructors called us, isn't it?—could outsmart the lot of you? It *was* a brilliant game I played, wasn't it?"

"Yes," Kreeger acknowledged, "but you made one helluva mistake, for such a brilliant gamester. You refused to believe that the Butler Administration would ever send troops into Mexico. You did not understand . . ."

"About the slut?" he interrupted. "About Señorita Hayes? Come on, Jim, we both know what she is. I knew something of her. Maybe not enough," he conceded. "And I confess, it is still difficult for me to understand how a bull from Texas—a President of the United States —can be terrorized by the threat that people could find out that he has a woman on the side. He should be scared of the reverse!" Fausto shook his head. "My worst mistake," he pursued, "was my reading of *you*. You trapped Ramírez. You had Fernando by the balls. Isn't that the dream of a man in our profession? To own a President? You could have done anything you wanted with Fernando, and with Mexico. And you abandoned it—for what? To install an impossible dreamer with a loud voice and a pretty face. A fellow who couldn't write an invoice for a box of avocados."

"You betrayed me, Fausto."

"It was a game. You have played by the same rules."

"You had my friend killed."

"I regret that. It was not a personal matter. And I never realized that you are fond of reporters."

The door was thrown open. Salazar, Fausto's former employee, thrust his bulk into the frame. He entered the room wearing a belted black leather coat. He was accompanied by a squad of Bookends in similar attire, openly flaunting machine pistols and pump shotguns.

The new masters of SIN showed no impatience. Fausto, for his part, showed no fear.

He said to Kreeger, with his upside-down smile, "They're not the kind you'll want to ask to dinner."

Fausto held Kreeger's arm, as the Station Chief turned to go.

"There's something I want to ask you. Something personal."

"That's okay."

"Do you believe in God, Jim?"

"I don't know what name to call Him."

"Do you believe in an afterlife?"

"I'm afraid I've mislaid the address."

"It makes a difference, what a man believes about such things. Have you been to the Maya country? Of course you have. The Mayas believe in an underworld called Xibalba. A place of ordeal and terror, ruled by gods who smell like shit. The Mayan mythology tells of heroes who journey to the underworld and are challenged by the Shit-Lords of Xibalba to a game of pelota. You know the rules of pelota."

"In fact, Karla gave me a lecture on that subject a while ago."

"There are still Indians in the north who play pelota the old way. It is the ancestor of all ball games. It is played with a rubber ball the size of a human head. For reasons you may imagine."

"And you lose if you're caught with your fingers on the ball."

"Exactly. Now, when the Mayan heroes went down to the underworld, they knew that they could never beat the Shit-Lords by strength and skill. After all, these beings are gods. The heroes could only beat them by trickery. By cheating. And that is how they escaped the shadow-world, and won immortal life."

Fausto stood watchful, allowing the moral to sink in. By games of trickery, a man schools himself to outwit the lords of the underworld.

"You see," Fausto pursued, "a man's actions in this life are always conditioned by what he believes about the life to come. Even when he does not believe. Especially, I might even say, when he does not believe. I have come to the opinion that you are a clandestine believer, Señor Kreeger."

5

Admiral Enright walked out the kitchen door of his white frame house in Arlington into watery sunlight. He was wearing longjohns under his jogging suit, added protection against the cold. Crystalline points flashed among the frost on the brown grass. A scum of ice by the woodshed was all that was left of the snow.

He loped around the side of the house. A gaggle of reporters surged from the cars and the TV vans that had been parked outside his picket fence since the President had announced the Admiral's resignation—an announcement made without informing Enright in advance. The press scented another Iran-Contra affair. He and Two Jacks Gilly were the available targets of opportunity, since Bill Wagoner had left for a sudden vacation.

Someone in the Administration was keeping the media fed with choice tidbits, so the reporters had new questions to hurl at Enright every day. Enright suspected Aaron Sturgiss, the Doctor Spin of the Butler Administration, as the prime leaker. But then, these days, the Admiral suspected almost everyone.

He ran the gauntlet of photographers and pressmen, making no effort to avoid them. It was necessary to show these bastards that his nerve was intact. Members of the Navy Association were collecting money for his legal defense, if that became necessary. A New York agent had called to say he could pull down twenty-five grand a pop, lecturing to patriotic groups on how he had tried to save the United States from another Noriega.

"Admiral Enright!" a young male reporter with a receding hairline yelled in his face. "We have information you diverted government funds in support of a Mexican group that includes a notorious cocaine trafficker. May we have your comments?"

"You're the one that seems to be doing dope."

Admiral Enright jogged up the street, pounding the sidewalk until he felt pleasurable jolts of pain shooting up his spine. Some of the reporters tried to keep up with him. That morning, they were not alone. He gradually became aware of several athletic young men in suits and trench coats. They had no difficulty matching his pace. They were all but treading on his heels.

Enright stopped and confronted them. "You guys from Central Casting? You want to show me some ID? Or do I call the cops and have you charged with harassment?"

"Your call, sir." The polite one flashed his FBI credentials.

"You better stop crowding me."

"We're just doing a job, sir."

What did they expect to accomplish with this obtrusive surveillance? To rattle him? To make him run for sanctuary?

It was dumb. They would never take him that easily. What did they have on him, anyway, except a chronicle of errors that had been authorized by the President of the United States?

The Admiral made a point of completing his five-mile run.

Back at the house, an unfamiliar reporter stuck a microphone in his face and shouted, "According to Administration sources, you were involved with a renegade CIA agent called Colgate in a drug-smuggling operation on the rivers of Indochina. This Colgate allegedly arranged the murder of U.S. citizens in Mexico. Do you know his whereabouts?"

Admiral Enright struggled to keep his composure. How the hell could they know that?

Inside the house, the kitchen phone was ringing. He left it unanswered. Some of the media people had gotten hold of his unlisted number. The phone rang again, just twice. Then once. Then twice again.

He recognized the signal. Emergency drill. A warning to get out at once, if that was possible. Colgate—and the Saigon Society—were still alive.

He walked slowly into his living room, unzipping his top. Something must have happened. After all the years of subterfuge, the bonds that had been forged in Saigon had become public knowledge. It occurred to him that the reporter's question about Colgate might be nothing more than a bluff, an inspired attempt to make him supply proof that the FBI lacked. Similar techniques had been tried before, with mixed results. Maybe Kreeger was at the back of it. Still, the phone signal indicated that the danger was real. He wondered which congressional committee would be first with a subpoena.

Did any of them understand what he was? Why he had acted as he had?

Admiral Enright stood in front of the banked coals in his grate, under his collection of samurai swords and antique Oriental weapons.

He believed that his forward policy in Mexico had been right, from day one until Harry Butler had chickened out. The next Middle East crisis would confirm it. The President had had the chance to make the United States virtually self-sufficient in oil, and he had blown it. He had also blown the opportunity to create a buffer state to staunch the tide of drugs and third world aliens pouring into the United States.

Beyond geo-economics, beyond his concerns about Mexican radicals and Japanese commercial warriors swamping America with cheap manufacturers from a forward base across the Rio Grande, Admiral Enright had glimpsed a chance of glory. That was dust and ashes now.

The things he had done, he told himself, had not been done with selfish motives. What he had stood to gain, in personal terms, was insignificant: a cushy retirement job with Colgate's company in Arlington, a nameplate on his desk, and an endless lunch hour.

Colgate had never threatened him, never pushed him beyond where he wanted to go. He tried to block out the memory of that unpleasant episode in Vietnam, when a preppie Navy lieutenant had filed a formal complaint that Commander Enright had taken advantage of his covert missions for Saigon Station to smuggle drugs and contraband down the rivers. Colgate had promised to bury the paperwork, and Enright had never had to face an inquiry.

Yet the story was out. He scripted, in his mind, the front-page headlines the newspapers would run. The shame would break his mother's heart. He pictured her, sitting alone in her expensive nursing home, staring at the TV.

The Admiral reached above the mantel and brought down a sixteenth-century samurai sword, a souvenir from his days as a naval attaché in Tokyo. He unsheathed the pressed steel, which he kept lovingly honed. The important thing was never to show a failure of nerve.

6

THERE was one thing more that Kreeger needed to do—for himself, for Judge Renwick, and for the secret lover who had gone missing in Vietnam. He needed to settle accounts with Art Colgate.

Colgate had done a professional disappearing act after the Safari Project had blown apart. Global Assistance Services, his Arlington consulting business, had been sealed up tight, its records carted away in cardboard boxes. Colgate's U.S. assets had been frozen—those that were immediately traceable, anyway—and FBI agents were pulling The Haven, his Fauquier County home, apart board by board. Federal warrants had been issued.

The investigative arm of the United States government had at last swung into action, but it had not turned up Colgate. With his fake passports, his numbered bank accounts, and his skill at crossing borders, Colgate could have gone to ground in a bolthole on the other side of the world.

Kreeger intended to set bait, in an effort to draw him out. The bait would be Rico Sanchez.

Sanchez was still under guard at a motel near the San Antonio airport. George Camacho had had the bright idea of flying Al Glass down to implant a miniaturized electronic homing device in Sanchez's right calf, just in case he succeeded in making a run.

Sanchez had a telephone number the FBI did not know about yet. It was the number of a commercial answering service in Miami that accepted messages for "Mr. Cantwell."

George Camacho elicited this information from Sanchez, in Kreeger's absence, by methods Kreeger did not ask about. When George called his boss at the Mexico Station to tell him what he had come up with, Kreeger took the next plane back to San Antonio.

At the Saguaro motel, he found Sanchez sulky and nervous.

"You promised a deal," Sanchez reminded him. "What I get is a working over and some Mengele type sticking metal in my leg."

"Would you rather go back to Fausto?"

"What about our deal?"

"You're holding out on us, Rico. I've talked to the President. He won't authorize any deals unless you cooperate fully."

This was hardly an accurate rendition of the conversation at the White House, but Kreeger was not going to lose any sleep over that.

"So what do you want?"

"I want Colgate. I want you to call his answering service. You will give them this number." He glanced at the dangling wires of the phone in the motel room, and Camacho gave a little nod. It could be easily reconnected. "When Colgate calls you back, you will give him a reason to come and see you."

"You're out of your fucking mind! Art's not dumb enough to do that!"

"We're going to test his survival instincts, okay?"

"What do I tell him?"

"You tell him you want the money he owes you. If you don't get it, you're going to sell your story to the magazines. Starting with the fact that Art Colgate ordered the murder of his ex-wife in Saigon."

KREEGER was trading on the fact that Colgate had no idea what had happened to Sanchez. It paid off. Colgate phoned the motel six hours after Sanchez left his message; he sounded scared and suspicious. He refused outright to come to the motel. Colgate was evidently holed up somewhere on the Mexican side of the border because, after much negotiation, he proposed a rendezvous out on the Amistad Dam, which lay between Del Rio and Ciudad Acuña. Colgate wanted to meet out on the water. That way, he could be certain that Sanchez was coming alone.

When Colgate rang off, Sanchez said to his captors, "You want me to do this, you let me go armed. You know what Art's gonna do? He's gonna try to kill me. He's too gutless to do it alone. He'll bring somebody with him. Maybe some of those gooks he shipped back from Nam."

Kreeger said he would think it over.

When the two CIA men were alone, Camacho raised a different question. How were they going to be able to stop Sanchez from making a break for the Mexican side if they allowed him out on the dam by himself in a power-boat?

Kreeger thought he might have an answer for that. He fished out the number Bob Culbertson had given him at Judge Renwick's memorial service.

KREEGER and Culbertson sat in a booth at Billybob's saloon in Del Rio, drinking Lone Star beer.

Kreeger said, "You once offered to help. I've got a shot at getting the man who arranged Hugh Renwick's murder."

"Count me in. What do you need?"

"I need a boat, and a man who's good in the water. And coverage of a rendezvous out on Amistad Dam."

"Where?"

"Four miles north of a place called Tlaloc Beach."

"Hell, that's Mexican water. Are the chili-bellies in on this?"

Kreeger shook his head. He described the procedure that Colgate had dictated. Two powerboats, converging at midnight. They were supposed to signal with infrared sensors.

"I know every place around the dam where a crab could take cover," Culbertson announced. "And I liked Hughie a lot. So I guess I'm your boy. But you gotta 'fess up to me, Jim. You're CIA, aren't you?"

Kreeger swilled his beer without responding.

"Have you guys got something dirty going down? Hell, you could just give a shout to the Air Force fly-boys over at Laughlin, and they'll rustle up a couple of chop-pers quicker than a shoat goes for slop. To get this done, you don't really need me."

"I don't want any noise. This is personal business."

"Gotcha."

"Do you have any suggestions?"

Culbertson thought about it for a moment. "Ever do any scuba diving?"

"YOU ought to let me do this," George Camacho told his boss, as he watched Kreeger struggling into a wetsuit. "I spent so long playing frogman down in the Keys, I must have grown gills."

"Sorry, George. Art Colgate belongs to *me*."

Camacho helped him to strap on the oxygen tank.

Two boats were tied up at the little dock at Black Brush Point, on the south side of the dam. Culbertson had hired the bigger one from the owner of the trailer camp up the road: cash down, no questions asked. It was a twenty-seven-foot Imperial XL, powered by Volvo engines, capable of doing fifty mph. Kreeger walked Sanchez on board, and chained his ankle to a metal handbar.

"What's this?" Sanchez groused.

"I want to know where to find you," Kreeger told him.

George boarded the second powerboat, which was Culbertson's own—a nineteen-foot Vindicator, slightly slower than the Imperial. The words "Yell Leader" had been painted on the stern. Camacho and Culbertson were both carrying hunting rifles with night scopes.

Kreeger tested the controls of the Imperial, kicked the engine into life, and followed the furrow of white water from Culbertson's stern into the narrows between Diamond Head Island and the jagged promontory of Diablo East. Culbertson led him a few miles further, into deep water west of the marina. Then the *Yell Leader* veered away—away from the curiosity of any concealed watcher with night vision goggles—and vanished into one of the inlets around Salem Point, which protruded from the northern shore like a bunch of stubby fingers.

Kreeger was left to navigate alone. The waning moon was hidden behind massive cloud banks. The waters of the dam rolled like pitch under the gusting wind from the north. Kreeger had tried to memorize every detail of his route, from maps and photos. His study was useless to him now. On either shore, none of the landmarks looked the way they were supposed to, even through infrared binoculars.

"Steer due west" had been Culbertson's parting words. Kreeger opened the throttle, lashed the wheel in place, and put his trust in the compass.

When he lowered himself to lie full-length beneath the starboard rail, Sanchez snickered at him from the other side of the boat.

"You think you can fool Colgate? You're out of your mind! He's chicken, and a coward always thinks of all the angles. And those gooks of his can smell a live body a mile away."

"Shut up," Kreeger growled back.

"Why'd you put this chain on me?"

"You'll see."

When Kreeger judged they had come about the right distance, he raised himself just enough to switch off the engine. He put the keys in the zipper pocket of his wetsuit.

Sanchez watched, disbelieving, as Kreeger proceeded to haul himself over the side.

"Hey! You can't just leave me like this! Colgate wants me dead! We got a deal, right?"

"I'll be watching," said Kreeger, before inserting his mouthpiece. He fell heavily into the water, and the force of his entry set the boat rocking.

He kicked with his flippers, pushing himself down fifteen or twenty feet. He idled among a shoal of small fish, silvery against the dark.

The minutes dragged. He was having trouble breathing. He tried to readjust his mouthpiece and sucked water into his lungs. For a moment, he felt he was choking, but resisted the urge to break surface. Above him, the powerboat was drifting quite fast—southward, toward Mexico.

Then Kreeger felt a new movement in the water.

Another powerboat was bouncing across the dam, homing in on the Imperial, moving at high speed. It made a complete circuit. When the engine was cut, the hull was bobbing above Kreeger's head. He swam toward its stern.

When he broke water, he heard Sanchez scream. He saw two small, slight figures in black, leaping like cats onto the deck of the Imperial. Behind them, at the rail of the new boat—an Australian-made Flightcraft 20XL—was Art Colgate, fitted out like a Rhode Island yacht captain. Colgate was cradling a mini machine gun, but seemed in no hurry to use it.

"Kreeger!" Sanchez screamed. "Where the fuck are you?"

Colgate jerked when he heard the name, as if he had touched a live wire.

"It's a trap!" he shrilled. "Finish Sanchez and we're out of here!"

Kreeger, hugging the side of Colgate's boat, saw the flash of the knife as one of the Vietnamese goons went for Sanchez. He had one dart in his underwater gun, and no doubt whose name was on it.

Colgate wheeled around, searching the shadows. Kreeger aimed for the shoulder. As the shaft sheared through muscle and sinew, Colgate squealed and dropped his weapon.

Kreeger dragged himself up over the rail and scrambled, hand over hand, for the gun. In peripheral vision, he saw the two Vietnamese on his own boat. One of them was hacking at the huddled body of Sanchez, as if he meant to eviscerate it. The other, alerted by the scuffle on Colgate's boat, was poised to leap back.

Colgate had regained the Uzi, but he was forced by the wound to use the wrong hand. That wouldn't matter, however, because he was too close to miss with an automatic weapon. Two bullets from his first clip tore through Kreeger's thigh.

With a tremendous effort of will, Kreeger flung himself sideways and forward, thrust out his hand, and took

Colgate by the throat. Colgate gagged and fell backward. Kreeger's forefinger and middle finger snapped into a V, bracketing Colgate's windpipe, choking off the air.

Behind him, one of the Vietnamese killers was advancing, knife in hand. Kreeger snatched up the fallen Uzi and spurted bullets across his attacker's midriff. In the process, however, he relaxed his grip on Colgate enough for the death merchant to break free.

The boat tossed and heaved. Kreeger, propped up on one knee, lost his balance and was hurled against the port rail. The bullets in his thigh stabbed like white-hot pokers.

Where were George and Culbertson?

He heard, or imagined, an approaching engine. He turned toward it, and found himself facing the second Vietnamese. The man's face was frozen in a victorious grin. He was swinging an ax—maybe a fire hatchet from the boat. Kreeger brought up the gun. It jammed. He gripped it by the muzzle and used it to ward off the ax blow.

The driving blade crashed against the gun barrel, flashing sparks.

Suddenly the Vietnamese, lither and faster than Kreeger, was under his guard, using the ax haft as a hammer against his throat. Kreeger's world dissolved into a spinning whorl, red within black. Then, from somewhere outside this world, he heard the crack of a rifle.

The pressure that was crushing his lungs slipped away. Groggy, he shrugged off the body that lay on top of his, snatched up the ax, and stumbled after Colgate.

In the harsh glare of the searchlight from Culbertson's boat, he could see his adversary clearly. Colgate was leaning against the wheel, hands raised in surrender.

On the *Yell Leader*, George Camacho lowered his hunting rifle and called, "Do it, Jim! There's nobody left who will talk! God knows the bastard deserves it!"

Kreeger looked at the gray man, the barb of the dart still impaled in his shoulder, his whole body shaking violently. Colgate dropped to his knees, blubbering and imploring.

Kreeger's eyes swiveled, in a kind of wonderment, to the ax in his hand.

He let it fall.

There had been enough killing, enough vengeance.

"You son of a bitch," Kreeger said to Colgate. "You'll stand trial for murder. In Texas. There's a death penalty in Texas."

Maybe they would not be able to charge Colgate with the assassinations of President Paz or Judge Renwick. Nor of the woman who had died in Saigon, so many years before. But Colgate would not be able to wriggle away from the mutilated corpse of Sanchez, in the black speedboat. That murder would be enough.

Bob Culbertson peered at the bodies of the Vietnamese.

He shouted at Kreeger, through the wind, "Hey, Jim! You're a real kick in the pants!"

7

THE Kreegers sat in the diplomatic stand at the inauguration of Emiliano Rojas as President of Mexico. The vast crowd heaved and rolled like ocean waves across the Zocalo. Miliano wore a plain black suit, a peasant's Sunday suit. He spoke softly, even shyly, of forgiveness and peace. Of a world in which common humanity would take precedence over politics and economics. Of a society beyond zero-sum games, in which one man's gain would enable others to benefit and grow. He spoke of the care of souls.

Kreeger inspected the faces of the visiting dignitaries. Some wizard of protocol had seated President Butler next to the premier of Japan. There was a large contingent of Japanese corporation chiefs. Maybe Harry Butler could live with them since Miliano had vowed to cancel the canal project and reserved the new oil fields in the northern Gulf—confirmed as one of the biggest finds since Spindletop—for Mexicans. In his speech, Miliano announced that his government would use the money saved from the canal scheme to create banks for the poor. Miliano might not be a free-marketeer, but he was already demonstrating that he was not an old-time socialist either. He promised that his first cabinet would include representatives of all democratic tendencies, from both right and left.

Miliano called his wife, Elena, up onto the podium. Another break with Mexican tradition. She was cradling a baby in her arms. She was wearing a simple flowered print dress. She was radiant.

She said, into the microphone, "God is slow, but He does not forget."